Daughter of the House

Victoria Cornwall

Cornish Tales Series

Books in the series:
The Thief's Daughter
The Captain's Daughter
The Daughter of River Valley
A Daughter's Christmas Wish
Daughter of the House
Daniel's Daughter

Where heroes are like chocolate – irrestible!

Copyright © 2019 Victoria Cornwall
Published 2019 by Choc Lit Limited
Penrose House, Crawley Drive, Camberley, Surrey GU15 2AB, UK
www.choc-lit.com

The right of Victoria Cornwall to be identified as the Author of this Work has been asserted by her in accordance with the Copyright, Designs and Patents Act 1988

All characters and events in this publication, other than those clearly in the public domain, are fictitious and any resemblance to actual persons, living or dead, is purely coincidental

All rights reserved. No part of this publication may be reproduced, stored in a retrieval system, or transmitted in any form or by any means, electronic, mechanical, photocopying, recording or otherwise, without the prior permission of the publisher or a licence permitting restricted copying. In the UK such licences are issued by the Copyright Licensing Agency, Barnards Inn, 86 Fetter Lane, London EC4A 1EN.

PRINT ISBN: 978-1-78189-090-5

I would like to dedicate Daughter of the House to all the men and women who, through campaigns, persistence and individual courage, have fought for gender equality so that future generations can enjoy the same rights and opportunities across all sectors of society.

Acknowledgements

There are many people who have supported me in my writing journey by offering encouraging words. They range from friends, relatives and neighbours, to novice writers and established authors who have become recognised household names. There are too many to name individually here, however many are members of the Romantic Novelists' Association, of which I am a member. Sensible advice and support, at just the right time, is as precious as gold. Thank you.

I would also like to acknowledge the two beautifully maintained gardens which inspired Drake's world:
The award-winning Victorian garden, The Lost Gardens of Heligan, near St.Austell, Cornwall and the formal gardens of Mount Edgcumbe House and Country Park, Torpoint, Cornwall.

I would also like to acknowledge two writers whose works also inspired *Daughter of the House*:-
The Yellow Wallpaper by Charlotte Perkins Gilman (short story).
The Angel in the House by Coventry Patmore (poem). An arguably, culturally significant poem which offers a Victorian perspective on the perfect woman.

I would also like to acknowledge and thank my publisher, Choc Lit, and their amazing team for selecting *Daughter of the House* for publication – with special thanks to Tasting Panel readers: Sallie D, Christina G, Elena B, Leanne F, Joy S, Jenny M, Barbara B, Jo L, Alma H, Barbara P, Isabelle D, Jenny K, Jo O and Katie P. I will be eternally grateful to you for bringing *Daughter of the House* to a wider audience.

Prologue

1870, Cornwall, England

'Has it started?'

'Four hours ago, Doctor Birch,' replied the butler, taking the man's hat and coat and immediately handing them on to a passing footman.

The doctor ran a trembling hand through his short white hair. 'Where is she? In her room?'

'Yes. The same room as you saw her in yesterday.' The doctor headed for the staircase with the butler hurrying in his wake. 'Let me show you the way,' he offered.

'I know the bloody way!' snapped the doctor. Much to his annoyance, the butler continued to follow him. 'You don't need to trail me like a puppy dog,' he complained loudly, without turning round.

The experienced butler faltered like a novice on the stair, his cheeks burning red by the reprimand. The doctor did not notice or care and continued to climb the stairs alone.

Doctor Birch had come to know Cedar Lodge well. Originally built in Tudor times, it had been extensively refurbished and modernised by its owner, Howard Pendragon, and was now an elegant country house, far grander than its modest name. Recently installed large bay windows encouraged more light into the rooms, which had been prone to darkness in the past, and a new wing had also been erected. However, despite Cedar Lodge growing in grandeur, compared to Carrack House, which belonged to his older brother, Sir Robert Pendragon, it would always be found lacking both in size and position. Cedar Lodge would always remain the smaller and more isolated of the two, and have the stigma of being the property of the 'spare heir' who had no role to fill.

'Doctor Birch, you are here!' The doctor's steps slowed at the sound of Howard's voice coming from the hall below. His grip tightened on the handle of his bag and he braced his shoulders. He silently waited as the owner approached him.

'Today is the day we have been waiting for, Doctor Birch.'

The doctor turned and smiled, his poor humour vanished, his bad manners replaced by a professional front.

'Indeed it is, Mr Pendragon. Indeed it is.'

Taking advantage of the diversion, the butler discreetly withdrew as Howard joined the doctor and proceeded to climb the staircase with him. Both men were in their forties and prone to portliness, but only one was in good spirits.

'I think it is time you called me Howard. Today, the Pendragon family will have an heir.'

'A happy day indeed,' agreed the doctor in a measured tone.

'More than happy,' replied Howard. 'This day will mark a major change.'

'Change?'

'For the future of Carrack House, of course.'

'Your brother's house?'

'Yes, of course.'

Doctor Birch's smile faded. He had spent the past six months tending this man's wife. No one, not even Mrs Pendragon herself, felt the pressure of delivering a live male heir as keenly as the doctor did himself. He stole a glance at the man by his side. He was beginning to resent ever setting foot within this splendid home, for over the past few months he had come to know about the bitter feelings that lay between the Pendragon brothers.

He had yet to meet Sir Robert Pendragon, 7th Baronet and owner of Carrack House and a vast acreage of Cornwall. The man who sought his skills now was his younger brother by no more than two minutes. The doctor had come to realise that despite today's bounce and swagger, beneath was a man filled with bitterness, a man who envied the inheritance and title his older brother had as his right. As if hearing his thoughts, Howard stopped, forcing the doctor to do the same out of politeness. A woman's cry came from one of the rooms above them, but both men ignored it.

'Give me a live boy, Doctor Birch. My wife is getting older and this might be our last chance. Do not fail us as other doctors have done.'

Doctor Birch felt the weight placed upon his shoulders. Howard Pendragon's wife had endured four pregnancies, none of which were carried to term. Doctor after doctor had walked this staircase, each assignment ending in a dismal failure and their careers blighted by their involvement. Now it was his turn and he had no plans to follow in their footsteps. Even so, a live child did not guarantee this man's hopes.

'Your brother may have a child of his own,' cautioned Doctor Birch.

Howard dismissed it with a snort. 'His first wife was barren. His second is no better.'

'She has a few more child-bearing years yet and their marriage is still fresh.'

Howard Pendragon waved his comment aside. 'It has been three years and she has not fallen yet. Besides, he needs a male heir as a daughter is of no use. A female cannot inherit the title leaving me or my son next in line. As for Carrack, my brother would never allow a woman to own and run the estate. Even he would not allow the bad feeling between us to overshadow his views on a woman's capability.'

Another cry echoed through the cut crystal prisms of the chandelier above. 'Your wife is in need of my services, Mr Pendragon ... Howard,' the doctor replied solemnly. 'If you wish a healthy child then I must be given leave to tend to her.'

Howard blinked. 'Yes, yes of course. Do what you need to do and give me a healthy son.'

The doctor turned and quickly proceeded up the stairs, all the while feeling Howard's eyes upon him.

'And when he is born,' called Howard, 'I shall name him Mawgan Charles Pendragon. And if I should die before I can claim my brother's title, it will be *my* son who will become the future Sir Mawgan Pendragon, 8th Baronet of Carrack!'

Moments later, Doctor Birch was at Mrs Pendragon's bedroom door. He stood for a moment to wipe the perspiration from his brow and straighten his cravat, before reaching for the doorknob. The door opened silently on well-oiled hinges, allowing him to stand unnoticed and survey the scene. All was quiet, but for a ticking clock hidden somewhere in the room.

Mrs Pendragon lay in her bed resting between pains as her loyal maid stood by her side and nursed her. Mrs Pendragon opened her eyes and looked at him. Sweat soaked hair framed her face, which was shiny from discomfort and a pale shade of crimson. She managed a smile, relieved he had arrived.

The doctor returned Mrs Pendragon's smile, but allowed his gaze to wander around the room. It finally came to rest on the dressing screen standing in the shadows to the right. Its presence gave him the courage to enter.

'It has begun, just as you predicted,' Mrs Pendragon said breathlessly, reaching out a hand to him.

He took it in his and patted it reassuringly. 'All that was needed was some of my mild tonics to build your strength,' he replied. His eyes searched for the bottles amongst the useless trinkets and ornaments that adorned her bedside table.

The maid noticed and found them hidden behind a silver framed photograph. 'Are these what you are looking—'

The doctor snatched the bottles from her and opened two of them to view their contents. They were empty. Mrs Pendragon had drunk them all, just as he had prescribed. Only the fragrant smell of angelica, and the faint minty aroma of pennyroyal remained to linger in the air. He opened the last bottle, which had contained blue cohosh. It too was empty. He puffed out his chest, satisfied that his concoctions had worked so efficiently.

Mrs Pendragon's hands clenched her blankets. The movement caught his eye and brought him back to the predicament he was in. The contraction was beginning to build again. It was strong, with little respite, indicating her time was near.

He slipped the bottles into his pocket, making a mental note to record the quantities for future use, and placed his bag in the shadows at the foot of the bed. He opened the bag briefly to check its contents, whilst the maid administered and soothed her mistress through the pain. When her mistress's writhing finally subsided he returned to her side with a Pinard Horn, to listen to the baby's heart.

'Now now, Mrs Pendragon,' he said, removing a handkerchief from his pocket and wiping his brow again, 'you would not wish to cause your husband undue concern by creating such a fuss.'

His patient dropped her head back on the pillow, exhausted. 'I'm sorry, Doctor,' she whispered between breaths. Her maid snorted in anger.

'Quiet please,' ordered the doctor. 'I must listen to the child's heart.'

He meticulously folded back the bed linen to expose her swollen abdomen and positioned the listening device against it. He bent forward and carefully placed his ear to it. The room fell silent as the occupants held their breaths. Doctor Birch listened intently and heard exactly what he expected to hear – nothing. He smiled.

'Your baby has a strong heartbeat, Mrs Pendragon, and is eager to meet you,' he said, carefully placing the horn on the bedside table.

Mrs Pendragon sighed, a smile of relief breaking through the exhaustion. 'I have not felt it move for two days,' she replied weakly. 'Thank you for coming to see me yesterday and putting my mind at rest. I have been so afraid. I could not bear to lose another child.'

'You will not lose another child, Mrs Pendragon,' said Doctor Birch, moving his gaze from the horn to his patient. 'All you needed were my tonics to boost your strength and now the baby is ready to come out. In fact, I think …' he said, looking at the intensity of the building pain etched on her face, 'it may be time to push.'

Doctor Birch repositioned the dressing screen a little nearer, and prepared himself to guide the baby out by carefully rolling up his sleeves.

He looked at the maid as he rolled up a cuff. 'Leave us, and do not return until I request it.'

The maid frowned. 'But, Doctor Birch, she needs me.'

'Allow your mistress to retain some dignity. She is not in the right frame of mind to make such decisions so I, as her physician, must do it for her.'

'But—'

Doctor Birch snared her with a dispassionate look. 'Are you refusing?'

She looked hesitantly at her mistress's face, contorted in pain, and did not move.

'I told you to leave us.'

'Ma'am?' she asked, hoping to hear a request to stay. None came.

Doctor Birch began to unroll his sleeve. 'If I do not have absolute authority and the conditions I require, Mrs Pendragon, then I cannot be responsible for the outcome.'

Mrs Pendragon's hand fluttered in the air between them. The maid caught it in hers.

'Do as Doctor Birch says, Mellin,' her mistress whispered hoarsely.

Mellin remained hesitant, her glance darting between doctor and patient, torn between the desire to give her employer comfort or obey her order to leave. The doctor waited, looking at her under heavy lids. A guttural cry came from the woman who lay between them. Bedclothes slipped away as their patient twisted in pain, exposing bent trembling legs, now slick with sweat. The message was clear; he would do nothing until she had left. Realising she had no choice, Mellin stifled a cry of her own and ran from the room.

Mellin did not go far. Not even a doctor's order would prevent her from being near to hand should her mistress have need of her. She began to pace the landing, waiting and praying for the joyous sound of a baby's cry. How dare the doctor refuse to have her present when it was clear that her mistress needed her! No one knew better than she the grief her mistress had endured in the past and the importance of having a healthy child. Mrs Pendragon's health and happiness were paramount and she would do anything for her in order to achieve it. Unfortunately, today it meant obeying an instruction that felt alien and wrong. As for maintaining her dignity, this was the fifth labour she had nursed Mrs Pendragon through. She had seen it all before.

The labour cries quietened. Mellin tilted her head to listen for a baby's cry, but was rewarded with an unnatural silence. The silence dragged on until she could bear it no longer. She returned to the door, quietly turned the handle and silently opened it. The maid surveyed the scene, just as the doctor had done not twenty minutes before. Her mistress lay exhausted, her head cushioned deep within creased, white, feather pillows. Her eyes were closed, but the maid noticed a faint smile upon her lips.

Mellin smiled too at what this might mean. Unwilling to disturb her mistress, she remained where she stood and eagerly looked to the doctor for news. She found him, crouching behind the dressing screen and tending to the needs of a new-born baby. The silence continued. Something was not quite right.

The screen's shadow must be playing tricks on her senses, she thought, casting an atmosphere of doom where none should exist. Yet, there was an unearthly stillness to the new-born. It lay flaccid, silent and abandoned by the doctor, who now showed more interest in the contents of his bag than the child he had just delivered. Mellin understood what this meant, for she had seen it four times before. The baby was dead.

However, something remained different and jarred against the normal order of things. There was not the usual grief filled aftermath and the doctor remained busy and focused. Muted in her growing horror, Mellin watched as the doctor carefully lifted a sleeping baby from his bag, and placed the stillborn inside.

Mellin, horrified, silently pulled the door closed again, her mind whirring with the implications of what she had just seen. Her stomach began to churn with shock. She remained still, as if frozen in time, reliving the scene in her head, yet at the same time doubting what she had seen.

Suddenly, the door opened and Doctor Birch came out. He walked briskly to the staircase with a confident stride and made short work of the stairs. Moments later he was greeting Howard Pendragon in the hall with the announcement he was now a father to a healthy son. The announcement sounded so genuine, so joyful, and so true. Mellin turned away, unable to watch.

Mellin edged towards the open door. The room was peaceful and all appeared as before, a mixture of dark shadows and shards of light spilling through the half drawn curtains. She saw the bag where the doctor had left it, on the floor, behind the screen.

What was she to do? Accuse a doctor of malpractice? Who would believe a servant over the word of a doctor? She heard her employer's laughter rise up from the hall. Her chaotic thoughts lurched from one direction to another, as she frantically tried to collect them together. Perhaps the macabre plan was carried out with the full knowledge of Mr Pendragon himself? Her position could be at risk if she disclosed what she saw. Yet, she could not forget what she had just witnessed. She had to do something. She must inform her mistress. She must learn of the truth and would know what to do.

Mrs Pendragon called her name, and she dragged her eyes from the bag to the woman in the bed.

'Mellin,' her mistress said smiling, her face rosy with joy. 'We have a son! God has given us a son.'

Mellin stepped forward, her feet heavy as lead.

'Look, Mellin,' her mistress encouraged, gently easing back the blanket that framed the bundle in her arms. 'Look,' her voice broke and Mellin could see pure joy glistening in her eyes and tears begin to flow down her cheeks. 'Look, Mellin, I am … a mother.'

Mellin looked at the baby in Mrs Pendragon's arms, his fair downy head being soothed by her loving hand. He was a beautiful baby, with good-sized limbs and a healthy glow, if somewhat sleepy. Mellin had devoted her adult life to Mrs Pendragon. Her mistress's happiness was her happiness and today, due to this baby lying in her arms, she was happier than she had ever seen her before. She could not break her heart now.

Only too aware of the bag that lay not ten feet away, Mellin forced a smile. 'Congratulations, ma'am,' she said quietly. 'You have a beautiful son.'

Doctor Birch could still taste the port on his tongue as he climbed into the waiting carriage. Although at first eager to leave, Howard had insisted he stay and join him in a celebratory drink. Praise for his professional expertise accompanied the glass handed to him, which swelled the doctor's chest and quickly diminished any desire to leave. For a while, as Howard showered him with thanks and pledged to recommend him to all of society, his bag and its cadaverous contents lay abandoned by his chair. Abandoned, but not forgotten.

Now sitting in the confines of the carriage, Doctor Birch nudged the bag with his toe in an attempt to arrange more room for his feet. Contented, he rested his head back and reflected on his achievement. The afternoon had gone according to plan. If he had known it would be so successful he would not have spent the previous night unable to sleep. It was to be expected, he comforted himself. He had never relied upon untested mixtures to induce labour before.

It had been part of an extraordinary plan to protect his good name and deliver a live child. He had suspected the child was already dead after receiving the request to visit. A baby that did not move was never a good sign. He had hurriedly acquired the mixtures from the strange old woman who frequented Cardon Woods. It was just one part of his plan, the other was obtaining a foundling new-born from a house of ill repute, quietening it with a dose of laudanum and passing it off as Pendragon's heir. The plan was a genius idea – and he had achieved it. The feeling of success it evoked was a heady tonic in itself.

A smile curved his lips as he congratulated himself. Only an experienced, intelligent man, such as he, could possibly have done it. He stroked his neat white beard as he realised he had always felt superior to the general society around him. His mother had believed it too, stroking his ego and moulding his character with undivided care. She called him 'extraordinary' and she was right. If he set his mind to it, he could achieve anything. He felt confident that the momentary self-doubt, which had disturbed his sleep, would never return.

The carriage had not yet set off, when voices outside caught his attention. He was about to lean forward to look out of the window when the carriage door was abruptly opened. A young man's face, breathless from running, came into view. From his clothes, the doctor soon realised he was no more than a neighbouring servant sent to fetch him. This method to request a visit from him was a common occurrence. Today, however, it was an annoyance. He would send him away. He reached for the door, but the servant blocked his way.

'Doctor Birch,' the servant pleaded breathlessly, 'Sir Robert Pendragon and Lady Pendragon of Carrack House request a visit from you.' He produced a letter for the doctor to read.

Doctor Birch looked at the envelope in the servant's trembling hand. 'Sir Robert Pendragon?' he repeated, snatching it from him. 'From Carrack House?'

The servant nodded eagerly.

Doctor Birch efficiently opened it with a square nailed thumb. He had not been asked to attend Carrack House before and the request not only intrigued him, but gave him hope. Doctor Lander usually frequented the place and, if the rumour was right, Lady Pendragon relied upon him heavily for advice on various minor ailments. However, Doctor Lander's own health was momentarily poor, and this request may be his only opportunity to usurp him. The headed paper sent a quiet thrill through his body.

Dear Doctor Birch,

I am sending this letter to request that you call upon us as soon as you are able.

My wife, Lady Pendragon, has lately suffered greatly from a poor appetite and bouts of sickness, which has a tendency to improve as the day progresses.

In all other ways she maintains she is well, leading us to come to the conclusion that she may be with child.

We would be grateful if you could visit us and put our minds at rest.

Yours sincerely,
Sir Robert Pendragon, Bt

Doctor Birch folded the letter thoughtfully. Despite all he had achieved today, it now appeared that Howard's older brother might succeed in producing an heir after all. The importance the doctor had placed on achieving the younger brother's patronage was now somewhat diminished. Being able to boast his older brother, a baronet, as a patient held significant more value. He banged the roof of the carriage, startling the harnessed horse who lifted its wide-eyed head high in readiness to flee. The driver above him fought to steady it.

'Take me to Carrack House,' the doctor shouted up to him, 'and be quick about it.'

The doctor pulled the door shut with a bang, frightening the already unsettled horse. The carriage lurched forward, but, thankfully, the experienced driver regained control almost immediately and began to turn the carriage in a semicircle within the courtyard of Cedar Lodge. The servant and stable boy retreated some distance, out of harm's way, to watch the hasty departure. Finally, amidst a flurry of stamping hooves and jingling harness, Doctor Birch was on his way to Carrack House and leaving Cedar Lodge behind him.

Chapter One

1886, Cornwall, England

Evelyn paused in the doorway and looked down the empty corridor. She tilted her head to listen. The house was unusually quiet, but for the tick-tock of the nursery clock and the rhythmical sighs and snorts of the woman sat by the fire. Evelyn's eyes brightened. It was the perfect time to escape. No one would notice she was gone – no one ever did. She silently closed the door behind her, ran along the empty corridor and down the back stairs, her feet tripping expertly over each step, rug and knotted floorboard. The warm summer breeze welcomed her outside. She slid the ribbons from her hair, shook her curls loose and began to run. She was free at last.

Evelyn followed the fragrance of her father's rose garden, gently trailing her scarlet ribbons from her fingertips as if they were her wings. Inspired by a statue of a unicorn she had seen in a book, she began to gallop. The illustration of the statue had awakened her vivid imagination, an imagination her parents had always discouraged. The statue's very existence, with its magical horn, hinted to Evelyn that the rest of the world was not like the world she knew. Someone, somewhere, had been commissioned to showcase their creative skills and in doing so expressed themselves, even though what they created was pure fantasy. It was a freedom Evelyn did not know existed, and yet subconsciously yearned for.

When Evelyn discovered that her newly appointed governess, Miss Brown, was afflicted with insomnia, she saw an opportunity to ease the restlessness she felt deep inside herself. Her devious behaviour, Evelyn reconciled to herself, would also help dear Miss Brown, who was often tired and pale through lack of sleep. Evelyn had discovered that during her reading lesson, if she read in a monotonous tone, she could sometimes induce Miss Brown to fall asleep. By the end of the second page, if she was lucky, her governess's lids would start to droop and by the end of the third page, a soft, vibrating snore would escape her lips. Evelyn could not predict when she would be successful, but the randomness of her successes made them all the sweeter. The governess's snoring signalled the start of forty-five minutes of precious freedom for Evelyn before she would begin to stir. When she did eventually open her eyes, Evelyn would be sitting opposite her, neat and tidy, reading studiously the last sentence of the chapter. It was not until Evelyn became an adult, did she begin to wonder who was fooling whom, and if the governess asked her to read in a desperate attempt to recoup lost sleep.

Evelyn headed towards the eighteenth century orangery, a tall, elegant, white building, one hundred feet by thirty feet, designed to appear like an elegant manor house rather than a glasshouse whose sole purpose was to ripen citrus fruit. Evelyn galloped through one door and down its centre path. The heat, intensified by the large windows, was stifling, but had no purpose as the orange trees had already been removed for the summer to line the gravelled paths leading to the Italian garden. Her footsteps echoed around her as she headed towards the door at the far end. Outside the warm breeze felt cooler compared to the orangery's tropical atmosphere and with renewed energy, she left it behind.

Evelyn's three beat gait skipped along the citrus scented gravel path and entered the next garden, one of many specifically designed by a long line of ancestors who wished to make their mark upon the land. Each area was different, brought to life as a reminder of humble beginnings, extraordinary travels, or lost loves. Evelyn knew all about how the Pendragons made their fortune, it was drummed into her brother Nicholas from an early age, and, by default, into her.

Once powerful merchants, the Pendragon family had accumulated much of their wealth during the reign of Henry VIII. Pendragon history and lineage was unquestioned and entrenched in Cornish society. It was a lineage to be proud of and an inheritance to be protected.

Carrack House, named after the distinct broad merchant ship with its tell-tale high sterncastle and even higher forecastle, was built in Georgian times on the same site as an earlier Elizabethan house. It was situated in the centre of the gardens, like a jewel sewn into sensuous, colourful embroidery of different fauna and flora.

It came as no surprise that Carrack House and Estate was passed down through the pedigree like a precious gift. It was a responsibility and a heavy burden that was both desired and feared, but had been successfully carried by a long line of male heirs. The house and gardens were envied by all who came to visit, but although beautiful, Evelyn knew from an early age, that every flower, every statue, every blade of grass had its place, specifically designed, commission, cultivated – and controlled. Her father, its current owner and guardian, was made for the task.

Statues of Apollo, Bacchus and Venus silently watched her pass by, inwardly frowning, no doubt, at the disturbance to their spiritually uplifting peace.

The French Garden welcomed her with vibrant colour of geometrically shaped flowerbeds trimmed with miniature hedges. At its centre stood a stone carved ornamental fountain of three cherubs pouring water. Evelyn let her fingers dip into its cool pool as she galloped by.

Evelyn passed the maze by. She had once gotten lost within its evergreen walls and had to be rescued by the head gardener, Timmins. The claustrophobic experience gave her nightmares for weeks and, in times of stress, she still dreamt of tall, laughing hedges closing in on her and draining her lungs of air.

The sombre Fern Garden was next and was nothing to fear, despite its shaded darkness, grotesque gargoyles and dark green ferns that rustled in the wind. Small gravestones marked the passing of beloved pets. They were no more than a melancholy curiosity to Evelyn, all of them dead long before Evelyn and her brother were born. She would have loved to have a pet of her own, but her mother would not allow it. 'Disease-ridden animals', her mother called them and 'a risk to one's health'. Mother must know, thought Evelyn, she was an expert in illness.

However, her mother's dire warnings did not stop Evelyn making friends with Duchess, the stray cat who had made her home in the outbuildings. Duchess was the closest she would get to having a pet, but when she was married, if her husband allowed it, she would have many.

Evelyn began to tire and headed towards Lady May's Garden. Named after the 4th baronet's wife, it could only be approached by way of a lengthy pagoda adorned with climbing ivy. Evelyn entered its leafy shadows and ran along its length. At the end she came out into the bright sunshine of Lady May's favourite place. She ignored the Japanese cedar, palms and magnolias and headed for the statue in the centre. Dropping her ribbons, she lifted her skirts and began to climb.

Evelyn straddled the lioness and lovingly stroked its noble head. It was her favourite statue to climb, partly because it gave her an unhindered view of the grounds and a better view of the sleeping cub between the lioness's front paws. The cub, lovingly protected by its devoted mother, appeared to have a smile on its face that never failed to bring a sigh of peace within Evelyn. Today, the sigh reached her lips.

Evelyn dragged her eyes away and looked about her. From her vantage point, she could see the house, many of the gardens and even The White Tower, an isolated folly, in the far distance. Built on the whim of some ancestor, it had no real purpose and stood at odds with the setting it found itself in, where everything had a reason, be it for colour, fragrance or design.

Evelyn had always felt an affiliation with the tower, although she could not explain why. Usually, it was rather plain to look at, but today its white stone walls shone brightly in the sunlight, emitting a quiet ambiance of strength, a stark contrast to the dark green trees around it, which waved their leaves in the breeze like swooning ladies. Beyond lay the expansive green lawns, dotted with grand oaks, wistful willows and towering ash and through it all cut a wide sweeping drive of gravel.

Something moved nearby. For the first time, Evelyn noticed she was not alone. Two gardeners, their backs bent, were quietly working in one of the gardens, pulling up weeds and throwing them into a wheelbarrow positioned between them. Evelyn watched and listened, fascinated, for normally gardeners would stop their work, remove their caps and drop their eyes in her presence – or simply disappear. Not today. From her vantage point, she watched them unobserved, as if they were wild animals in their natural habitat. They were talking and although it was only idle chatter to help pass the time, their banter humanised them in a way that their doffing of caps and averting of eyes had failed to do in the past.

Evelyn felt a jab of guilt as she realised that, although she knew their faces, she did not know their names, or anything about them. Until now she had not really thought of them at all. They were like moving furniture, taken for granted, but missed when not fulfilling their role. She did not even know how many gardeners they had. She wasn't even sure if Father did. Timmins, the head gardener, dealt with the gardening staff. At least she knew *his* name.

Evelyn looked about and found him inspecting the rose garden. She could tell it was him. He always wore his distinct wide brim hat and walked with the rounded shoulders of a man who had spent much of his life out in all weathers. She had known of his presence all her life and envied him his wisdom and gift to turn an area of soil into a fragrant kaleidoscope of colour, but most of all she envied him for the respect and time her father gave him.

Her father had spent more time in Timmins' presence than he had ever done with her. Her time was between five and five-thirty in the evening, when she was presented to her parents before bed. In addition to this precious interview, for that was how she saw it, she was allowed to accompany them to the Sunday service in the Pendragon private chapel.

The service was a small, chilly affair but always well attended as the seats behind the Pendragon pew were filled with indoor and outdoor staff. They all listened in silence to the pulpit thumping vicar, warning of fire and brimstone raining down upon them if they did not mend their ways, which always confused Evelyn as she did not know their ways were broken, whatever *ways* were.

Evelyn longed to turn around and look at the interesting faces behind her. It was an urge hard to resist, particularly since Nicholas had told her they were obliged to attend or their wages would be docked. She had always thought they wanted to attend. Knowing they were forced, as she was, made her feel she had more in common with them than her parents. Did they show the same boredom as she felt inside? She was tempted to find out.

Up to the age of twelve, her brother fared no better and saw as little of their parents as she did. Then, one day, Father took it upon himself to prepare him further for the responsibilities ahead. The best tutors were no longer adequate, now he insisted Nicholas learnt about the estate and accompanied him when visiting his tenants. Evelyn was filled with quiet envy each time she watched the trap pull away with her father and brother sitting side by side, enjoying time in each other's company that she could only imagine.

She did not blame Nicholas for this. She loved him too much. Although he was only two years older than her and small for his age, he seemed to have the wisdom of an adult that she could only admire. She also knew, without a doubt, he loved her too. This, unfortunately, she could not say about her parents.

They were not cruel, just distant, and they valued Nicholas more. She learnt that lesson when she reached her twelfth birthday. Desperate to spend time with them, Evelyn asked her father if she could accompany them on a visit to a tenant. Her father had looked at her and laughed. He rarely laughed. The sound should have been joyful to her ears, but instead her cheeks burned. He returned to his book almost immediately, shaking his head in bewilderment. His lack of reply marked the contrast between what he expected from a son, compared to a daughter and Evelyn, with ribbons in her hair, felt stupid for not knowing the difference before.

'Have you bored Brown to sleep again?' Evelyn turned to look behind her. Her brother was looking up at her, shielding his eyes against the bright sun. 'One day, Effy, she will wake up and find you gone,' he warned.

Evelyn glanced at the clock tower above the main door. 'I have another twenty minutes before she will stir.'

'The clock might be wrong,' teased Nicholas.

'The clock is never wrong. Father would not allow it.' Evelyn began to climb down, her dress riding up behind her. She landed on the ground beside him and smoothed her dress down with brisk, matter-of-fact strokes of her hands. 'Why aren't you in your lessons?' she asked, without glancing up.

Nicholas leaned back against the base of the statue and crossed his ankles.

'How many times have you climbed that statue?'

She looked at him and smiled. 'Lots.'

'I thought so. Word reached Mother that Mr Burrows had a cold.'

'Oh dear. Did she send him away?'

Her brother nodded. 'With strict instructions not to return until he had written confirmation from Doctor Birch that he was healthy again.' Nicholas spied a small patch of lichen on the lion's paw and attempted to scrape it off with a nail. 'Despite Mother's earlier concerns, she has since discovered that there is an advantage to not having a live-in tutor for me.' He glanced at Evie and smiled. 'Mother can quarantine me far more efficiently than if Mr Burrows was wandering the house.'

'Was he terribly upset?'

'He was more upset that it was Mother who gave the order. I think he hates women.' He gave up on the lichen and scraped a blade of grass off his shoe instead. 'Mother was upset too. I have just been subjected to one of her interrogations.'

'Oh dear.'

Evelyn could picture it, her mother feeling the heat of Nicholas's brow and firing endless questions at him regarding the state of his health. Her 'panics', as Evelyn and Nicholas called them, were becoming more and more frequent. Mother always had a mild preoccupation with her own health, but now her anxieties were well and truly transferred to Nicholas.

It started last winter, when Nicholas fell ill with rheumatic fever and almost died.

It had been a worrying time for all the family, but fortunately, after several months, Nicholas had recovered. However, the illness had subtly left its mark and the energetic brother Evelyn had known all her life, had failed to return. These days he was slower and exuded a quiet dignity that was beyond his years. His eyes held a grave wisdom she had not seen before and he no longer shared his thoughts as readily as he once had.

Her governess, Miss Brown, believed it was because he had had a brush with death and had grown up, but this reason made no sense to Evelyn. Surely if he had escaped the clutches of death he would be filled with joy that he had survived. Mother did not help matters by constantly worrying about him and treating him like an invalid. Doctor Birch was frequently called upon for advice and tonics, which he happily provided for an exorbitant price.

Nicholas thought the fuss their mother made was silly too. When questioned, he reassured his sister that he felt quite recovered and their mother had nothing to fear. He even joked that the only time he felt unwell was after one of their mother's interrogations and it was only as a direct result of it and not any lingering illness. Evelyn was only too happy to believe him, eager to put the dark phase of his illness behind them. So eager, in fact, that she did not think to question why he obediently took all the foul smelling tonics if he did not feel unwell.

'So I have found myself without a tutor,' Nicholas was saying, 'and came to look for you. Brown has a loud snore, doesn't she?'

'Sometimes she makes a sound like a pig.'

'A little one or a big one?'

Evelyn did an impression for him.

Nicholas couldn't help smiling at his sister. 'That's definitely a big one! Seriously, Effy, you will get into trouble one day.'

'I am careful. No one will find out.'

Nicholas sighed. 'We are surrounded by people. You think the servants don't talk, but they do. One day someone will tell Mother and Father.'

Evelyn began to tie the ribbons back into her hair. 'I will be more careful.'

'One day they will notice your skin is burnt from the sun.'

Evelyn rolled her eyes in reply.

'Your face will turn brown like a pair of old leather boots.'

Evelyn poked out her tongue and began to stroke the lion's paw as if it was a real animal.

'And your hands will look like they belong to a labourer.'

'I don't mind that,' said Evelyn.

'And your face will become wrinkled like Timmins'.'

Evelyn stopped stroking. 'Our Timmins?'

'Yes, our Timmins.'

'I want to see.' Evelyn abruptly turned and began to walk briskly down the path towards the rose garden.

Exasperated, Nicholas followed. 'Where are you going?'

'To see Timmins' face.' She beckoned him to catch up with her. 'Come on. He's working in the rose garden.'

Shaking his head, Nicholas walked a little quicker. 'I'm only coming to keep you out of trouble.'

'Liar,' accused Evelyn. 'You want to see his wrinkled brown face as much as I do!'

They heard Timmins' shovel methodically cutting and turning the soil, long before they saw his hat above the rose bushes. Nicholas and Evelyn confidently approached him with a plan to engage him in conversation so they could look at his face more clearly. They were on a mission, bonded like soldiers, but at the last moment, when they saw the gardener's head turn in their direction, they panicked and found themselves crouching behind a bush.

Their bodies heaved and hiccupped with stifled laughter at their sudden act of cowardice. Gradually their giggles subsided and they sat for a moment looking at each other, their cheeks flushed, their eyes glistening with excitement, just like it had been between them before his illness. Timmins was momentarily forgotten as other forms of mischief sparked in their minds. The sparks did not last long.

'Hush,' whispered Evelyn. 'Was that Mother?'

They tilted their heads to listen, their bodies mirrored but for Nicholas's rapid breathing. As if on cue, their mother called out again. Evelyn's eyes widened.

'It's all right, Effy,' he whispered. 'She is looking for me. I will go and divert her.'

'No, stay.'

Nicholas shook his head. 'I have no tutor to occupy me so I am in no trouble. You, on the other hand, should be at your lessons.'

Nicholas heaved himself to standing as if he was an old man. It marked the end of their silly adventure that had hardly begun. Evelyn looked up at him gloomily.

'Don't frown so, Effy. You have no reason to look so glum.'

'I have every reason,' she mouthed at him.

He shook his head solemnly. 'No, you don't, Effy. You really don't.'

Evelyn, stiff with anger at her mother for ruining their fun and at Nicholas for allowing her to, sulkily watched him leave. She hugged her knees tightly and listened to her mother's footsteps grinding on the gravelled drive as she approached her brother. She heard her fuss, as if he was a new-born, offering him her shawl and insisting he rested. Her brother's curt refusal helped to smooth Evelyn's frown and she immediately forgave him for leaving her. Their voices grew more distant as he encouraged their mother back to the house. She went willingly and Evelyn, who should have been pleased, felt a stab of hurt at the realisation her mother had not noticed she was missing too.

Evelyn remained seated, toying with the idea of hiding until dark, just to see if anyone would miss her. She would have to find another place to hide. Somewhere the ground was not as hard or littered with broken thorns. The fragrant scent of roses was pleasant enough, but from her position, she could not see them and had to make do with their twisting stems casting her in shadow. She was imprisoned to the spot, bars of needle sharp stems to her left, her mother's distant fussing voice to her right.

She looked through the spikey stems to spy on Timmins. He had stopped working and was leaning casually on the handle of his shovel. His back was to her, so she was unable to see his weathered face, but she could tell that he was looking towards the entrance of the rose garden. She followed his gaze, eager to see what had interrupted his work.

Standing in the rose archway was a boy she did not recognise. Despite keeping his eyes respectfully lowered, Evelyn could see a deep militant furrow marking his brow. He stood quite still, his serviceable dull clothes and pubescent body a stark contrast to the floral garlands that framed him.

Filled with curiosity, Evelyn lengthened her neck to get a better view. The boy looked too uncomfortable in his surroundings to be a member of the outdoor staff. He must be looking for work. Unfortunately, thought

Evelyn, he looked too angry, his chin too stubborn and his stance too militant to please Timmins, who despised insolence in all its forms. It would be best if the boy turned away now and saved himself an ear bashing.

A muscle worked in the boy's jaw as he lifted his gaze to look at Timmins. To Evelyn's surprise, he nervously cleared his throat. The subconscious act enabled Evelyn to see what she had not seen before. It was not obstinacy she was witnessing, but paralysing unease at the fear of rejection.

A wave of empathy for him rose up inside Evelyn, filling every empty part of her. She could feel what he was feeling, as surely as if she was standing in his place, every rapid beat of his heart, every breath that he took which did not seem to quench the thirst for air. She felt it all, as she knew the fear so well.

'What do you want?'

'To see you, sir.' The boy jerked his head in the direction of the main house, but Evelyn knew he was really indicating the outbuildings beyond. 'They said you were working around the front today.'

The gardener began to dig again. 'You have no business coming around the front.'

'I was told to, sir.'

'And they probably laughed behind your back as you left.'

The boy did not leave.

Timmins looked up. 'Did you not hear me?'

'There is only one way to wipe the smile from their faces, sir.'

'I have no work for you. Clear off.'

'I'm a good worker, Mr Timmins. You'll find none better.'

'They all say that.'

'Or as keen to learn as I.' The boy walked forward, slipping his cap from his head to reveal black unruly hair, which curled about his ears and stroked his collar as he walked.

Evelyn found herself rooting for him and silently applauding his courage. Her eyes grew wide and she felt, inexplicably, a little breathless.

He was quite handsome for a boy who had yet to grow into his features, with clear skin, a shapely jaw and an attempt at facial hair that only a youth could be proud of. He stopped a few feet in front of the head gardener; his body obscured from Evelyn's view by the older man's broad back. She had to make do with seeing glimpses of the boy's arm, or the side of his head, as he spoke in his recently broken voice.

'I won't be any trouble, sir,' the boy insisted.

'I have five orphanage boys living in, a visiting journeyman and eighteen permanent workers under me. I need no more like them.'

'I'm different.'

'You are no better than all those who have come before you, desperate for work so you can put food on the table.'

'I'm not looking for work, sir. I want an apprenticeship.'

Timmins snorted. 'I've not taken on an apprentice for years. The training is too hard and long for most.' He stopped digging and took a cloth from his pocket. 'More trouble than they're worth,' he muttered, wiping his forehead and stuffing it back into his trouser pocket. 'To train to become a head gardener you have to love the feel of soil in your hands and have a passion to grow, create, experiment and improve what nature has given us.' He looked closely at the boy for the first time. 'The hours are long and the work hard, but at the end of the day, when your body is aching for sleep, you will have studying to do.' He returned to his digging. 'The pay is poor. You would do better seeking a labouring job at another garden.'

The boy did not move to leave, but Evelyn could see his chin lowering.

'How many brothers or sisters have you got to support? Five? Six?'

'None, sir. There is just my mother and I. I know it will be hard, Mr Timmins, but I want to be a great landscape gardener one day.'

Timmins arched his back to ease his muscles and studied him for a moment.

'I know what will be expected of me, sir,' the boy pressed.

'Do you now.'

'I've asked around. One year as a pot boy doing all the jobs no one wants, then three years learning how to grow things.'

'It's four years and you'll learn a lot more than just that.'

'And then two as a journeyman working at different places.'

'Could be as long as three before you are in charge of your own place or take commissions.'

The boy lifted his chin defiantly. 'I'll train twice as long and twice as hard if it means I can become a great landscape gardener one day.'

Timmins frowned as he studied him. He is wavering, thought Evelyn. He is beginning to consider the boy's request.

'Can you name one?' asked Timmins.

'A great landscape gardener?'

Timmins nodded.

'Capability Brown, sir ...'

'Everyone knows him.'

'London and Wise.'

'They were nurserymen.'

'Mr Steven Switzer and ... and I have an old copy of John Loudon's *Encyclopaedia of Gardening*.'

'That's a big book. You would do better by reading Keane's *The Young Gardener's Educator*.'

The boy grew brave and took a step towards him.

'I have wanted to be a gardener since I could walk, sir. Mother says I have soil in my veins.'

Timmins did not answer immediately. Instead he moved to a rose bush to look at the flowers. The movement finally allowed Evelyn a clear view of the boy again. His eyes flickered briefly and she wondered if he had seen her, but instead he turned his head to watch Timmins. He appeared calm, but Evelyn could see that his fingers were blanched white as he held his cloth cap tightly by his side.

Eventually, Timmins sighed. 'What's your name, boy?' he asked quietly, without turning around.

'Drake Vennor, sir.'

Evelyn smiled. The name suits him, she thought. It was straightforward, strong and close to nature, just like him. He was the exact opposite of her brother in looks and frame, and his tousled hair and rough clothes indicated he was far below her own class. Yet all of the things that should have repelled her interest made him more of a curiosity and a pleasure to study.

'Where do you live?'

'Perran Village, sir. On the corner of Piggy Lane.'

'Leads onto Miller Road?'

'Yes, sir.'

Timmins cut three wilting roses from their stalks. 'I know it,' he said, dropping them onto the ground. 'Vennor, you say. Are you the preacher's son?'

'You knew my father?'

'Knew?'

'He died three years ago.'

'I'm sorry to hear it.' Evelyn didn't think he sounded sorry. 'I attended his bible classes for a time, but I found the preaching hard to stomach in the end. Has your mother remarried?'

Drake shook his head.

'Why did she move to Piggy Lane?'

'Father had died and the rent was cheaper. One day I will buy my mother a house which will be twice as big.'

'She will have a long wait, boy. As an apprentice you are expected to live here – in the bothy. How would your mother feel about that?'

'She expects it. She will leave fresh eggs on your doorstep each week, as a way of a thank you, if you take me on.'

'I don't take bribery, Vennor.'

'I meant no offence, sir.'

Timmins cut off the head of another flower then turned back to the boy. 'There will be a fee up front.'

'I know, sir.'

'The wages are low, starting at three shillings a week. If you do well they could rise to four.'

'It's still a wage, sir. I would do it for nothing.'

'Which would make you a fool.' Timmins frowned. 'But you are no fool, are you, Vennor? I see something in you that I can't quite figure out. I'm not sure if you have a stubborn streak or you are resilient. One you must tame, the other you must nurture.' Timmins nodded decisively. 'We will see how long you last. Collect your things, boy. You can start tomorrow.'

'Thank you, sir. You won't regret it.'

'I will be the judge of that. Now go. I have work to do.'

Evelyn smiled as she watched Drake leave. He was in a hurry, afraid, perhaps, that if he lingered the offer would be snatched back again. Evelyn had no such fear. She had known Timmins all her life. He was reliable and as good as his word, so she was confident the apprenticeship position was Drake's.

She hugged her knees. The thought of seeing the boy again conjured up a feeling of nervous excitement she did not fully understand and made her feel a little nauseous.

Timmins picked up his shovel and turned it in his hands, preparing to slice it into the soil.

'Your mother has gone, Miss Evelyn,' said the head gardener quietly, without taking his eyes from the spade in his hand. 'Your governess will be wondering where you are. I have no wish to lose my job by being party to your absence. You'd better go back inside.'

Evelyn guiltily rose up from her hiding place. A dead leaf fell from her dishevelled hair and her dress became snagged on a thorn. Evelyn carefully untangled herself, nervously glancing up at him and pricking her finger in the process. The head gardener appeared not to have noticed, preferring to concentrate on his digging, but as Evelyn walked away she felt sure she had seen a faint smile upon his lips.

Chapter Two

Drake slowly opened the door and paused on the threshold of his home. They had moved to the house shortly after his father had died and over the last few years he had grown accustomed to its small size and blind to its flaws. Now that he had seen Carrack House, albeit from only the outside, he viewed his home with different eyes. He was reminded how old and basic it was, with only two rooms downstairs and two bedrooms upstairs. On the other side of the house was a small backyard, where the ground turned hard and slippery with ice during the winter. At the far end was the privy, a small brick building housing nothing more than a wooden bench with a hole cut in it, placed over an ash pit, which needed emptying every day. The yard backed onto farmland. It was there, on a small fenced off area, the farmer allowed his mother to keep a few hens. His mother was proud of her hens, for the eggs earned her a few pennies and kept food on their table. However, despite lacking in grandeur, the old house was tidy and homely, with home-made curtains at the window, a rug made out of rags by the fire and his mother where he knew he would find her, on her hands and knees scrubbing the floor with vigorous, well-practiced strokes.

The floor always got a good cleaning when his mother was anxious, whether it needed it or not. She found the chore oddly comforting and he, in turn, found his mother's predictable behaviour equally so. His mother, sensing she was not alone, looked up at him and sat back on her heels.

'Well?' she asked anxiously, brushing a stray hair away from her cheek with her forearm.

He smiled and offered her his hand, which she accepted. She stood; hope lighting up her eyes as she waited for his answer. Her patience quickly ran out.

'What did Mr Timmins say?' she pressed.

Drake turned away and sat down at the table. His mother eagerly followed, wiping her hands on her apron before sitting opposite him. She pushed a plate of bread towards him and waited patiently for his reply as Drake cut himself a slice.

'He has agreed to take me on,' he said, spreading the bread with butter.

'He has?' His mother looked quite shaken with the news. It was as if she couldn't quite believe it.

Drake nodded calmly and took a bite. Their eyes met over the crusty slice and she saw that his news was true. 'Oh! This is wonderful news!' she exclaimed. Drake saw the years fall from her features and he was able to glimpse the young woman she had once been before widowhood had taken its toll. He was pleased his news had been the cause of the change.

'Your father would have been so proud.'

'He would have been prouder if I had followed in his footsteps.'

His mother laughed. 'I think even your father knew you would never make a preacher.'

They fell into silence as they both thought of him. Richard Vennor had been a kindly man, who often remarked that prudence, sobriety and a calling from God in his darkest hour, set him on the path to Methodism. Life could be wicked, he had often warned. His cousin was proof. Anne had been abandoned to bear an illegitimate child alone. The circumstance of Anne's eventual demise was pitiful. If she had placed her faith in God and asked for forgiveness, his father had often lamented, he would have protected her and she'd have lived to a ripe age.

By the time Richard was in his mid-twenties he had become a lay preacher, walking for miles to preach the gospel in neighbouring villages. Mother estimated he took sixty services a year, weekly Sunday Schools and evening bible classes, as well as his labouring jobs. It was at such a class he had met Drake's mother, a shy young woman who was oblivious to her own beauty, or so his father had often recalled. Drake would squirm with embarrassment, as children often do when they are confronted by their parents' intimate teasing. At the time his mother's fine looks were diminished by being seen through a son's eyes. Now, sitting opposite her and a little older, he could see his father had been right. His mother could turn heads if she had a mind to, but her love for his father endured beyond his death and she would never marry again. Drake felt a frisson of surprise at the realisation that he was glad she would never replace him.

'I will have to live there,' Drake warned her.

His mother nodded. 'I knew it would have to be so.'

'It will not be easy.'

'You knew that.'

'Twelve hours a day, six days a week, although if something happens, frost or high winds, I will be called upon at all hours.'

'Tell me about the training,' she asked, folding her arms on the table and leaning forward expectantly.

'One year as a pot boy,' he replied, with a mouth full of bread. In answer to his mother's raised eyebrows, he swallowed before he spoke again. 'I will be washing pots, stoking boilers and studying at night. Then I will spend four years learning the basics of gardening in all the different areas ... kitchen, ornamental, glasshouses.'

'And then what?'

'I will have to go away as a journeyman, to work on other grand estates.'

'Go away?'

'For only two or three years. And then I will gain a position of a head gardener. Nowhere grand at first, but in time it will come. One day they will be requesting my services. It will be my name that will go down in history as the designer of the greatest gardens in the county. I will buy you a grand house, Mother. Just like the one I saw today.'

He saw his mother's eyes sparkle with curiosity.

'Did you see anyone from the big house?' she asked.

Drake thought of the fair-haired girl hiding in the bushes.

'No.' Drake took another bite, a large one that would take a while to eat.

'How was Mr Timmins?'

Drake shrugged in reply.

'Did he question you about your background?'

Drake shrugged again.

'Drake?'

'A bit.'

His mother got up and walked to the window to look out onto the road. 'Does he look healthy?'

Drake laughed. 'I don't want him to drop dead just yet, perhaps when I am fully trained and then I can have his job.'

His mother shot him an angry look. 'That is not what I meant.'

'He *is* old.'

'He is not much older than me, so mind your tongue.'

Drake frowned at her sharp retort. 'Do you know him?'

His mother unrolled the sleeves of her dress. 'Not well,' she said, fussing with the buttons on one of her sleeves. 'He went to bible classes once, but not for long.'

Drake nodded. 'Yes, he did mention that.'

His mother returned to the table and began to gather up invisible crumbs using sharp flicks of one hand to sweep them into her other cupped one. 'Did he now?' she muttered. She removed Drake's plate, forcing him to rescue his bread as it passed under his nose.

'I will have to pay him a fee upfront, but after that I will earn about three or four shillings a week. He does not want any eggs from you. He calls it bribery.'

'I see,' his mother replied quietly. She stood for a moment, as if deep in thought, his empty plate tilted slightly in her hand. Suddenly she came back to life. 'So, Mr Timmins thinks my eggs aren't good enough for him,' she fumed. 'Well, if he changes his mind, he knows where to find me. But he will have to ask nicely, or I will give him half a dozen addled ones. Bribery indeed!' She turned and, to Drake's surprise, dropped the plate into the pig pale used for peelings. 'Silly man!' he heard her mutter. 'Silly foolish man!'

At dawn, Drake left his home and walked the quiet, narrow road from Perran Village to Carrack Estate to start his apprenticeship. Drake eventually found the building that would become his new home. Known as a 'bothy', it was built in the shadow of the kitchen garden's north facing wall. To the gentry, it was ideally situated. It made use of land that was constantly in shadow, yet it was at close quarters to the vital, but vulnerable, vegetables and herbs that required constant monitoring and protecting.

The small building was originally built to accommodate up to eight apprentices. After forty years in constant shadow, its weakened rafters now creaked and groaned under its dipping slate roof. Drake wondered if Timmins' reluctance to take on more apprentices was partly due to the poor state of the bothy, rather than his unwillingness to teach a student.

Drake tentatively opened the door. It was colder and darker inside than out, thanks to its thick granite walls and small windows. Drake paused, squinting until his eyes grew accustomed to the poorly lit rooms. In fact, the downstairs was made up of two rooms, one was sparsely furnished with two long benches and a wooden table for eating and study, the other professed to be a rudimentary kitchen and bathhouse. A ladder led to the upper floor and one large room. Here there was evidence that the place was inhabited. Seven beds, made of coarse, unplaned planks of pine, neatly lined the wall of each room, and beside each bed was a wooden box with a hinged lid where belongings could be stored. Dirty bed linen littered the floor, as if tossed aside in a hurry by the inhabitants. However, the smell of sleeping bodies still lingered in the air and Drake could see clearly the indents of their bodies in six of the straw mattresses, as if their spirits still slept while their bodies toiled outside.

Drake picked his way carefully through their scattered belongings and found an empty bed. He sat down on it and began to unpack the few items he had brought with him, a change of working clothes, books and journals on gardening and finally three gifts from his mother; a notebook, a pen and a pot of ink. He placed them carefully in his box and looked around him, unsure what to do next.

The sound of boots entering the room below resonated up through the floorboards. An old woman's voice followed, accompanied by the smell of milk and oatmeal. Breakfast was being served downstairs. He was about to meet his fellow workers.

Drake later learnt that the bothy was home to one visiting journeyman and five boys who came from the local orphanage and had been sent to Carrack Estate to learn a trade. Four of the boys had arrived at the orphanage as babies, all within a month of each other, and the staff, either lacking imagination or motivation, had named them after the gospels, Matthew, Mark, Luke and John. The fifth, Abel Hicks, had arrived at the age of five and was the elder by two years. On reaching the age of twelve, they had started work at Carrack Estate and they, like most children who had lived their lives in an orphanage, considered themselves fortunate to find bed, board and employment working out of doors upon leaving the institution. However, Drake was soon to learn that they were not so keen to welcome a newcomer into their group. Particularly one who had a home, a mother and an apprenticeship, all of which they lacked. Their opinion of him, Drake came to realise, had been made before his arrival and whatever he said or did would not change it for the better.

It was Luke who climbed the ladder first and found Drake sitting on the bed. The boy was slight in frame, with sandy hair and a thin, pinched face. He looked at Drake warily and called to the others who had remained below.

'He's arrived.'

The tone of his voice had little warmth and told Drake he was not welcome. Drake heard the others gather at the bottom, their voices a mixture of questions and orders. Someone must have tugged on Luke's leg from below, for he looked down and silently retreated back down the ladder.

Another head appeared and looked at him. This boy was stockier than the first, with hair so short that Drake wondered if he had taken a razor to it the week before. His face was pitted and his nose was large and flat as if it had been broken. The boy looked at him through cold eyes partially hidden under heavy lids. He heaved himself into the room, stood up and braced himself. Those cold eyes stared back at him again. They were evenly matched in height, although Drake thought the boy was probably older by a year or two.

'What's your name?' asked the boy, who Drake would later learn was Abel Hicks.

'Drake Vennor.'

Abel's gaze traced the length of his body, taking in his clean hair, clothes and boots. He sniffed and walked around him whilst the other four climbed the ladder and settled on their beds to watch. Unconsciously, the muscles in Drake's body tightened in readiness. It was not the welcome he had hoped for.

Abel looked over his belongings, his gaze finally settling on Drake's books. Drake braced himself but held his tongue. The boy had not done anything yet, best not jump to conclusions as to what he might do.

Abel picked a book up, opened it and began to roughly flick through the pages. Finally, he settled on a page. Imitating a gentleman's accent, Abel began to read. The orphanage taught him to read, thought Drake, but not how to be friendly.

'Using the es-pal-ier technique allows the growth of fruit trees to grow effi-ciently in a limited space.'

The boys laughed at his impersonation as they turned expectant eyes on Drake.

'Espalier?' asked Luke between gasps. 'What's espalier?' His neighbour, Matthew, sobered and dug him in the ribs to be quiet.

'Binding and trimming the branches of fruit trees to increase yield in a limited space,' replied Drake evenly. He reached out his hand for the book, mindful that Abel had already soiled two of the pages with his earth-covered fingers.

Abel closed the book noisily and dropped it on the floor before Drake could take it. The book landed with a thud. Mark, the only boy still laughing, fell silent.

'Fancy words are of no use when there is work to be done.' Abel tilted his chin and looked at Drake down the bridge of his nose. 'You ain't anyone special, Vennor. You will have to work the same as we. Your books ain't going to help you shovel shit and don't you forget it.'

Drake tightened his jaw, but said nothing. Abel waited, but the tempting smell of breakfast reminded him of his hunger, and he suddenly ended the standoff before it really began.

Abel shouldered past Drake and climbed down the ladder. The others obediently followed leaving Drake alone. Their first meeting had not gone how Drake would have hoped, but it was early days and perhaps they would warm to him in time. Drake soon discovered it would not be so.

The bothy boys' contempt for him only increased when they discovered that Drake would be supplied with extra candles to aide his evening study, a privilege they did not have. They could not refuse to work with him, or risk their jobs by being openly hostile, but they found other ways to alienate him and did not wait to use them.

They began by excluding him from their conversations. Drake did not care. He thought their conversations were crude and often offensive to women, and as Drake's only experience of the gender was his mother, who was both virtuous and kind, he was glad to play no part in it. Drake's reaction, or lack of it, troubled the boys even more. From being ignored, he became their main focus and a subject for their taunts and tricks.

If Drake had been weaker in mind and spirit, he would have left his apprenticeship within a few weeks and returned home. The bothy boys had spent their early lives as outcasts of society, but now, with only a temporary journeyman staying and an old woman visiting twice a day to cook, they were their own masters behind the closed bothy door. It was a potent position to find themselves in. They became a pack, whose bond strengthened with each effort to tease the newcomer. His books were hidden, his food spat in and his clothes trampled on. Drake tried to ignore them, but he was no actor. In those first few weeks it grew harder to hide his frustration and disappointment at their juvenile behaviour and although he consoled himself that he was not there to make friends, he knew he would give anything for it not to be so.

Dick, the journeyman, was a good deal older and a little friendlier. For Drake, his presence was a constant reminder of what he hoped to achieve and the career that would be available to him beyond the role of journeyman. Dick had spent the last two years moving from estate to estate in pursuit of horticultural experience and had grown accustomed to meeting and leaving the staff of each place. He had honed his skills well, becoming friends with everyone, but a true friend to no one. However, when he left the following month, he saw fit to offer Drake some words of advice. For once, Drake had risen to the bothy boys' teasing and lunged at the nearest one. Dick returned just in time to pull Drake off Abel before the others felt it their duty to join in. He dragged the furious teenager aside as he ordered the others to leave. Dick looked about him and saw the cause of the incident. Drake's bed was soaked in urine.

'Did they do this?' asked Dick, indicating towards the bed with a jerk of his head.

Drake refused to answer, his eyes pinned mutinously to the floor.

'Your nose is bleeding.'

Drake dabbed at it with the back of his hand and looked at the scarlet stain on his skin, but said nothing. Dick waited for the bothy boys to leave the building. Finally they heard their low grumbling voices receding into the distance as they crossed the yard and headed towards the village.

'You have years of this.' Dick threw him a cloth to wipe his nose. 'Best keep your head down and out of trouble.'

Drake turned away. 'It was not of my making.'

Dick grabbed his shirt. 'Listen, boy,' he hissed under his breath, 'you will meet many people during your apprenticeship that will tempt you to do wrong.' He snapped his fingers in Drake's face, making him jump. 'Your apprenticeship will end, just like that and no one will take you on again.'

Dick's warning felt like a punch to the stomach. Any doubts Drake had whether to continue with his apprenticeship quickly disappeared with the threat of having it taken from him.

'Ahhh,' said Dick, 'that's scared you, hasn't it?'

Dick was right. The thought did scare him, something the bothy boys' teasing had failed to do.

The journeyman's face softened. 'I don't have much longer here and I have no wish to be dragged into your fights. But I also don't want to see good talent go to waste.' He turned and began to rummage through his belongings. When he found what he was searching for, he abruptly stopped and stood up, forcing Drake to step back warily. 'Study hard, Vennor,' he said, thrusting a well-thumbed book towards him. Drake read the title, *The Garden Designs of John Fleming*. It was a book he had been saving to buy. 'Pay no heed to those who do not dream big,' said Dick. He smiled and jabbed the book painfully into Drake's ribs. 'You will never get a chance like this again. Don't let anyone stop you making the most of it.'

Drake looked down at the book and nodded, his throat too clogged with emotion to thank him. He hastily wiped the blood off his hand and took it. Dick was right, he thought as he reread the title. He had to be careful not to put his apprenticeship at risk. He would not let it happen again.

Dick left shortly after for a job as a foreman on an estate in Devon. The journeyman would never know that Drake's retaliation *did* instigate a change in the bothy boys' behaviour towards him. They were no friendlier, but their teasing did stop and they grew wary of the sullen boy. They had come to realise that although Drake was quiet and studious, and his punches were unskilled, his fist felt like granite and had the power to knock out two teeth should he have the mind to use it.

Chapter Three

'Quickly, quickly. They are waiting for you.'

Evelyn ran to the window and looked down onto the great lawn. To her surprise, her parents seemed quite settled. Cups of tea and plates of food were already being served and Nicky and her cousin, Mawgan, were playing ball on the grass. Her earlier excitement quickly dampened. She was aware that Uncle Howard, Aunt Edith and Mawgan were visiting today. It was such a rare event that an intangible tension had hung in the air all morning, similar to that experienced before an approaching storm. Their last visit, when Evelyn was no more than five years old, had ended in a row and resulted in her father vowing that his brother would never set foot inside Carrack House again. It seemed her father was still keeping to his vow. Uncle Howard may have been permitted to visit, but the refreshments of tea and cake were being served on the lawn, which ensured their visitors remained outside of the great house.

'How long have they been here?' Evelyn asked her governess. She was pleased she had been invited to join them, but now it appeared the invitation was more of an afterthought.

Dear Miss Brown tried to cheerfully console her. 'Not long. Your mother wants you to wear your blue dress. Now where is it?'

Evelyn allowed herself to be dressed, obediently stepping out of her old dress, and into a circle of blue material, which was immediately lifted up so she could thread her arms through the sleeves. She stood for a moment as a maid buttoned her up.

'It feels tight,' Evelyn muttered, 'and it will be too hot.'

Miss Brown's worried expression told Evelyn that she thought the same. 'You *have* grown since you last wore it. But your mother insisted upon it and I dare not go against her wishes.'

Evelyn looked down at her chest. Her budding breasts felt tender as they strained against the tight fabric. 'I shall get all sweaty,' she grumbled, wondering if the new apprentice gardener would be working near the lawn today. She did not want to appear sweaty in front of him.

'Hush. A young lady must not talk of bodily functions. Now hurry, put your boots on, or your mother will grow anxious.' Evelyn did as she was told and waited in silence as the maid buttoned them up. 'You must wear a hat. We can't let your freckles come out.'

After another flurry of activity, a hat was produced from a hatbox and placed on Evelyn's head. Evelyn stood still and tried her best not to fidget in order for Miss Brown to give her a final look over as the maid tidied the scattered clothes and boxes round them. Miss Brown bit her lip as she examined her charge. She looked worried so Evelyn gave her, what she hoped, was a charming smile.

Miss Brown couldn't help but return it. 'They will be proud of you. They *should* be proud of you. Now hurry. Hurry!'

Her governess flapped her hands, ushering Evelyn out of the bedroom and down the stairs to the waiting party below. Evelyn felt nervous with excitement. Although her parents often entertained, they were usually evening affairs, which excluded their children. It was most unusual for them to have tea in the afternoon on the great lawn and for her father's relatives to be present. As Evelyn approached the gathering, her steps slowed. Doctor Birch was sitting by her mother's side and, if the crumbs on his plate were anything to go by, had been present for some time. Everyone had been there for some time, except for Evelyn.

Her mother noticed her arrival and indicated to the vacant seat next to her.

'Evelyn, dear, come and sit next to me. Brown, fetch her one of my parasols.' She gave Evelyn one of her fleeting, sideways, glances as she sat down. 'We must buy you a new dress,' she said through a tight smile, before returning her gaze back to Nicholas.

Her mother's remark, although kindly meant, ensured that Evelyn felt even more conspicuous than her late arrival had made her feel. It seemed to Evelyn that her dress grew tighter, and she was sure that if anyone cared to look in her direction they would see what a spectacle she must be. A parasol was placed in her hands. Again, she heard her mother's quiet voice, spoken from the corner of her smile and in the manner she reserved for Sunday service.

'Evelyn, dearest, you are holding it like a placard. Tilt it, like so.'

Evelyn carefully imitated her mother's demonstration and copied how she placed her feet. Her mother's final sideways glance lingered this time, and her smile softened. She gave her a single, gracefully tilted, nod. Her wordless praise meant everything to Evelyn, as it gave her the consent that she could stay.

More tea and cakes were served and Evelyn found herself successfully juggling parasol, a teacup and eating a slice of cake, without disgracing herself. While her confidence grew, she remained silent, just as her father would wish. Besides, she had little to say that would be of interest and she was content to watch and learn.

She looked at her father over the brim of her teacup. Her father's brow was permanently in a frown, which was all the more prominent due to his receding hairline. Where he lacked hair on his head, his sideburns remained as thick as ever, framing his cheeks like two gloved hands. It was as if, Evelyn thought, his hair had slipped down his cheeks from the top of his head and got lodged on his starched collar. Perhaps the stiffness in his posture was due to his facial hair, she thought suddenly, and if he did not have it he would be more relaxed like Nicholas.

Evelyn turned her attention to her uncle. She remembered little about him, except for one vivid memory of his large bushy moustache. She was pleased to see her memory had served her well. It had not changed, remaining as thick as she recalled and still resembled the bristles of a brush. Today it moved like a caterpillar as he spoke and Evelyn was surprised that she had not remembered that too.

Mother and Aunt Edith were content to admire their sons playing ball. Mother was in her best afternoon dress and Evelyn suspected Aunt Edith was too. Their hair was equally dressed to perfection and their impeccable manners and politeness to one another could not be faulted. However, their behaviour lacked the relaxed manner that came with true friendship and Evelyn could not help but feel an underlying tension weave its way around the party.

The only person who seemed at ease was Doctor Birch. In fact, thought Evelyn, if a stranger was to arrive at this very moment, they could easily mistake him for the owner of Carrack House, for he sat amidst the party emanating confidence and power that even seemed to eclipse her father's. Evelyn likened it to a magical aura that surrounded him and was ever present. She knew she was not the only one to be in awe of him. His presence cast a spell on her mother whenever they met, leaving her moronic, amenable, but always grateful. Evelyn felt all of those things too, but unlike her mother, she felt ultimately fearful.

'Which school does Nicholas attend?' asked Uncle Howard.

Her father carefully placed his cup onto the saucer, without making a sound, and sat back in his chair. 'We have a home tutor for Nicholas.'

'Mr Burrows was highly recommended to us,' interjected her mother. 'In addition to Greek and Latin, he is a master of two additional languages. He is in great demand for his knowledge of science. We are fortunate to have him.'

'But a home tutor is no substitute for the benefits of a boarded education. To be educated away from home develops ones character, principles and ability to govern. Nicholas would benefit from the sport that is on offer. It will help build a healthier body.'

'Nicholas is healthy,' came her father's curt reply.

'I'm sure he is,' soothed Aunt Edith. She turned to Doctor Birch. 'We were terribly worried when we heard of his illness last year.'

'Worried he would survive,' her father muttered under his breath. Evelyn's fearful glance round the gathering told her that she was the only one to have heard him.

'We all were,' replied her mother. 'And I, for one, thank God every day that Doctor Birch was on hand to attend him.' She gave Doctor Birch a warm smile.

He accepted her praise with a smile of his own, confident that he deserved the compliment.

Not wishing to be outdone, Aunt Edith added, 'I also have much to be grateful to Doctor Birch for.' Both women turned their heads towards their sons. No more needed to be said. They all knew that Doctor Birch was the only doctor to deliver them a live child.

Evelyn watched the two boys play. Mawgan was sixteen and a good deal taller than her brother. He had fine features, with hair the colour of caramel and eyes to match. He was much better at handling a ball, and probably excelled in sport, but he rarely smiled, and there was a stiffness about him, which gave the appearance of containment and aloofness.

'May I play ball with Nicholas and Mawgan, Mother?' asked Evelyn, without thinking.

Her mother answered without looking at her, 'No, dear.' She turned towards her sister-in-law. 'Ladies do not play ball, do they, Edith?' The two women laughed, as did the men. For the first time, there was a tangible softening in the tension that had coiled around them. Evelyn felt her cheeks burn and wished she had the power to disappear. The boys heard the laughter and stopped their game. She saw Nicholas scan the party until his searching look settled on her glum, red face. After a short exchange of words, Nicholas and Mawgan approached, coming to her rescue.

'I would like to show Mawgan the gardens, Father,' said Nicholas, breathless from their game. He addressed Evelyn with a twinkle in his eye that told her he knew what her answer would be before he asked the question. 'Effy, would you like to come too?'

Evelyn exerted all the control she could muster not to run into his arms. 'Father, may I?' she asked politely.

For five long heartbeats, her father considered her request. The children's departure would leave a void. The admiration of the boys, the discussion of their education, even the teasing of Evelyn's innocence, provided a much-needed buffer between the families. Evelyn found herself holding her breath.

Finally, her father gave a curt nod of his head. 'You may.'

Their parents silently watched the children leave; contemplating how they would manage without them, yet resigned to the fact it would be churlish to call them back.

Evelyn heard Doctor Birch's cultured voice break the silence, as he began to recount about his latest trip to London. His monologue filled the vacancy to perfection, both in subject and interest, as he had attended a lecture on the affliction of insanity.

Although no one owned it, every family had a distant relative who had suffered the weakness. Evelyn suspected her mother's aunt had turned mad following the loss of her child. She had withdrawn from society quite suddenly and was never mentioned again. It was as if she had disappeared, even her portrait was removed from the wall and stored away. Evelyn stole a glance over her shoulder as she walked away and noted the interest in his captive audience's eyes. Yes, Doctor Birch had chosen his topic well, thought Evelyn, as it tapped into their fears and gave him centre stage.

'I hope you will not leave Cornwall to attend the elite in London,' Evelyn heard her mother ask nervously.

Doctor Birch's chuckle drifted across the lawn to the children. 'Of course not. My loyalty is to Cornwall,' he replied. Evelyn heard a murmur of delight at his answer, but in truth no one believed him.

The children walked at the pace set by Nicholas, and followed the meandering path through the gardens. Even Evelyn, who knew the gardens well, enjoyed the tour, seeing it through new eyes just as Mawgan was now. For the first time that afternoon, she began to relax. Her dress felt less constricted now that she was standing. She also felt in more control of her mother's parasol, so much so that she began to twist its handle in her fingers so it spun daintily on her shoulder.

'You should visit us more often,' she ventured, squinting up at her cousin's tall frame.

He looked down at her with eyes that observed rather than welcomed a connection.

'I think we should be thankful Mawgan is here at all,' answered Nicholas for him.

'Why?'

'Because Uncle Howard does not wish to visit more often,' said Nicholas. 'Cedar Lodge is situated at the boundary of Carrack Estate. This means that much of the adjacent countryside belongs to Father and is a constant reminder to Uncle Howard of his misfortune at being born second by only a few minutes.'

'Uncle Howard is jealous? Is that why he won't let you visit more often?'

'I would not call it jealousy,' replied Mawgan as he looked out towards the distant parkland.

Keen to find a solution, Evelyn said, 'The estate is so big that I'm sure Nicholas would be happy to give you half when he inherits.' She turned to her brother. 'You wouldn't mind, would you Nicky?'

Nicholas's face paled.

Mawgan came to his rescue. 'I don't think it will have to come to that,' he said as he looked down at her. 'Time has a way of sorting things out.'

Evelyn smiled nervously. She did not understand what he meant, but his unwavering look made her feel like a curious object being studied by a scientist.

'All this talk about inheritance is depressing,' said Nicholas. 'Let me show you the greenhouses where the tropical fruits are grown. Father would be most disappointed if I did not show them to you.'

The children skirted the side of Carrack House and headed towards the working gardens. It was not an area that Evelyn often explored, as it was usually too busy with gardeners potting, planting, pruning and harvesting. Suddenly she felt a thrill of nervous excitement for going there. She had not seen the new boy for almost a month, even though she had often looked down on the established gardens from her nursery window.

'We have twenty-five gardeners to tend to the gardens near the house, the parkland and wild gardens further north,' said Nicholas as they entered the first walled garden through an open wooden door. 'Most live out and come from the nearby villages. We have a few who live in, but not many.'

'We also have an apprentice,' said Evelyn proudly, glad to have something to contribute for once. The boys silently surveyed the scene.

They had entered the fruit garden. South facing sloping glasshouses lined the far redbrick wall, tempting the children to explore them. The north and east facing walls were lined with stone buildings used for storing implements, fruit and, according to Nicholas, provided a home to some of the boys. Evelyn found herself searching the small windows for a glimpse of the new apprentice, yet knowing full well he would not be there at that time of day.

Nicholas called to Evelyn to follow. Reluctantly, she dragged her eyes away and shadowed the boys along the path through the centre of the yard. Low slanting glass pineapple houses occupied each quadrant. At the centre of the yard was a man-made pond, a valuable source of water for the tender plants. Evelyn felt hot. Concerned she may break out into a sweat, she dipped her fingers into the cold water and dabbed her neck as she passed.

The children entered each glasshouse in turn, too inquisitive to pass them by. Trained branches of three peach trees skimmed the glass ceilings, like a fan, above their heads. Grapes, not yet ripe, hung tantalisingly within reach in the vinery, and melons, growing ever plumper, were like merry, round faces watching them pass through. Evelyn was the only one who paid attention to the gardeners who worked around them. She found herself waiting with a hesitant breath, until she could dismiss them as not being the boy called Drake Vennor.

They left the heat of the glasshouses behind them, and headed for the next walled garden, dedicated to vegetables. They passed by Mr Timmins' office, unaware he was watching them stroll by.

The vegetable garden was large and precise in its design. Rows upon rows of leafy plants stretched before them like soldiers. Large, orange clay pots stood amongst the rhubarb, waiting to be used later in the year and a scarecrow stood sentry near the middle. Apple trees, their branches trained to form a tunnel, framed the centre path and dangled small, green, unripe apples. More gardeners were at work here, digging, weeding and harvesting. None of them were Drake.

They followed the path around the side of the gardens and back to the house. The boys were in deep conversation, but Evelyn had lost interest and trailed behind them, disappointed at not seeing the new apprentice. When she noticed they had disappeared from view, she quickened her pace and followed their voices to catch them. Suddenly she was entering another yard she had never visited before. The handle of her parasol stilled in her fingers.

Almost two hundred orange pots lined the wall, waiting to be washed and refilled, but Evelyn did not notice one of them, for it was the boy drawing water from the well that held her attention.

The bucket looked heavy, as he lifted it from the well and carried it to a battered tin bath, where he set about cleaning each pot. He crouched, scrubbed and stretched for another, unaware he was being watched. His movements were agile, and although he was no more than fourteen, Evelyn could see the emerging strength of the man he would become. His trousers were dirty, his forearms smudged with soil and his face was set in a deep frown of concentration, but the way his body moved transfixed her. Her brother noticed.

'Is this *your* apprentice?' he asked.

The boy looked up.

'He's not *my* apprentice,' said Evelyn under her breath. 'Let's go.'

Mawgan ignored her and continued to stare at the boy. Nicholas, concerned at the edge in her tone, stood in his sister's way.

'What's the matter, Effy?' he asked, intrigued. 'Why have you gone red?'

'I am not red. You are *embarrassing* me.'

'In front of whom? There is nobody here but us.'

How could Evelyn tell her brother it was the gardener she wanted to hide from? She couldn't, for he was meant to be of no consequence. Reluctantly she turned back and looked at everything but Drake. The pots, the soil, the water, the walls – anywhere but into those dark brown eyes.

Amused by her reaction, Mawgan approached Drake, who was obliged to stand and remove his cap. His dark tousled hair gave him a wild, dangerous look that suited him. In comparison Evelyn felt her body was nothing but a mismatch of long limbs, big hands and sweaty armpits.

'What's your name?' Mawgan asked as he looked him over with an arrogant tilt of his chin.

Evelyn cringed with discomfort.

'Drake Vennor, sir.'

'How long have you been in employment here?'

'I started my apprenticeship a month ago.'

Mawgan acknowledged his answer with a nod of his head. He turned to Evelyn.

'Nicholas was right. It appears that Vennor here is *your* apprentice, Evelyn.'

Evelyn lifted a furtive glance in his direction. The set of his mouth in a firm narrow line told her he was not taking kindly to being a butt of their joke. She wanted to die.

'Father will be wondering where we are,' she muttered.

Nicholas disagreed. 'We have plenty of time yet, Effy.'

Mawgan continued his questioning. 'Are you enjoying your apprenticeship?'

Drake gave a single nod of his head.

'Is there a need for study?'

Another nod.

'It seems we are studying the wrong subjects, cousin,' teased Mawgan. 'We spend our time studying Latin when we could pass our time learning how to grow grapes? Much less taxing and we will have something to eat at the end of it.'

Pleased with his joke, Mawgan's eyes lingered on the boy for his reaction, but received none. Mawgan's cheeks reddened. 'Let's leave him to his chores,' he said, suddenly tiring of Drake. He turned abruptly and led the way out of the yard. Nicholas quickly followed.

Evelyn wanted to apologise for her cousin's behaviour, yet felt ill-equipped to do it. She had been taught that one did not apologise to staff and a woman must never apologise for a man's behaviour, for it would demean him and in doing so disgrace the woman. It did not help that Drake was a fine-looking boy.

She stood looking at him, unable to move. She felt awkward and clumsy in his presence, as her body strained against the stitching of her dress. She attempted an apologetic, but feeble smile and then thought better of it. She was too late. He saw it and misread that she was laughing at him, just as she feared. His frown deepened as he forced his cap on his head and returned to his work, effectively dismissing her from his company.

Nicholas called for her. She hesitated for a moment, torn between her brother's company and this boy in dirty clothes. She wanted to leave on friendlier terms, yet he was not even acknowledging her presence. Her brother called again. Reluctantly she left.

The children rejoined their parents on the grand lawn. Polite conversation continued to flow, as did the tea and impeccable manners. Evelyn sat quietly next to her mother, filled with tangled emotions she felt unable to unravel.

Chapter Four

'He is like a vulture circling above us. He wishes me dead. He wishes our son dead.' Sir Robert watched the servants clear away the table and chairs from the great lawn, his hands clasped tightly behind his back, his shoulders pulled back as if bracing himself for a fight. 'It was a mistake to invite him here,' he concluded. 'A mistake, I tell you.' He poured himself some brandy, drank it with a jerk of his head and returned to the window. 'Bloody servants. They are making a mess of the lawn. Can't they remove the furniture without traipsing back and forth so much?' He turned away from the window, unable to watch.

'Why did you invite him?' asked Lady Pendragon as she sat nursing a headache. 'You have not seen him in years.'

'I thought it would be a good opportunity to show him how much Nicholas has recovered from his illness.'

'Nicholas has not fully recovered. I have been telling you this for months.'

For once his wife was right.

'I can see that now. Compared to Mawgan, he looks frail and breathless. He needs more exercise to build up his muscles.'

'He needs more rest,' argued Lady Pendragon. 'Doctor Birch recommends a new tincture.'

'Another concoction bought at an extortionate price. Nicholas has had enough of his potions.'

'He does not need exertion, Robert. I worry for him enough without your ideas adding to my burden.'

Lady Pendragon sat in a chair, nervously plucking at her handkerchief. Her distress did not help her husband's mood. He returned to the window. To his relief, the furniture had been removed and his garden was back to how it had been prior to his brother's visit; colourful, fragrant, but most importantly, neat and orderly.

'Howard's hope to claim Carrack House for himself may be fading, but his hope for Mawgan to replace Nicholas has grown. I know what is in his mind. It won't happen. I won't allow it.' He turned to his wife. 'We will build up Nicholas's strength so there will be no doubt. Let the vulture dine elsewhere.'

Evelyn read the last sentence of her book and looked up at her governess. Miss Brown's head nestled in the wings of her favourite armchair as she snored rhythmically into her chest. She looked so peaceful. Every line on her face had been ironed away as her responsibilities were forgotten.

On previous occasions, Evelyn would already be exploring the gardens, but her mindset had changed since her last encounter with Drake and she would no longer take advantage of her governess's affliction. Bearing witness to her cousin's teasing of Drake had, inadvertently, held a mirror up to her own behaviour. She had been unfair and cruel to make fun of her beloved governess and she would not do it again.

Miss Brown was the kindest woman to be appointed to the nursery and Evelyn had grown fond of her. Dare she admit to it, but she thought she might even love her more than her own mother, for it was Miss Brown who comforted her when she was upset and wiped away her tears.

Of course, it was easier to remain seated and behave well, when the mere thought of seeing the boy again filled her with trepidation.

Miss Brown stirred in her sleep. Evelyn smiled and wondered, not for the first time, why her governess had remained a spinster. She was not unattractive and Evelyn felt sure she would have had a proposal at some point in her youth. As it was a woman's duty to marry – and marry well – Miss Brown's misfortune hid a mysterious tale. She knew she was the youngest of five daughters and her mother was a widow, perhaps her mother had simply lost motivation by the time it was Miss Brown's turn to marry. Evelyn gave a start when she realised Miss Brown had woken and was looking at her.

Two pink spots glowed on Miss Brown's cheeks as she straightened herself in her chair. 'It is rather warm in here. I must have fallen asleep,' she said, fussing with her hair. She found a stray lock and smoothed it back into place. 'I do apologise. It is no reflection on your reading. Your mother … it would be best if she did not find out.'

Evelyn would not have told her, she cared for Miss Brown too much. Even so, perhaps now was a good time to ask her why she was not married.

Miss Brown raised an eyebrow at her impertinent question. An unspoken understanding passed between them. Evelyn would not report her governess and Miss Brown would not report her pupil for her poor manners. Miss Brown considered her answer, every train of thought reflected in her face and watched carefully by Evelyn.

'I chose not to marry,' she replied crisply, taking a sudden interest in the folds of her skirt.

Evelyn was shocked. 'You *chose* not to marry!'

Miss Brown nodded.

'I thought no one had asked you,' blurted out Evelyn.

'I have been asked, twice, but one was rather old … the other rather … hairy.'

An image of a monkey came to Evelyn's mind.

'The truth is,' continued Miss Brown, 'I have never met a man I had an inclination to marry. Mother despaired. I felt it was more conducive to maintaining a cordial relationship with her if I left home.' She pushed herself up from the chair and collected the book, which lay forgotten on Evelyn's lap. 'I found employment as a governess with a family in Falmouth,' she said, inspecting the cover, 'and resolved that marriage was not for me.' She returned it to the bookshelf, taking a moment to line it up neatly.

'How awful for you!' exclaimed Evelyn.

'Awful?'

'To have never fallen in love.'

Miss Brown began to neaten all of the books on view. 'I never said I have never fallen in love.'

Miss Brown was a mystery after all. Evelyn jumped to her feet and ran to her.

'How many times?'

'Once.'

'What was he called?'

Miss Brown gave her a coquettish glance over her shoulder. 'Francis.'

Evelyn could not contain her excitement and began to follow her around the room as she pretended to tidy.

'What did he look like?'

'A little taller than me, with thick dark hair and the most beautiful eyes I had ever seen.' She paused for a moment, a whimsical smile lit up her face.

Evelyn was intrigued. She had never seen this side to her governess before.

'What was he like?'

'Francis was educated, quite the activist and very courageous. Francis feared no one, which is the complete opposite to me.'

She began to rearrange Evelyn's paintbrushes. 'We must start a new painting project. Your father is very proud of his garden and I think documenting it through the seasons would make a wonderful collection.'

'Why didn't you marry him?'

Miss Brown carefully closed the lid of the paint box.

'Marriage was not an option.'

'Did he ask you?'

'No. I told you, it was not an option. Anyway, Mother would never have accepted our feelings for one another.'

'He was married! Oh, Miss Brown!'

'Hush, before someone hears you.'

'Oh, but—'

'No more questions,' whispered Miss Brown.

Evelyn tried not to speak, but failed. 'How can you bear not to be with him?'

'I have you to love.'

'That is not the same and you know it.'

'If we remained together we would have become outcasts of society. I was not brave enough to endure that.'

Evelyn felt her heart break for her. 'Do you regret the choice you made?' she asked.

Miss Brown paused in her tidying of Evelyn's paintbrushes. 'Do I regret my decision?' she asked herself as she traced her finger across the bristles of one of them. She sighed. 'Yes, Evelyn. Every day of my life.'

Autumn announced its arrival with the appearance of migrant redwing and ripe black sloes lining the hedgerows. Green leaves turned to scarlet, orange and yellow, adorning the trees like coins of gold and ruby gems. Despite nature's preparations for dormancy, the gardeners continued to battle against it within the glasshouses. Eventually autumn came to a temperate end, leaving in its wake memories of abundant harvests of sweet pineapples, figs and grapes it had unknowingly helped to nurture.

On the last day of November, a heavyset horse pulled a cart filled with seaweed into the yard. As the horse was led away to be fed and watered, Drake was given the unpleasant task of unloading it. He climbed on-board, his feet slipping on the tangled, sand peppered weed. The seaweed had been collected from the west coast of Cornwall and brought to the estate to nourish the soil in the vegetable garden. Drake had studied its properties, but it was the first time he had seen the alien plant and smelt its shoreline aroma. It was heavy, slippery and back-breaking work, so it was no surprise he did not notice Miss Evelyn and her governess arrive in the garden next door.

Drake eventually stopped, resting his forearm on his fork handle to catch his breath. The height of the cart allowed him a fine view over the red brick wall and the gardens beyond. He looked about him with a critical eye. In the midst of the earthy browns and dark green leaves of the cabbages, he saw the girl who had laughed at him and made him feel a fool.

She sat at her easel, her face serious with concentration as she attempted to faithfully replicate the rows of vegetables in front of her. She wore a warm coat and gloves, but no hat. Her fair hair, the colour of ripe wheat ready for harvesting, hung down her back in a thick plait. He had heard from the other gardeners that she had been seen painting, but she had not ventured this near to the work yard before. The humiliation he had been subjected to at their last encounter still felt surprisingly raw. He turned his attention back to his chore, each stab of the fork an attempt to spend his pent-up anger – no frustration – at not being able to argue back the last time they had met. He did not notice the girl exchange words with her governess, leave her easel and take a walk towards the yard.

'Hello.'

He paused for half a breath and then stabbed the fork into the stinking mess at his feet.

The girl tried again, this time a little louder. 'Hello.'

'I heard you,' he replied curtly, straightening to look at her. He gave her his meanest stare. She had the good grace to look a little nervous.

'Don't stop working on my account.'

She expects me to say, 'It's all right, miss. I'll stop for you, miss. I'll doff my cap to you, miss,' thought Drake. *She'll get none of that bowing and scraping from me.*

He stabbed his fork into the seaweed again.

'What are you doing?' she asked.

'What does it look like?' he asked rudely, lifting a fork laden with seaweed and dropping it over the side.

She fell silent. Drake tried to concentrate on his job, but remained acutely aware that she continued to watch him as she absently twisted the heel of her right foot into the ground. Eventually she tried again.

'I am painting the vegetable garden for my father. I have painted most of the others already. I plan to show the gardens in the different seasons, but Miss Brown says I won't be able to spend so much time in the garden during the winter.'

Drake ignored her. He did not care what she chose to do with her time.

'Can you paint?' she asked. The absurd question almost made him laugh.

'When do I have time to paint?' he retorted angrily. Her nervousness turned to hurt and for the first time he felt he had gone too far, but then her questioning began again.

'How is your apprenticeship training?' she asked quietly.

Her interest confused him, almost as much as her manner. He grew wary. No one, except his mother, had ever asked him that question. No one else really cared.

'Why?'

'I would like to know. Nicholas is taught lots of things, but I'm a girl.' She did not explain further. 'Is it difficult?'

Drake thought for a moment. 'The bothy's cold, my bed is hard and I am running out of ink.'

'Oh, I could get you more ink,' she said, looking hopeful.

Drake felt he had worked her out. He went back to his task. 'And be dismissed for stealing from you when you inform your parents that I have ink from your father's desk.'

To her credit, she sounded horrified. 'I would never do that!' she said, climbing the wheel of the cart.

Her sudden appearance unsteadied him. He felt his foot slide.

'Why are you so mean?' she asked as he landed on his bottom.

'You were the one who laughed at me.'

She watched him get up. 'I was not laughing at you. Don't roll your eyes at me.'

Drake returned to his chore, lifting the heavy seaweed over the opposite side of the cart to where Miss Evelyn clung to the side, glaring at him. Mr Timmins could arrive at any moment. If he was not finished, he would have some explaining to do. Miss Evelyn, however, had other ideas.

'I did not laugh,' she insisted. 'I smiled. It was a gesture of friendship.'

The girl was clearly mad.

'Why would you do that?'

Her eyes widened, as if she was unsure herself. She shrugged her shoulders. 'I would like us to be friends.'

They could never be friends. It was impossible and he didn't even want to anyway. He could easily put an end to her absurd idea.

'I don't need a new friend. Least of all a child.'

'You aren't much older than me,' she argued. 'I am thirteen – almost fourteen. Mother says I can move out of the nursery soon and have my own bedroom. I will be able to see Lady May's lion from my window.'

Drake did not answer. She was much younger than him with regard to experience of life. However, her ramblings had given him a glimpse into her life behind the walls of the grand house and it left him with more questions than he cared to admit to. Why, when she lived in such a large house, did she not have a bedroom of her own? What was a nursery? Why would a girl who has everything, want to talk to him? He was too proud to ask them, conscious that he might appear ignorant in her eyes.

'I'm sorry that my cousin made fun of you.' He knew she was watching him, waiting for a flicker of forgiveness. He did not give it.

She attempted conversation again. 'Miss Brown says it will be too cold to paint in the gardens again. I will paint from my window until spring.'

She waited for his reply, but received none. Drake heard her sigh and felt the cart shift as she climbed down.

'Goodbye, Drake.' He jabbed the seaweed with his fork, but his action lacked both energy and purpose. She was finally leaving.

Drake lifted his gaze to watch her walk away. She had been the only one to use his first name and in doing so made him feel valued as an individual for the first time since his arrival. A sense of unease swept through him. Had he been wrong about her after all?

If any doubts lingered in Drake's mind regarding Miss Evelyn's remorsefulness, they were swept away the following week with the arrival of thick blankets for the bothy workers. The blankets were, undoubtedly, cast-offs from Carrack House's well-stocked linen store, but despite being faded and well used, they were still serviceable and provided much needed warmth as the winter chill set in. The other bothy boys whooped with joy when they discovered the new bedding. Their gratefulness did not last long. Their resentment of their employer's wealth soon resurfaced and their earlier enthusiasm quickly changed to grumbles that it had taken so long to receive adequate bedding in the first place.

Drake turned his back to them and snuggled deep down into the warmth provided by the blankets. Only Evelyn knew that they lacked blankets, he thought, she must have arranged their delivery. Perhaps he had misjudged her. He cringed when he remembered how rude he had been to her. He wanted to take it back and thank her for the blankets, but knew that he probably wouldn't see her again until spring. Spring seemed so far away. Strangely, the thought of having to wait so long marred the joy the arrival of the blankets had brought.

Chapter Five

As a first year apprentice, Drake was given the responsibility of maintaining the temperatures in the glasshouses and pineapple pits. He spent most of December and January carrying sacks of bark for the pits and coal for the boilers. The rest of the time he was a slave to the thermometer, either stoking the boilers to increase the heat or opening the glass vents should it reach too high. Outside, biting frosts blanched his fingers and stung his cheeks, whilst the heat of the glasshouses and sheer exertion of shovelling coal, caused sweat to trickle down his back.

The gruelling work built muscle, chiselling his arms and legs as his body grew taller. He turned fifteen and thought of Miss Evelyn, wondering if she had also had her birthday.

February brought a night of heavy snow. It fell silently, watched only by Drake as he made his final check on the glasshouse's temperature during the night. By the morning the landscape was covered in a diamond encrusted blanket of thick, white snow. It glistened in the sun and provided the perfect backdrop to the flowering camellias, hellebores and daffodils.

It was within this enticing scene that he saw her again, picking her way carefully through the snow covered path, with Master Nicholas by her side. They walked slowly, their heads bowed, their arms interlinked, ready to support one another should either of them slip. Drake stopped what he was doing to watch her. She wore a deep burgundy coat, with mink fur cuffs, brown buttoned boots and matching gloves and hat. She was a flash of vibrant colour in a white sea and he wondered if this might be his opportunity to thank her for the blankets. He wiped his hands on his trousers as he rehearsed in his head what he would say if he got a chance, but all his good intentions were forgotten when he saw Master Nicholas collapse.

Drake was already running before she called for help and was the first to arrive. She was kneeling in the snow and looked up at him as he approached. She looked stricken.

'Nicky's not well,' she needlessly explained. 'He wanted to see the snow.' Master Nicholas's head lay in her lap. There was a blue tinge to his lips as his chest heaved for breath. 'Nicky! Nicky! Wake up!' she pleaded.

His eyes moved beneath their lids and flickered open. He looked about him, confused. His wide-eyed stare frightened them both.

'Fetch Father and Mother!' cried Evelyn.

Drake did not need to be asked a second time and sprinted towards the house.

He ran to the nearest entrance, the grand front door, and banged on its oak panels with the side of his fist. Too impatient to wait for an answer, he pushed open the door and ran into the hall, leaving a trail of snow to melt on the marble floor in his wake.

He hesitated, momentarily overwhelmed by the opulence of his surroundings. Statues stood in alcoves and looked at him with disdain and the high ceiling, decorated with ribbons and swag mouldings, made him feel small. A footman's loud reprimand brought him to his senses. He ran to the nearest door and pushed it open.

Sir Robert Pendragon stood by a large white marble fireplace, with a letter in his hand. Lady Pendragon sat at her writing desk, penning one of her own.

'It's Master Nicholas, sir. He has been taken ill.'

Lady Pendragon abruptly stood, causing sheets of paper to flutter to the floor from her desk.

'Where is he?' asked Sir Robert, striding for the door.

Drake followed him out into the hall. 'On the east lawn … with Miss Evelyn.'

They ran outside, quickly followed by the butler who had appeared from nowhere. Two garden workers reached Evelyn at the same time as Drake and her parents. More indoor staff arrived and a commotion ensued. Sir Robert finally brought some order.

'Allow my son some air!' he barked.

Lady Pendragon arrived, parting the crowd with her mere presence. For the first time, she could see her son's oddly coloured lips.

'Somebody fetch Doctor Birch,' she cried, reaching for Nicholas.

Her husband barred her with an outstretched arm. 'We need to bring him inside.' He addressed his staff. 'Inside! Now!'

Nicholas was lifted into the air and carried towards the house on a moving bed of people and flanked by his parents. Evelyn, who had been largely ignored, was finally helped to her feet by Timmins. He picked up her hat from the bed of snow and returned it to her. She looked at it with glazed eyes.

'Thank you, Timmins,' she murmured and stiffly turned, intending to follow the procession.

Drake noticed her chin dimple when she saw Nicholas's pale hand lying limp and unsupported amongst the eager hands that carried him. Drake felt her sadness and stepped forward to support it, but someone, with cleaner hands than he, pushed him away. The message was clear. He was no longer needed. He watched, solemnly, the tangle of human bodies carrying their precious cargo, followed sombrely by Evelyn in her vibrant red coat. In her hand she held her hat, its red ribbons trailing in the snow like streaks of blood.

'How long were you out there?'

Tears stung the back of Evelyn's eyes. 'No more than a few minutes, Father.' She watched him pace the floor. His anxiety frightened her.

'Nicholas must have overexerted himself.'

'It was only a walk, Father.'

'I don't believe it.' He didn't want to believe it. 'What were you doing? Playing one of your silly games, no doubt?'

She wished they had, but Nicholas had lost interest of late.

'Nicholas asked if I would like to go outside to look at the snow. I said yes, Father. How is Nicholas? What is wrong with him?'

'I don't know.' He sat down and massaged his knotted brow with his fingertips. 'Doctor Birch is with him.'

Lady Pendragon entered the room. 'You know exactly what is wrong with him,' she accused her husband. She addressed her daughter, but the words were for him. 'Vital medicine has been withheld from him. Now he is ill. From today, we do everything Doctor Birch recommends. *Everything.*'

'That is unfair, Beatrice. Nicholas has had the best medicine money can buy. He has not been right since his illness last year. His heart has been weakened and he is tired of taking Doctor Birch's miracle cures. No amount of potions will bring about a cure.'

'He *can* be cured. He *will* be cured. Doctor Birch says he can.'

'And the poor will be showered in gold,' scoffed her father.

Her mother ran from the room, weeping. Evelyn was horrified. Her parents never argued, Doctor Birch's skills were never in question and, worst of all, Nicholas *was* ill, despite his reassurances to the contrary. Her safe world suddenly felt uncertain. It was all her fault. She should never have agreed to see the snow.

Nicholas was taken to his bed and Miss Brown summoned to remain on hand until a more suitable person was found. Her temporary removal meant Evelyn was left alone with her guilty thoughts and with no sensible voice to rebalance her. She paced the hall outside her brother's door, eager for good news, but none came. Instead, the servants talked in whispers and gave her pitying looks, which stoked her feelings of guilt.

To everyone's relief, Doctor Birch arrived within the hour. The household seemed to hold its breath as it waited for his diagnosis, but if he had made one, no one told Evelyn. She had finally been sent to her room where she sat on her bed, hugging her knees, waiting – and praying – for the nightmare to end. The winter sky had grown dark before Miss Brown returned to her and gave her the comfort she craved.

'A nurse has arrived to tend to Nicholas,' she told her as she stroked her hair. 'He is in good hands now.'

'Will he recover?' Evelyn asked hopefully.

Miss Brown smiled a little too brightly. 'Oh, I'm sure he will.' Her forced smile frightened Evelyn. She looked tired, worried – defeated.

Evelyn just wanted everything to return to normal. 'Shall I get ready to visit Mother and Father?' she asked. Her allotted time with her parents was part of her daily routine and something to cling to.

Her governess, unable to hold her gaze any longer, looked down at her hands. 'No,' she replied gently, 'your mother and father are too distressed with the events of the day.'

Evelyn felt their rejection as keenly as if they had shut a door in her face. Her eyes brimmed with burning tears. 'They blame me, don't they?'

'No,' Miss Brown said sternly.

'They must.'

'My dear—'

The endearment brought tears to Evelyn's eyes. Miss Brown opened her arms and Evelyn threw herself into her embrace.

'It is all my fault,' Evelyn sobbed into her governess's dress.

'No, my dear Evelyn. No. Your brother has been unwell for some time.'

So it was true. He had lied to her.

'Why didn't he tell me?' she asked, between hiccupping sobs. 'I asked him but he said it was all in Mother's head.'

'He didn't tell you because he didn't want you to be upset.'

'But I could have stopped him from going outside. Now Mother and Father blame me.' Her throat felt raw with distress, yet she couldn't help feeling angry with her brother for not telling her. It was cowardly to hate him, for she should have realised his health was failing. Perhaps, deep down inside, she had, but didn't want to acknowledge it. A fresh bout of sobbing, louder than before, poured out of her. Tears for herself, tears for Nicholas, and tears for her mother and father.

'They do not blame you,' soothed Miss Brown as she stroked her head.

Evelyn pulled away to look at her. 'Then why won't they see me?'

Miss Brown cupped her tearstained face. 'Their hearts are breaking, Evelyn. Just as yours is.'

Evelyn tried to catch her breath between sobs. 'I don't want their hearts to break.'

'Then you must be strong and wipe away your tears,' said Miss Brown, delicately dabbing away Evelyn's tears with a handkerchief. 'They have enough to worry about without seeing you upset too.'

Evelyn wiped her face with her hands, eager to help in any way she could and have things return to normal again.

Miss Brown smiled fondly at her. 'No one wants their heart broken, but we all will at some time in our lives. It is the price for loving someone.'

'Is Nicholas's heart breaking?'

'Yes, my dear. Yes it is.'

Evelyn snuggled into her governess's embrace again. 'I hope it will mend. Having a broken heart hurts.'

'But we can lessen the pain.'

'How?'

'By caring for those that we love. By appreciating them while we are with them. By giving our love freely and unconditionally.'

'How will that lessen the pain?' asked Evelyn.

'Because your memories of them are not tinged with regret. You see, Evelyn, regret makes the pain so much harder to bear.'

Fearful that her son's recovery would be hindered by overexcitement, Lady Pendragon banned Evelyn from visiting him. Miss Brown disagreed with the order. The following day she took it upon herself to champion Evelyn's need to see him. She left Evelyn painting while she went to see her parents. Politely, she pointed out to Sir Robert and Lady Pendragon that keeping the children apart benefitted neither. After all, she reasoned, Evelyn was old enough to sit quietly by Nicholas's side and cheer his spirits without overtaxing him.

Her impassioned plea made no difference. Lady Pendragon remained adamant that Nicholas would receive no visitors until his health improved and, unfortunately, despite Doctor Birch's 'solicitous care', she had seen no improvement so far. The health of her family was of the utmost importance to her, she told the governess, and she would not risk it for the whims of her daughter. Miss Brown left the room, defeated. She had taken a risk by questioning her employers' instructions. Now that she had failed in her quest, she had the unnerving feeling that she had risked more than just being denied.

Evelyn looked down the stone steps into the gloom. Warm air rose up and caressed her face, telling her that she had come to the right place. She heard movement and the sound of a shovel scraping out coal from a pail. Suddenly the boiler door opened, exposing red flames and silhouetting Drake's figure as he threw coal into the furnace. The door closed with a bang, plunging the area at the bottom of the steps into blackness again, yet the flames and his shape still remained in her mind.

She took a step back, as he emerged into the daylight. He appeared startled to see her.

'Hello,' she said suppressing a nervous smile.

He looked about warily.

'It's all right; Timmins told me you were here.' Drake followed her gaze and saw Mr Timmins nodding his approval before he left the melon yard. 'He's going to see Cook,' she added needlessly. 'He wants to discuss the households' requirements for the coming year.' She looked back at Drake and found he was staring at her. He looked uncomfortable at being caught and she found his discomfort touching. 'I want to thank you for fetching Mother and Father.'

He moved past her and plunged his hands in a trough of water. 'There's no need. Anyone would have done the same.'

He washed the coal from his hands and dried them roughly on his trouser legs. His movements mesmerised her. When he had finished he glanced up and Evelyn quickly looked away.

'I've brought you a gift,' she said, feeling flustered and pulling out a flat package from inside her coat. She held it out to him.

'I want no gift.'

'I've written on it that it is a gift from me for coming to my assistance. No one can accuse you of stealing it.'

'I didn't mean that.'

'Then what did you mean?'

'I don't know.'

She jerked it towards him. 'Take it. If you don't want it, give it to your parents.'

'Father's dead.'

'I'm sorry to hear that.' Evelyn realised she really meant the platitude. Poor Drake, to suffer such a loss so young. 'You could give it to your mother.'

He reluctantly reached for it and held it carefully in his hands.

'Don't seem right, Miss Evelyn. I've not thanked you for the blankets yet.'

'You have now.' She tried to smile, but couldn't quite manage it this time.

He must have noticed for he asked, 'How is Master Nicholas?'

'I don't know. I am not allowed to see him and no one tells me anything.'

'That must be hard.'

Her bottom lip began to quiver. Someone, other than Miss Brown, finally understood.

'Don't cry,' he said, alarmed.

She tilted her chin, bravely. She didn't want him to feel embarrassed by her tears. 'I won't.'

Drake did not look reassured. She tried another smile, but failed miserably.

Drake's eyes darted around the yard. 'Are you sure Mr Timmins has gone to the big house?' he asked. Evelyn nodded. 'Then come with me. I know what will cheer you.' When she didn't follow, he looked back at her, surprised, 'Come on, before we are missed.'

'Where are you taking me?'

'To the storehouse. I want to show you something.'

Evelyn did not move. It was wrong to go into a building alone with him. If someone found them, they would both be punished. Yet – she looked at his dark brown eyes and felt a frisson of excitement which ignited every fibre of her soul. His invitation offered her a ray of sunshine to light up her bleak world. The temptation was too great.

She followed him into the next building. Like the neighbouring bothy, it was a two-storey house made of granite. Drake ignored the rooms on the lower floor and headed for a wooden ladder. She watched his legs disappear through the hatch in the ceiling. Evelyn lifted her hem and followed. A faint aroma of apples greeted her as she poked her head up through the floor and into the room. For a storeroom, it looked very empty.

'We store apples and pears in here over the winter. There are only a few left now.'

Evelyn followed his gaze and saw a row of apples at eye level at the far end of the room. She climbed the last few rungs of the ladder and into the room to get a better look.

'Where are the others?'

Drake gave her a boyish smile. 'Your family and staff have eaten them.'

'Oh.' Memories of apple sauce, pies and fruit filled bowls came to mind. She should have realised, she thought, suddenly feeling stupid. However, Drake did not appear to have noticed. He was already walking toward a pile of sacking and beckoning her to follow. He moved one of the sacks and revealed a cat, curled up and purring. Evelyn squinted in the darkness. 'It's Duchess!'

'You know her?' he asked, surprised.

She nodded enthusiastically. 'And she's had kittens!'

They watched, in silence, the squirming balls of fur foraging for milk, climbing and rolling over one another in their quest. Finally they settled into rows and sucked hungrily at their mother's milk.

Evelyn sighed. 'They are so sweet.'

'Would you like to hold one?' She looked at Drake to find him watching her. She smiled and nodded enthusiastically. Drake placed the gift she had given him near the window and out of harm's way. He picked up a discarded sack, gave it a shake and laid it down on the floor next to the kittens. 'Sit on this and I will pass you one.'

Evelyn obeyed, eagerly watching Drake's every move, as he carefully selected a kitten.

'This one has finished feeding,' he told her as he handed her a black one.

Evelyn held the kitten carefully in her cupped hands, afraid she might hurt it. It felt warm and soft, with fragile claws that pricked her skin and tickled her palms. His head, which seemed large compared to his little body, featured a pink button nose and wide blue-black eyes that stared blindly at her. It was the sweetest thing she had ever seen. For a moment Nicholas's illness and her parents' distress were forgotten as her eyes drank in the miracle of nature. Drake came to sit beside her and, once again, they lapsed into silence as they watched the kitten settle down to sleep.

Growing in confidence, Evelyn eased the kitten to one palm and began to stroke it with a single finger. Drake did the same.

'Why don't you go to church on Sundays?' asked Evelyn after a while. She didn't care that her question showed she had looked for him.

'I was bought up a Methodist. My father was a lay preacher. Besides, someone has to keep an eye on the glasshouses until the others return. Sunday afternoon I visit my mother.'

'Do you have any brothers or sisters?'

'No.'

Their fingers touched briefly, bringing a flush to both their cheeks. He withdrew his finger and left her to tend the kitten on her own. They sat in silence again as Duchess's loud, vibrating purr brought a soothing ambience to the room and wrapped them in a comforting blanket neither had a wish to leave.

Eventually, Evelyn spoke, her voice barely a whisper. 'He's very ill.' She felt no need to explain who she was talking about. 'I'm afraid he will die.'

'Do you think he will?' asked Drake.

'I don't know,' said Evelyn, as a wave of misery engulfed her again. 'If he does it will be my fault.'

'Why would you say that?' asked Drake.

If she told him, he would blame her too. She glanced up at him but only saw concern in his eyes. 'Because I wanted to see the snow and didn't stop him from going outside.'

'Did he want to go outside too?'

Evelyn nodded. If he hadn't been watching her so intently, he would have missed it.

'Master Nicholas is older than you. You would not have been able to stop him even if you wanted to. Besides,' said Drake, reaching to stroke one of the kittens, 'going outside to see the snow did not make him fall ill. You had not walked far.'

'Do you think so?' she asked hopefully.

Drake nodded confidently. He lifted one of the kittens. 'We should give the kittens names.'

Evelyn smiled at Drake's attempt to distract her. Perhaps it would do her good to think of something else. They agreed on some names that suited each kitten, before lapsing into a companionable silence again. However, Nicky was never far from her thoughts and she still feared for his future.

'What is it like when someone you love dies?' Drake would know. His father had died, hadn't he? Drake leaned back and thought for a moment, trying to remember. She could see that he was struggling to put his memories into words that made sense.

'Life changes,' he said eventually. 'What was normal is lost forever and a new normal replaces it.'

He looked sad, but she had to know more. Drake was the only one she felt she could ask. Who else would know? Who else would tell her the truth?

'What did it feel like to lose someone so close to you?'

'It felt ... it felt ...' he took a deep breath and sighed away the painful memory '... unfair. Very unfair.' He looked at her and smiled. 'I'm meant to be cheering you up. Besides,' said Drake, trying to make light of things, 'Nicholas is young and has the best medicine available. He will get better.'

Evelyn lifted the sleeping kitten to her lips and kissed it. 'Yes. You are probably right.' She handed the kitten back to him. 'I'd better go.'

'Yes, me too.'

They touched hands again as the kitten was passed from one to the other. This time there was no embarrassment as they had just shared more than an accidental touch. They made their way carefully down the ladder, pausing at the door to see if the yard remained clear of workers. There was no one to see them, so Evelyn made to leave first.

'Thank you,' she said. 'For showing me the kittens.'

'There is no need to thank me, Miss Evelyn.'

She didn't want him to call her Miss Evelyn. She wanted them to be friends and true friends don't use formal address.

'My name is Evelyn.'

'I couldn't call you that. I'm not of your class. It wouldn't seem right to call you the name your parents gave you.'

She didn't care. Having a friend was more important than etiquette. 'Then call me something else, just not Effy. Nicholas calls me Effy.'

'I'll think on it,' he replied. He was unsure – she could see it in his eyes. She would not press him further. A fledgling friendship was forming and she did not want to ruin it before it had really begun.

Chapter Six

Following her visit, Drake found himself taking an avid interest in the comings and goings of Carrack House. Doctor Birch visited daily, arriving late in the afternoon and, on occasions, staying for dinner. As always, Doctor Birch appeared confident and relaxed when he disembarked from his carriage. Filled with port and good food, his countenance remained unchanged when he left a few hours later. Drake saw this as a good sign that Master Nicholas would soon recover, for who could remain unmoved when a child remained so ill?

The following Sunday, Drake arrived at his mother's house, hungry and pleased to see her. Drake shrugged off his coat and followed his nose to his mother's range, where a pot of stew simmered. He lifted the lid as his mother asked the usual questions. He answered each one, pre-empting some. It was a weekly routine that both frustrated and amused him.

'Do they feed you enough? Your work is physical and you need a full belly.'

'We have enough, just not as tasty as yours.'

Pleased with the compliment, she made a show of tidying the table in preparation for their meal.

'What's this?' she asked, holding up the thin parcel Evelyn had given him.

He quickly explained, playing down his part in fetching her parents, for he had done nothing out of the ordinary.

'It was nothing,' he added. 'Anyone would have done the same.' He dipped a spoon in the pot and blew on the stew, before taking it into his mouth. He waved the spoon at her. 'Open it. It's for you.'

'Only because you refused it. I'm right, aren't I?' she said, opening it. Inside was a single sheet of paper. She carefully unfolded it. 'It's a painting,' she said, surprised.

He thought as much. 'Miss Evelyn paints,' he explained.

'She did this? She is very good.'

Drake watched his mother's eyes as she studied it. He saw her face fall. She looked worried.

'What is the matter? Don't you like it?'

'I'm just used to seeing you as a boy. I have never looked upon you like this … as a man.'

Drake left the stew and joined her.

'She painted me?'

'You have not seen it?'

'No.'

His mother showed him. Miss Evelyn had captured his likeness in minute detail. He was digging, with a focused look upon his face and each muscle taut with tension. His sleeves were rolled up exposing skin tanned from the sun and scattered with fine dark hair. His brow was furrowed, his unruly hair as black as coal with a similar sheen. Yet, at his feet sat a squirrel indicating that despite the predatory nature of humans, an animal recognised his kindness and felt safe enough to stay and watch.

'How old is Miss Evelyn?' his mother asked.

He shrugged, pretending he didn't know for sure. 'About fourteen, no more.'

'Did you sit for her?'

'No.'

'She painted this from memory?'

'She must have.'

His mother fell quiet as Drake busied himself sorting his study notes that were, in truth, already in order.

His mother looked up. 'She may be fourteen but she is becoming a woman.'

He didn't like where this was going. They were friends, no more. Not even friends really. 'No, she's a girl.'

'Yes she is, Drake,' his mother replied calmly. 'She looks at you with the eyes of a young woman. She has painted you as a man.'

Drake felt his cheeks burn. 'I am one. I'm fifteen now.'

'You are right. You are growing up before my very eyes.' His mother's gaze returned to the painting. 'All the more reason for you to mind yourself, Drake. Your apprenticeship with Mr Timmins is too important to risk for an infatuation of a girl you can never have a future with.'

'You are reading too much into it, Mother. She is a good painter and she was just as happy for you to have it as me.' He felt embarrassed. Speaking of such things with his mother did not come naturally. 'Besides, what would you know of infatuation?'

His mother gave him a reproachful glare for his sharp retort.

Drake felt a stab of guilt. After all, her warning had been kindly meant. 'I'm sorry. I promise I won't risk my apprenticeship,' he replied more gently. 'You have nothing to fear. It's a painting. Do not read more into it. I do not.' He didn't want to talk about Evelyn with his mother any more. He didn't know why, he just didn't. 'Besides,' he added quietly, 'I see no reason for us to speak again so there is no need for you to worry.' Strangely, the thought saddened him

Evelyn's fingers itched to play something more jovial, but Miss Brown thought it more fitting, given Master Nicholas's illness, to learn a sombre melody for her piano lesson. The lesson went well, and as a reward Evelyn was allowed to have her wish and play one short jovial tune. It was in the midst of this that her mother came into the room. Evelyn froze, her fingers curled in play. Her mother rarely came to the nursery to see her. She looked tired and pale, as her eyes flicked nervously about the room yet never settling on Evelyn.

'You can visit Nicholas now.'

Evelyn looked at her governess, unsure what this meant. Was Nicholas better? From the sadness in her mother's eyes, it did not appear so. She saw the same sorrow in Miss Brown's. Obediently, Evelyn silently got up from the piano and left the room. Her mother did not follow.

It did not take long for Evelyn to reach her brother's room. The nurse discreetly left as she approached the open door. Her departure substantiated Evelyn's growing suspicion that Nicholas had asked to see her. Evelyn entered, satisfied that she would no longer be banned from his company. They had all been wrong. She *was* needed to aid his recovery after all.

The heavy curtains were drawn to ward off the drafts. By his bed, a single oil lamp burned, its note-less whistle providing a comforting purr whilst its harsh white light, softened by the pink, glass shade, cast his frail body in a false healthy glow. His frail body. Her confidence drained away as she drew closer.

It had been almost a month since their walk in the snow. They had been laughing, trying not to slip on the frozen path. Now Nicholas lay quiet, no more than skin and bone, and too weak to raise his head from the pillow.

She sat down carefully in the chair beside him, unsure if she should wake him. She decided to wait and as she did so, became aware of another noise coming from somewhere in the room. It burbled and crackled, like a rhythmical rattle, and it was only when Nicholas opened his eyes and coughed, did she realise it was coming from him.

She smiled brightly as he looked blankly at her. Eventually he recognised her and attempted a fragile smile. It gave her hope.

'Effy?' whispered Nicholas.

She could barely hear him. It almost broke her heart. She attempted to remain strong. She did not want to distress him with her tears.

'Is this how you spend your days?' she said brightly, looking about the room. 'Lazing around in bed, having everyone at your beck and call.'

Nicholas did not reply, but his eyes crinkled at her humour.

'From the look of you,' she added, 'you need one of cook's meat and potato pies.'

Her comment made him chuckle, for when they were younger they had once stolen a pie from cook's pantry and eaten it all. They spent the next day in their sickbeds with stomach pains, much to their mother's distress. Doctor Birch diagnosed food poisoning, but they both knew it was no more than overindulgence.

'It's good … to see you,' he croaked.

Evelyn felt extraordinarily pleased at his effort to speak. He was already improving.

'Duchess has had a litter. They are beautiful.'

He sighed 'I wish … I could …' he rested for a moment before taking in a deep breath '… see them.'

'When you are well, you will be able to see them.' He shook his head. Evelyn ignored him. 'There are four. I've named two, Topsy and Turvy, because they keep falling over one another.'

'I'm dying, Effy.'

'Drake has named one, Blackie, because he's black—'

'Effy—'

'You can name the other.' They stared at each other. 'How long have you known?'

'Long … time.'

'Does Mother and Father know?'

'Everyone—'

'—knows but me.' Now was the time to cry, wasn't it? When your worst fears have come true. Nothing came. She felt numb. 'Are you afraid?'

He shook his head.

'I think I would be.'

'I will be in … heaven.'

'Heaven must be full of people. God doesn't need you too … and then there are all the animals from the Fern garden, tripping everyone up.' Nicholas smiled, but Evelyn wasn't trying to be funny – she meant every word.

Nicholas rallied what little strength he had left. 'I'm afraid for you, Effy.'

Evelyn, taken by surprise at his warning, stopped her grumbling. 'What do you mean?' she asked.

'My health has occupied Mother.' He paused to take a breath. 'I fear … her focus will turn on you.'

'Rubbish. I'm healthy as an ox.'

'And Father …' A tear trickled down the side of his nose. 'I have let … him down.'

'Don't distress yourself, Nicky,' she soothed, dabbing at his face with her handkerchief. She pretended to make light of it all. 'We shall be all right. It's about time I had more of their attention, anyway.' She didn't mean it. She would willingly trade her parents' company for Nicholas's any day, but her reassurances seemed to comfort him. The strength he had mustered began to drain away and he closed his eyes. Alarmingly, the rattle in his lungs sounded louder.

'Don't change, Effy,' he whispered between breaths. 'Don't let *them* … change you.'

'Who?' she asked, puzzled, but he did not answer. He had fallen asleep, exhausted from the effort of speaking. Her precious time with him had come to an end.

Evelyn had just returned from a morning walk with her governess when an unearthly wail echoed down the stairs and greeted her in the hall. Evelyn exchanged an anxious look with Miss Brown. She had hoped to visit Nicholas again, but the strange noise upstairs sounded as if a wild animal was loose somewhere in the house and in great distress.

Her governess took her firmly by the hand. 'Straight to the nursery, Evelyn. We must not disturb your mother.'

Evelyn resisted Miss Brown's hold and did not move. 'Do you think that is Mother?' It didn't sound like her. It was too guttural, too animalistic – unless something terrible had happened.

Evelyn tugged her hand away. 'Nicholas!' Miss Brown reached for her arm to prevent her from leaving, but Evelyn broke away. 'I must see him!'

She left Miss Brown behind as she ran up the stairs and along the corridor to Nicholas's room. Three sombre servants stood outside his door and were unable to meet her gaze. It was as if fate was playing a cruel trick, replaying the day he had fallen ill. If it was true, she would see her parents standing by her brother's bedside, watching him sleep, just like before.

The door was open and she cautiously approached. The scene was similar, but not the same. How she wished it had been the same. Her mother lay across Nicholas, her body heaving with each sob, her hands clawing the bed linen on either side. Her father was trying to console her, but was ill-equipped to do so. In desperation, he ordered the nurse, her maid and Miss Brown, who had just arrived, to escort his wife to her room.

Evelyn stepped aside as Lady Pendragon was walked, half carried, from the room, on legs that threatened to crumple beneath her like paper. Her cries, which were no longer muffled by her son's body, pierced the air and echoed around them.

Her father followed them, walking like a drunkard, reaching for furniture and door frame, as if for support. The room fell quiet, but for the ghostly whistle of the oil lamp by the side of her brother's bed. Evelyn stepped inside and silently shut the door behind her.

Nicholas appeared asleep, but for his chest failing to rise and fall. Evelyn quietly approached and sat down beside him in her mother's vacant chair. She waited for his translucent eyelids to open and for him to smile at her. She swallowed down the rising lump in her throat when they didn't.

'I've brought you something,' she said, gently withdrawing a kitten from her fur muff. The kitten yawned and stretched in her hand as she placed it on the bed beside him. She looked up, expectantly, with a fragile smile on her lips. Nicholas did not turn his head to look. Evelyn returned her gaze to the kitten, her smile fading as quickly as it had come.

'I told Miss Brown you would like to see them, so we fetched one for you. Here, let me help you hold it.' She lifted her brother's fingers, so they might curl in rest around the kitten. 'Can you feel how soft his fur is,

Nicky?' Tears welled up in her eyes and threatened to turn everything into a blur. Stubbornly she wiped them away and continued on.

'Isn't he sweet?' She heard her voice crack with emotion in a way she had never heard it do before. The unfamiliar sound made everything more real and frightened her. She cleared her throat and braced herself. 'I will call this one Nicky, because he is the laziest,' she said decisively. Her brother did not laugh at her teasing, not even a smile.

Tears threatened to rise up again. She stared at the kitten and attempted to swallow their saltiness down. The kitten stretched out a soft claw beneath his frail hand and, momentarily, snagged on her brother's skin. His fingers blurred before her eyes for he had not moved at all. He was indeed dead and she realised she would never laugh with him again.

Chapter Seven

Evelyn did not have to adopt full mourning. Given her young age, half mourning for a six-month duration would suffice. Within days of Nicholas's death, her clothes, including her new burgundy coat, were replaced with greys and mauves trimmed in black. They would be a constant reminder of her bereavement, not that she needed it.

On the day of his funeral, Evelyn stood at her window and watched the people gather on the drive below. Although united in grief, her parents had spent the week disagreeing about the finer details of their son's funeral. For several days the house reverberated with their arguments, as minor details took on a greater significance and shielded them from facing their true loss.

Her mother wanted Nicholas to be buried as befitting a child and to adopt the growing preference for less extravagant affairs. Sir Robert, on the other hand, wanted him to be buried with all the pomp and ceremony an adult would expect in years gone by in order to reflect his position as the heir of Carrack Estate. 'Had he not been in training for the position?' he had argued. 'Did the tenants and workers not respect him as such?' Evelyn could now see, as she watched the procession assemble below her, that they had come to a compromise.

Four black horses were harnessed to a hearse. They waited quietly, an occasional nod of their heads the only sign of their impatience. Through its glass windows, Evelyn could see Nicholas's shiny, black coffin, adorned with gold mouldings and surrounded by flowers. Two gowned mutes, four pages, two coachmen and a single feather-man were to accompany it. They waited, poised for the occasion, holding their truncheons, wands and top hats tied with black silk. A further three coaches, hired for the extended family mourners, waited to follow, their blinds pulled shut to offer the occupants sitting inside some privacy.

Her father had indeed spared no expense for the burial of his son, but no spectator would be in doubt that the heir had been taken too soon, for the horses wore white ostrich plumes, instead of black, indicating to all who saw the procession that behind the glass window, they carried a child.

Her mother had planned to attend the service, although not the burial. The interment, Miss Brown had told Evelyn, was thought too distressing for women and therefore attended only by men. However, on the day of

Nicholas's funeral, her mother went to her bed, exhausted in both mind and body and feeling unequal to the task of attending the service itself.

Evelyn was not invited. Being afflicted with both the female gender and lack of years, she was considered deficient in both self-control and the ability to comprehend the gravity of the situation. 'One could not be confident that she would not disrupt the solemnity of the occasion,' she overheard her father say. 'She must stay at home with Miss Brown.'

The workers had gathered to line the drive, each wearing a black armband as a mark of condolence. Evelyn saw Drake amongst them, his cap respectfully removed and held in his hands. He waited patiently for the mourners to climb aboard the waiting coaches, although Evelyn noticed that his gaze kept returning to the black wreath on their door. Her heart lurched. He was looking for her. What must he think of her not attending her own brother's funeral?

A signal was given for the procession to set off, snapping their attention back to the hearse. The long, solemn journey would take it through two villages, before returning to the little church on the estate. The meandering route offered the opportunity for the villagers to pay their respects and Evelyn had heard that some had already been seen gathering by the roadside.

The estate workers bowed their heads as the procession passed and Evelyn, not knowing what to do, followed suit from her bedroom window. Finally, she lifted her head to watch the procession grow smaller with each horse's stride.

'I wonder how many of the villagers have met Nicholas,' Evelyn said sadly.

Miss Brown came to stand by her. 'Why do you ask?'

'Because I envy them. They have been invited to pay their respects, while I am shut away.'

She felt Miss Brown place a hand on her shoulder. No words of comfort were spoken as none would suffice.

'Nicholas's death is a tragedy.'

Sir Robert stopped tapping his fingertips on the curved wood of the chaise longue. 'It is tragic, not a tragedy,' he corrected. The tapping began again. *Tap, tap, tap.*

Howard ignored him. 'A terrible business. Just terrible,' he said, shaking his head and withdrawing a letter from his jacket pocket. He placed it on the table. 'A letter from Edith. She offers her condolences. Nicholas's passing has brought back some unhappy memories for her so she is not up to visiting at the moment.' He patted the pockets of his jacket searching for his cigars. Finally he located them, withdrew the brown tortoiseshell case and selected one from the three he had brought with him. He made himself comfortable in an armchair by the fire. 'Where is Beatrice?'

'In her room. She is not up to visitors yet.'

Howard raised his eyebrows. Beatrice had suffered several convenient maladies of late, but now was not the time to voice it.

'Nicholas never fully recovered from his illness last year. I saw it. Your wife feared it. I believe even Nicholas knew it. It was only you who kept your head buried in the sand.'

Sir Robert said nothing. *Tap, tap, tap.*

'I do understand what you are going through,' Howard continued as he located his matches. 'I know we have not seen eye to eye, but I would never have wished this to have happened.'

'No one can understand.'

'I do,' said Howard, sucking loudly on his cigar to encourage it to light. He settled back in his chair amidst a cloud of grey smoke. 'We lost four babies before Mawgan.'

None of which even drew breath, thought Sir Robert, bitterly. Nicholas had not long turned sixteen years old. He was on the verge of manhood. Now we have nothing. Nothing! *Tap, tap, tap.*

'But one must be sensible and not let grief overrun us.' Howard watched the smoke rise. 'Life must go on.'

'Which is why you are here.'

Howard had the good grace to look embarrassed. 'Well no, I came to offer my support.'

'And talk of the future of Carrack Estate.'

'Well, it must be a worry for you.'

The tapping stopped. 'Spit it out, Howard. We know this is not a visit of condolence.'

'There is no need to be quarrelsome.'

They sat in silence for a moment. Sir Robert ran a hand over his brow in defeat. Not long ago everything was in order and the future mapped out, now everything was in chaos.

'Carrack Estate is a heavy burden, Robert,' Howard said as he surveyed the room. 'Each owner never truly owns Carrack. They are its guardians, to care for it until it moves on to the next generation in the family. You do the job well.' He looked around the room, blowing a trail of smoke as he did so. 'I see not much has changed here since the last time I was invited inside.'

Sir Robert, feeling stifled, got up briskly and walked to his desk. Some of Evelyn's paintings were strewn across the polished surface, a gift from her the evening before. He had barely looked at them. He did so now for the want of something to do as his brother droned on behind him.

'No one wants to go down in history as the person who lost it to another family,' Howard was saying. 'Upon your death, and in accordance to the remainder in default of a male issue, the title of baronet will pass to me, or if I am already dead, to Mawgan.' In the absence of a reply, Howard continued. 'I think we agree that the latter is the more likely to occur as, out of the two of us, you have enjoyed better health than I. It is only right for the future baronet to live at Carrack House.' Howard smiled, confident that his own demise was some years off yet, but Sir Robert did not notice. His attention was held by his daughter's paintings. He selected one to look at it more closely. They were surprisingly good, capturing both the vibrant colours of summer, and the rich golds of autumn in delicate watercolour. The work was detailed, yet dreamlike, devotedly painted by someone who loved the gardens as much as he. He looked up. As if on cue, Evelyn strolled across the grand lawn, accompanied by her governess.

'My son will make a fine custodian. It might be best if he spends more time here. He will need to learn, at first hand, about the running of the estate …'

His daughter stopped to talk to a young gardener with black hair. It was breezy outside, but his daughter did not seem to mind the chill. She appeared at ease, taking the lead in the conversation as if she was a lady asking questions of her staff, not a child guided by the adult in her company. Sir Robert frowned. For the first time he saw his daughter as the woman she would become, not the child he thought he still had.

'I will help, of course,' his brother was saying. 'I can introduce him to his future tenants—'

Sir Robert bristled at the thought. 'No!' he blurted out. He turned to face a shocked Howard. For the first time in weeks, he felt he was regaining some control. Some may call him radical, others foolhardy – but in truth he was being plain obstinate. He would never leave Carrack House in the hands of his brother's child – even if it meant bequeathing it to a woman.

'Carrack has a guardian for the future.'

'Who?'

'Evelyn.'

Howard tried to laugh, but failed. 'You can't be serious?'

The look of horror on Howard's face reflected the ridiculousness of the proposal. Sir Robert realised he had spoken without caution or thought, but he would not back down now. Sounding more confident than he felt, Sir Robert added, 'I am serious, so there is no need to be concerned.'

Howard stubbed out his cigar with violent stabs and stood. 'Look here, Robert. You cannot leave a woman to run things. Dance steps and piano pieces have no place in understanding ledgers and tenancy agreements.'

'She will learn.'

'She cannot.'

'It is not your concern.'

Howard shook his head in disbelief. 'Grief has turned your mind. You have gone quite mad. There is no talking to you when you are in this state.'

'Evelyn will inherit Carrack House and Estate. There is no more to be said on the matter.'

'Your decision is based on spite not sound judgement!' shouted Howard. Sir Robert returned his gaze to the painting in his hand. Howard let out a guttural growl of contempt. Sir Robert ignored him. Howard swore and swept from the room. His raised voice continued in the hall as servants hurried to bring him his hat and coat. 'A woman is ill-equipped to have such a responsibility!' he shouted, shouldering himself into his coat. 'You are a fool, Robert!' He slammed his hat on his head. 'And I will enjoy gloating when I have been proved right!'

'I will ensure Evelyn is equipped,' Sir Robert shouted back. He took a deep breath and placed the paintings carefully on his desk, 'She won't fail!' he muttered to himself. He looked at his trembling hands and pressed them firmly on the polished wood to still them. 'She can't fail. I won't let her.'

Miss Brown stood before Sir Robert and stole a nervous glance towards his wife. Lady Pendragon remained silent and her masked expression gave no hint to the governess why she had been summoned. He had informed his wife of his decision only moments before and although she expressed concern, these days she lacked the energy to argue. However, her cold silence told him she refused to take part.

Sir Robert cleared his throat. 'Did Evelyn enjoy her walk?'

Miss Brown remained wary. 'Yes, Sir Robert. We walked around the gardens and towards the Melon Yard. A cat on the estate has recently had some kittens and Evelyn finds some comfort in seeing them.'

It was an unusual situation and he understood Miss Brown's apprehension. This was the first time he had summoned her as there had been no need to before. Circumstances had changed and the situation he now found himself in was too serious for small talk. Sir Robert decided to get straight to the point.

'Do you think Evelyn is intelligent?'

Miss Brown looked somewhat puzzled with his question. She glanced again to his wife, which irritated him.

'Well?' he snapped.

Miss Brown straightened, growing an inch before his eyes. 'Yes, Sir Robert. Your daughter is very intelligent.'

'Is she capable?'

Miss Brown raised an eyebrow. 'Capable of what, sir?'

There was an edge to her voice he did not like. On this occasion he would ignore it.

'Does she have strength in her character? Resilience? The capability to learn?'

'Your daughter is an exceptional young lady, Sir Robert. She is kind, thoughtful and tries so hard to please.'

Sir Robert waved his hand. This was not going well. He had made a terrible mistake. In truth, his opinion of a woman's role in life was no different to that of his brother. Howard had been right; grief had turned his mind and made him speak hastily. Unfortunately, it was too late now.

'I plan to leave Carrack House and its estate to Evelyn, but I need to be sure she is capable of the responsibility it entails.'

The governess, who had remained wary since entering the drawing room, suddenly smiled. 'She is more than capable, Sir Robert. She would enjoy learning about the estate and spending time in your company. I have no doubt that Evelyn would devote her life to it.'

Sir Robert let out the breath he had been holding. This was good news. Very good news indeed.

'We have much to do,' Sir Robert said as he began to pace out his thoughts. 'Up till now she has been trained for marriage, but we must mould her to be as equal to any man with regards to intelligence.'

'She will relish the challenge, Sir Robert.'

'People will think I have lost my mind when it becomes known that I am to leave it to her. We must silence the doubters.' He paused for a moment. 'Perhaps "equal" is not good enough.'

Miss Brown's brows pinched together, as she looked at him.

'I'm not sure I understand.'

'The Pendragon name must not be made a laughing stock and Carrack Estate must grow in strength. Do you speak Latin?'

Miss Brown shook her head. 'I can speak a little French.'

'Nicholas was learning Latin and Greek. Evelyn must do so too … and French.'

'Three languages at once. Is that really necessary?' questioned Miss Brown.

'She must be better than average. She must excel. Silence the doubters, Miss Brown,' said Sir Robert, wagging his finger at her. 'Silence the doubters.'

'*I* do not doubt her, Sir Robert.'

There was that edge again. He stopped pacing and looked at her.

'Perhaps it's you who is not up to the task,' he challenged. He did not wait for a reply. He felt energised and needed to expel it. He began to pace again; aware Miss Brown watched his every move. 'What do young men learn in college today? A fit body nourishes a fit mind and sport is recommended. I will reinstate Nicholas's tutor as soon as possible.'

'Mr Burrows?' Miss Brown's frown deepened. 'He prides himself on educating young men, Sir Robert. I do not think he values the education of women.'

'He will value his employment continuing.'

'Even so, I don't think he will bring the best out in Evelyn.'

'You think I do not know my own child?' blasted Sir Robert. Miss Brown's shocked expression brought a heated flush to his cheeks. He had lost his temper in front of his wife, something he had wanted to avoid.

'I do not think Mr Burrows is …' he saw her searching for the right words '… a good match for Evelyn.'

A good match? What was she talking about? Tutors were employed for their ability to teach, not how they formed relationships with their pupils.

'You are only saying this because you fear for your own position.'

Miss Brown raised an eyebrow. 'I was not aware my position was in jeopardy.'

'It is if I do not feel you can support me in this,' he challenged.

'It is growing harder by the minute,' retorted Miss Brown. Miss Brown addressed his wife as if he no longer mattered. 'Lady Pendragon, Evelyn is a sweet-natured child, eager to do well. I have no doubt that Mr Burrows is a great teacher, but he has always looked down upon the education of girls. He certainly has no respect for my position as a governess.'

'Now I understand,' said Sir Robert. 'You have a personal grudge against Mr Burrows.'

'No, I do not, sir.'

'Mr Burrows takes great pride in his profession.'

'I know he does—'

'So you do not disagree with me.'

'—but he will resent having to educate Evelyn.'

'He educates to a high level,' argued Sir Robert.

'I fear he will—'

'He will bring the best out in Evelyn.'

'No, sir! He will challenge her confidence and relish doing it.' Miss Brown turned to his wife for support. 'Lady Pendragon, Evelyn is in mourning. She grieves for Nicholas as deeply as you do. She needs tender care, love, support and encouragement. What is being suggested resembles a harsh regime.'

His wife slowly raised herself out of her chair. Her interest spurred the governess on.

'Three languages, years of education consolidated in one or two, a tutor who will show her no patience. If you care for your daughter, as I do, you will stop this.'

'You care for my daughter?' his wife asked.

'Deeply, Lady Pendragon. I love her as if she was my own.'

'She is not,' Lady Pendragon snapped. '*I* am her mother.'

'Then love her as a mother should!' blurted out Miss Brown. The governess gasped in horror and clamped her hand to her mouth, but it was too late, the words were out.

Sir Robert's eyes grew hard. 'You have insulted my wife and you have insulted me.'

'I did not mean to offend, Sir Robert. I spoke in haste.'

'And without substance. I cannot have your attitude poisoning our daughter against us.' Miss Brown began to protest, but he ignored her. She was an obstacle to his plan and must be removed. 'You will go to your room, pack your bags and leave this house immediately.'

'I am being dismissed? But what about Evelyn?'

'As of now, Miss Evelyn is of no concern of yours.'

Miss Brown did not move. 'Sir Robert,' she pleaded, 'I spoke out of turn and deserve to be dismissed, but I implore you to reconsider Evelyn's education and the demands you mean to place upon her at this time. She will make a fine heiress one day, but at the moment all she needs is your love or she will—'

'Will what?'

'—fade away.'

'As Nicholas did,' replied his wife. 'You think we are to blame for our son's death.' She had come to his side and he had not noticed. He felt her hand slip round his arm. He looked down at the white handkerchief, trimmed in black lace, clutched in her fingers. She was supporting him at last.

'No. No.' The governess turned to him. 'Sir Robert, you cannot think I—'

'Get out.'

'I never meant—'

'Get out.'

'But, sir—'

'Get out!' he shouted, his whole body shaking with the anger.

They were as strangers, with no common understanding between them and no desire to nurture one. Miss Brown clenched her teeth to stem the tears that threatened to fall. Her distress did nothing to quell his anger.

'You are never to see my daughter again or attempt to correspond with her. Now leave before I have you removed from the premises.' His daughter's governess looked stricken. Seeing her distress reminded him of his own loss, for it was how he truly felt inside. He looked away, as she walked briskly from the room.

Chapter Eight

Tired of waiting for Miss Brown to return, Evelyn laid down her sampler and went in search of her. She found her in her bedroom, packing.

'What are you doing?' she asked. 'Are we going somewhere?'

'I am going somewhere, Evelyn. You are not.' Miss Brown busied herself folding and refolding her clothes. 'Your parents have great plans for your future,' she added brightly, 'which do not involve me.' She lifted a pile of clothing and placed them carefully into her trunk, sniffing rather loudly as she did so. 'It is a wonderful opportunity for you.'

If it was so wonderful, why was her governess trying to avoid looking at her? Evelyn said as much. Miss Brown turned and smiled, but Evelyn saw that the smile did not reach her eyes.

'You are to have a private tutor. Isn't that wonderful?'

'A private tutor,' Evelyn repeated. The opportunity of learning more than the basics filled her with a surge of nervous excitement. It meant that her parents thought her worthy of an education beyond what was required for a wife. 'But why must you leave?'

'I am not qualified to deliver the education that they now wish for you.'

Evelyn grew concerned. 'Will I see you again?' Her governess shook her head. 'But where will you go?'

'To Francis,' she said, tearing a page from her journal and writing down the address. She pressed it into Evelyn's hand and squeezed it for good measure. 'So you see, Evelyn, there is no need for you to worry about me.' The strength in her parting touch, conveyed more than any words she had spoken. Evelyn felt her heart breaking.

'Have you been dismissed?' asked Evelyn.

Miss Brown sniffed again and gave a curt nod. The packing resumed.

Any joy Evelyn had felt about her future plans began to drain away as Miss Brown was leaving and would not be part of them. A sense of panic surged through her as she realised she may never see her again. She flung her arms round her governess and buried her face into the crook of her shoulder.

'Are they dismissing you because you fell asleep? I did not tell them. I didn't.'

Miss Brown stroked her hair. 'I know you did not. It is not because of that.'

A sob escaped Evelyn. 'So why are you leaving me?'

'Because I have to.' Miss Brown stepped back from her embrace and held her hands. 'You have hidden strengths to call upon should you need them, Evelyn. Remember that.'

They did not notice her father standing at the door. His sudden appearance gave them both a start.

'It is time you were gone, Miss Brown. You are no longer welcome in this house.'

Miss Brown released Evelyn's hands and squared up to Sir Robert. 'Am I to be escorted from the house like a criminal?'

'If needs be,' her father replied.

The tense exchange frightened Evelyn. Why had her beloved governess fallen out of favour so quickly? She watched, confused, as Miss Brown picked up one of her bags.

'I will make arrangements for my trunks to be collected,' her governess said primly. 'I have left my forwarding address with Evelyn.' Without looking at either of them, she marched from the room.

Evelyn opened her hand. A name she recognised was neatly written on the crumpled paper. Below it was an address, but before she could read it, her father snatched the note from her. She continued to stare at her empty palm, confused and terrified by the speed of Miss Brown's departure. She had to speak to her, despite what her father might say.

Evelyn ran from the room, ignoring her father's orders for her to stop. She caught up with Miss Brown at the top of the stairs and flung herself into her arms. They silently embraced as Evelyn tried to memorise everything about her, the feel of her hair against her cheek, the warmth and comfort her body offered, the fragrance of lemon and bergamot that often tickled her nose. She squeezed her eyes shut as she locked the memories away one by one. One day she would revisit them when the pain was not so great. She wanted to tell her how much she loved her and would miss her, but all she could do was hold on to her while she was here. Finally, she knew what to say.

'I hope you have a happy life, Miss Brown,' whispered Evelyn, her voice ragged with emotion.

Miss Brown squeezed her tightly, before letting her go. She gave her a trembling smile as she picked up the bag she had dropped. It was the last time Evelyn would see her, but she could see from her expression that

Evelyn's parting words meant the world to her and would be forever remembered.

Drake removed his coat and shook the scattering of raindrops from it, before hanging it on a rusty nail. Mr Timmins had given him the afternoon off to study, but the old cleaning woman had chosen today to turn the bothy upside down. The storeroom was a good alternative. It was dry and quiet and the kittens would make good company, that's if there was not already someone up there. He instinctively tilted an ear to listen, alert for the noise he thought he had heard. Yes, it was a shuffling noise, made by something far bigger than any kitten or rat.

 Concerned for the kittens' safety, he climbed the ladder. Miss Evelyn sat in the far corner with a kitten on her lap. She was on her own. He had not seen her alone since the first day he had shown her the kittens. He knew a girl of her standing would not normally be left alone in a boy's company. He looked around, half expecting someone to jump out upon them.

 'Where is Miss Brown?' he asked.

 Miss Evelyn continued to stroke the kitten. She did not look at him.

 'She has been dismissed.'

 She offered no more explanation and he felt it was not his place to ask. He was intruding and his mother's warning came to mind. He began to climb down.

 'Don't go.'

 Drake hesitated, unsure what to do.

 'Please, sit with me a while,' pleaded Evelyn.

 What was he to do? She was still mourning the death of her brother. It would be unfeeling to leave her now when she looked so wretched. He retraced his steps up the ladder and, with a well-practiced movement, transferred from ladder to floor. He felt rather pleased with himself how easy he had made it look. He stole a glance at her to see if she had noticed, but she hadn't, preferring to care for the kitten on her lap.

 'Where is Turvy and Nicholas?' she asked him.

 Drake came to sit beside her, although he ensured he was not too close.

 'The head groom has rats in his stables. He took them.'

 Topsy yawned, her pale pink tongue matched the colour of her button nose.

'They are too young to catch rats,' replied Evelyn, miserably.

'He will look after them until they can fend for themselves.' Drake had made sure of it, hiding the kittens until he had promised to care for them, much to the head groom's frustration.

'Topsy will be lost without them.'

'She will learn to live without them. She is stronger than she looks.'

Their eyes met. Was he talking about her? Perhaps he was. He suddenly felt hot.

Evelyn returned her attention to the kitten in her hands. 'I am to have a new tutor.'

'To replace your governess?'

She nodded. 'I think he will hate me.'

Drake couldn't imagine anyone hating Miss Evelyn. 'Why would you think that?'

'Something Nicholas once said,' she replied. She sounded miserable and Drake felt at a loss how to reassure her on the matter. He was glad when she changed the subject back to the kittens. 'Did you come to see them too?'

'Yes. No.' He sounded like an idiot. 'I came to study.'

She appeared impressed. He felt absurdly pleased, but thought it best not show it. He shook it off with a nonchalant shrug. 'I have a lot to study.'

'Don't let me stop you,' she said, settling back on the sacking. 'I won't disturb you.' Her lashes fanned her cheeks as she returned her loving attention back to the kitten. He should decline and leave, but instead Drake removed his study notes from his pocket.

The Latin names of well over fifty plants were listed on the paper in his neat copperplate writing. By each name were brief notes on their descriptions and the season of their lifecycle. At first he felt awkward trying to memorise them in her company, but he soon found himself relaxing, for she did not disturb, irritate or tease him about his study. Occasionally, he found his eyes straying from the paper, to ensure she was still there. Strangely, he began to find her continual presence oddly comforting.

It was inevitable she would catch him looking at her eventually. When their eyes met, she did not mock him, but offered to help. He found himself cautiously accepting.

They fell into their new roles with ease, forgetting the world outside the old apple scented storeroom. Initially, she struggled with the pronunciation and he found himself smiling inwardly as he watched her lips twist over their long Latin names. However, she was the first to laugh at her mistakes, a quality he liked, and she refused to give up, a quality he shared, which made the experience far more pleasant than he expected. He soon discovered that she was a quick learner, had a good memory and had a methodical and sharp mind. Her questioning tested his memory and common sense in a way that studying alone would not. The time passed quickly, his mother's words of warning all but forgotten.

'I have to go,' Evelyn said, suddenly getting up and returning his study notes. Drake looked up at her, reluctantly taking them from her outstretched hand. 'Will you look after Topsy and Blackie for me?'

Drake scrambled to his feet. 'Yes, but why? Are you going to stop visiting them?'

'I think I will be too busy.'

How she chose to spend her time should not bother him, yet her announcement disturbed him. 'Why?' he asked again. There was desperation to his voice he was not proud of.

'Father has arranged a timetable of study which will fill my day,' she replied, brushing the kittens' hairs from her dress. 'I will be busy studying myself. I don't want to let my parents down.' She looked up and smiled. It was a smile just for him. His heart flipped in his chest and he began to feel hot again. He wondered if she noticed the effect her smile had on him. Did he look as out of control as he felt? She turned away. 'It will be fun.'

It didn't sound like fun. He was going to say as much but she was already walking to the ladder. He hastily followed and climbed down after her. He found Evelyn waiting for him at the bottom.

'Goodbye, Drake.' A fragile smile played on her quivering pink lips. 'I will miss the kittens.'

'I will look after them. Goodbye, Evie.'

She looked at him shyly through her lashes, a slight blush colouring her cheeks. 'Evie,' she said, testing the name on her lips. 'I like Evie.'

'I like Evie too,' he said, without thinking.

He had told his mother they were barely friends. He could not claim that any more.

Drake waited for several minutes, before he ventured outside. To his surprise Timmins was waiting for him. The head gardener looked towards Carrack House, but his words were for Drake.

'Tomorrow you will start clearing the gullies and paths in the valley gardens,' he told him, solemnly. 'It will keep you out of the way – and keep us all out of trouble.'

The head gardener left without explaining further. He had seen Evie leave and wanted to keep them apart. Drake watched him go, aware he had been temporarily banished from the gardens as a warning and a punishment. He was about to leave too when he noticed Abel standing by the far wall. His leisurely stance and the confident twisting and flipping of a broken twig in his mouth told Drake that he had probably been there for some time. Abel suddenly taunted him with a smirk, before removing the piece of wood, spitting on the ground and walking away.

Chapter Nine

The emergence of the narcissus flower heralded the arrival of spring, draping the lawns and flowerbeds in sheets of fragrant yellows and whites. The name originated from Greek mythology, where the young Narcissus fell in love with his own image. It seemed fitting that the arrival of the fragrant blooms corresponded with the reinstatement of the narcissistic tutor, Mr Burrows, whose self-absorption was only rivalled by his hatred of the female gender.

Little was known about the private life of Mr Burrows. His teaching career, on the other hand, was better known, or at least what he chose to share of it. He had obeyed his overbearing father's orders and entered the profession at a young age. It was thanks to his father's influence, as a member of the board of governors, that he secured his first teaching post at an exclusive school for boys in London.

The reason for his sudden departure, some years later, was somewhat hazier. An incident had occurred, which, if he was to be believed, he found intolerable and led to his abrupt resignation. He moved to Cornwall with a glowing reference in his pocket from the board of governors, but no invitation to return. His father had not spoken to him since.

He eventually found a position in a small village school, but teaching the children of farm labourers lacked the prestige he felt was due to him. He often remarked on his experience, saying the children 'were deficient in basic intelligence' and that 'one cannot build an education on a foundation of sludge'.

Securing a position as Nicholas Pendragon's private tutor fulfilled all his desires. Teaching the son and heir to the most respected and wealthy family in Cornwall lifted him above his peers, gave him the power of autonomy and a good annual income. Nicholas's deterioration in health, and subsequent death, was both a shock and an inconvenience to him. He accepted the role as a private tutor to Miss Evelyn Pendragon with a mixture of relief and reluctance. Although it carried the same benefits he had previously enjoyed, the position was marred by the fact that she was a girl.

There appeared a marked absence of the female gender in his life, for he never mentioned a wife, sister or mother. Although he was once seen coming out of a seedy establishment in the town of Saltash, an incident which fuelled gossip amongst the servants who held a distinct dislike for him.

Evelyn overheard their whispers, but did not understand, whilst her parents never learnt of them. Needless to say, his clandestine trips continued, while the more sordid details of his private life remained unknown and unchallenged. Yes, there was far more to the private life of Mr Burrows, more than even the servants were aware.

Although Mr Burrows was Nicholas's only tutor since his bout of rheumatic fever, Evelyn had had little to do with him until now. Nicholas had found him tolerable, although a little odd, so Evelyn, although apprehensive about her future education, was eager to meet him and begin her studies.

Her father formally introduced Mr Burrows to her at the beginning of her first lesson. She remembered the meeting clearly. In order to convince her new tutor, or perhaps himself, her father endorsed her abilities to her new tutor with a nervous eagerness she had not witnessed before. He presented her as if she was a gifted protégé. It was a lot to live up to and a long way to fall.

As her father stood between them and talked, Evelyn and Mr Burrows studied each other. He was short for a man, not much taller than his new pupil. He had fair red hair and light lashes which appeared almost transparent and not of this world. His eyebrows were almost white and, to her surprise, appeared dusted with powder. He had pale skin, as smooth as porcelain, with a straight nose and grey eyes, which could penetrate one like a knife. A large neatly trimmed moustache topped the mouth that never smiled, and always near to hand was his cane, made of birch, which she would later learn he called 'The Master'.

During the first month of his appointment, Mr Burrows was all Evelyn hoped he would be. He was knowledgeable, kind, patient and encouraging. As a result, Evelyn's confidence in her abilities grew with each day that passed. Whenever her parents ventured into the schoolroom, which was often in the first few weeks, he would turn his charm on them, calming their nerves and providing the reassurance they craved.

For the first time since Nicholas's death, Evelyn could see that her parents' suffering had lessened. Although they still grieved, they were reassured by Mr Burrows that their daughter was well cared for, enjoying her new studies and might achieve success as an heir. Their visits stopped, confident that all was well. They were right to think that, for in the first month she had reassured them herself. She would have shared her happiness with Drake, if he could be found. She did not realise then that things were about to change.

Evelyn looked out of her bedroom window and up at the dark grey clouds in the sky. The north facing schoolroom will be dark today, she thought, smiling. On such days, when everything was cast in a gloomy, chilling shadow, the lamps in the schoolroom were lit early to provide much needed light for study. Their soft golden glow made the sparsely furnished room cosy and welcoming, which Evelyn loved. She left her bedroom and practically skipped to her lessons where she knew Mr Burrows would be waiting for her. A few minutes later and a little breathless, Evelyn entered the small schoolroom. Her jaunty steps faltered as she saw the unlit lamps and realised Mr Burrows had no plans to use them today. She tried not to let his decision dampen her mood and bid him a polite 'good morning' and her brightest smile before sitting down at her desk to wait his instruction.

This morning Mr Burrows did not return her greeting as he usually did. Instead he remained seated at his desk and stared at her with narrowed eyes. He remained strangely still and quiet for some moments, which unnerved Evelyn. She grew increasingly self-conscious under his gaze, but dared not question his odd behaviour. Instead she offered him a nervous smile. He abruptly stood, making Evelyn jump.

'Our lesson today is writing,' said Mr Burrows as he came round to the front and sat on the corner of the desk.

To Evelyn, he resembled a doll that had been awkwardly placed there, as his back was too rigid and his legs too short. She wanted to giggle, but knew her manners and did not allow her thoughts to show.

'I want you to write about Nicholas,' ordered Mr Burrows.

The mention of her brother caught Evelyn unaware and at first she thought she had misheard.

'Write about Nicholas?' she repeated unnecessarily.

'Yes, I want you to write about Nicholas,' he replied slowly as if talking to a half-wit. Uneasily, Evelyn looked about her. The schoolroom had been *his* schoolroom, but as Evelyn had never entered it until after his death, somehow the connection never really felt real. Suddenly, hearing his name in this room, spoken by his tutor, the connection felt very real indeed. Only Nicholas wasn't here any more—

She wasn't sure she was up to the task. Nicky's passing had left a gaping wound in her heart that was yet to heal. She dared not examine and prod it while she was in company. It was too painful – too raw. Remembering Nicky was something she only dared to do when she was alone and no one could hear her cry. She thought of Drake. She had spoken to Drake about him, but he was different from everyone else.

'I think it will be good for you to write about your brother,' insisted Mr Burrows.

Perhaps Mr Burrows was right. Not wishing to displease him, Evelyn slowly lifted the lid of her desk and withdrew a sheet of paper, an inkpot and her pen. She placed them carefully on the closed lid and looked at them. Yes, perhaps he was right. She would think of all the good times they had together and how much she missed him. She dipped her pen in the inkpot, aware of an aching sadness in her chest that threatened to rise up to claw at her throat. Evelyn swallowed it down. She would write about the time they found a sickly bird and Nicky had taken it to the stables to nurse it back to health.

'I want you to write about the times you hated your brother,' interrupted her tutor. 'I want you to list all those bad memories so you can cleanse yourself of such feelings.'

Evelyn paused and looked up. Had she heard him right? 'But I didn't hate him, Mr Burrows. I don't want to write bad things about him.'

'Are you refusing?' he asked evenly.

His tone was ambiguous, his mood unclear, but Evelyn saw a steely hardness to his pale grey eyes, which she had not seen before. She must have displeased him.

'No, Mr Burrows. It just feels wrong.'

He did not answer as he considered her reply. Suddenly his expression softened as he eased himself off the desk.

'It will help you in your time of grief. I understand you are suffering. You do well not to show it, but I can see that Nicholas's death has come as a blow to you. Nicholas was an exceptional child. You must miss him greatly, but I truly believe that if you vent your anger and express your hatred for him ...' he saw Evelyn's horrified expression '... you will feel better for it. There is no need to feel ashamed. We all feel hatred, Evelyn. Some people more than others.'

Tears threatened. Again Evelyn swallowed them down. Mr Burrows had acknowledged her grief, something her own parents had difficulty doing. Perhaps he was right. Perhaps doing as he said would help – somehow. Evelyn hesitantly took up her pen. There was the time he had hidden her doll. He had given it back to her, but it had upset her greatly at the time. She began to write, her pen moving haltingly across the paper. She looked up, anxious to see if her tutor was content. Mr Burrows gave a rigid nod for more. Evelyn refocused her thoughts on her memories. Then there was the time they had rowed. She couldn't remember what it was about, but they had rowed – once or twice. She began to write again.

If writing about such memories were meant to help her, she did not feel the benefit of it. With each word her wretchedness grew, with each thought her loss felt more raw and during the entire ordeal she felt Nicky was watching over her and feeling more and more betrayed with each stroke of her pen. Finally it was over and Evelyn waited in glum silence as Mr Burrows collected her work and returned to his desk. Even her natural desire for his good opinion had deserted her and she was unable to look as he put on his spectacles to examine her work. When he had finished, he lowered the paper and carefully removed them.

'Well, Miss Evelyn. I am surprised by this,' he said, indicating to the paper in his hand with a wave of the other. 'I knew Nicholas well. This is nothing short of a character assassination.'

Evelyn felt terrible. She had gone too far when all the time she had been fearful Mr Burrows would expect more from her than she could bring herself to write. She had confided too much and now he was appalled by her thoughts. She was a very bad sister to say such things. An invisible blanket of shame quickly settled over Evelyn. Her shoulders rounded as she felt its heavy weight and sunk lower in her chair.

Mr Burrows approached her desk and lent over it. She could feel his warm breath on her face as he reproached her. 'These accusations are made out of jealousy and envy, not grief! You are a sinful child.'

Hair rose on the back of her neck, like a wave of fine needles pricking at her skin. Jealousy? Envy? At the time, perhaps, she had felt such emotions during their petty, although infrequent, arguments. Sins she had been warned about at every Sunday Service she had attended. She must be very wicked. Evelyn wanted the lesson to end.

Abruptly, Mr Burrows straightened and returned to his desk. 'We will not discuss this again,' he remarked, settling himself behind the desk, 'other than to say, you have disappointed me, Evelyn. Disappointed me very much indeed.'

Mr Burrows did not speak of it again and the lesson subject seamlessly changed to mathematics. The remainder of the day went by without incident, but Evelyn found it difficult to shake off the sadness that she felt. Later, she reflected on the task Mr Burrows had set her. Mr Burrows had only been trying to help her, she concluded, but she had misunderstood and taken his direction too literally. She had done the task poorly and been too sensitive to his criticism and she must try harder to not let him down next time. However, Evelyn did not know it, but Mr Burrows' challenging tasks had only just begun.

Mr Burrows was a clever man for he had carefully set the landscape on which to play his twisted games. Just like a boy who is entertained by pulling the legs from a spider, there was no reason for his cruelty other than his own enjoyment at seeing Evelyn suffer.

In the first few months of educating Evelyn, he had secured her parents trust and gratitude, so should any future changes in his manner be reported, it would be hard to understand the reason unless there was a just cause. And as Evelyn was his only pupil, the just cause would naturally point to Evelyn herself.

The writing lesson was the beginning of his game, which gained momentum with well-practiced, insidious moves on his part. At first he increased her workload, by the amount, then difficulty and then the time given to complete it. Initially she was able to keep up, but eventually she began to struggle. Mistakes were made, tidiness suffered and each time Mr Burrows compared her to her beloved brother and found her wanting.

'Nicholas would never make such a silly mistake,' he would remark as he examined her work. 'Nicholas knew this answer.' 'I can see Nicholas was the one gifted with the brains.'

His scornful remarks were cloaked in a tone full of pity, and Evelyn began to believe him, for he was the teacher with far more experience of the abilities of others than she. She was failing and her failure was seen by the servants, for Mr Burrows did not refrain from making his comments in their presence. She began to believe herself stupid, but dared not confess it to her parents. Her confidence was whittled away by each mistake and each comment and, worst of all, she even began to resent dear Nicholas himself.

At the beginning of the third month she was introduced to 'The Master'. It entered her life suddenly, cracking the air and slamming down on her desk to mark the end of a test, narrowly missing her fingers in the process. From then on it was used frequently, whether on her desk, on her chair, on her palms or the backs of her legs, it made no difference. Each and every time surprised her, frightened her, hurt her and set her frazzled nerves even more on edge. 'If only you would make more effort,' she was told, 'I would not have to discipline you in this way.'

By the fourth month she was made to march on the spot, 'in order to improve your health'. He drilled her daily, for an hour, beating a rhythm out on his shoe with his cane as he sat with one leg hitched over the corner of his desk. Although it was now summer, she still wore her half-mourning which had been made in the colder months. He knew this and appeared to enjoy her discomfort, as she marched to his tune and grew hotter with each step.

By the time she finally found the courage to tell her parents, Mr Burrows had made his mark upon her. She became tongue-tied, expressed herself badly and her complaints even sounded lame to her own ears. It was difficult to convey the fear she felt, when the actual words her teacher spoke were harmless and not untrue.

Her parents listened with the knowledge that Nicholas had excelled in Mr Burrows care, but their daughter was not. Her father, fearful that she was not up to the task, suggested she should try harder. 'There is nothing wrong with a flick of the cane, if it is used sparingly,' he reassured her. 'The threat of punishment is commonly used. Did we not both experience it at some point in our life?' he said, turning to his wife. 'And for the marching, if it helped to improve one's fitness, that was all to the good.'

The opportunity to seek help was soon over and she returned to her room. And when Mr Burrows heard of her complaints the next day, he took out 'The Master' and with each swipe on her calves, warned her never to tell lies again.

Evelyn ran and did not look back. She dared not, as the mere hesitation would slow her progress. She knew it was an impossible task she had been set, as the time she was given to complete the trail was far less than she needed. For each minute she was late, she would have one lash from 'The Master'. She could feel her calves stinging in anticipation of the beating already.

From the moment Evelyn heard that her parents were going out for the day, she knew what Mr Burrows held in store for her. His new amusement entailed Evelyn running the two mile trail through the valley gardens, whilst he idled away his time waiting for her return. Her stomach had churned throughout the morning, as she waited for her new torture to begin. The final countdown began when she heard the wheels of her parents' coach rattle over the courtyard cobbles. Mr Burrows had silently watched their departure from the schoolroom window. When they had gone, he had turned and settled his cold gaze on her. As usual, it had brought the inevitable, and now familiar, chill to her bones as she waited for him to speak.

'Two o'clock,' he had said, holding up his fob watch by its gold chain. That was all; two words, and she had started to run, with no time to look back.

The valley gardens were entered by a steep downward trail, and exited on the far side by an equally steep upward path. Between the two, and sheltered by the wind, were acres of microclimate habitat, where exotic plants from around the world flourished; palms, conifers and bamboos grew tall and splendid rhododendrons added colour to the greens of the jungle. But Evelyn appreciated none of it. She just ran and ran and ran.

It started to rain. Water began to trickle down the banks of the valley, gaining momentum to become gushing streams. The deeper ruts in the path filled with rain, disguising them as shallow, harmless puddles. Evelyn tried to jump or dart around them, fearful she may twist an ankle, but her petticoats and dress grew wet and heavy, dragging at her and sapping her strength. She felt herself tiring, but continued on, gasping for air as if she was drowning. She thought of what waited for her at the end as tears of frustration and panic mingled with the raindrops on her face.

Evelyn looked ahead. The dark clouds had absorbed all the light in the valley, turning it into a colourless world. Yet in the distance, standing in the rain as if waiting for her, she saw a figure of a man. He stood quite still, his feet and shoulders braced against the heavy rain and a dark frown upon his face. As she approached, she realised it was Drake. A new panic seized her. She could not stop now.

'Evelyn. What are you doing?'

Evelyn attempted to pass him, but he grabbed her wrist.

'Evie, it's raining. What are you doing?'

Evelyn tried to pull away. 'Don't, Drake. Let me go.' Her wet wrist slipped from his grasp and she stumbled on, but he soon blocked her path again. This time he had no intention of letting her slip past. He grabbed both her shoulders and turned her to face him.

'Look at me. Look at me!'

Reluctantly she did so, eager to be gone. She had not seen him in several months. He looked older, but perhaps so did she. Raindrops hung from the peak of his sodden cap and the tip of his nose and although his cheeks were wet, his eyelids and lashes remained dry. He was looking at her intently and in their depths she saw only his concern for her. She wanted to weep.

'Why are you out in the rain?' he asked. 'Why are you running?' She wanted to lean against him and tell him everything but she didn't have time. A hurried explanation would have to do.

'If I am not back when the clock strikes two Mr Burrows will beat me.' She tried to pull away, but Drake's hold on her tightened.

'Why?' he asked.

'Please, Drake. I don't have time. Please let me pass.' She tried to shake him off, but he would not let go. Panic overtook her. Drake would never understand and she was already late. She began to struggle, kicking and hitting her dear friend in an attempt to break free. Drake held her tight, pinning her arms to her sides. He nestled his face against hers as she struggled, his warm breath brushing her ear. Finally she stilled in his arms.

'I know a shortcut,' he whispered. 'It will give you time to spare, shelter and a place for us to talk.' She felt her legs begin to sag with relief, as he let her go to grab her hand. 'Follow me,' he said, and led her back along the path she had come.

They did not retrace her steps for long before Drake led her off the main path and up a narrow trail made by woodland animals. It rose steeply, taking them out of the valley. If it had not been for Drake's firm grip pulling her along, she would have soon tired. Gradually the ground became firmer beneath their feet and began to level. Near the top was the wooden shelter he had spoken of and when they arrived, Drake wasted no time in yanking the door open and leading her inside. They took off their wet coats and wrapped themselves in the blankets kept at the shelter to be used in times of frost.

'It's used by the gardeners,' Drake explained as he brushed the surface of the wooden bench with his sleeve for her to sit down, which she did. 'The shortcut is too.' He looked around at the untidy room. 'Not exactly what you are used to.' He opened a tin and offered her the contents. Inside were two slices of bread, an apple and a slice of cake. She refused with a shake of her head, so he closed it again and set it aside. He sat down beside her. Evelyn wished the kittens were with them too. It would give them both something to do and look at. Here, it was just the two of them in a bare wooden shed and her odd behaviour to explain.

'Timmins saw us together,' Drake said, breaking the silence. 'He sent me here to get me away from the house … and you. I've been here for four months now. I have watched you on the path several times. Thought it best to stay away and not interfere, although what you were doing made no sense.' Evelyn looked away, embarrassed. 'I don't pretend to understand what you told me just now, but it sounds like torture. This man called Burrows, is he your tutor?'

Evelyn nodded.

'Tell me what this is all about?' She could not look at him, but he would not be put off. 'Evie, look at me,' he coaxed.

She had asked for help before and what did that achieve but bruised legs? And besides, what could Drake do to help? She would reassure him so he would delve no deeper, she decided.

She met his gaze, but saw only concern and a readiness to listen. She knew, without doubt, he would believe her and, even more importantly, his concern told her that she did not deserve such treatment. A wave of enlightenment flowed through her. How had she become so low to believe that she did? She felt angry, and with it came a new strength. She wanted someone else to know of the injustice she had suffered and, as they sat side by side, with the rain beating down on the little slate roof, Evelyn told Drake everything.

Chapter Ten

Evelyn received four lashes from 'The Master', but for once she did not mind. The reprimand was worth the extra minutes she had with Drake. After the beating she returned to her room and hugged her knees to soothe the stinging of her calves. She thought of Drake and remembered how he had wrapped her in his arms after she had finished confiding in him. She smiled as she recalled the warmth of his body, the smell of burnt charcoal on his clothes and the feel of his heart pounding in his chest. They had stayed like this for some moments, hidden from the outside world. At one point, Evelyn was sure she felt a soft pressure upon the top of her head. She hoped, no prayed, Drake had kissed her. Suddenly, the importance of Mr Burrows' timekeeping no longer held any significance for her. Being with Drake was all that mattered as, for the first time in a long time, she felt at peace, happy – and something else that both excited and unnerved her.

'You have to tell your parents,' he had finally advised her.

'I have. They did not believe me.'

'Then tell them again or I will tell them for you.'

She had shaken her head. 'They will question how an apprentice gardener would know. They will dismiss you if they find out we meet. I couldn't bear that.'

They had fallen into a silence. Eventually he had asked, 'Does he touch you?'

The question had puzzled her. 'What do you mean?' she'd asked him.

Drake had swallowed as he struggled to find the right words. Now, the memory of his discomfort made her smile.

'In womanly places where only your husband should touch you.'

At the time, she had felt her cheeks burn with embarrassment and was eager to reassure him. Now, looking back, she felt pleased that he thought of her as a woman and no longer a child. She felt a glow of joy warm her inside at the thought of Drake. He was a good friend. No, he was more than a friend and, of course, he was right. She must tell her parents about Mr Burrows again. This time she must make them understand, but she needed time to prepare herself as she could not afford to fail again. She would tell them tomorrow and this time they must listen to her.

Drake knocked on Mr Timmins' office door and listened for his curt order to enter. When it came, he slipped the cap from his head and went in. The room was smaller than he had expected. It had a single, north-facing window and white lime washed walls, which brought much needed light to the room. Shelves skirted one wall. Glass jars, filled with an assortment of seeds, were neatly arranged on each one and beneath stood a wooden workbench. The room was serviceable and lacked comfort. If it had not been for the unlit fireplace in the corner or the desk scattered with lists, books and ledgers, it would have passed for a storeroom. The Head Gardener looked up from his order book. It was evident that he had disturbed him.

'What do you want, Vennor?'

'There's talk amongst the servants, Mr Timmins.'

Timmins sat back in his chair to study him. 'What talk?'

'That someone in Sir Robert's employment has been seen coming out of a whorehouse in Saltash.'

Timmins expression did not change. 'One of my staff?' he asked.

'No, sir.'

'Then it is no concern of mine.' Timmins returned to his desk. 'Shut the door when you leave.' Drake did not move, forcing Timmins to glance up. The little patience he had was already wearing thin. 'Well, boy? Spit it out. You obviously have more to say on the matter.'

'I'm telling you because you have a special relationship with Sir Robert. He trusts you. He will believe you.'

Just as before, Timmins sat back in his chair to study him. It was true, the Head Gardener's relationship with Sir Robert was close. It was of many years standing and was built on trust and respect for the gardener's knowledge and skills. Drake saw Timmins' chest rise with pride.

'And why should I bother Sir Robert with such sordid tales?'

'I believe he would want to know.'

Timmins snorted. 'There are many men, and gentlemen too, who visit such places. To discuss such matters would be embarrassing.'

'Something needs to be done.'

Timmins eyes narrowed. 'Who was it? Who has got you so heated up?'

'The private tutor to Miss Evelyn, Mr Burrows.'

Drake did not need to explain further. A private tutor held a position of responsibility. Great trust was placed upon them, as the child in their care spent much of the day with them, unchaperoned and under their sole influence. The tutor a family employed reflected on their good name. They must be honourable and their behaviour exemplary. If he was not, Sir Robert's judgement for employing such a man would be in question. Of course, there was also Miss Evelyn to consider. To be taught by a man who frequents a whorehouse would also tarnish her reputation. Even so, one cannot accuse a man on evidence based on rumours.

'Who saw him?'

'I don't know, sir. I only heard the gossip from some of the bothy lads. They were only retelling indoor gossip.'

'When does he visit this establishment?'

'Most weeks. Tonight, if he keeps to his regular routine.'

Timmins chewed his bottom lip as he stared at the floor and mulled over the problem. Drake clenched his teeth as he waited. If Timmins did not help, he would have to take matters into his own hands.

Timmins sniffed, and returned his attention back to his ledger. 'I'll not talk to Sir Robert.'

'But, sir!'

'There are other ways to sort this out, Vennor. Meet me at the stables in half an hour. There is an errand that needs doing and I want you to come with me.'

Mr Burrows looked in the mirror as he straightened his waistcoat and necktie. He tilted his head, this way and that, to see if there was room for improvement. Deciding there was, he licked his fingers and raked them lightly through his hair with short jabs, finishing with gentle strokes on his moustache. Finally content with his appearance, he put on his bowler and manoeuvred it with the finest of precision, all the while ignoring the reflection of the unconscious woman in the bed behind him.

Outside, Mr Burrows saw that night had already fallen. Half the street remained in darkness, whilst the other half hissed with the sound of gaslights, their bright glow illuminating the cobbled street below. A man, carrying a ladder and lamp, passed him on his way to light the rest. Mr Burrows was about to leave, when he noticed his way was blocked. Two men, one young, the other in his early fifties, stood shoulder to shoulder glaring at him. Mr Burrows automatically reached for his pocketbook to ensure his money was safe.

'If you will excuse me, gentlemen, I will be on my way,' he said, touching the brim of his bowler and attempting to sidestep them. The younger man was quicker and blocked his path again.

'We want a word or, so help me, I will lay you out right here,' warned the youth.

The threat would have been more ominous if they were not standing in a street full of witnesses. Mr Burrows looked at him with a haughty tilt of his chin, ready to scoff and put him in his place. Instead he saw the young man's struggle to hold on to an immature temper. The lad really did want to beat him and he did not care who would see him do it. Mr Burrows' mouth turned dry as his confidence drained away. Perhaps he had misjudged the danger he was in.

'What do you want?'

It was the older man who replied. 'We know who you are, Burrows, and the company you like to keep. If you value your reputation, you will do as we say.'

'I don't know what you mean,' replied Mr Burrows, as he kept his eyes on the younger, more unpredictable one of the two.

'Do you think Sir Robert, or any other family of consequence, would knowingly entrust their child's care to a patron of a whoring establishment?'

So this is what the confrontation was about. Blackmail.

'You want money to keep silent?' He withdrew his pocketbook and took out some coins. The men, no doubt, wanted some money for a drink. This was a problem he could sort; after all he had done it before. 'How much do you want?' he asked, selecting a few coins.

The boy would have lunged at him, if the older man had not steadied his temper with a firm hold on his arm.

'We don't want your money,' the older of the two replied calmly. 'We want you to resign from your post and move away from here.'

Mr Burrows paused in his searching and looked up. His fingers curled round a coin. This was more serious than he first thought.

'And why would I do as you say?'

'It would be for the best,' ground out the older man.

Mr Burrows' eyes darted nervously from one to the other. He swallowed noisily. He had thought the younger one was the bigger threat, but there was something in the other man's tone that carried a stark warning. Yet he did not want to leave his employment. The money was good and the position was envied. Their demands were ludicrous.

'And what do you propose I say is the reason for my sudden departure?' he challenged.

'Family commitments have called you away and you do not intend returning. We do not care, as long as you leave.'

'And what if I refuse? Will you set your mongrel on me?' said Mr Burrows. He tried to laugh, but even to his own ears it sounded forced and pathetically dwindled away before it had begun.

'Sordid stories sell newspapers, Mr Burrows. I'm sure I can find a newspaper editor who will be happy to hear your story. I can see the headline now. "Respectable tutor finds gratification between the sheets and legs of Cornwall's finest whores."'

For the first time, the younger man was forgotten as Mr Burrows turned his full attention to the older man. A weathered face looked back at him from the shadows of a wide brimmed hat. His straight, firm mouth did not invite further negotiation. This man meant every word he said and he was prepared to do anything to be rid of him. It was happening again and if an eager journalist delved further, it would not be long before his other sordid secrets were revealed. Mr Burrows paled at the thought.

'Is there no other way? No agreement we can come to?' The two men glared back at him. 'I have no choice, do I?'

'You have no choice,' said the youth.

'Then there is no more to be said. I will send a note to Sir Robert tonight and be gone by the morning. Now get out of my way. You have won and I hope you both rot in hell!'

Mr Burrows walked briskly to a waiting coach. He informed the driver of his address and climbed inside. He reached for a handkerchief and mopped his brow with a trembling hand, before resting his head back against his seat. Mr Burrows was not a brave man and the incident had shaken him. It had also changed everything.

He would have to leave Cornwall, he decided. The county was nothing more than a backwater, where life remained stagnant and nothing progressed. He would return to London. Yes, that is what he would do. He would seek his father's help to obtain another position. He had helped once before, perhaps he would help again. Somewhere he could blend in and people did not give two curses for their neighbour's troubles. Not like this provincial place, where curtains twitched and everyone was either related or knew one another. Where else would you have two labourers caring for the reputation of a man like Sir Robert? Mr Burrows frowned as he thought of the mounting difficulties in his future that needed to be overcome. Sir Robert, on the other hand, would remain oblivious to his hardship and continue to enjoy the comforts of his ostentatious house. He knew it would not take him long to employ another tutor for his pampered daughter. There were many who would clamber over bodies to obtain it. Mr Burrows' dedication to his son would soon be forgotten. Well, perhaps he would leave a few chosen words for Sir Robert to ponder on. Why should he be the only one to suffer?

Mr Burrows craned his neck to watch the two men who had challenged him. They were walking back to the hole they had crawled out of with their heads bowed against the growing breeze and their hands thrust deep in their pockets. As the coach passed them, they briefly lifted their heads and noticed him sitting inside. He tilted his chin and looked the other way.

After confronting Mr Burrows, Timmins and Drake failed to find a ride home and were forced to walk; Drake to the bothy, Timmins to his small house on the grounds of Carrack House. A full moon lit their journey as the sound of their boots marked the speed of their progress. Despite their prior alliance, an awkward silence quickly settled between them. Timmins was not a talkative man and Drake was at a loss how to converse with the head gardener. In truth, Drake was a little shaken. Not by the pompous man, Burrows, but the realisation he was prepared to beat the man if he did not leave Evie alone. He had never felt such hatred or a desire to protect another. Evie had brought that out in him. What did that mean? He could hardly discuss it with Timmins.

They had walked a mile when Timmins finally broke the silence. 'You did well tonight, Vennor,' he said in a measured tone. Drake looked up, surprised at his praise. 'You have shown responsibility by bringing a delicate matter to my attention. They are qualities that few labourers have.'

The compliment moved Drake more than he cared to admit and whether it was a change in him, or a change in Timmins, conversation began to flow more easily as their difference in rank was temporarily set aside. Granted, their topic of conversation remained firmly on horticulture, but it was a passion they both shared in equal measures and it allowed Drake respite from examining his own feelings for a girl he could never have.

They eventually left the road to follow a cross-country footpath, which led them through streams, over stiles and across fields left to lie fallow. The path reduced their journey by many miles, but the light from the moon, smothered by thickening cloud, no longer lit their way and put their surefootedness at risk. On several occasions a hand of support was needed, offered and gratefully accepted by each of them, in order to avoid serious injury. Each offer of support unconsciously helped lay the foundations for a new relationship between them. Eventually Carrack House came into view. They paused to look at its silhouette filled with golden-lit Georgian windows.

'It's time,' said the head gardener as he chewed on a blade of grass. 'Up till now I have given you jobs that any unskilled labourer can do. All apprenticeships start at the bottom and those that can stomach it and are willing to study hard can work their way to the top. You have worked hard and done well. It is time your learning really began. We will start tomorrow and I will teach you all I know.'

Sir Robert removed his reading glasses and pinched the bridge of his nose to stem the headache that would surely come. He stole a glance at his wife across the table. She had barely touched her breakfast. Grief continued to affect her and it was not only her appetite outside the bedroom that remained poor. He could not remember the last time she had invited him into her bed or allowed his comforting touch to stray. She needed a diversion from the loss of her son, although this was not what he had in mind. Even so, he could not hide the latest calamity to befall them, grief or no grief.

'Mr Burrows has resigned from his post,' he said, pushing his plate of haddock away. 'Our daughter is without a tutor.'

'With no explanation?' asked his wife. At least the news had shocked her out of her usual malignant trance.

'Oh, he has explained. Quite thoroughly, in fact, but I have no wish to repeat it.'

Lady Pendragon plucked the letter from his hand. 'Is this his letter?' She did not wait for her husband's answer. Her eyes traced the tutor's neat handwriting with lightning speed. 'Can this be true?' She looked up, puzzled. 'I find this hard to believe.' She looked down again, her eyes darting to the words used to describe her daughter. 'Insolent, lazy, rude, contrary. He says she lacks motivation and a desire to learn. But Evelyn is so quiet. No, this cannot be true.'

'I thought so too, so I went to the schoolroom and searched her desk. Her work is of a very poor standard. Mr Burrows' corrections are all over her work and clearly highlights the fact it is unsatisfactory.' One essay, about Nicholas, was particularly unpleasant to read, but he would not distress his wife with that particular discovery. Sir Robert rang for the butler, who quickly appeared. 'Fetch my daughter,' ordered Sir Robert. 'I want to speak with her.'

The butler gave a curt bow of his head and immediately left the room.

'A few months ago she told us he had punished her for not completing her work. She was quite open with the fact that she found the work he gave her too much and too challenging.' He retrieved the evidence to his daughter's poor behaviour and studied it for a moment. 'I should have listened,' he said to himself. 'Perhaps if I had shown some understanding of Mr Burrows' difficulties and intervened, he would not have left.'

'But she appeared eager to improve,' argued his wife.

'To us, perhaps, but it seems she showed a more petulant side to Mr Burrows.'

'Nicholas always spoke highly of him, although Miss Brown did not like him.'

'Miss Brown did not want to lose her position.'

'She did think rather highly of herself towards the end. How dare she be so carefree with her opinions and tell us how to bring up our daughter.'

Sir Robert discarded the last remark. He had noticed his wife's growing jealousy where the governess had been concerned. It proved useful when he wanted to replace her, but it served no purpose here. He had another problem to deal with now.

'Evelyn is growing up and testing the boundaries. I will not tolerate rude and contrary behaviour.'

Lady Pendragon looked at the letter she still held in her hand. 'The situation must have been quite dire for him to leave without speaking to us first.'

'He has always been most agreeable, but I can see that it would have been very difficult for him to broach the subject with us, considering our recent bereavement.'

His wife's bottom lip began to tremble. He plucked the letter from her hand and offered her a handkerchief. She refused, but withdrew one of her own from her sleeve. He left the table, so she could dab her tears alone. He had seen her weep so much of late that he was becoming immune, even irritated, by her frail emotions.

'I was afraid Evelyn would not be up to the task,' he said as he took up his position in the centre of the room to wait for her arrival. 'Mr Burrows expressed his doubts, but I insisted that my daughter was not like other girls. I told him that she was able to cope.' He looked at the letter in his hand. 'Howard will find this fiasco amusing.' He waved it at his wife. 'I can see him now, sharing the news with his friends at the club, scornful of my ability to secure a future for Carrack. Laughing at me.' He scrunched the letter in his hand and threw it across the room. 'Evelyn has let me down. She has let us both down. And she has made me look like a fool.'

'Don't distress yourself, Robert.'

He looked at his wife in some surprise. 'I am not distressed. I am bloody furious.'

Evelyn stared at the schoolroom clock. Mr Burrows was late. He was never late. Was this a new ploy to trick her? The thought unnerved her. Had he told her to meet him somewhere? Was he going to use her failure as a reason for 'The Master' to visit? She tried frantically to recall their last conversation for some clue to his whereabouts. Suddenly, the door opened. It was the butler. Her parents wanted to see her.

Her father was waiting for her with a stern expression on his face. Her mother stood behind him and to one side, her hands clasped at her waist, a frown pinching her brow. A sense of foreboding filled Evelyn as she entered the room. Something was wrong and she felt instinctively that Mr Burrows was involved.

'Do you know why you have been summoned?' asked her father.

She shook her head, glancing at her mother for a clue. Her mother remained silent.

'No, Father,' replied Evelyn.

'Mr Burrows has left and will not be returning.'

The news was so welcome, Evelyn gasped with delight.

'You look pleased,' observed her father.

'I am!' Her delight made her forget her well-rehearsed lines. 'I'm sorry, Father, but I did not like him.'

'You insolent pup!' Evelyn looked at him, wide-eyed with shock. 'Your behaviour has placed us all in an insufferable position, Evelyn. How are we to face society when it becomes known that our daughter caused the resignation of her own tutor?' Evelyn's mouth dropped open, her mind dazed from his onslaught. 'You have behaved badly, young lady. Very badly indeed! You have been lazy in your studies and shown nothing but contempt for the opportunity I—'

'No! Whatever you have been told, it is untr—'

'Selfish child! You have taken advantage of our suffering and made me look like a fool in the process.'

'I would never do that. Father he was—'

'This interview is over. Go to your room, Evelyn.'

'No!'

Her father's rage was barely concealed. 'Do not answer me back. If this is an example of your behaviour, I do not blame him for leaving. Now go. I cannot bear to look at you.'

Her father turned away from her. She had been dismissed. The sight of his broad back, impermeable to her pleas, ignited a sudden rage of injustice inside her. She would *make* him listen and she would not leave until he had heard her.

Struggling to know where to begin, for her rage went much deeper than mere words could relate, she reached for the nearest object and smashed it on the floor.

Crystal cut glass showered the parquet floor at their feet, to leave a pool of shards glinting in the morning sun. Her parents looked at her in dismay and, for the first time in her life, Evelyn felt she had their attention. They were both looking at her. They saw her. They actually *saw* her.

'I am not to blame for his leaving!' shouted Evelyn. 'He was a horrible man and I am glad he is gone. I tried to tell you, but you wouldn't listen. You never listen!'

Her father's face turned red, but the tone of his voice remained calm and razor-sharp. 'How dare you. Go to your room.'

'If you really knew me, you would know I am not to blame!' screamed Evelyn.

'I said, go to your room.'

She would not be dismissed, but realised shouting would not help her case. She tried to calm herself. Her nostrils flared with the effort.

'The truth is,' she said unsteadily, 'I don't think you really know me at all.'

Her father shook his head. 'I'm not listening to this.' He looked towards the door and shouted for a servant to clear up the mess, but no one dared to come.

Evelyn grew bolder. 'I was of no importance when Nicholas lived. I am not sure I am now. You don't know what my hopes and dreams are because you have never asked me.' She moved towards him, her feet crunching on the scattered glass between them. 'I want you to know, Father. Ask me.'

'Leave, before I lose my temper,' warned her father through gritted teeth.

Evelyn ignored the threat. She wanted to be heard. 'I hate embroidery, Father. It bores me,' she said firmly. 'I dislike learning slow piano pieces. I love to paint ... but I hate painting landscapes.'

'Enough!' He took a step back, warding her off with an outstretched hand.

Evelyn followed him. 'Did you hear me? I hate painting landscapes.' She looked to her mother. 'I like chocolate and rhubarb, Mother, but hate almond and cherry. And when Miss Brown fell asleep, I would sneak out of the nursery to play in the gardens.' Evelyn turned back to her father. 'I want an education—'

'You had an education and threw it away.'

'—but not one where my confidence is whittled away!' shouted Evelyn, upset.

'Miss Brown was lax in her duties,' said her mother, coming towards her.

She is coming to comfort me, thought Evelyn, as her eyes began to fill with tears.

'No, Mother. Miss Brown was kind and good,' she tried to reassure her. 'She was like a mother to me.'

Her mother's stinging slap violently jerked Evelyn's head to the right and shocked her into silence. Slowly, hesitantly, Evelyn touched her burning cheek with her hand and looked at her mother in disbelief. Wild eyes stared back at her.

'I am your mother. *I am*!' her mother shouted at her.

Evelyn, who had never been struck by her parents before, felt its pain more deeply than any punishment Mr Burrows had meted out.

Confused, she looked to her father for support, but he refused to look at her. It was as if she had become invisible once more. Nothing she had said had made a difference. It was as if she had not spoken at all. She would not have it. Not again. The anger she had tried her very best to control suddenly broke forth like a raging bull. It overwhelmed her, tearing her common sense to shreds and deluding her to the good it could do. She reached for another glass and smashed it on the floor.

This time the rebellious act, and the sound of it smashing, sent a thrill through her and brightened her eyes. She reached for another, insensible to her parents' retreat as they protected their faces from the showering glass. She turned to the breakfast table. Cutlery, plates and teacups were rapidly sliding in a tangle of white linen before Evelyn realised what she had done, but she did not care.

She had swept the crowded sideboard clear of ornaments and trinkets, and was in the midst of pulling books from the shelves, when the door opened. In her frenzy, she did not hear anyone enter or feel their hands upon her until it was too late.

Suddenly, the room was tilting. The solid ground beneath her feet fell away and she was falling backwards, backwards, into a bed of hands. Angry faces looked down upon her. She was being carried away, but to where? Frightened, she began to struggle, jerking and flaying like a floundering, landed fish. The hands tightened, pinching her tender flesh and finally bringing her back to her senses.

Evelyn realised that her dress was about her waist, exposing her drawers to the servants who carried her. She tried to pull it down, twisting and turning in acute embarrassment, but their grip only tightened further.

They think I am violent. They think I am mad!

Evelyn tried to explain her actions as they carried her unceremoniously from the room, but as she saw the destruction around her she knew, with a sinking heart, her efforts would be futile.

Chapter Eleven

Sir Robert and Lady Pendragon sat stiffly, side by side, waiting for the closed door of their drawing room to open. Whilst Sir Robert rapidly tapped his fingers on the walnut wood arm of their leather sofa, his wife kneaded her handkerchief into her lap with the vigour of a nervous woman.

'He can't be much longer,' Sir Robert muttered to himself. 'What is taking him so long?'

He did not expect an answer. They had both witnessed their daughter's odd behaviour, the whole damn house had witnessed it, and such a serious decline would take time to assess. Even so, his wife did reply, in her clipped, uptight tone that offered no reassurance.

'He is very thorough. Whatever he prescribes, we must follow it to the letter.'

'Is that a jibe at me?'

'It was *you* who declined his tonic for Nicholas,' snapped his wife.

Sir Robert stood abruptly and walked to the window. 'Nicholas was dying. We knew that long before his relapse.'

'He may have lived longer.'

Sir Robert turned on his wife. 'Don't you dare lay his death at my door! He had the best treatment money could buy. You are not the only one who grieves! He was my son too! At least I can say I have never raised a hand to my children.'

His retort struck his wife like the slap she had given. 'I am her mother! I love Evelyn!'

'And slapping our daughter's face proved that?'

Silence fell heavy upon the room and shone a light on the void between them. Lady Pendragon's appetite to fight faded as suddenly as it began. She stood and stiffly turned to face him.

'I have lost one child, Robert, and I felt like I was losing another. I slapped Evelyn because I was jealous of Miss Brown. It was shameful and wrong. We should not be baiting one another. Our daughter is ill and needs our help.'

Sir Robert's shoulders began to shudder. His wife came to his side to see what was ailing him. She lifted his bowed head to find his cheeks wet with tears. She had never seen him cry before because he never had. Embarrassed, he tried to turn away, but she would not let him.

'Robert, my dearest love.'

He felt a sob rising in his chest and felt helpless to quench it. 'Poor Evelyn. I have never seen her so wild and feral. What are we to do?'

'Doctor Birch will help Evelyn,' she soothed, wiping away his tears as if he was a child. And like a child, he allowed her to do it. To both their relief, his tears stopped as suddenly as they had begun. They would never speak of his moment of weakness again. They stood for a moment, arm in arm, looking out onto the gardens that their daughter had so vividly captured in watercolour.

Eventually, his wife spoke her thoughts aloud. 'The things she said ... were so very cruel.'

Her husband laid his arm around her shoulder. 'She was not in her right mind, my dear.'

'She hates us.'

'No. She thinks we do not care.'

'But we do.'

Sir Robert stroked his wife's arm. 'We do. And we will prove it. We will stand by her and give her the best and most up-to-date treatment available.'

'Doctor Birch will know what to do.'

'And whatever he prescribes, we will ensure that she has it.'

From their window, they could see vibrant fuchsias and hydrangeas in full bloom.

'One would never guess she did not like painting landscapes,' said his wife thoughtfully.

'No,' replied Sir Robert. 'However, she is not her normal self at the moment and what she says cannot be relied upon. I have learnt that our daughter hides her troubles very well.'

Doctor Birch stood in the hall, savouring the moment of his dramatic return. He knew Sir Robert and Lady Pendragon waited anxiously for his opinion on their daughter's mental state, but he did not care. Let them wait a little longer, he thought, as he considered his next move. After all, they had made him wait long enough.

In truth, he still smarted at their lack of contact since their son's death. Before and during Nicholas's illness he received constant invitations to dine with them, which he used to his advantage and often boasted about. However, since Nicholas's death he had received none. Their silence had been deafening and caused him great concern. He did not think for one minute that they blamed him for the child's demise, for the boy had a weak heart that should have killed him months ago. No, he was apprehensive that he had lost their patronage and the commendation that went with it.

True, attending social engagements and entertaining guests during deep mourning could be considered inappropriate. He had also heard tales of patients withdrawing from all contacts who reminded them of a tragic time. Yet, he truly believed that his position within the Pendragon family was on firmer ground. To be so brutally dismissed from their lives, like a trader whose wares were no longer required, fuelled a resentment that still burned daily in his gut. Fortunately, this new crisis had them crawling back to him and the nature of it excited him greatly.

Several years ago he had developed an interest in the disorders of the mind. It followed an incident in Truro, where a terrified woman, who felt persecuted by demons, ran through the streets clawing at her own face. A crowd had followed her all the way to the quay, but was unable to persuade her otherwise or save her when she finally jumped into the water. The affliction of madness controlled thought and body. To be able to cure it would hold much power. Frequent trips to sideshows and asylums followed, where he spent hours observing the wild existence of the mad. Now Evelyn had shown signs of hysteria. How fortunate he had an interest in the subject and understood more than most.

Her parents' anxious attentiveness, when he entered the drawing room, helped stroke his ego and made him feel generous enough to offer a morsel of reassurance, although in reality their prior indifference would not be forgotten lightly.

'Your daughter is sleeping peacefully, Robert,' he said, determined to make the point that titles were for society to use, not him. He turned to Lady Pendragon and addressed her in a similar vein. 'I gave her some laudanum, Beatrice. It has helped settle her nerves.'

He took the glass of port offered and sat down in a large, winged chair. Evelyn's parents sat opposite him on the sofa, leg to leg, shoulder to shoulder, with no stomach for drink.

'How did you find her?' asked Lady Pendragon.

'Highly agitated and confused. She even expressed feelings of paranoia.'

Lady Pendragon stifled a sob. 'Our daughter has always been such a good child.'

'When did you first notice this change?'

It was Sir Robert who answered, as he felt he was to blame. 'In truth we have only now become aware of the extent of the change. Following Nicholas's death, I engaged our son's former tutor for Evelyn. I hoped that if she had the best education, she may be better equipped to be my heir.' He frowned at the recollection. 'Mr Burrows, her tutor, found her lazy and lacking motivation. In the end, it was her insolence towards him that made him leave. We challenged Evelyn this morning. She became hysterical, cruel and quite violent. We had to call for help to restrain her.'

Doctor Birch studied the remains of his port as he enjoyed its astringent aftertaste on his teeth and gums. It was a very fine wine indeed and he was secretly pleased that they had remembered his preference for it, despite the early hour.

'Evelyn tells me she is fourteen.' Her parents nodded. 'A female's nature is inextricably linked to her reproductive organs,' said the doctor. 'Hysteria, nervous excitability and great irregularities of temper can cause irritation to these sexual organs and, if untreated, lead to madness.'

'You think our daughter is mad?'

Doctor Birch afforded them a smile. 'No, Beatrice, at least, not yet. Does madness run in the family?' He listened patiently to the scanty information they had regarding a distant relative. There was always someone in a family, a secret never to be mentioned, lurking in the background somewhere. 'From your testimony and her very own lips, Evelyn has certainly exhibited behaviour that is sociably unacceptable and must never be repeated. Should this behaviour continue into adulthood, well it would be social suicide for her.' He lifted his empty glass. It was immediately filled by Lady Pendragon. He took a sip and savoured it, knowing that they waited anxiously for him to continue. 'It is well recorded in medical journals, that females are uniquely vulnerable to mental instability. Their character is weaker and must therefore be protected. I have studied the work of many psychiatrists—'

'Alienists?' cried Lady Pendragon.

'Yes, they are one of the same. Have you heard of Doctor Silas Weir Mitchell?' He smiled inwardly, of course she had not. He would be the one to enlighten her. 'He is an American neurologist and an expert in the field of hysteria and neurasthenia. He has developed a treatment for these ailments which have proved most successful.'

Sir Robert remained wary. 'He is an American?'

Doctor Birch expected Sir Robert's response. For someone whose fortunes were made on trade with other countries, he had a healthy suspicion of all things foreign.

'He is a prominent physician who has written many books on the subject,' explained Doctor Birch. 'I have been aware of him for some time. His treatment resonates with me more than any other.'

Lady Pendragon leant forward. 'What is the treatment?'

'He calls his treatment The Rest Cure. It heals the patient's physical and moral degeneration and is very simple. It involves complete rest of the mind and body.'

Sir Robert noted his wife's interest, she understood these things far better than he. Even so, his guilt made him err on the side of caution. 'I will not have her committed to an asylum.'

Doctor Birch smiled, as if he was an endearing child. 'That will not be necessary. The treatment can be given here.'

'This treatment,' ventured Lady Pendragon, 'what does it entail?'

'Complete isolation, bed rest and a high fat diet to enrich the blood.'

'Bed rest does not seem too harsh, Robert,' she said, turning to her husband. 'She can paint and read. I will spend more time with her and help her to pass the time.'

'I'm afraid that is not possible,' said Doctor Birch. 'As I have already mentioned, both the mind and body requires rest. She must be in complete isolation, but for the maid who cares for her.' He placed his empty glass on the table at his side. 'Evelyn is very ill, Beatrice. Reading, painting and visitors are to be banned; even the burden of personal care must be lifted from her tired shoulders. This means that washing, eating, even turning in bed will have to be done for her.'

Evelyn's parents looked stricken. He must convince them to accept if he was to secure this opportunity to recreate Weir's treatment.

'Your daughter's wellbeing is teetering on the abyss. The respite will give her body the time to heal and at the end of this treatment, she will be your dutiful daughter again. However, I require your full co-operation and my directions must be followed to the letter. We must not let her down in her time of need.' He looked at them through his eyebrows. '*You* must not let her down.'

The inference that they had let Nicholas down hung in the air between them. Sir Robert, laden with the guilt of a bereaved parent, allowed it to go unchallenged and accepted his recommendation. Both parents were unaware that Evelyn no longer teetered on the edge of the abyss, but was about to fall headlong into it.

Chapter Twelve

Following their visit to Mr Burrows, Timmins had kept his word and Drake's apprenticeship changed for the better, starting with him being recalled from the valley gardens. Heavy chores, which relied on muscle rather than wit, were no longer delegated to him and the hours he had spent studying the theory of gardening was now called upon and used in practice.

The weeks that followed revitalised Drake's passion for the land, as the head gardener was as eager to share his knowledge as Drake was to absorb it. For the first time his dream to emulate the finest landscape gardeners in England looked possible, he just had to work hard, remain focused and put Miss Evelyn out of his mind. Only Miss Evelyn – Evie – refused to leave his thoughts.

Drake found his eyes often straying from the task at hand, hoping to catch a glimpse of her painting at her easel or strolling through the gardens with a parasol resting on her shoulder. He was no longer concerned for her welfare, as he knew she was safe from Mr Burrows. The tutor had ceased visiting Carrack House immediately after their confrontation. Drake knew this as every morning since their encounter, he had waited for the tutor's horse and gig to drive up the gravelled road and felt a great sense of relief when he did not appear.

At night, as he cradled his head in his bent arm and listened to the soft snores of the bothy boys, his mind would relive the day, but inevitably return to Evie and her unexplained absence. She had not visited to tell him the news of her tutor's departure or thank him for helping her that day he found her running in the rain. She had not even visited the kittens, which were now young cats with long gangly legs and an appetite for mice. He couldn't help wondering if she had forgotten him and the thought hurt him more than he cared to admit. He could not really blame her. She was the daughter of a titled man and he was a nobody – but he would be *somebody* one day.

As always his thoughts turned to the memory of holding her. He hadn't planned for it to happen. He had just reached for her and she had stepped forward, fitting perfectly within his arms as if she had been made for them. Holding her made him light-headed and weak, yet he had felt strong enough to take on the world should the need arise in order to protect her. He frowned. It made no sense to feel such intense, contradictory feelings. If he was to make a success of himself, he could not afford to risk his apprenticeship again for a relationship that had no future. Next time, being banished to the valley gardens may not be good enough. It would be, 'Goodbye, Drake Vennor, and good riddance.' He should be glad she was not around. Yet, as always, he could not help wondering what she was doing or feeling hurt that she had not sought him out. He wanted to hate her for her cold-heartedness. He wanted to, but he couldn't. He just *couldn't*.

One could hear Mrs Beecham, long before one stepped inside Carrack House's large kitchen, for the cook shouted rather than spoke and lacked the skill of listening. Drake had accompanied Timmins on his early winter visit to the kitchens to discuss the household's requirements for the coming spring. They exchanged amused glances as the cook's billowing voice greeted them at the door.

Mrs Beecham, all sweat and flour, was stirring the contents of a mixing bowl with such ferocity that her whole body rocked and twisted with surprising agility. Neither man, for that was how Drake now saw himself, dared to interrupt.

As her speed slowed, they removed their caps. Mrs Beecham saw the movement and looked up. Her feelings of irritation changed to bashfulness when she saw Timmins. A rosy glow lit up her rounded cheeks as she pushed the bowl aside and self-consciously patted her stray hair into place.

'Why, Mr Timmins,' she said, untying her apron and giving her dress a cursory brush. 'Is it that time of year already?' She gave him a coy smile. 'I must look a right mess.'

Timmins reassured her. 'Mrs Beecham, you can never look a mess.'

The cook smiled. 'Oh, Mr Timmins, you are like a ray of sunshine on a dark day and the Lord knows there have been too many of those.'

The cook is smitten with the old man, thought Drake, amused. The revelation made him look at his boss with new eyes. For the first time, Drake saw beneath the weathered face and realised he was not as old as he first thought.

'What dark days have you had to endure?' Timmins asked, returning her smile with an indulgent one of his own.

'Oh, not me, Mr Timmins. It is the woes of others I speak of, but thank you, your concern warms my heart.' She mopped her brow. 'Can I tempt you to an iced fancy? They go down very well with a nice cup of tea.' She looked at Drake and her smile dropped a little. 'And who do we have here?'

'This is Vennor. He has been my apprentice for well over a year now.'

Drake placed the basket of root vegetables he was carrying onto the table for the cook to inspect and retreated to the door. The cook looked them over, selecting several for further examination. Her knowledge and experience made it a speedy task.

'Very nice ... as always, Mr Timmins,' said the cook as she studied Drake over the parsnip in her hand. He had the feeling she preferred he was not present. 'The boy looks like he could do with a rest and a slice of cake. He can stay here while we go next door to discuss next year's supplies.'

'I had hoped he could be present,' ventured Timmins.

'Perhaps another time, Mr Timmins,' said the cook as she led the way from the kitchen. She turned to look at the head gardener, expecting him to have followed. 'The truth is,' she said, giving him a doleful look, 'last spring I had problems with my curly kale. It is a matter best discussed alone ... over an iced finger and a cup of tea.'

Drake smiled at Timmins' discomfort. The head gardener was about to protest, when a maid entered carrying a tray laden with remnants of a meal, although it was unclear what the meal had been. The cook's flirtatious demeanour disappeared at the sight of it.

'Did they force her to eat it?' The jarring question shocked Drake and wiped the smile from his face.

The maid shook her head. 'Not this time, Mrs Beecham.'

'Thank the Lord for small mercies.' She turned to Timmins, her smile less broad. 'This way, Mr Timmins. This way.' Timmins raised his eyebrows at Drake and obediently followed her.

Drake remained by the kitchen door, his gaze rooted on the plate on the tray. Cook had said 'her'. Who was she talking about? He had to ask. The maid looked up at his question, surprised to find she was not alone. In any other circumstances Drake would have found it amusing when her pale cheeks flamed red, but the subject of Mrs Beecham's question was all he could think about.

'Who are you?' asked the maid.

'My name is Drake. I work in the gardens.'

'I'm Tilly,' replied the girl, self-consciously touching her hair, just as Mrs Beecham had done not a few minutes ago. 'I've not seen you here before.'

He jerked his head towards the basket of vegetables. 'You may see more of me from now on.' Tilly smiled shyly as the blush on her cheeks rose to inflame the tips of her ears. He had not meant it as a flirtatious promise, but she had taken it as such. 'Who was Mrs Beecham talking about?' asked Drake again.

'I am not sure if I should tell you. We have been warned not to gossip.'

Fingers of fear trailed up Drake's spine. What was happening in the house that the staff had been instructed not to speak of it? Did it involve Evie? Drake tried to keep his mounting concern in check, as it would do neither Evie nor himself any good if their friendship was discovered. However, he had to know or Mrs Beecham's remark would eat him up inside.

'Mrs Beecham brought up the subject in front of me,' he reasoned. 'She does not appear to think I should not know.'

Tilly remained reticent. If she would not tell he would find out another way. Drake prepared to leave.

'No matter,' he said, reaching for the door. 'I will ask one of the other maids.'

To his relief, Tilly suddenly changed her mind. 'If I tell you, you must promise not to tell anyone else?'

Drake turned to look at her. 'I promise.'

Tilly smiled shyly under his steady gaze. 'She was talking about Miss Evelyn.'

It was as he had feared. A hundred questions came to mind, scrambling for attention but he was unsure how much interest he could safely show. Instead he stood there, dumbly staring at Tilly as she quietly set about clearing the tray. She glanced up and found him watching her, her smile broadened, pleased to have his interest. Manners told him he should return the smile, but he just couldn't.

'Did Mrs Beecham offer you some cake?' asked Tilly.

'She did, but I'm not hungry.' It was true. He felt sick.

'I will wrap you a slice so you can take it with you,' offered Tilly. She selected a knife, sliced into the fruit cake on the table and carefully began wrapping it in baking parchment.

'Why did Mrs Beecham ask if she had been forced to eat it?' asked Drake. He wasn't sure if he wanted to hear the answer.

Tilly reached for his hands and placed the small parcel in them. 'Because she once refused to eat,' she said, holding his hand a breath longer than was necessary.

'Why?'

'Because it's no better than pig swill,' said Tilly, oblivious to his pain. She returned to her work, laying a new tray with crockery and fetching a kettle from the range. 'Cook gets very upset. She says it's not natural to eat so much fat and dairy.' Tilly poured hot water onto the tea leaves in the pot and leaned back to avoid the cloud of steam that rose up between them. The sweet, woody aroma of tea filled the room. 'Milk, milk puddings, bread and more milk. Mutton chops if Miss Evelyn is lucky, then more milk. I feel sorry for her.'

Drake's stomach churned at the thought of such a restricted diet. 'And if she refuses, how do they force her to eat it?'

Tilly returned the kettle to the range and paused for a moment as she remembered. 'It has only happened once. Doctor Birch put a tube down Miss Evelyn's nose and poured the milk into her.' Drake was horrified. He must have looked it, for Tilly added, 'I know it sounds awful. It was awful. We were all upset by it ... even Mrs Beecham went to her office for a cry and she never cries. Miss Evelyn hasn't refused again.'

Drake had a sudden need for escape and fresh air, but he could not leave. Evie was somewhere in the house living a new kind of hell, while he stood in her kitchen, holding a slice of freshly baked fruit cake which probably, under normal circumstances, would be intended for her.

'Why are they doing this to her?' Nicholas came to mind and a new fear gripped him. 'Is she ill? Is she dying?'

Tilly shook her head. 'No, she's not dying. As to whether she is ill, that depends on who you ask.'

'I'm asking you.'

Tilly blinked at his directness. She did not answer immediately, preferring to move the plates and saucers on the tray so they lined up neatly.

'No, I don't think she is ill. Miss Evelyn was in the drawing room with her parents, when she began to break everything in sight. Sir Robert had to call for the servants to control her and carry her to her room. She destroyed most of the china, glass and books in the room. She left a terrible mess.' Such behaviour didn't sound like something Evie would do, thought Drake. 'Cook thinks Miss Evelyn had a hissy fit and says, "Nothing that a slice of fruit cake and a kindly ear could not have sorted out."'

'Do you agree with her?'

'I've seen plenty of hissy fits. My sister has them all the time. I've been known to have one or two in my time. Pa or Ma would give me a cuff around the ear and that would be the end of it.'

'What did Miss Evelyn's parents do?'

'Sent for Doctor Birch who said she was as good as mad. She has been confined to her room ever since.'

No wonder he had not seen her. All these weeks he had thought she had forgotten him. How wrong he had been. Drake leaned against the table in what he hoped appeared a nonchalant manner, but in truth it was for much needed support. Tilly rattled on beside him. What was she saying? Drake tried hard to concentrate.

'Doctor Birch wants her to rest her mind and body. She has to remain in bed and do nothing for herself. It would turn my mind if I was not allowed to move. Mrs Beecham says it's enough to send any sane person mad.'

'How is she now?'

'Miserable. She is finding it very hard. Sometimes she refuses to lie still and often begs for something to do, but when she fights against Doctor Birch's treatment, it does no good. It only prolongs it. You should eat your cake. You look quite pale.'

Drake shook his head. 'I have no appetite for it now.'

Concerned, Tilly laid her hand on his arm. 'You look upset, Drake. Have you met Miss Evelyn?'

Drake had not had another girl touch him since Evie. Tilly was not as pretty, her features were too sharp and her hair too fine to attract him, however her harmless touch still stirred his youthful body and he felt as if he was betraying Evie. He slid his hand over hers and gently removed it from his arm.

'I've seen her about, no more,' he replied.

'You feel things deeply, don't you?'

Drake pushed himself away from the table. He did not deserve her kind words. His body had reacted to another girl's touch, whilst Evie was suffering. He was shallower than she thought he was.

'The boys I know think only about themselves,' continued Tilly. 'Some don't grow out of it. Mr Burrows was like that. He was her tutor. He thought a lot of himself. Everyone disliked him. But he is gone now. He resigned as he found it impossible to teach Miss Evelyn. I don't think he was very nice to her. At least that is what I have heard from some of the staff.'

Had he made things worse by forcing Burrows to leave?

'I'd better go,' said Drake. 'It is too hot in here. I need to get some fresh air.' He paused in the doorway. He could still feel the whisper of her touch on his sleeve and he hated himself for still being aware of it. 'Tilly, will you do something for me?' he asked

'What Drake?'

'Will you tell Miss Evelyn that the outdoor staff wish her well.'

'I will if you want me to.'

'And Tilly.'

'Yes?'

Drake winced at the hopeful lift in her voice. 'Tell Miss Evelyn that the kittens in the barn miss her.'

'Oh.'

She sounded disappointed. Drake thought she would be. He rubbed the imprint of her touch off his arm with his hand.

'Especially Blackie,' he said firmly. 'Blackie misses her the most.'

It was several hours later when Drake realised he had left the slice of cake behind. He did not care, as he did not want it, yet oddly he could not recall putting it down. The shock at learning of Evie's plight had robbed the visit of its finer details. However, every aspect of Evie's treatment remained clearly etched in his mind and he could not help but torture himself with the belief that her plight was as a direct result of his well-intentioned meddling.

Chapter Thirteen

Evelyn's lids felt strangely heavy, as if her lashes were laden with beads of lead. She tried to lift them again, but her attempt only succeeded in resembling the feeble fluttering of a caged bird rather than the simple act of opening one's eyes. The struggle quickly tired her and she felt herself falling back into the familiar darkness of a drug-induced sleep.

Sometime later, for it could have been minutes, hours, days or months for all Evelyn knew, she awakened to fingers pinching at her calves. She instantly recognised the pain. It was the nurse massaging her calves to reduce muscle wasting in her legs. Evelyn was relieved to feel the discomfort, as it rescued her from the darkness and anchored her in the world of the living. This time she was able to open her eyes with ease and bright light streamed in forcing her to squint. She looked up and recognised the familiar bedroom ceiling above her.

As the nurse continued to work on her legs, Evelyn's eyes searched for the crack in the corner. She always looked for the crack in the corner. Its constant presence was a reassuring sign in a world that had changed so much. She traced the black line with her eyes, which resembled a profile of a face with a bulbous nose and lips, similar to a caricature. Perhaps she should give the face a friendly name, thought Evelyn, before it began to resemble a more sinister entity in her mind.

She looked for, and found, her next anchor, the spider who never ventured lower than the height of the door. It remained motionless, perhaps feeding on something, or taking a rest, Evelyn could not tell. Then there were the curtains, which did not move but for the far bottom right corner, which swayed slightly, like an incoming wave, should the door open. The shadows between the folds provided much needed stimulus to occupy her mind as they changed each day when the curtains were drawn open. She would spend hours familiarising herself with the twists of the pattern and the folds of the fabric, in a desperate attempt to pass the time.

Yet, each day the four walls of her bedroom appeared to move closer and squeeze her world ever smaller. When she was alone, she would spend her time sitting up in bed and hugging her knees for comfort as she looked about her empty room. Furniture, books, papers, ink, sewing, painting, clothes and company, anything that might enrich her life, had all been taken from her. It was no wonder she devoured each new stimulus she discovered like a hungry animal as she tried not to lift a hand or turn her head, just as Doctor Birch had instructed.

She tried her best, but inside her youthful energy would rise up and scream to be freed, taking over her body so she would sit up and shout out in frustration, or fall weeping at the sight of a tray laden with milk. Her rebellious outbursts made her feel alive, but ultimately they signalled her failure. If Doctor Birch should hear about them, he would come with a tincture that she would have to take. Later, perhaps minutes, perhaps hours, perhaps months later, she did not know, she would open her eyelids, which felt beaded with lead, and see the familiar ceiling above her that now resembled the lid of a coffin. The nightmare that was now her existence had come full circle and was about to begin again and she would desperately search for the crack in the corner in the hope of anchoring herself against the madness that threatened. The crack, which had resembled a face, was beginning to change over time. Any day now it would turn and laugh at her.

Evelyn could not bear to look at the glass of milk the maid carried. She turned her head away. 'What time is it?'

'Midday, Miss Evelyn.'

Midday? Was it only midday! As if to prove the maid right, she heard the distant tower clock sombrely strike the hour.

'Please, take it away.'

'I've had instructions not to.'

Evelyn opened her eyes and saw the nurse's vacant chair. The nurse had taken advantage of the maid's arrival to stretch her legs. Evelyn thought it strange how she was deemed too mad to be left alone during the day, yet sane enough to be left at night. They believed she slept soundly, but they were wrong. With nothing to tire her, her sleep pattern was all over the place and a constant torment. Poor Miss Brown, thought Evelyn. How did her beloved governess remain so cheerful and focused when she lacked sleep, whilst Evelyn's mind had become a whirling, thick fog, where clear thought was near on impossible.

Evelyn turned to look at the maid. 'I've already drunk a quart of milk today, two quarts yesterday and two the day before. Please, I beg you, take it away.' Evelyn sunk below the covers.

'I can't take it away,' said the maid. 'They might see and then they will force you to drink it.'

'I will fight them,' came Evelyn's muffled reply.

'And they will win.' Evelyn heard the maid pick up the glass. 'But I could drink it for you.'

Was she testing her? Were *they* waiting for her answer? Were *they* listening at the door? Evelyn, suddenly alert and wide-eyed, looked over the brim of the sheet. The maid, who was not much older than her, smiled at her. She did not look like she was trying to trick her. Evelyn glanced nervously at the door and back at the maid, who appeared quite calm. Evelyn dared to nod her consent. The movement was so slight and hurried; one could have easily missed it. The maid drank quickly and placed the milk stained glass back on the tray. There was never such a simple act that bared more significance.

'You do not think I am mad?'

'No, I do not.'

Evelyn found it hard to breathe, for in recent times she had begun to doubt her own sanity.

'And the other staff?'

'I think most do not. They just wish you well.'

'Who? Who wishes me well?' asked Evelyn, desperate for confirmation that she was not alone.

'The cook, Mrs Beecham, the chamber maids, the housekeeper, Miss Robbins.'

Tears stabbed at Evelyn's eyes.

'So many ...' she whispered.

'Even a gardener asked after you. He sends his good wishes and hopes you will soon be well enough to see the kittens again.'

Salty tears clogged Evelyn's throat. Drake had asked after her. How she longed to see him again.

Her voice, raw with emotion, was barely audible. 'I hope to see the kittens again too.'

'You will, one day.'

Evelyn looked at the maid. 'What's your name?' In the past she would have known, now the world had seemed to pass her by.

'Tilly, Miss Evelyn.'

'Thank you.'

'I've done nothing, miss, but drink some milk.'

You have done more than that, thought Evelyn. You have given me hope.

Something small and hard hit the windowpane, seizing Evelyn's attention as if Drake himself had walked into the room. The noise was slight and sudden, like the chinking of wine glasses. She sat up and strained to listen for it again, her body prickling with alertness. If the sound had occurred during the day, with the hustle and bustle of the thirty indoor servants, Evelyn may have missed it. However, darkness had fallen some time ago and the house had retired to bed. Only the odd servant, silently and efficiently undertaking the last ministrations of their master and mistress, walked the corridors now. The tower clock chimed eleven. Yesterday, she would have begun to doubt what she had heard, but not now. Not any more. This time, a wave of small stones hit the window. She knew it must be Drake and he wanted to see her. And she wanted to see him.

She scrambled out of bed, forgetting her weakened state. The act of standing had been denied her for so long that the muscles in her legs, robbed of their purpose, had withered despite the nurse's attempts to maintain them. Evelyn teetered briefly, before her legs gave way, crumpling beneath her like a pack of cards. She fell to the oak floor with a jaw wrenching jolt and lay for a moment, shaken, wide-eyed and trying to make sense of the world which was now tilted on its side.

Chink, chink. Drake was calling for her. She must get to the window, now, before he gave up and left. She may not get a chance to see him again. Evelyn began to crawl on her hands and knees despite her thighs shaking from the exertion. The window seemed so far away, yet with each grunt and soft moan, it came nearer, until finally the curtains and sill were within her reach. She wrapped one arm in a curtain and grasped the wooden sill with the other. With all the strength she could muster, she heaved herself up, to stand on her wobbly legs, before laying her body against the sill for support.

A bright moon greeted her. She looked down at the gardens beneath her window searching for movement. The night was cold, still and devoid of colour. The gardens appeared empty. Then a movement caught her eye and she saw Drake's figure emerge from shadows of the old birch tree. He wore a large coat, with an upturned collar and was taller than she remembered. The vision began to fade until she could not see him any more. Realising what had happened, Evelyn frantically wiped the condensation, caused by her rapid breaths, from the ice-cold glass. His image, tall, sturdy and unmoving, re-emerged between the smudged droplets of water. He slowly lifted his hand and she knew he had seen her too.

She rested for a moment, her fingertips touching the glass, fearful he would think she had left. She took a deep breath to gather the little strength she had and reached for the latch. The window opened and cold air swept over her face, like a welcoming kiss. She gasped and felt alive again. She looked for Drake, her heart hammering so loud that surely he must hear it, but he was no longer looking up at her. His head was bent, his attention taken by something hidden beneath the warm weave of his coat.

Gradually a cat's head emerged and looked about, as Drake unfastened the remainder of his buttons to reveal its body. It was Nicky, the kitten she had named after her brother and was taken to live in the stables. How he had grown! He had been no bigger than the palm of one's hand, but now he snuggled against Drake's chest and rubbed his face along his jawline. All the kittens would be the same size by now, she realised. She had missed out on seeing them grow. She had missed out on so much since her confinement.

Drake looked up and their eyes locked. Even in the darkness she could see his face. She had missed Drake so much, more than she had dared to examine before. Her body pulsed with each beat of her heart, its potency reaching every extremity and every secret place. Her body's reaction, both unbidden and instinctual, frightened and thrilled her.

Where Tilly had given her hope, Drake's visit had given her a goal – to escape this room and step into his arms – and to feel the provocative warmth of his body against her own.

For weeks, if not months, her days had merged into a continuous loop of despair, where any means of escape seemed lost to her in a fog of self-doubt. But now, with Drake's eyes upon hers, the fog slipped away and her thinking became crystal clear.

She would survive this treatment and emerge stronger than before, but not because of Doctor Birch's Rest Cure ministrations, but *despite* them. She will play his game until he pronounced her cured and she will listen gravely when her parents congratulate him for saving her soul. But Evelyn's soul had changed, indelibly, resentfully.

She would never forget the tutor who had crushed her confidence and optimism for learning or that her parents had chosen not to believe her and later abandoned her to the mercy of Doctor Birch's arrogance. She would not forget that the servants, who had known her all her life and had witnessed her humiliation at his hands, had chosen not to speak out. The people in her life that she should have been able to trust, had failed her. Only Drake and Tilly were her allies now. There was no one else.

Drake lifted his hand in farewell. Evelyn smiled and raised her own. Suddenly, he was gone, his dark, shadowy figure merging into the blackness of the night. It was as if he had never been there, waiting for her to appear. She lowered her hand and absently touched the dull ache in her chest as a new resolution formed in her mind.

One day she would walk her own path in life. Even dance along it if it took her fancy. And it would be the path she chose, not one that was made for her by others. Where would the path lead? Wherever her instinct and own judgement told her to go, even if it meant disregarding the rules of society, for society's rules, which were aimed at protecting her from harm and ruin, had already let her down.

Each night that followed, as the distant tower clock struck eleven, Evelyn found Drake waiting for her in the shadow of the tree. His visits were short and wordless, but his silent and reliable presence brought her precious comfort and fed her resolve to survive. They also excited her for she never knew what he would do next to cheer her. He brought all the cats in turn to see her. Their visits made her smile as their inquisitive faces peeped out from behind his heavy coat. One night he brought a hedgehog and on another an indignant duck he had smuggled in from the wider estate. Unfortunately, amidst a flurry of flapping wings, the feathered creature broke free, landing with a thud and a squawk on the grass at his feet, before waddling away at a surprising speed. Drake gave chase and disappeared into the night, leaving Evelyn shaking with stifled laughter as she listened to distant quacking floating out of the darkness.

It was the last time Drake brought an animal to show her, but it did not matter. Spring had arrived and the garden and grounds offered up their booty to aide her recovery and bring colour into her life. He brought her peach blossoms, apple blossoms and the flowers of the rhododendrons and Sweet Williams. She could not touch them or smell their honey-like fragrance, but she appreciated their fragile beauty and that Drake had thought of her sometime during the day.

And then there were the nights he came bearing nothing and those were the visits she liked best of all. She would look down from her window to find him waiting, his hands in his pockets and his collar turned up to ward off the night-time chill, and he would tilt his face upwards, his dark eyes would look upon her, and he would smile. Fine drizzle, heavy rain and bitter cold nights that heralded mornings of biting frosts, did not deter him. He would always come to see her – and she would smile too and feel fulfilled.

When Drake left, Evelyn's new, self-designed regime would begin. She spent the long dark hours exercising her mind and body, with the aim of passing time and strengthening her weakened muscles. By the morning she was exhausted and, under the watchful eye of her daytime nurse, she would spend large parts of the day sleeping. This was the only way she could tolerate her enforced bed rest. Her young teenage body no longer wanted to kick and scream in frustration one minute or want to die the next. She escaped to her dreams, dreams that were filled with Drake.

Her only other ally was the servant, Tilly. A tentative friendship formed, built on need and empathy. Whenever the nurse left them alone, Tilly would help Evelyn consume the high fat diet. Glasses of milk, milk pudding and fatty meat were hastily shared and although it was not every day, as the nurse did not always leave the room when Tilly arrived with a tray, it helped. On other days Tilly smuggled in extra candles, a book, or something small and tasty from the kitchen to tease her palate. Such precious gifts were slipped between the hair and spring mattresses and brought out at night to help pass the hours.

However, the most precious gift Tilly brought Evelyn was news of Drake for she often mentioned his visits to the kitchens. Evelyn eagerly listened and later, when left alone, recalled and re-examined each word she had heard. Hearing snippets of his day through Tilly brought Drake closer to her, yet she remained too wary to share her own friendship with Drake to Tilly. She had to remain content to see Drake's kitchen visits through Tilly's eyes, eyes that appreciated his looks as well as she did.

Chapter Fourteen

Turning up his collar, Drake looked up at the sky. He was glad to see that although it was thick with cloud, there was no sign of rain. This week the walk to Perran would be a dryer one than his last, which had left his clothes sodden and his mother worrying he would catch a chill. For the most part, Drake enjoyed the weekly walk to his mother's house. In total the journey took over an hour, which was as long as the time he spent with his mother, but it gave him precious respite away from Carrack Estate, work and study and some peace to think about Evie.

He had not gone far from the bothy door, when he heard Tilly calling to him. He wanted to ignore her and keep walking, but he did not have the heart to do so. Besides, she might have news about Evie. He turned to look at her. Unusually, she was dressed in what looked like her best hat and coat.

'I thought I could walk with you to Perran,' said Tilly, smiling brightly as she approached.

Abel appeared to lounge against the bothy door.

'And why would you be going to Perran today?' he asked Tilly, as she walked past him.

'Because I have every other Sunday afternoon off now,' answered Tilly, still smiling at Drake.

Abel frowned and followed her. 'Since when?'

'Since you last decided to wash, Abel Hicks.' Her retort stopped him in his tracks. Her smile widened further as she approached Drake. 'Fancy some company, Drake?'

Drake's heart sank a little. He liked Tilly, but he wasn't sure he wanted her company right now. He had seen her yesterday as he delivered the supplies to the kitchen. They had chatted, as they usually did each morning, and he had gone away content he had found out all he could about Evie without asking too many questions. Now Tilly wanted to walk with him and their conversation would naturally turn to other things unrelated to the goings-on within the walls of Carrack House.

'I didn't know you had relatives in Perran.'

'There is a lot you don't know about me,' said Tilly, looking up at him through her lashes. 'Besides, it would seem silly not to walk together when we are going in the same direction.'

Drake felt Abel's stare burrowing into his head. 'Abel doesn't look too happy,' he said, lifting his gaze over her head to look at him.

'Abel never looks happy.'

They both looked back at him. He scowled at them, before turning and walking away. Tilly had a point, Abel only laughed when it was at someone's expense. Drake smiled. Tilly, taking it as his consent, immediately fell into step beside him. He noticed that her smile grew even brighter than it had been before and her head held a little higher. She quickly filled the silence with idle chat that required no response and Drake, who usually used the journey to think, found it was now impossible to do so. It felt strange to be alone with a young woman. His visits to the kitchen meant they saw each other often, but he hadn't really considered Tilly a friend up to now. If someone saw them, they would think they were walking out together, which they weren't. Yet, he had the feeling that his agreement to her company had set a new precedent that he could not easily change without hurting her feelings. And he did not want to hurt her feelings, as she was kind to Evie when Evie most needed a friend. He might as well make the best of the situation he had found himself in. He looked at Tilly as she walked beside him and tried to concentrate on what she was saying.

Doctor Birch declared Evelyn cured on the 19th March, four months after Drake's first visit, just over six months after Doctor Birch first diagnosed her with nervous hysteria, an affliction, he often said, the female gender was particularly prone to.

Ironically, it was her female body that provided the key to her release, for on the 19th March Evelyn Pendragon experienced her first menstrual flow. Innocent of such things, Evelyn thought she was dying when she discovered the scarlet stain on her sheets. Doctor Birch, however, had no such concerns. In fact, he was delighted, explaining to the nurse that the reproductive organs were intimately entwined with the emotional and mental health of a woman. The appearance of her monthly curse, he explained, was a sign that her womb no longer wandered about her body and that stability had been restored. Evelyn silently lay between their exchanges, daring to hope that her torture was coming to an end.

'Evelyn has finally passed through the dark phase of emotional instability and emerged a young woman,' he later told her parents, 'and she appears the healthier for it, for her eyes are bright, her muscles are strong and her motivation to spend time downstairs again is unquestionable. She is cured and her treatment is a worthy subject for a paper. In fact, I will submit it for publication to the Journal of Mental Science, which is one of the best resources around. I shall not mention her identity, of course,' he added as an afterthought as he accepted a glass of port.

The nurse provided the knowledge that Evelyn lacked. At the age of fifteen, she was now a young woman, she was told. Childhood, and all that went with it, was behind her. Lost forever, thought Evelyn sombrely, but at least the treatment would now end.

Her cure did not bring about instant freedom for her, but each day brought it a step closer. She was allowed to dress, read openly, embroider and receive visitors again. Her parents were the first to come to her room. Silver threads in their hair and lines of worry on their faces had aged them. Was it her confinement that had caused the changes or simply the passage of time? She wondered how she must look to them. Did they see the change in her outlook on life? Did they see cynicism in her eyes when they looked upon her?

They entered the room with a mixture of caution and curiosity, as if she was a bearded lady in a sideshow they had just paid money to see. The conversation that followed was painfully polite, with no hugs or loving words to soften their first meeting. Her mother fidgeted. Her father constantly cleared his throat with stifled coughs. Evelyn quickly realised the cause of their unease.

'Do you fear I may suddenly relapse?' asked Evelyn boldly.

Her parents had the grace to look embarrassed, although they attempted to deny it. Evelyn looked to the window and longed to be outside.

'We have missed you, Evelyn,' replied her mother. 'It is difficult to know ...' Her mother's voice faded into embarrassed silence.

'How to treat me,' said Evelyn, finishing her sentence for her.

'Well ... yes.'

'Treat me as *you* would wish to be treated, Mother.'

'As a woman?'

As a human being, thought Evelyn. Instead she just nodded.

'We are glad you are now well. We did not expect the treatment to be so long,' said Sir Robert.

'Doctor Birch's visits must have been very costly for you, Father.'

'The cost does not matter. We were worried for you. You were like an animal. It was very upsetting for your mother.'

'And for your father,' interjected her mother.

'And for me,' added Evelyn. 'I was upset too.'

They sat in silence, her parents united in their belief that what they had done had been the right thing to do. Evelyn realised she would never convince them otherwise or make them understand the betrayal she felt. She needed fresh air. She needed to see Drake.

'I understand your concern that I may relapse again.' Her parents looked up at her, surprised. 'I would if I was in your shoes,' she continued. 'To see your only child writhing like … an animal … must have been truly upsetting for you both.' She hoped they did not hear the bitterness she felt. 'Doctor Birch has been most … helpful,' said Evelyn, 'and now it's my turn to do all I can to aid my recovery.' She looked at her mother. 'I must do all I can to remain healthy.'

'It is all I have ever wanted,' replied her mother. 'Doctor Birch can advise us.'

'I have spoken to Doctor Birch. He feels there is a strong link to exercise and health. I thought I should undertake a daily walk in the gardens. Doctor Birch suggested an hour.'

'That sounds like a splendid idea. I shall walk with you.'

'No, Father. I should like to walk alone. I think it would help me to reflect on the past and look forward to the future.'

Her father, who was not a great walker, accepted her suggestion. 'Well, if you insist. I think a long walk will be most beneficial.'

Her mother was less enthusiastic. 'I'm not so sure. You may catch a chill.'

For once, her father came to her rescue. 'I think the benefits of taking a turn in the grounds will be far greater than recuperating indoors, my dear.'

Evelyn pressed her advantage. 'The gardens are beautiful. They will help me return to full health and fall in love with life again … and all it can offer.'

Her father smiled broadly. Evelyn knew what he was thinking. His daughter was clearly recovered as she appreciated the beauty of his gardens as much as he did. Now he could put the whole sorry episode behind him and never talk of it again. Evelyn turned to her mother, who still appeared unsure.

'I promise I will wrap up warmly,' reassured Evelyn. 'I have taken my health for granted in the past. I will not do it again.'

'Well, if Doctor Birch thinks it is helpful.' Her mother's smile matched her husband's. 'It has been a difficult time for all of us. A daily walk will show the servants you are in good health and we can start spreading the news you have recovered from your bout of pneumonia.'

'Pneumonia?' asked Evelyn.

'Only those who attended you knew of your … episode. We explained your absence to family and friends as lingering pneumonia. It was too shameful to tell them the truth.'

'Yes,' said Evelyn, thoughtfully. 'It was a shameful episode. Very shameful indeed.'

Evelyn felt nervous as she stepped out of Carrack House for the first time. She had been indoors for so long that, at first, the bombardment on her senses threatened to overwhelm her. Vibrant shades of green foliage and blue sky strained her eyes, the aroma of freshly cut grass brazenly invaded her nostrils and the gentle heat of the sun touched her skin but was too weak to warm the spring chill in the breeze. She shivered, closed her eyes and took a deep breath, holding it for a moment to make sense of it all. She could hear cheerful birdsong in the distance and a bumblebee desperately searching for a suitable nesting spot. Their sounds, as they went about their daily tasks, cheered her and her initial nervousness began to melt away. She opened her eyes again. The colours of the outside world that had, only moments before, assaulted her eyes, grew less harsh and more beautiful. She savoured the view and allowed herself to feel thrilled by it. It feels good to be outside, thought Evelyn. It feels good to be alive.

Evelyn followed the path looking for Drake. Her eyes searched for his familiar figure stretching tall in the orangery, digging or weeding in the Italian and French gardens, or tying the climbing roses to their supports in the rose garden. Each step became faster, fuelled by her eagerness to see him again. And then, quite suddenly, he was there, standing at the entrance of the maze trimming the hedge with a large pair of shears in his hands. When he saw her, the task was forgotten. They both froze, neither noticing the shears fall from his hand and thud on the grass at their feet. A bird flew low nearby and brought them to their senses. Without speaking, he entered the maze and turned to wait for her.

Evelyn's breath caught in her throat as she looked at him. He was sixteen now. The winter had been good to him as his body had grown and matured in the most delightful way. He was as handsome as she had pictured in her dreams, but there was more to notice that only being with him could provide. A powerful attraction that both frightened and tempted her, an earthy ruggedness, a quiet confidence, a steely determination in his eyes to be alone with her – all this and more robbed her of any words she might say. No servant should dare hold such thoughts or look at her in such a way, yet it thrilled and excited her. To love him was shameful, a dangerous game she must not play, yet she knew, instinctively, she was powerless to resist the attraction she felt for him.

He tilted his head for her to follow him into the maze she had always feared. She looked back at Carrack House, imposing, solid and steeped in history and tradition. She looked at Drake, her confidante, her rock, her love. He was offering her the freedom to be herself. He held out his hand to her. Needing no further encouragement; she lifted the hem of her dress, stepped over the shears and followed him inside.

He seized her hand and led her along convoluted paths hedged with tightly trimmed thicket. Finally they came to a dead end where the world was shut out and no one could see them. He turned abruptly, took her in his arms and buried his face into the nape of her neck.

'I'm sorry, Evie. I am so sorry,' he whispered hoarsely, his warm breath caressing her delicate skin. 'It's all my fault.'

His heartfelt apology surprised her. She pressed his chest away and looked up into his anguished face. He really believed he was responsible.

'Why do you say that?' she asked.

'I went to see Burrows and forced him to leave his post. I thought it would stop him. I didn't know he was going to blame you. I am so sorry.'

'But you *did* stop him, Drake.'

He shook his head. 'No, I made things worse. Tilly told me what they did to you.'

'It was not your fault,' she soothed. 'I, and I alone, am responsible for my behaviour. It was my parents who called Doctor Birch and it was Doctor Birch who prescribed the Rest Cure.' Evelyn framed his face with her hands so he could not turn away from her. 'Your visits helped me through it, Drake. You were the only one to believe in me. You helped me.'

He slid her hands from his face and held them tightly in his. He looked down at them. 'I have thought about you so much.'

'And I you.'

He looked back at her and she was pleased to see the frown on his brow had lessened. He even managed a smile.

'You look well.'

She did not believe him. 'I look pale and feel bloated.'

'Not to me you don't.'

His compliment made her glow inwardly. Already, she felt better for seeing him again. 'I have convinced my parents that walking would be good for my health.'

'In the gardens?'

Evie nodded. 'Every day.' She saw Drake's eyes light up. He appeared to like the idea too.

'I will watch out for you,' he promised.

'I would like that.' Dare she ask him? His dark eyes melted her inside. Yes she dare. 'Where shall we meet?'

How bold she had become. An unspoken understanding passed between them as she waited for an answer. They both knew their meeting was laden with danger. He would be placing his apprenticeship at great risk if they were caught. Had she asked too much of him? It seemed she had not.

He pulled her into his arms and rested his chin on the top of her head. 'I will leave a message to tell you where I will be,' he promised, 'and if I will be working alone.'

Their stolen moments together were precious indeed, to be enjoyed and later relived in the dark hour before sleep. Every accidental touch, every conversation shared, were remembered with a smile and a desire for more.

Drake left word where she could find him by way of a note hidden under a stone at the entrance to the maze. Sometimes their meetings were no more than a brushing of hands as they passed one another, both wary of the other outdoor staff working all around them. Yet, even those short brief moments ignited a strange, sparking energy between them, which fed something deep inside her.

Other times were truly stolen, clandestine meetings at an agreed place: the White Tower, the folly in a hidden, neglected corner of the grounds where they were shielded from view by hedges and trees; the grotto, a gardener's hut; and so many more. Yet, the best times were the months Drake was sent to the country parkland. There, they could spend a full hour together, shielded by great oaks and ash, weeping willows and hedgerows. In the parkland they were quite alone, but for the sheep that kept the grass low by their constant grazing. In this idyllic world, *their* world, she was able to watch him openly as he worked, stripped to the waist, sweat shining in the sun, sawing and inspecting the ancient fallen trees. Other times they sat together in silence on shaded wooden stumps, while he rested or Evelyn shared something she had brought from the kitchen. Sometimes they talked, other times they remained silent, just content to be in each other's company. Occasionally they would tease each other, but neither took offence. It was their way, comfortable, safe, as friends should be together.

One day, he had finally reached for her hand and pulled her to him. They had looked at one another, their laughter fading suddenly until they both felt quite sober. She had felt a change in their relationship looming, but his reaching for her told her he felt it too. It was powerful, all-consuming and drew them together for their first much longed-for kiss.

Although tentative at first, their kiss quickly developed to hold a maturity and depth of desire beyond their teenage years. It was illicit and scandalous, and all the more thrilling because of it. Yet, their kiss, and those that followed, left them with only memories and a yearning to meet again.

As season followed season, budding, ripening and maturing in the only way nature can, so did their love for one another.

At times, Evelyn saw a struggle in Drake she did not fully understand. He tried to explain by telling her that he felt a hunger for her that sometimes threatened to overtake him. She told him she felt it too. He had only shook his head.

'You are still young and need protecting,' he had told her. 'You will understand one day.'

'I am sixteen now, only a year younger than you. I don't need protecting,' she had argued.

'You are young in your experience of life,' Drake had said, sounding very wise. Suddenly, he had smiled and she had smiled too. It was enough to break the tension, which had been building since the end of their last kiss. He lay back on the grass and looked up at her with eyes that tugged at her heart. 'I love you, Evelyn Pendragon,' he had said, without thinking. His smile faded and he frowned. 'I know I shouldn't,' he said more seriously, 'but I can't stop – or will ever want to.'

Yes, the glorious months when he was allocated to the country parkland were the best, but at the end of each day, Evelyn had to leave Drake and pretend she did not know him well. She joined her parents for their evening meal and pretended to enjoy their company as she ate braised veal with a silver knife and fork engraved with their family name. However, locked in her head were her secret memories and she could not help but find herself lost in them, while her mother sipped her wine and her father chewed his meat. Instead she was with Drake again, listening to his whispered words and remembering his kisses on her lips.

'Evelyn looks well,' observed Howard as he watched his son, Mawgan, take a turn of the gardens with her. 'How long has it been since her ... illness?'

'Pneumonia. She had pneumonia.'

'Ah yes ... pneumonia.'

'It's been over a year since her recovery.'

'She has grown into a beautiful woman.'

Sir Robert glanced at his brother, expecting to see a hint of malice. There was none. He returned his gaze to his daughter, content. Why would there be? The last twelve months had seen his daughter bloom in the most extraordinary way. He watched the young couple taking a turn in the grounds, their leisurely steps matching, their gazes in opposite directions as they admired the opposing views.

Eventually, Sir Robert said, 'I'm sorry to hear about Edith.'

'We feared the worst.' A crease shadowed his brow. 'Weight loss is never a good sign. We have been told that she does not have long.'

Sir Robert felt a lump fill his throat. When he had heard of his sister-in-law's illness he had felt some sympathy towards his brother and offered an invitation for him to visit. However, he had not expected the news to be so bad. He cleared his throat.

'How long?'

'Months. And I do not expect to survive her by very many years.'

'Now you are being maudlin.'

'It is the truth. Neither of us is getting any younger. They ...' Howard jerked his head to their offspring '... are the future.'

Sir Robert watched his daughter and nephew stop to admire a bed of flowers. He suddenly felt very old.

'Robert,' said Howard, interrupting his thoughts, 'we have spent our best years bickering. I have had an idea that will soothe the troubled waters between us.' He sighed, as if he felt exhausted from their fighting too. 'Being the younger brother, and having to bear the younger son's lot, has always stuck in my throat. I have made no secret of this.'

Sir Robert sombrely nodded in agreement, wary of what was to come. His brother did not usually show his vulnerable side.

'And you also have a heavy burden to bear,' said Howard, giving him a sympathetic smile. Sir Robert stiffened. He had been right to remain wary. 'When Evelyn marries,' continued Howard, 'she will take her husband's name and the Pendragon line will be severed, if not in blood, certainly in the documentation relating to the history of Carrack Estate.' Howard turned to Sir Robert. A curt nod of his head was his only answer, but it was the only encouragement he needed to continue. 'If Evelyn remains a spinster—'

'She is only sixteen.'

'—there will be no offspring to take over the estate. An inheritance this size is a heavy burden. She is a woman prone to illness. She will always be at risk of a relapse.'

What could he say? His brother had voiced the concerns that kept him awake at night. His attempt to prepare her had dismally failed, as he feared they might.

'What do you propose?'

'Mawgan and Evelyn should marry. It will solve all our problems. He has the Pendragon name to hand down and she has your blood. Our bloodline will continue through our children.'

Sir Robert considered his brother's proposal. Mawgan and Evelyn did make a handsome couple.

'Does Mawgan know? Has he declared an interest?'

'No. He does not appear to enjoy the usual gentlemanly pursuits a young man enjoys.'

'As you enjoyed.'

'As I enjoyed in my youth. He prefers his own company and is more studious than I ever was. He takes after his mother. However, I think he will be amenable to the suggestion. What of Evelyn?'

'Evelyn is still too young.'

'Old enough.'

'The last few years have been turbulent, what with Nicholas's illness and … passing.'

'And Evelyn's illness.'

'Quite. This past year has been calmer. I like the fact that our day-to-day life is now more orderly. Evelyn now accompanies me on my trips to our tenants. She converses with them with an ease I can only admire. They respect her for who she is, not the position she holds in their lives.'

'You think she is capable of running the estate when you have gone? Even if that means losing the Pendragon name to another family?'

'No.' Sir Robert sighed. He had foolishly hoped that once, but not any more. 'No, I do not. At least, not alone. With a reliable and wise husband by her side taking the lead, I think Carrack House and Estate will be in safe hands. However, given her age and innocence, I think she is too young to consider the proposal of marriage with a logical eye at the moment.'

'So my suggestion is worth considering?'

Sir Robert watched Evelyn and Mawgan turn and walk slowly away from them, his daughter's fair hair hidden behind a lace parasol. Mawgan, twenty years old and a few inches taller, walking steadily by her side. The number of occasions they had met could be counted on one hand. They barely knew one another.

Howard refilled their glasses and re-joined him by the window. 'Tell me my proposal is not off the table.'

Sir Robert thrust out his chin. The cousins were finally out of sight and it became easier to consider his brother's suggestion seriously. Howard was right; their marriage would be a solution to all their problems, yet he was still reluctant to give his full acceptance.

'I'm not sure, Howard. She is so innocent.'

Howard drank from his glass and cleared his throat. 'I was thinking of sending Mawgan on a tour of the Empire after he has finished his studies at Oxford. A year or two spent travelling will provide the experience a gentleman of good standing requires.' He looked pointedly at his brother. 'Experience will mould him into a loyal husband, one who appreciates his roots and his home.' Sir Robert met his gaze. 'Give him the wisdom a husband requires … that Evelyn requires. But perhaps when he returns?'

Sir Robert returned his gaze to the gardens laid out below and drank deeply from his brandy glass.

'Robert, is it off the table?' pressed Howard.

Sir Robert suddenly felt tired, feeling every ache in his bones anew. 'No,' he replied. He met his brother's gaze. 'It is not off the table.'

Chapter Fifteen

Samuel Timmins, his hands thrust into deep pockets and his shoulders hunched against the evening chill, had lost track of time a while back. He had found the house easily, its situation, warped stony walls and little windows that allowed little light inside. He had often visited Perran Village when he was a young man and knew its tangled lanes and quaint little houses well. Nothing had changed, yet everything had.

He was aware of the fragility of life. He saw it every day, a thriving plant dead within hours of a morning frost, or a bountiful crop diseased and rotting at the turn of the weather. Yet, it always surprised him how a man's world could change on a spoken word, an object found, a discovery of the truth or in the belief of someone's lies. This morning he had been ignorant of the facts or he had put them to the back of his mind and ignored them. A man is good at ignoring what he does not want to face. He was the best. He had perfected the skill for a long time now. Not any more.

It was Abel who had inadvertently forced his hand this morning. He had reported to him that he had seen Drake speaking to Miss Evelyn in a too familiar tone. On further questioning, he admitted that Miss Evelyn had not been insulted by his lack of respect, but Abel felt it was his duty to report Drake for overstepping the mark. He had expected the head gardener to dismiss Drake, but it was his accusations Timmins chose to ignore, much to the lad's irritation. However, unknown to Abel, his words had played on his mind long after the boy had left his office. The truth was Abel had only voiced his own growing suspicions.

On several occasions he had come upon Drake hard at work, appearing oblivious to Miss Evelyn walking away in the distance. He had not caught them talking, as Abel had done, or even close enough to hold a conversation, but something unnerved him and made the hairs at the back of his neck prickle. If they had been found alone, her reputation would be compromised and Drake's apprenticeship would be terminated. He had grown fond of Drake and did not want his training to end. So he had spent the latter part of the morning compiling a list of suitable establishments and a reference to his good character. Drake could undertake his final year of basic training elsewhere and then he would be ready to be a journeyman, the next step in his apprenticeship that would take him from mere gardener to the path of head gardener and, eventually, landscape architect, the profession he hoped to achieve.

He had summoned the boy to his office and told him the good news, fully expecting Drake to be grateful and enthusiastic about the next phase of his apprenticeship. He was wrong. The boy, nay the man, looked him in the eye and refused to go. For a moment Timmins was lost for words. This was what Drake had wanted. This was what he deserved. The familiar feeling of unease resurfaced. If Drake thought he had a choice in the matter, he would be sorely disappointed.

Drake had left then, his fists clenched and a stubborn frown marking his brow. Timmins had watched him through the window of his office, half angry, half inwardly admiring the boy's growing confidence and ability to argue his point. Drake had a stubborn streak that he recognised and he found himself smiling at the thought. It was in that moment his world changed forever, brought about by enlightenment he had not been searching for.

The legs that had held him up for most of his fifty-four years suddenly felt as weak as a new-born babe's. He reached blindly for the chair and sat heavily upon it, pale and stricken. There, he remained for the rest of the day, uncharacteristically idle as he was unable to concentrate on the ledgers in front of him. His absence outside went unnoticed by his staff as plants continued to be tended, crops harvested and produce prepared. The gardens' routine remained unchanged, but inside the head gardener's office, everything had.

Timmins banged on the door with his weathered knuckles and waited. He heard the light footsteps of a woman approach the door. The door opened only wide enough for a woman's face to look out. Her eyes immediately lifted to meet his.

'Samuel,' whispered the woman, wide-eyed at his sudden appearance.

'Your boy, Drake,' he muttered, feeling suddenly breathless again. 'I know he's mine.'

Drake turned the page in the hope it would ignite his interest, but it was not long before his mind had begun to wander again. Instead of trying to memorise a list of Latin plant names, he was thinking of Evie. It had been a frustrating month. He had been allocated to work with Mr Timmins. An excellent learning opportunity, but it meant that he was unable to meet Evie in secret as she took her daily walk. Today, feeling the separation as keenly as he did, she had dared to visit him as he worked in the glasshouses. She sought him out under the pretext of sampling some strawberries, but he was not alone. Timmins stood between them like a cuckoo in their nest. Their conversation was formal, but beneath each word they spoke was a silent heartfelt message.

'You look busy,' she said.

When can we meet again? I miss you.

'Yes, Miss Evelyn. There is much to keep the gardeners busy.'

I want to see you, but Timmins has me working here and I cannot get away. I miss you too.

She addressed Timmins. 'I hope you are not working your staff too hard, Mr Timmins, or they will leave us,' she cautioned him with a smile.

You are spoiling things for us. Allow Drake time off so we can meet.

'Vennor needs my guidance, Miss Evelyn,' Timmins replied solemnly, 'or he will not achieve all that he is capable of achieving.'

Stay away Miss Evelyn or you will ruin his future with your games.

Evie and Drake stiffened, as if they were rabbits caught in a lamping light. Did Timmins know? His reply hung between them like a warning, until Drake defiantly picked up a basket of strawberries and offered her one – right under his nose.

Drake closed the book with a thud. It held no interest for him tonight. He was reliving the moment Evie had reached to sample a strawberry and their fingers had touched. It had taken all his strength not to take her hand and pull her towards him right in front of Timmins. In front of the whole damn lot of them. He hadn't and now he ached with frustration at not doing so. He raked a hand through his hair. He was not sure how much longer he could continue like this.

The bothy boys entered, making Drake sit up again and feign interest in the pages in front of him. Abel Hicks knocked his chair as he passed, but the rest of the bothy boys ignored him, as they usually did. One by one they climbed the ladder to the loft above, leaving Drake alone to listen to their voices above.

'I'm telling you the truth,' said Mark. 'Saw it with my own eyes.'

'What were you doing there?' asked Luke.

'Fetching the shears old Murphy repaired.'

'That was last week.'

'Aye. According to Murphy he's been visiting every Thursday for the past month.'

Drake closed the book and made for bed, only half listening to the gossip above his head. He stepped onto the first rung of the ladder, but climbed no further.

'Old Timmins is like the rest of us after all,' scoffed Abel.

Abel started to laugh, followed, no doubt, by a lurid re-enactment. Another burst of laughter rang out above his head, which was joined by the other bothy boys.

Drake smiled too. Old Timmins was not so old after all.

'Who's the unlucky woman?' asked Matthew. Drake tilted his head, listening intently. It was the question he would have liked to have asked.

'This is the best part,' replied Mark. 'She is the local lay preacher's widow. She spends her life opening her heart to God, but on Thursday night she opens her legs to Timmins.'

As more laughter rang out above his head, Drake remained at the bottom of the ladder, unnoticed and in shock. They were talking about his mother. *His* mother. He should confront them and force them to take back their lies, yet he could not move, fearful that their gossip was grounded in truth. He clutched the rung of the ladder even tighter and stared at his blanched knuckles and bulging veins that threaded beneath his skin. The pain from the effort told him this was real, but he did not want it to be so. He rested his head on his fists and closed his eyes to shut out the world. It was a lie. It had to be. More laughter broke out above.

'Hey, Vennor, wasn't your old man a preacher?' Abel's voice became clearer as he approached the hatch. 'Is Timmins sticking your mother?' Drake did not move. He could not move. 'How desperate must old Timmins be?' Abel asked his friends as he gloated over Drake's bowed head. The mocking laughter that followed ignited Drake's anger. He suddenly lunged upwards, with the aim of dragging Abel through the small hatch. He wanted to break every bone in his body. He wanted to silence him forever. Abel darted away from his desperate reach and joined the others, their raucous laughter quickly bursting out again above his head. Drake could take no more. As bile rose in his throat, he ran outside for some air.

Drake stood opposite his old home, watching. The hour was late and there was a night chill to the air. Only a stray dog searching for food and the soft glow from a candle in the upper window indicated any signs of life.

So Mother was still awake, that meant nothing, thought Drake. Even so, a sense of unease continued to linger in every fibre of his body.

He silently crossed the road and opened the door, careful to muffle the sound of the latch. He carefully climbed the steep, narrow stairs. He knew every creaking floorboard, every uneven plank and was able to avoid them with ease. A chink of light spilled onto the floor at her door. He heard her soft murmur and her turning in bed. Still hopeful that the gossip had been wrong, he swallowed and eased open the door.

Tangled sheets, naked limbs, two lust filled bodies exploring, invading, oblivious to everything but their own carnal needs. Drake blinked, his gaze settling on his mother's enraptured face. Bile rose in his throat at their betrayal. He thought he had earned the right to be an apprentice. He thought Timmins had seen something in him. He believed Timmins when he thought he had the gift. In reality, Timmins was open to bribery and his mother was willing to pay by lying on her back. He had lied. They both had.

Drake closed the door and stumbled down the stairs. He stepped outside just in time to retch into a bush. Afterwards he stood as if he was an old man, bent over, his hands resting on his thighs trying his best to recover, but his body continued to let him down. It began to tremble as feelings of hurt were replaced by anger. It seeped into every vein, filling him up and urging him to return and tear them apart. He wanted to, Lord knows he wanted to, but he couldn't. Despite his anger towards his mother, he would not embarrass her by challenging her while she was naked. He straightened and breathed in deeply, trying to calm the volcano raging inside him. He turned towards Carrack Estate and began to run. He ran and ran and ran, until he felt his heart might explode with the pain of it all and then he ran some more.

Drake stood in the potting shed, looking at the rows of small, terracotta pots that were lined up like soldiers along the wooden bench. Fragile shoots, in a variety of stages, sprouted from each one. They were emblems of his close relationship with the head gardener as it was only their labour, their sharing of ideas, their experimentation in propagation and cultivation that had brought life to these rare specimens. He saw Timmins approaching. Not now, Drake thought, I cannot face him now. It was too late, Timmins had blocked his escape, oblivious to Drake's simmering anger.

'Why are you here?' asked Timmins, casting a glance over the pots. 'There's work to be done on the east side.' He left, expecting the boy to follow, but when he didn't Timmins was forced to turn back. 'Come on, Vennor,' he ordered, with a jerk of his head. 'I'll not ask you again.'

'Then don't. Go dig your own pits.'

Timmins stepped inside. Heat blasted down on them through the glass panes.

'Watch your tongue, boy,' warned the head gardener.

'Or what? You will stop bedding my mother?'

Drake still hoped that he had misinterpreted what he had seen, but Timmins expression quickly destroyed that. It was written plainly on his face. He had not been mistaken.

'When did you find out?'

'Last night.'

'You came to the house?'

Drake nodded.

'You came to the room?'

He nodded again. 'What sort of man are you?' spat Drake.

'What do you mean?'

'Taking advantage of my mother like that.'

'Don't talk to me like that, boy.'

'Well, I won't let you any more.'

'You have no say in what I do in my free time.'

'I have every say. I'll find work somewhere else.'

Timmins grew angry. 'You foolish boy. Have you no respect for your mother?'

'I have more respect than you do. How long has it been going on? Sneaking off ... lifting her skirts at any opportunity. The thought of it ... Seeing you both ... It makes me sick to think of it.'

Timmins stepped closer and pointed his finger at Drake. 'I care for your mother.'

'You hardly know her! You are here most of the time!'

'I knew her before you were born.'

Drake hesitated. He had not expected that. 'You lie. My mother would have told me.'

'It's the truth.'

'Is that why you took me on? Not because you thought I would make a good head gardener one day, but because you wanted to get into bed with my mother?' Timmins' struggle to reply was clear upon his face. 'You bastard!'

'Now steady, lad.'

'Don't call me that!'

'I've loved your mother for years.'

'I don't believe you.'

'It's true.'

'Then why didn't you marry her? Why? Look at you! Floundering for excuses to cover your lies!' shouted Drake as his anger exploded.

'I don't need to explain myself to you.'

Drake lunged towards him and grabbed his collar. 'I saw you with my mother!' shouted Drake as he locked eyes with him. Their faces were so close he could feel the man's breath on his skin. He had respected him. Now he despised him. 'You are no more than a dog on heat!'

'I didn't marry her because she was already married,' replied Timmins, calmly. Drake hesitated; his fists grew weak and slowly unfurled. Surely he had misheard him. 'Her husband was always away preaching. We met at bible class. I thought she was the prettiest thing I'd ever set eyes on. She was lonely. I was lonely.'

Drake stepped away, shaking his head. His mother had an affair? *His* mother?

'Suddenly she didn't want to see me any more. I didn't want it to end, but she did and I had to walk away. Later, I found out they were going to have a child and consoled myself that she probably grew frightened that if we were discovered, folk would forever question if the baby was her husband's. She did not want to humiliate him. She always said he was a good man and he did not deserve her betrayal. It was only the other day that I discovered that the baby was mine.'

'What baby?' Drake stepped back, dazed from the revelation. 'What happened to the baby?' Timmins did not answer. 'Tell me.' Why did his voice sound like a bewildered child? 'Tell me what happened to the baby!'

'I'm looking at him,' replied Timmins.

Too many lies had been exposed. Too many questions that needed to be asked. It was too much to take in. His world had changed and he did not know how to change it back. An angry yell escaped him as he lunged at his father and punched him hard on the jaw. Timmins' head jerked to the side and for a moment time stood still. Drake wanted him to retaliate;

he wanted the fight to continue so he could discharge his anger, but Timmins did not. Instead he straightened and looked him in the eyes.

'I loved your mother.'

'You know nothing of love!'

'I know more than you. I loved her enough to walk away. Can you say that?'

'What do you mean?'

'I've seen you both. You can never have a future together.'

'What are you talking about?'

'You and Miss Evelyn. I know you think you have feelings for her—'

'Shut up!'

'—and she might enjoy your company—'

'You don't know what you're talking about!' Drake turned away, but Timmins grabbed his arm and made him face him again.

'—but you can never be together. She is not of our class. She is used to a way of life that you can never provide. She is playing with you, like a curiosity, but she would never lower herself to marry someone like you.'

Drake shook his arm off. 'Don't …'

'She is young and beautiful and you are a handsome lad. I can see why you are both attracted to one another, but it is a flirtation and a dangerous one.' Timmins placed his hand on his shoulder. 'Listen to me. If your secret liaisons are discovered, her reputation will be destroyed. What gentleman would want to marry a woman who has been cavorting with a labourer? I loved your mother enough to walk away and save her marriage. If you care anything for Miss Evelyn, end it, before you ruin her.'

Drake shrugged him off. 'We are not playing a game! We love each other!' he shouted. The words were out and he could not take them back, but his feelings for Evie were more serious than mere cavorting and Timmins needed to know that.

'Love is not enough. There will be other girls. What about Tilly from the house? I have seen you both walking to Perran. She has a soft spot for you. She is always making eyes at you.'

Timmins didn't understand. He never would. 'I'm not interested in Tilly.'

'You are a fine looking young man. You can have your pick.'

Drake had had enough. 'This isn't about Tilly and Evie! This is about *you* bedding my mother!'

'What do you think Sir Robert would say if he knew you called her Evie?' Timmins pointed his finger at Drake. 'What you want should not be more important than Miss Evelyn's future. She will be disowned by her family. She will lose her inheritance. She will be shunned by society,' he warned him. 'She is young, her head is full of fairy tales, but life isn't a fairy tale, Drake. You have learnt that today.'

Drake turned his back on him. 'Go away. Leave me be.'

Timmins dabbed his lip with the back of his hand and looked at the blood on his skin. He nodded. 'Think about what I said. I know what I'm talking about.'

Drake watched him leave. The situation was impossible. How could he face his mother again or work with the man who had come between his parents' marriage? Only they both weren't his parents, were they? Only his mother – who had lied to him his whole life.

Drake turned and looked at the rows of neatly lined pots and fledgling plants, picked up a stick and began to scythe the bench top. The pots were dragged off the wooden surface and smashed onto the floor, their contents spilling out like entrails from a slain animal. Another row and another, until nothing remained but a floor of broken terracotta, soil and wilting, fragile stems.

'Drake?' Evelyn stood at the entrance, concern etched on her face. 'What's wrong?' She knelt down and began to collect the terracotta fragments. 'You will lose your job if Timmins or Father finds out you have done this.' He watched her trembling fingers as she grew frantic. 'Quickly, Drake, we must tidy this up before someone comes.'

'Leave it,' he demanded, breathless from the destruction he'd caused. He dropped the stick on the ground in front of her, but Evie ignored him.

'Why would you do this? Why?' she asked.

The soil dirtied her fingers and dress as she scrabbled desperately to clean up his mess. He had brought her to this.

He took her arm. 'Leave it, Evie. I don't care who sees it.'

She looked up, upset. 'Why wouldn't you care?'

Evelyn slowly stood with several shards from a pot still in her hands. She deserved an explanation.

'I hate him.'

'Who?'

'Timmins.'

'Why?'

'Because …' how could he explain it? '… I saw him with my mother.'

'What is wrong with that?'

'Doing things with my mother … to my mother.'

'What things?'

'*Things* … in bed.'

'What things?'

Drake looked at her. She is so innocent and does not understand what I am talking about. She only knows about kisses and embraces.

'Drake?'

Timmins was right. They were playing with fire and she did not realise how badly she would get burnt.

'What things?' Evelyn touched his arm. He eased it away and took a step back. *Don't ask, Evie. Don't ask.* He turned away from her. 'Drake, tell me.' He felt her touch his arm again. 'What things?'

Drake turned on her. 'He was doing things to my mother that I want to do to *you*!'

He knew she didn't really understand – not the details, but he saw something pass in her eyes, the shudder of her breath that showed what he had said had shaken her, thrilled her, frightened her – and he suddenly felt terrified that she would one day understand and want it too. He had to put a stop to it, before he destroyed her.

'I'm leaving.'

'No! You can't!'

'I can and I will. I can't work with him any more.'

'But what about us?'

Drake turned away, he could not stand to see the pain he was inflicting on her. He picked up his jacket and put it on. Keep busy Drake. Don't look at her.

'There is no "us", Evie. There can never be an "us".'

Her voice became a little frantic, her words a little rushed. 'You are upset about Timmins. Your feelings are still raw. Time will settle—'

'Time will settle nothing.'

'But I love you. You said you loved me.'

Drake swallowed. 'I lied.'

He attempted to leave. The heat from the glasshouse made him feel claustrophobic. Evelyn stepped into his path, blocking his way.

'You didn't lie. I know you didn't.'

'We are too different. You think life is a fairy tale, but it isn't.'

'I love you.'

'No, you don't. You think you do because I was there when you had no one to turn to. There is no future for us and if your parents find out we have been meeting I will never be able to find work again. If you love me, you will let me walk away.'

'I don't believe you. You are only saying that to make me want to end it, but I don't want to. I don't.'

'But I do, Evie. I do.'

Drake looked over her shoulder. Evelyn followed his gaze and saw the head gardener approaching. He came to the door and solemnly surveyed the destruction at their feet.

'He wants to leave, Mr Timmins,' said Evelyn. 'Tell him he can't. He has a duty to remain and replant what he has destroyed.'

Timmins removed an envelope from his pocket and placed it in Drake's hand.

'What's that?' asked Evelyn. Drake knew without opening it.

'It's a list of places he can apply for work to finish his apprenticeship and a letter of recommendation from me.' The two men, mirror images but for time's unkind hand, looked at one another. 'I'm sorry, Miss Evelyn, but I'll not ask him to stay. It is time he moved on.'

It didn't take long for Drake to pack. He had few belongings and the speed of a man who wanted to be gone. The bothy boys will not miss me, he thought as he rammed another book into his bag and searched for another. He imagined Abel Hicks finding him gone. No doubt Hicks would be very happy to be rid of him. He could imagine him laughing now. He hated his laughter. It sounded like he was trying to clear his throat. Drake found the book he had been searching for and put it in his bag. None of them made him feel welcome or understood his desire to study. He threw his blankets over in the direction of their beds and imagined them fighting over them after he was gone. Well he had news for them. He would not miss them either.

He climbed down the ladder and walked through the old building, which had been his home for over three years. He left the dark room behind him and walked out into the sunshine. He would miss the gardens of Carrack House, which had served as a living encyclopaedia for his apprenticeship. He had enjoyed every minute of his time in them, from the heavy labour of transporting wet seaweed, to carrying sacks of pine needles during the winter frosts that were so cold they bit at your fingers and gnawed at your toes.

And, of course, he would miss Evie the most. The anticipation he felt that he might see her again. The thrill when he saw her walking his way and the anxiety of being discovered. Seeing her face, touching her hand, holding her body that had changed over the years in the most enticing way. The sound of her voice, the feel of her breath on his lips, the taste of her kiss … He would miss them all. God, he would even miss seeing those silly feminine accessories she carried or wore: her fan, the combs in her hair, her white lace parasol. Objects he had never seen up close before or would ever hold his interest, but in Evie's possession they held a curious fascination as they were all connected to her. He would even miss seeing her walk away from him and watching the delightful swing of all that material at the back of her dress – what did she call it? A bustle?

He wiped his eyes roughly with the sleeve of his shirt. He must leave her a note to soften his harsh goodbye. He had been cruel and she did not deserve that. Saying goodbye was bad enough, he did not have to deny that he loved her. He went back inside and sat down at the bench table, took out his inkpot and pen and wrote her name. He found it difficult to start. How do you explain your leaving while trying to keep your mother's secrets? He tried, but ultimately it was still a goodbye letter. What do I want her to know? Drake asked himself as he looked at it. The answer was easy. He dipped his pen and began to write again. This time the words flowed more easily as they came from his heart. Satisfied, he folded it up carefully and headed for the kitchens in search of Tilly. Tilly was their friend. He would ask her to pass it on to Evie.

'Are you leaving?' Drake looked up and into Abel's cold eyes. He tried to pass him, but Abel stepped in his way. 'Well?' he asked.

'Yes.'

'Studying's not got you anywhere then.'

Drake was in no mood to argue. Abel's opinion meant nothing to him. He tried to go round him but Abel blocked his path with a single step to the side.

'Get out of my way, Hicks,' Drake ground out, without looking up.

Abel tilted his head with curiosity. 'How long will you be gone?'

Drake looked up. 'Why do you care?'

Abel's smile held no warmth. 'I don't, but Tilly might need some comforting. And I reckon I'm the man to do it.'

'Get out of my way.' Abel's smile widened, but he still did not move. Drake lost his patience and shouldered his way past him. He headed for the kitchens with Abel's grating laughter still ringing in his ears.

Evelyn looked at herself in the mirror, her head tilting with each of Tilly's slow strokes. Evelyn normally enjoyed the nightly routine of having her hair brushed by Tilly. It was comforting, peaceful and sometimes filled with laughter as a result of hearing Tilly's gossip from the servants' quarters. Sometimes Evelyn would share her own thoughts, confident that Tilly would not repeat them, although a protective instinct prevented her from sharing her meetings and feelings for Drake. Tonight, Tilly was unusually silent, which suited Evelyn as her own thoughts were too fragile to absorb trivial gossip and her heart too shattered to carry another's concerns.

Drake's parting words kept running through her head as she looked at her own face staring back at her. He had been so angry and upset and she had not been wise enough, or grown up enough, to know how to handle him or understand what he was trying to say. Suddenly it was too late to do either and the damage was done. Perhaps if she had handled it differently she would have provided the comfort he needed. She had failed him when he needed her most.

While she had wittered on about tidying up the glasshouse, too fearful she would lose him if he was dismissed, she hadn't realised she had already lost him. He saw her in a different light now, a silly child who repelled him. There were moments when he could not look at her. She understood his need to leave, but the rest of it – that he felt nothing for her – that she meant nothing to him. He might as well have ripped out her heart, thrown it on the floor at their feet and ground his heel into it. How old she looked now, she thought as she studied her miserable reflection in the mirror. I have aged ten years. She looked up and realised Tilly was watching her. Her eyes looked as sad as her own.

She realised Tilly had stopped brushing her hair. 'Thank you,' said Evelyn.

Evelyn watched Tilly in the mirror as she picked up Evelyn's discarded dress and hung it up in the wardrobe. How she longed to share her pain with Tilly, but she had never shared her secret friendship with

Drake with her before and to do so now, when it had come to an end, seemed to flaunt the fact that she did not trust her with the secret before. Evelyn noticed something slip from Tilly's apron pocket and flutter to the ground.

'Tilly.' The maid turned and their gazes met in the mirror. 'You have dropped something. Is it for me?'

Tilly bent down slowly, picked it up and held it in her hands for a moment before slipping it into her pocket. 'No,' she said, turning away. 'It is just a list of chores to do. Nothing of great importance.'

She sounds miserable too, thought Evelyn and, despite her own distress, she found herself asking Tilly if she was unwell.

'I am well, Miss Evelyn,' replied Tilly.

Evelyn recognised the clipped tone and understood. Tilly had a right to her private life. She would not pry further. Evelyn watched her maid turn away and energetically fold back the bed covers. How she wished she had that energy. Drake's departure had sucked all of her vitality and joy from her. Somehow, she must learn to survive without him, because one day she was sure that they would meet again and she wanted to be strong enough to bear it.

Chapter Sixteen

1896, Cornwall, England

Glistening pearls of rain balanced precariously on each petal and leaf, as if part of some game of endurance. A slight breeze and the mere touch from an insect coming in to land, was enough to tilt the status quo and the velvet surface beneath. The decorative droplets, perfect in shape and purity, merged into larger ones, drawn together by an invisible force. They began to roll, gaining speed and chaos, as if fleeing from some danger that could not be seen. Falling, falling, one after another onto the ground beneath, absorbed into the earth, their glistening orbs destroyed by the beat of an insect's wing.

Timmins dragged his eyes away. Sir Robert was expecting him to follow and it would not do to keep his employer waiting. They had spent the morning inspecting the gardens. March, with its late wintery gales, had not been kind to nature's gifts and the great storm in early July had damaged many trees and several panes in the orangery. However, summer had finally arrived, despite the early morning shower, and now the heat of the sun was providing a comforting hug, which relaxed the muscles, eased the joints and lifted the spirits.

They were heading for the north-east patch, an area laid to grass not a five minute walk from Carrack House. It was flat, too flat to be of visual interest, and its location on the other side of the potting sheds, bothy and glasshouses, made it inaccessible to house guests. However, Sir Robert had a mind to do something with it, which was the main purpose of their meeting today.

The two men surveyed the land. It was a daunting project; even for Timmins who knew all there was to know about gardening. They would have to employ more men, which in itself was a difficult task. It was hard to find reliable workers. Only this morning he had dismissed Abel Hicks. He had been a good worker in the past, but in recent times, thanks to his growing fondness for drink, he had become more and more unreliable.

It would also take an artistic flare to design and sculpt the land; yet give the illusion that man had no hand in it. Not for the first time he thought of Drake. He would be twenty-four years old by now. He had completed his basic apprenticeship and, as a journeyman, he had excelled. He had secured work at some of the places the head gardener had recommended, but he'd also made his own connections and his abilities were quickly recognised by others. Soon head gardeners were seeking him out, which was unheard of for someone so young. Timmins acknowledged that Drake was unlike any apprentice he had taught before. He was intelligent and had used his knowledge and connections wisely. He'd spent time at Kew Gardens and on the infamous Warwick Estate and the Duke of Westminster's Estate, where he drew up plans for the new parkland. Not that Drake kept him up-to-date with his commissions. There had been no communication between them since the day he left six years ago.

News of Drake's progress came from his mother, who received regular letters from him in the absence of any visit. In fact, Drake had not returned to Cornwall in all the years he had been away and they both carried the blame for this.

Timmins still visited the widow and probably always would, but marriage was out of the question. Their relationship had changed to one of friendship, as both felt the weight of guilt that their previous passion had swept aside. She would never marry him, she had told him once, not unless Drake was ready to accept him. 'How are father and son ever to reconcile if he will not even speak to me?' he had argued at the time. Perhaps it was not only Drake who did not want them to marry.

'I want to make this area somewhere my wife would enjoy,' said Sir Robert as he surveyed the field. 'You know the sort of thing; grottos, waterfalls, a gazebo or two. I thought it would encourage her to come outside.'

Rumour had it Lady Pendragon spent much of her time in bed again. Without anyone to lavish her health fears upon she had turned them onto herself. The death of her sister-in-law five years ago, and her brother-in-law, Howard Pendragon, last autumn, did not help matters. Doctor Birch regularly attended her and was often seen in his gig, rattling along the drive with his top hat firmly on his head, his cane held like a staff as if ready to part even the highest biblical waters in his path.

Sir Robert coped by doing what he always did, retreating to his gardens, where any chaos was as a result of cultivation and where every border provided a frame and an order. The tempestuous relationship he had with his brother ended with his death and it left a gaping void Timmins suspected Sir Robert felt more deeply than he cared to admit. It had manifested in the commission of two lions, carved in stone, to be placed on either side of the main entrance to the estate. Both were to be equal in size and roaring as if they were protecting the estate with a fierce loyalty, like brothers-in-arms, Sir Robert had instructed the stonemason.

During their inspection, Sir Robert had also confided in Timmins that he was encouraging a relationship between his daughter and his nephew, Mawgan. It explained why Timmins had seen Mawgan call on Miss Evelyn in recent months and suspected Sir Robert felt an obligation to look after his nephew now that both his parents were dead. Whatever the reason for his matchmaking Timmins felt a sense of relief that all was working out well after all. Miss Evelyn had forgotten about Drake, just as he knew she would and Drake was doing well in his chosen profession.

Perhaps it was this new-found relief and confidence that made him speak of Drake, or perhaps it was the pride of a father wanting to boast of his son's achievements. Whatever it was, his intentions were as harmless as a beat of an insect's wing.

'My s— former apprentice would have ideas for the land. His name is Drake Vennor and he is currently advising on the new Lawton Manor gardens in Kent. His skills are in great demand. He has worked with the botanists in Kew. I could send him plans of the area and see what he suggests.'

Sir Robert thought for a moment. 'Lawton Manor, I have heard of it. He must be good if they have commissioned him. I do not remember this boy.'

'He was here for three years but left to complete his training. He must be …' he pretended to work out the age, but in truth he knew it well '… twenty-four.'

'Young.'

'In years, perhaps, but not in knowledge.'

'I will invite him to visit.'

'No,' Timmins replied a little too quickly. Sir Robert threw him a glance. 'He will be too busy to visit. I will write to him and send him the plans of the area. He knows this land well enough. He will be able to make some suggestions.'

Sir Robert agreed and they retraced their steps, leaving the vast grassland behind them. Timmins felt hopeful. The redesign of the land would give him a reason to contact Drake and, God willing, build a bridge between them. He glanced at Sir Robert. They were men of different classes, yet their shared passion for the soil had forged a respectful relationship which now spanned almost thirty years. Perhaps the same could happen between him and his son.

Sir Robert and Timmins walked side by side in companionable silence until they reached the main entrance to Carrack House. Timmins doffed his cap before turning away and walking towards the granite steps. As he took the first step, a dull pain pressed hard against the centre of his chest, like a hard walnut being pushed through to his back. By the second step he felt nauseous and light-headed as the pain intensified. His third step was no more than a stumble as he clutched at his chest and bent double with pain. He missed the fourth step, his body rolling over it as he fell to the ground. He heard Sir Robert calling, but turned his head away. If he was about to die, he wanted to see the gardens he had lovingly tended over the years. A crimson haze of pelargoniums filled his line of sight. He smiled at their beauty and radiance, and then slowly closed his eyes forever.

Drake made his way down Miller Road. It was reassuring to see that Perran Village had not changed during the last six years. The same mismatched houses still lined the road, whilst narrow footpaths meandered behind and between the houses, following the route of an ancient stream that had long since dried up. He came to the end and turned onto Piggy Lane. On the corner was his mother's familiar granite house welcoming him to step inside.

'My, don't you look dandy.'

Drake turned to the man who had spoken. Abel Hicks emerged from the shadow of another doorway, pushing himself forward so he took several steps in quick succession before he came to a swaying halt. He stood for a moment, before lurching forward. He had lost weight since they had last met and was in need of a good scrub and a sobering. Drake waited as Abel attempted to make his way across the road to him, his body swaying with each unpredictable step he took. Drake could smell the alcohol on his breath long before he reached him.

'My, don't you look …' Abel waved a finger over him '… the proper gentleman now.'

Drake thought better of attempting a civil conversation with him. 'We have nothing to say to one another, Hicks,' said Drake, turning away.

Abel stepped forward and lifted his arms dramatically, barring his way. 'No. No, no, no.' He started to laugh, then thought better of it. 'Sshhhh,' he reprimanded himself, holding a grimy finger to his own lips.

Drake waited patiently. Abel indicated to himself and Drake in turn with a wave of his hand. 'Me and you ... both dismissed from Carrack House by Timmins.' He noticed the cloth of Drake's coat, frowned and touched it with his finger. 'That is expensive.'

Drake glanced down at Abel's finger. 'I was not dismissed,' he said quietly. 'I left to finish my apprenticeship.'

Abel wasn't listening. 'The old beggar is dead now.'

'I know,' said Drake, losing his patience. He removed Abel's hand from his coat and brushed past him. He did not want to listen to the ramblings of a drunkard, particularly when it involved insulting Timmins.

'You're no better than me, Vennor!' shouted Abel, stumbling slightly with the effort. 'Think you can wheedle your way into rich houses, with all your *studying.*' He lurched forward two steps, before stopping again. 'Well, I have news for you ... you are neither one thing nor the other.' He tapped his temple. 'I know what you really are. You are a nobody! A *nobody!*' Abel's voice echoed along the street and came back to him. He turned to look around, surprised to find that the street was now empty. A movement caught his eye. It was the door of the house Drake had entered as it closed behind him. Abel remained for a moment, staring at the house on the corner of Piggy Lane. His frown deepened, as he wondered who Drake was visiting. The name of the road sounded familiar. The effort of thinking was too much for him. Shrugging his shoulders, he turned and stumbled away.

'Mother.' Drake's mother looked up, but did not speak. It was as if she was not sure whether to trust what she saw. The dark shadows lining her eyes gave the impression she had lost a little weight. When she eventually smiled and ran into his arms he could feel that she had.

'Drake! Why didn't you tell me you were coming home?'

'I didn't know I was.'

'Never mind, you are here now.' Her words were muffled as she pressed her face against his chest. How small she seems, thought Drake as he towered above her. They stood, holding one another. Too much time had passed, he realised. The longer he had avoided coming home, the harder it had been to return.

'Come, sit down,' said his mother, hurriedly wiping away her tears with her apron. 'Let me get you something to eat.' Drake was not hungry, but he did not refuse. He was just happy to be here and she was content to busy herself trying to find something suitable.

'I baked some bread yesterday and I might have some cheese left.' She turned, her face much brighter than only moments ago. 'Or would you like me to cook you a meal?' Her eagerness to make his stay pleasant was palpable. 'Soup or a stew … Oh! I have a nice bit of mutton I bought yesterday at the market.' She went to a barrel and lifted the lid. 'I waited until the end of the day for the prices to drop. Go too early and you are paying the same for half as much.'

Drake came over and stood beside her. He took the lid from her hands and carefully replaced it, covering the wrapped meat soaking in brine. 'Bread and cheese will suffice. There is no need to take it out if you have gone to the trouble of salting it. Keep it for another time.' He looked at her. 'Come, sit down. How are you?'

He led her to a chair at the table and she did as she was told. He sat down opposite her. She looked frail, but she continued to hold his hand with a vice-like grip, with no intention of letting him go.

'Oh, so and so. You received my letter?' Drake nodded. 'It was sudden. One minute he was fine, the next he was dead. I thought you would want to know.'

She was right, he did want to know that Timmins had died, but it was not the reason he had come back. He wondered if Timmins had ever told her that her son had caught them in bed together. He hoped not. She would feel humiliated and he wanted to spare her that. Even so, there was still a part of him that was still angry at his mother. He had always thought she was loyal, good and trustworthy, not someone who could betray his father and lie to her son.

'You have done so well,' she was saying. 'Your father would have been so proud of you.'

'Which one?' retorted Drake. He saw his mother's face fall and immediately apologised. He shouldn't keep raking over old coals. He had told his mother of his discovery by letter shortly after he had left. He should leave it in the past, but sometimes he still found it hard to do.

'Don't be sorry.' She looked at his hand in hers and smoothed the skin as if it was precious silk. 'You have a right to be angry, but in answer to your question, they both would have been proud of you. They both were.'

He withdrew his hand from hers. This is why he had not returned sooner, he wasn't sure if he could talk face-to-face with her about

Timmins, despite having so many questions to ask. Instead he said, 'I can send you more money. You shouldn't have to wait until the end of the day for the prices to drop. I'm earning good money now.'

'You send me plenty and pay my rent. I have no complaints.'

'But it was no more than a scrag end.'

'Talk to me, Drake,' interrupted his mother. 'It is not my choice of cuts that plays on your mind. I can't guarantee you I will have the right words to explain things, but I am willing to try and not hold back.'

His mother was right. It was the only way to move forward. 'Why?' asked Drake. 'Why did you have an affair?' His mother looked down at her clasped hands resting on the table surface. She carries her bereavement well, thought Drake, although he could still see that Timmins' passing had left a mark on her.

'Your father was often away preaching. Sometimes he would be away for days. I was young, lonely and fell in love. He sensed something had changed between us and one day he asked me directly. I could not lie to him. He was very upset and I realised what I had done. I wish he had been angrier, I deserved it, but he forgave me.'

'And life carried on.'

'Yes, of sorts.'

'What about Timmins?'

'I ended the affair and told him I didn't want to see him again. He accepted it and did not try to make things difficult for me. I now know I hurt him very much too. Things changed and your father only took services within an hour's ride so he could come home by nightfall, but by then you were on your way.'

'Did Father know that I was not his?'

She nodded. 'I told him that you may not be. He said he would accept what God had given us and love you as if you were his own. We never spoke of it again and he was as good as his word.'

Drake nodded. 'He was a good man, which makes it harder for me to understand why you would betray him.'

'Yes ... and kind too. I did love him, but Samuel—'

'Samuel?' Drake sat back. Three years working together and he did not know Timmins' first name. Learning it now suddenly brought the gardener's youthful past to life. He seemed more human, more virile, more like himself. Drake's throat grew dry.

'Mr Timmins. He was so different from anyone I had ever known. When he was younger, he was so handsome.' His mother smiled. 'You look so much like him, Drake. I thought he would see that from the very beginning, but he didn't. Men can be so blind sometimes.'

'Is that why you allowed me to ask him for an apprenticeship? So he would finally learn the truth?'

'I seem to recall the idea of asking him for an apprenticeship was yours and I had little say in the matter. You informed me that you wanted to be "taught by the best in the area and work at Carrack House".'

'But you could have refused. Did you hope that Timmins would realise I was his son?'

'No. Yes.' She shook her head. 'I don't know. Part of me feared the discovery; part of me yearned for it.' She looked away again, preferring to stare out of the window and see things that Drake could not see. 'At the time I only had my memories of the man I fell in love with, not the man he had become. I had no idea what his reaction would be to discovering he had a son, so I was torn. Samuel was so different from my husband. They were both clever and gentle,' she mused, 'but Samuel was tough too. He made me nervous ... not in a bad way but in an exciting way. He made everyone else seem so bland.' She chuckled at a memory. 'He was so active and full of energy. Talking to him, just seeing him, made me feel ... alive. I wasn't lonely any more.' She stole a glance at her son. 'It sounds so silly now.'

'No, it doesn't,' said Drake. He knew exactly what she meant and it wasn't silly at all. It was real, every heart pounding, nerve tingling, moment of it.

'We let our passions run away with us. It was foolish and shameful.'

'Did you love my father?'

His mother frowned as she considered his question. 'I loved him very much, Drake. At times it frightened me and made me want to run, at other times it made me feel as if anything was possible. Being in love is like a madness taking hold of you. It makes us do silly things.'

Drake wondered who she was talking about, his father or Timmins. He decided it was better not to know. It did not matter now. His mother was suffering enough. She had lost them both and to love someone and then never have the chance to see them again was unbearable. Drake knew the feeling from experience. He remembered the letter in his pocket.

'I think Timmins must have had something to do with this,' said Drake, removing the letter and placing it on the table between them. 'It is a letter from Sir Robert Pendragon. He wants to commission my services. I am meeting him tomorrow.'

His mother's eyes grew wide, making him smile.

'That is wonderful news!' She touched the letter cautiously with her fingers as if it might dissolve in front of her.

'I am not going to accept it,' said Drake. He saw her face fall. 'I know the land he is talking about and it is a large project which will take at least a year. I have commitments planned and cannot take on such a large commission.'

'So why are you seeing him?'

Drake slid the letter from beneath her fingers and placed it into his pocket.

'I don't know. The sensible thing would have been to send a reply rejecting his request, but I had a yearning to see the place again and to see if much has changed. I can offer him some advice.'

'It has been a long time. You may see Tilly. She is a lady's maid now, to Miss Evelyn Pendragon, although she will be leaving the post soon. She is to be married.'

Drake felt as if someone had just slapped him in the face. 'Miss Evelyn is to be married?'

'No, Tilly, come next spring. You have lost your chance with her. She is to be married to the baker's son.'

Drake felt his racing heart begin to slow to a steady beat again. Dear Lord, he had not expected to feel like this on hearing news of Evie. But she was not engaged, there was no need for alarm. His mother was talking again. He tried to concentrate on what she was saying.

'Spring is always a nice season to be wed. However, I would not be surprised if Sir Robert makes a similar announcement very soon. Miss Evelyn has been seen out in the company of her cousin. They make a handsome couple and rumour has it that Sir Robert is encouraging the match.'

Drake rocked back in his chair and gravely imagined the 'handsome couple' walking out together. Unaware of the effect her idle gossip had on her son, his mother moved on to another subject, something to do with wood for the fire, or was it wood as in woodland? He did not care any more, his thoughts were elsewhere.

Mawgan and Evelyn Pendragon. Cousins made for one another. A wiser man should walk away. *I* should walk away. Drake wrapped his fingers around the letter buried deep in his pocket. The new garden was his only reason for the visit, but now there was an added urgency to it. He wanted to discover if the news was true. Had Evie fallen in love with her cousin? He should feel happy that Evie had found happiness with another man and was planning a future. But he did not. He did not at all.

Chapter Seventeen

Drake looked at the lions guarding the entrance. They were new, so new in fact that one of them was still being erected. The stonemason's skill in creating the lifelike creatures could only be admired, but for all their intricate carvings, they were an unwelcoming pair. If it were not for the letter inviting him to visit, Drake would have felt their snarling mouths were directed at him.

Drake dismounted the gig and dismissed the driver, telling him he had the desire to walk the rest of the way to Carrack House. He had arrived in plenty of time and was curious to see how the grounds had matured. He was glad to see that the old oak and beech trees still lined the drive leading to the great house. They provided a warmer welcome than the lions at the gate and, in his mind, were more beautiful. Their dappled shadows offered shade, as their branches, heavy with rustling leaves, helped to calm Drake's nerves. He looked up to the clear blue sky as he passed beneath each one, and admired the delicate network of brown lace formed by their branches. It felt good to be back. He had not expected to feel this way.

Gradually, bit by bit, Carrack House grew more visible between the trees, rising up at the end of the grand, trailing drive, like a magnificent blossom. It would not be long before he was walking up the main steps to the house. Drake realised he was not ready for that – not yet.

He left the drive and soon found himself wandering the gardens, passing by the glasshouses and through the yards. Eventually he arrived at Timmins' office, his jars of seeds still lined the shelves and the cushion in his chair still had the imprint of a man's body upon it. This visit was going to be harder than he had anticipated.

Drake turned away to look at the next building, his former home, the bothy. It was empty. Slates were missing from the roof and some windows were broken. Drake, who had always found it a cold and miserable place, now felt sorry to see that it had no purpose at all. He wondered where Matthew, Mark, Luke and John were now. Were they married and renting elsewhere? He looked at the gardeners labouring on the land. He was not close enough to recognise any of them or for them to recognise him, yet he had been left unchallenged. His fine clothes and smart footwear were all the evidence they required that he was to be trusted. They had never met Evie's old tutor, thought Drake.

Drake had expected to see some changes and his sharp eyes were quick to spot them. He also noticed what areas were already showing signs of Timmins' absence and if a new head gardener were not appointed soon, the land and harvest would quickly degenerate. The tour of the grounds was a haunting experience. No familiar cats came to greet him and he wondered what had happened to them all. Ghosts and memories lingered in every part. He saw Timmins working, teaching, scowling or coaxing his workers at every turn. The knowledge he had acquired was a constant reminder of all he owed the man, and how much his betrayal had hurt.

He had expected to be reminded of his time as an apprentice during his visit; however, he had not expected to see Evie everywhere he walked. He saw her as a child chasing her brother with ribbons dangling from her fingers. He saw her as an awkward, shy girl, attempting to make a friend of him despite his wariness of her. He saw her as a teenager, on the verge of womanhood, smiling at him through the glass panes of the orangery. Finally, he saw her looking up at him, with her wide, searching eyes, earth staining her hem and broken pot fragments in her hand.

Drake pinched the bridge of his nose as if it would remove her from his mind. Why had he come back? Because of Sir Robert? There was only one thing left to do, get the visit over with and leave. He turned and headed towards Carrack House.

Drake was shown into the hall and told to wait while Sir Robert was informed of his arrival. He looked about him. The last time he was here, he was just a young lad fetching help for Evie's brother. At the time he had been overawed by the opulence, yet due to the circumstances had really noticed very little of the grandeur of the hall. He had not noticed its wide sweeping staircase, large oil paintings or fully appreciated the beautifully carved statues lining the walls. Back then he had been too frightened and hurried. Nicholas had fallen ill and Evie had needed help. Today, he had time and was no longer overawed by the experience. Over the last few years he had secured many commissions where visits to such houses were not uncommon. He had grown used to the splendour of the rich, however he still felt on edge as he was aware that Evie might appear at any moment.

'What are you doing here?'

Drake turned to see Tilly descending the stairs. As her eyes swept over his smart clothes and back up to his face, Drake realised the real reason why he had come. He wanted to show Evie that he was no longer a labourer, but had done well for himself. Stupid pride. Stupid, stupid pride.

'Leave, now,' said Tilly, 'before someone sees you.'

Drake smiled, it was good to see a familiar face, although he had hoped for a warmer greeting. 'I have been invited by Sir Robert so there is no need to fret, Tilly.'

The anxiety did not leave Tilly's face. 'Why? What have you done?'

'Nothing yet. He wants me to look at some land that he wants to develop.' Tilly did not appear impressed. She threw a nervous glance towards the stairs. He wondered if Evie would soon arrive. 'I hear you are to be wed soon,' said Drake, hoping to change the subject. 'Congratulations.'

Tilly was in no mood for Sunday talk. 'You are not wanted here, Drake. Tell Sir Robert you can't help and leave.' She stepped forward and for the first time he saw anger in her eyes. 'Why are you raking over old coals, Drake? Don't you think your leaving was painful enough?'

Had Evie confided in her? 'How much do you know?' he asked.

'She told me nothing, she didn't have to, but I'm her maid, I have eyes. She's older now and not a foolish girl thinking herself in love. She can see what you really are. Not good enough for her to step over.'

Her scorn took Drake by surprise. 'Tilly!'

Exasperated, Tilly turned and walked briskly away towards a door that looked as if it might lead to the servants' quarters. She paused at the threshold.

'Why did you not want what was in front of you, Drake?' she asked wearily. She half turned her head, preferring to stare at the door frame rather than turn around to look at him. 'Why do you think I walked with you to Perran every other Sunday?'

He could only see the profile of her face, her back remained turned to him. He frowned at her odd question.

'I thought you were visiting your sister.'

Tilly let out an exacerbated sigh. 'My sister lives in Redruth, Drake. I visited no one. I only said that so I could walk with you.'

'What did you do with yourself?'

'I sat in the graveyard waiting for you to leave … so I could walk back with you.'

How had he not realised? 'I'm sorry. I didn't mean to lead you to think—'

'Oh you didn't. We both know that you only had eyes for someone you could never have. You are a fool, Drake, a fool. She is over you now so it would be best if you go. Best for all of us.' She stepped into the darkness beyond the door, leaving Drake alone in the hall with his growing self-doubt.

'Sir Robert is ready to see you now, Mr Vennor.' Drake did not move. I should leave. Now, before she arrives. 'Mr Vennor?' prompted the butler, lifting his hand to indicate the way.

Drake lifted his head and looked towards the voice. The butler, stiff in his uniform and manner, was waiting patiently for him to follow. 'Love consumed and controlled me,' his mother had said, 'it frightened me and made me want to run, at other times it made me feel as if anything was possible.' Anything is possible. Drake understood what she meant.

'Thank you,' said Drake. 'Please, lead the way.'

To Drake's surprise, Sir Robert was not alone. Mawgan rose from the chair to greet him, unfurling his legs like a cat disturbed from his resting place. It was the first time Drake had seen Mawgan Pendragon, face-to-face, since their encounter all those years ago. The memory of being the butt of his joke still remained vivid. He did not expect Mawgan to remember him, but to his surprise, he did.

'Drake Vennor,' said Mawgan, reaching out his hand. 'The boy gardener.'

'No longer a boy,' said Drake, taking his hand. They shook as their faces drew level. Drake saw the look in his eyes that he remembered so well. Curiosity, scrutiny, that lingering look that had judged and unnerved him as a boy. At the time he had felt like a specimen being examined, but now he was a man and the feeling of inferiority no longer clouded his judgement. He had seen that look somewhere before. He let his hand go.

'I am surprised you remember me,' replied Drake.

Mawgan smiled. 'I have a good memory for faces. Something I discovered during my travels. Brief encounters made in busy cities can reap benefits if one can only recall their names.'

'I don't doubt it.' Their gazes remained locked, each man trying to work the other out. It was Sir Robert who broke the deadlock.

'My nephew has been touring the Empire. I was beginning to wonder if he was ever going to come home.' They shook hands. 'I am glad you are here, Mr Vennor. You were recommended to me by my head gardener.'

'You mentioned this in your letter.'

'I have land—'

'The north-east field. I know it. Good soil but the land is flat and the drainage poor.'

Sir Robert looked pleased. 'Of course, you would know it well having worked here once.'

Drake nodded. He glanced at the closed door. *Where was Evie?*

'We could take a walk out there and discuss your ideas,' suggested Mawgan, his smile broadening. Why does he still smile, thought Drake? Has Evie confessed everything to him? Is she now embarrassed by her childish crush? Is Mawgan Pendragon finding the whole situation rather amusing?

'I would be happy to,' said Drake, 'but I cannot remain in Cornwall to carry out the project. I already have commitments for later in the year.' Drake saw the disappointment in Sir Robert's face. For a man so devoted to his gardens, Drake had rarely seen Sir Robert take a walk in them. The man preferred to enjoy them from a distance, preferably through a glass window. However, he had an obsession to have the best gardens in Cornwall and he had the passion and money to achieve it. His latest project meant a lot to him. Drake relented. 'I can suggest things and draw up detailed plans that any competent landscaper can carry out. I can even recommend someone to you.'

The door opened, drawing the men's attention to the woman who stood on the threshold. It was Evie and Drake knew, in that moment, why he had really come.

She hadn't said a word since entering the room, just a slight inclination of her head at her father's introduction and a nervous glance at Mawgan, as she accepted the chair offered by him. Since then, she had been sitting bolt upright, ignoring Drake and taking no part in the conversation that followed. She appeared as tense as his stomach felt and he regretted not warning her of his arrival. In his haste to visit, and all the occasions he had examined his own reasons for coming, he had not thought how she might feel. He was glad to see that her complexion, which had drained of all colour at her first sight of him, was slowly returning to a gentle pink blush.

Despite the conversation requiring Drake's full attention, he found his eyes straying to Evelyn to only look away quickly in fear he may be caught. She looked even more beautiful than he remembered, with skin as smooth as cream and hair like spun gold. She was now an adult with all the allure of a woman in her prime. He had not prepared himself for this new power she had over him. A drink was offered to him by Sir Robert. He took it, but had no idea what he had agreed to have. He realised, belatedly, that Sir Robert was talking to him.

'I would like a water feature of some sort.'

Drake composed himself. 'A fountain or perhaps a stream passing through?'

'Is it possible?'

Drake nodded. 'There is a spring in the top corner that can be diverted.'

Drake found himself looking at her again. She wore a pale blue and white dress, buttoned high at the neck and nipped in tight at her waist. He noticed her breasts heaved a little faster than normal, drawing his attention to them time and time again. Dear God don't let me lose control and reach for her, he thought. He took a drink and swallowed, the liquid burned his throat all the way down to the pit in his stomach.

'I want it to be envied.'

Drake looked at Sir Robert. 'It will take time for it to mature, but I will ensure it will make a fitting legacy.'

Sir Robert turned to Mawgan and the conversation momentarily turned to family history. Thankful that he was temporarily excluded, Drake found himself looking at Evelyn again. He felt a need to absorb every detail of her while he was in her presence, her wrists framed by lace, the curve of her dress hiding the splay of her hips beneath its folds. He felt as needy as a child for her approval. Was she impressed by the change in him? Was she pleased he had done so well? Was she ashamed that they had once kissed? Why could she not bring herself to look at him? Did she hate him so much?

As if she heard him, Evelyn lifted her gaze and turned her green eyes upon him. He felt his heart heave as he looked into them. He still loved her, but how did she feel? Her stony expression told him nothing.

Sir Robert rose to his feet. 'It is time to show you the land, Mr Vennor. I have high hopes for this project. They say you are this century's Capability Brown.'

'Your enquiries have gone further than your former head gardener's recommendation,' replied Drake, rising himself. Evelyn rose too and he found himself briefly facing her, too far away to touch, but not too far away to see every exquisite detail of her face. She has grown taller, thought Drake, just the right height for kissing.

'This will be one of the biggest changes to the gardens since my grandfather's day. I want it to be done right.'

'Will Lady Pendragon accompany us?' Drake asked Evelyn, unable to drag his gaze away from her face.

It was Sir Robert who answered. 'She will not. She has one of her headaches. Let me show you the way.' Sir Robert and Mawgan prepared to leave.

'Then perhaps Miss Evelyn will.' The words were out before he had a chance to filter them.

He saw her stiffen and realised she had hoped to slip away and leave them to their talk. He may not get the opportunity to see her again if she had her way. 'It would be helpful to obtain a woman's perspective.'

'A woman's perspective is rarely sought, Mr Vennor,' replied Evelyn. Unable to hold his gaze she blinked and fixed it upon her father who was speaking to Mawgan near the door. Her voice had not changed and hearing it again unleashed another set of memories for Drake. Shared confidences, reassuring words, help with his studies. How did he find the strength to walk away all those years ago?

'This is true …' he almost did not recognise the tenderness in his own voice '… but I am seeking your opinion nonetheless.'

She looked at him. 'Why?'

'Because they are worthy of being heard.'

Evelyn blinked. 'Not everyone will agree with you, Mr Vennor.'

'I have never lived my life trying to please others.'

'You are fortunate. A woman has little choice in the matter,' she replied, before following her father and cousin out of the room.

Evelyn did accompany them, but refrained from making suggestions. She listened to their discussions and occasionally agreed to a suggestion made by her father with just a slight nod of her head. Otherwise she remained distant in mind and body and Drake often saw her gazing into the distance as if she wished she were anywhere but with them.

With a sinking heart Drake realised she had only come to please her father and he felt responsible for placing her in such a position. The only time he saw any reaction, was when her father invited him to stay in the house. The project was large and the completion of a comprehensive survey and plans would take several weeks, so it was only natural that such an invitation would come. Even so it caught both Evelyn and Drake off guard. Evelyn hid her distress well, but Drake still noticed. Wishing not to cause her further distress he politely declined. Their reunion was not going as well as he had hoped, not that he knew what his hopes had been.

'Then stay in Timmins' old house,' suggested Sir Robert. 'I have not appointed a replacement for him yet and an empty building soon deteriorates. Having it inhabited for a few weeks will give it some much needed airing.'

'The cottage will give you the space to draw your designs,' said Mawgan as he offered his arm to Evelyn. Drake clenched his teeth as her arm slid easily through her cousin's. 'Unless you do not feel you are up to the task and wish to refuse the commission.'

Drake dragged his eyes away from Evelyn's arm nestled in Mawgan's. 'Is that a challenge?' asked Drake.

Mawgan smiled. 'Perhaps.'

What was the man up to? 'Then it is a challenge I cannot ignore,' said Drake. 'Thank you, Sir Robert, the use of the head gardener's cottage would be most welcome.'

Evelyn's silence and pressed lips told him what he already knew about her feelings on the matter. Her anger was palpable. He had not planned to accept the commission, just offer some words of advice, but seeing Evie again only confirmed what he had always known deep inside, that he would always compare every woman he met to her … just as he had done these past six years. Today he saw that he was close to losing her forever and that realisation felt like he was dying. He had no choice. He had to stay.

Chapter Eighteen

The paintbrush felt heavy as lead in Evelyn's hand and her strokes grew clumsier to her critical eye. He was standing too close. So close that Evelyn swore that she could feel an invisible pull towards him. She fought the urge with every fibre of her being, but it came at a cost. She could neither concentrate nor paint the landscape Drake was describing to her.

Evelyn glanced up at her mother who sat quietly reading in the corner. She had made a remarkable recovery over the last week and now played the part of chaperone well. Having a garden designed in her name was a powerful diversion from her own health worries and more potent than any tonic Doctor Birch had prescribed. Her father had come to know his wife well.

Drake leaned closer. 'This ground level needs to be higher,' he instructed, indicating an area on the paper with his sun-kissed hand.

His calm, softly spoken tone only succeeded in making Evelyn tenser, clenching her jaw, she did what he had asked.

'Higher.'

'The land is *flat*,' Evelyn ground out under her breath.

He bent down closer so she could almost feel the warmth of his spoken words. 'It can be changed.'

She raised it a little more. Could he see the tremor in her hand?

'A little higher ...'

Evelyn swept the brush upwards with an angry stroke, shocking Drake into silence. He straightened.

'You wanted it higher,' said Evelyn, dropping her brush into the jar of water at her side.

'I wanted a hill ... not a volcano.'

Lady Pendragon lifted her gaze. 'Is something the matter?'

Drake smiled reassuringly. 'Nothing that cannot be remedied.'

'Don't be so sure,' muttered Evelyn under her breath.

Evelyn had still not fully recovered from finding Drake standing in her drawing room a week ago. The sight of him had robbed her of voice, thought and reason. He looked even more handsome than she had remembered. His black tousled hair, dark serious brows and firm jaw remained the same, but now he was a man, more chiselled, more experienced and more confident in his own skin.

She thought she would be immune to the spell Drake Vennor, the boy, had cast over her as a child. She was wrong. The spell he cast today was even more intense, arousing every nerve in her body and setting her on edge. While she had fallen to pieces, he had remained calm at their meeting. It was painful, upsetting. She had made up her mind not to repeat the tortuous experience again.

She successfully avoided seeing him in the days that followed, but this morning her father had called her into his study. 'Mr Vennor has drawn up some basic designs,' her father had informed her, 'but lacks the skill to translate them into a landscape. He asked if I knew someone who could paint. I have offered your services.'

Evelyn had no grounds to refuse, at least none that she could offer. And so she found herself in his company, resenting him, hating him – and far too close to him.

Evelyn stood up suddenly; knocking the leg of the easel with her own. The easel teetered and the painting she had been working on began to slip. Drake reached to steady it.

Her mother looked up, exasperated to have been disturbed for a second time. 'What is the matter, Evelyn? You look a little pale.'

'I am just a little hot, Mother.'

Eager to prevent a possible fainting fit, Lady Pendragon rose from her chair. 'I will send someone to fetch some water.' She rang the bell and they waited in awkward silence for a servant to come. No one did. Lady Pendragon began to fidget with her lace handkerchief, embarrassed by her staff's poor attendance when they had a guest present. Eventually she could tolerate it no more. 'You cannot find reliable staff these days,' she said as she went to the door. She paused to look at them. 'I will leave the door open,' she added, her chaperone duties still firmly in her mind.

Feeling stifled, Evelyn moved to the other side of the room. It was the furthest she could be away from Drake without leaving.

She began to pace the floor before the bay window, aware Drake's eyes followed her every move. She shot him an angry glance. He appeared so calm, while she felt like prey caged with a predator.

'Why have you come back?'

His answer was well rehearsed. 'Your father has commissioned me to—'

'Save your excuses for someone who will believe them,' she retorted angrily. 'How could you without warning me first?'

'I had begun to think you did not care.'

'It is *you* who does not care!'

'I care very much.'

'Don't pretend to have a heart now, Drake. If you did you would have thought of my feelings in all of this.' Evelyn helped herself to some of her father's brandy, carefully positioning her body between the glass and Drake to hide her trembling hands.

'Steady,' he warned. 'You are not used to—'

Evelyn ignored him. Jerking her head backwards, she swallowed the small amount in one large gulp. She braced herself as she felt the burning flame travel through her. It tasted awful, but she would not give him the pleasure of seeing her disgust. She blinked away the pain.

'I began to worry you had lost your spark,' he said gently.

'If I had it was you who extinguished it.'

'I'm sorry for how we parted. It was poorly done.'

Evelyn turned, surprised at his apology and was even more so to see the sincerity on his handsome face. The taste of the brandy still lingered on her tongue, but the pain it had caused began to melt away. Her anger, however, remained.

'I had to leave. I thought by leaving quickly it would make it easier,' offered Drake.

'Easier? For who? Certainly not for me.'

'For both of us,' said Drake, walking towards her.

'You left me wondering what I had done.'

'I tried to explain. I had just found out Timmins was seeing my mother ... that he was my father. It was too much. Besides, you knew I would have to leave.'

'I knew you would have to leave Carrack House as part of your apprenticeship, but not Cornwall. Not me. And now you are back as if nothing happened between us.'

Drake reached for her, but Evelyn stepped away. 'Conceited, arrogant, self-centred man.'

'Evie ... please.'

'I hated you for leaving me. I hate you now.'

She could see her words were hurting him, each well-aimed phrase finding their mark. He deserved it.

'Then there is nothing I can say or do to make it better.' He picked up her painting. 'At least my return has awakened your spirit.' He paused and looked at her thoughtfully. 'Mawgan will never make you happy, Evie.'

'Mawgan is ten times the man you are!' retorted Evelyn. She only wished Mawgan was here now making demands for her company, but recently he had been too busy to see her and with no one to occupy her time, she did not have the excuse to avoid painting for Drake.

'Where is he now?'

'An old university friend has arrived in town and he felt obliged to entertain him.' If Mawgan was here, she thought angrily, he would wipe that look of sympathy from Drake's face. At least she hoped he would.

'You are angry with me,' observed Drake. Evelyn looked up to the ceiling in mock gratitude that he was beginning to understand. 'Curse me all you like if it makes you feel better. I can take it. I probably deserve it—'

'Probably?' scoffed Evelyn.

'—but whether you believe me or not, I left to save *you* as well as myself.'

Evelyn turned on him. 'I did not need saving.'

Drake glanced at the door. Satisfied no one was listening he stepped forward and touched her elbow. 'You did need saving … from me. I would have ruined your life.'

She looked at his hand, its warmth moving up through her arm in a most pleasurable way.

'As a child I had no voice or control of my life. My opinions were not worth considering, my cry for help not worth hearing. My crime?' She eased her arm away and took a step back. 'I was a girl and incapable of independent thought.' She watched his gaze lift to hers. 'I thought you were different, Drake. I thought you treated me as an equal, but I can see now that I was mistaken. You left to save me, but did not ask my opinion. My thoughts were not worthy of consideration.'

Unconsciously, as if requiring some protection, Evelyn stood behind a chair and rested her hands on the back hoping she could calm her beating heart.

'Should a woman dare to step out of line, she is labelled, ostracised, stripped of everything she holds dear. I know. I have experienced it. So we do as we are told and walk the narrow path of propriety, dedicating our lives to pleasing others. God forbid we should aspire to achieve anything more than a suitable marriage. So we are told who to love and I, like many others, have resolved to abide by our families' wishes for the good of the family name. And then I find you standing in my home, after all these years. I have lost count of how many times I have turned your parting words over and over in my head.'

'I'm sorry, Evie.'

'I deserve the truth, Drake. Why have you come back? Is it to soothe your conscience? To quell your curiosity? To close a chapter? How fortunate that you are also being paid for your time.'

They could hear her mother's voice in the hall. Their time alone was drawing to a close.

Drake raked a hand through his hair. For the first time she saw that he trembled too.

'I came back to see you, Evie.'

'And what do you see?'

'A woman who has lost her rebellious streak. A woman who is going to marry a man she does not love and who will never love her the way I do.'

Her breath caught in her throat, turning her voice to no more than a whisper. 'Don't preach to me about what real love is.'

'I loved you enough to leave you.'

'But you did not love me enough to stay.'

It seemed ironic that Evelyn found herself looking at her reflection and reliving every word of their parting, just as she had done on the day Drake had left all those years ago. Back then Tilly was unpinning her hair in preparation for bed and today was no different. Evelyn would probably not be seeing Drake again.

Her mother had returned abruptly ending what had never really begun.

'I think it has been a tiring day for all of us, Lady Pendragon,' Drake had said, bowing over her mother's hand. 'I think I can complete the designs from now on.'

In the hall, he stole a moment to whisper. 'Where is the Evie I used to know, who escaped her governess's company and ran free through the grounds?'

'I'm no longer a child,' she had replied through tight lips.

'It is not the child I am talking about, it is the spirit inside,' Drake had answered.

Evelyn looked at herself and wondered the same thing now.

'I can manage now, Tilly,' she said, breaking free of her maid's brush to stand up.

Tilly froze in surprise, the hairbrush aloft in readiness for another stroke.

'I'm sorry, Tilly. I am not myself.'

'You have not been yourself since Drake Vennor arrived.'

Evelyn stared at her maid. Did she know about her love for Drake? Was it that obvious?

'I am not sure what you mean,' said Evelyn carefully.

Tilly began to turn down the bed. 'It must be terrible being told how to paint by someone who, not long ago, dug holes for a living.' She extracted Evelyn's nightgown from a drawer and gave it a vigorous shake. 'The arrogance of the man. I don't know how you manage to bear it.' She laid the nightgown on the bed, splaying out its white cotton panels. Evelyn's cheeks burned. She was glad Tilly had her back to her and was taking such an interest in the floral embroidery that lined the modest neckline. 'He has no respect for his betters ... or women. I knew it the first time he walked into the kitchen.'

'You sound like you do not like him,' said Evelyn, surprised at her maid's dislike for Drake. She had always thought they worked well together. It appeared that way when Tilly tended her during her Rest Cure treatment.

'I've seen the likes of him before. They leave a trail of broken hearts behind them.'

Evelyn didn't want to hear any more. 'I would like to undress myself tonight. You may go, Tilly.' Evelyn smiled to soften her dismissal. 'It is nothing you have done or said,' she reassured her. 'I just want some time alone. I am sure I am quite capable of undressing myself for once. Thank you.'

Tilly left, her brow knotted with concern.

My maid thinks I am acting oddly, thought Evelyn, all because I wish to prepare myself for bed. Perhaps she was, but did it matter? Evelyn suddenly felt the urge to scream, or laugh, or both, at the ridiculousness of the situation. The expectations placed on a lady of her breeding were heavy and, in truth, not funny at all. She felt the invisible shackles that censored her every deed, thought and word, more keenly than ever before ... and Drake was to blame.

Tilly had been right, ever since Drake had returned her equilibrium had been disrupted. She felt unsettled and dissatisfied. It was cruel of him to return and remind her of everything she could never have.

It was raining by the time Evelyn reached the head gardener's lodge. Her decision to come was so sudden, that she took neither jacket nor shawl. She stood on the threshold, shaking with an emotion she could not name and dared not examine. She lifted her fist and banged angrily on the door. Drake opened it almost immediately and, for the first time, as his eyes raked over her, she became aware of her rain soaked dress, her loose fair hair beaded with droplets of rain and her shocking behaviour of visiting a man alone. She felt that her heart would burst from the thrill that coursed through her.

Without speaking, she pushed past him and went inside. She spotted his drawings immediately. Three detailed landscapes, which translated his plans to perfection, lay on the table. She moved closer to look at them. He had not needed her to paint for him at all.

'You were avoiding me,' said Drake behind her. 'I had to think of something.'

Her anger began to slowly drain away from her. She began to shake, but it was not from the cold. 'You told me you left to save me.'

'It was better for you that I left.'

'Don't tell me what is best for me, Drake. I have been told my whole life what would be best for me.'

'Why are you here?'

'Because I was angry with you!'

'Are you angry with me now?'

Was she? She shook her head. There was no point in lying.

He took a step towards her. 'I came back to see you because I still love you. I should have returned a long time ago, but I was afraid.' He touched her arm and this time she did not flinch away. 'Afraid you would have come to your senses and see me for who I was … a filthy labourer with no future.'

Evelyn stared at his hand on her arm. She dared not look at him, too frightened that she would see he was lying, but then his hand slipped around her and she felt his cheek against hers. A sigh escaped her. He spoke the truth, she could feel it.

'I have thought of you every day,' whispered Drake into her hair. 'When I received your father's letter I thought, maybe I am now worthy to return.'

His mouth sought hers, but it was too much, too soon. She pushed him away and took a step back. It was what her father and Mawgan would expect her to do. It was what Tilly would expect her to do.

Drake was looking at her, his brows creased with worry, his mind trying to read hers. 'I'm sorry. I should not have done that.' He raked a hand through his hair. 'You came here to see me tonight, Evie. Why are you here?' He raised his dark eyes to meet hers and braced himself. 'What does Miss Evelyn Pendragon want?'

What did she want? No one had ever asked her before. Her heart thumped so loudly she felt her body vibrate with each beat. She recognised the soul in his eyes and felt the pull of desire for his body. The first she knew so well, the second she longed to discover. Neither, she was permitted to do.

'She wants to be free.' Her uncensored answer surprised them both. Something changed between them.

'And what does Evie want?' asked Drake softly.

Evelyn no longer had the strength to pretend. She knew he saw through her.

'She wants you, Drake. She has always wanted you.'

She did not know who moved first, only that the space between them disappeared and she was in his arms, feeling the warmth of his body, his breath in her hair and his evening stubble against her cheek. For a moment neither spoke. They remained still, wrapped in each other's arms and listening to their beating hearts. The past forgotten, the future ignored, just the two of them alone.

Evelyn was the first to speak, her voice quiet, vulnerable, confessional. 'I've missed you so much, Drake. So much it hurt.'

'You don't have to hurt any more,' whispered Drake, running a hand through her hair. 'I am here.'

'You broke my heart when you left.'

'I broke my own too.'

This time she did not refuse his kiss, which ended in a smile before they broke apart. Nothing had changed. It was as if they were children again, meeting secretly in the parkland, stealing thrilling, forbidden kisses during those warm summer months. Their smiles were ones of relief. It felt as if they had come home.

Another kiss followed, slower than the last. Evelyn began to tremble as she was reminded of all that she had missed. Drake sensed the change in her. He framed her face with his hands and looked at her. His steady gaze told her he understood and felt the same. His gentle smile calmed her and stilled the squirming snakes in her belly. She returned a shaky smile of her own.

He kissed her lips before her smile faded. This time he was teasing and playful, attempting to lighten the mood and relax her. It worked. The tension she unknowingly held deep within, slowly uncoiled and slinked away.

She allowed herself to rest against him. She could feel his solid frame against her body. It was beautiful, muscular and largely unknown to her. She felt a desperate desire to discover how the years had changed him. Evelyn's breath grew shallower as she grew braver. Her fingers threaded between the buttons of his shirt in search of the skin beneath. She heard his breath catch, or was it her own?

Wantonly, she had shown him what was on her mind and from their breathless kisses that followed; she knew he felt the same. Drake broke away first.

'Evie …' he whispered as he rested his cheek against hers. 'I want you so much.'

She heard his pain and felt it too. Dear Lord, wasn't every part of her body crying out for him too? It was a need that was primal, instinctive and more potent than mere desire, ignoring all other thoughts in the quest to be even closer.

'He was doing things to my mother that I want to do to you.'

Evelyn finally understood what he meant all those years ago. Poor Drake. Poor, darling Drake. How he must have suffered.

Evelyn touched his cheek. 'I want you too, Drake.' She was offering more than he expected, she could see it in his face. Losing her maidenhead would ruin her marriage prospects – ruin her. It was a secret she could not hide on her wedding night. There would be no going back for either of them. Yet, he looked hopeful, or perhaps he was fearful that he might have misheard. She wanted there to be no confusion. 'Make love to me, Drake.'

His reply came out in an anguished rush. 'Do not say this on my account. I have no wish to cause you harm.'

'Then be gentle.'

'That is not what I meant and you know it.' He raked his hand through his hair again. 'Evie, stop this now, because I am not sure that I can. I can never give you the life you deserve. Your family will never allow it. Society will never allow it. Your reputation will be the price for making love with me.'

'I don't care. Life can change in an instant.'

'Life would not be worth living if you were not in it.'

'Then why should we wait?'

He had no answer, or perhaps like her, did not want to find one.

'I cannot work out if we are brave or foolish,' he said.

'Does it matter as long as we are together?'

He took her hand to lead the way upstairs, but she resisted and shook her head.

'No … not the bedroom. Let's stay here, by the fire.' How brave she had become in such a short time. Drake did not argue, instead he gently pulled her towards him so he could kiss her again.

Evelyn broke away and breathlessly reached for the pearl buttons at her collar. As Evelyn worked to undo them, Drake traced the curve of her neck with his kisses. Her fingers worked more efficiently than she dared hope, for her clothing was stifling and she longed to escape it. Button by button, she was freed from her bodice and skirt. Drake untied her petticoat laces, as she traced her fingers over his broad shoulders and marvelled at the movement of his muscle beneath his shirt. He eased her petticoats and crinoline over her hips until they pooled at her feet.

Drake stepped back to look at her. No man had ever seen her like this. No man had looked at her the way Drake was looking at her now. Her public façade had been peeled away one layer at a time and his desire for her had not diminished. Under his gaze, her body tingled with expectation.

'Beautiful,' whispered Drake. 'I've lost count of the number of nights I have lain awake imagining you like this.' He must have felt overdressed, for he hastily pulled off his shirt and cast it aside. For the first time she could see the man that lay beneath. The muscles and tanned skin of a labourer, the strength of an adult, the allure of the unknown. The glow of the evening fire cast shadows on his skin and invited her to touch him. She reached out and ran her fingers across the contours of his chest. He watched her hand stroke his skin. 'I have wanted to feel your touch for so long,' he said, with a curve to his lips. He lifted his gaze to look at her. She knew what he was thinking, he wanted to touch her and she wanted it too.

She turned around so he could loosen her corset while she fumbled with the fastenings in the front. Her corset came away, as he kissed the crook of her neck and slid his arms around her. She leant backwards against his chest, glorying in his touch.

'I've thought of you often. Just like this. I don't deserve you.'

'Hush, Drake,' soothed Evelyn, turning in his arms. 'Such thoughts have kept us apart.'

'Nothing will keep us apart. Nothing.'

His next kiss was as determined as his promise. It left her breathless and shaking, as he lifted her chemise from her body and pulled her close before it touched the floor. They knelt before the fire, both naked to the waist, skin on skin, whilst the gentle warmth of the fire warmed their bodies.

She felt his hand trace the curve of her spine and finally come to rest on her drawers trimmed with lace. The hand stilled and she wondered what he was thinking.

She loved this man so much. How could one night ever be enough? How could she live without him in her life? She felt the waist of her drawers loosen and his hands begin to ease them over her hips. She sat back on her heels, halting the fabric from falling lower.

'Promise me you will never leave me again, Drake. I couldn't bear it again.'

He looked at her, surprised. He saw her fear and his eyes filled with tenderness.

'I promise, Evie. I love you. Always have. Always will.'

She reached to touch his cheek, but he took her hand instead and pulled her gently towards his embrace. They were together, skin on skin, with a mutual desire for more and prepared to damn the consequences. Her worries were forgotten, her bad memories laid to rest. All that mattered was the present, where sight captured memories and touch, whether by hand, tongue or breath, awakened intoxicating sensations. Finally, when she felt there was no more to be discovered, Drake took her to a world beyond her imagination, where she felt powerful, yet powerless, enslaved, yet free, and when she felt she could take no more, yet fearful that it would end – he joined her.

Evelyn woke to find Drake lying beside her, his head resting on the heel of his hand, his dark eyes tracing the length of her hair. Whatever he was thinking had brought a slight curve to his lips. He sensed he was being watched and looked at her. 'I love the colour of your hair. It glistens in the sun.'

Evelyn lifted her hand and brushed one of his stray black curls away from his cheek. 'And I love yours.'

'My hair is not like a gentleman's. It is too wild and long.'

She smiled. 'Which is why I love it. It will not be tamed. Just like you.'

'You could tame me.'

'I don't want to. Perhaps I want you to un-tame me.' Drake threw his head back and laughed. Evelyn watched, fascinated. It had been years since she had last heard him laugh and told him so. 'I am falling in love with you all over again,' she teased.

'I have fallen in love with you a hundred times,' said Drake, turning onto his back and using his bent arm as a pillow.

Evelyn rolled over onto her front and look down on him. 'Tell me. What makes you fall in love with me again and again?'

'Each time I discover there is something new to love.'

'Such as?'

He looked up at her. His penetrating gaze tugged at something deep inside her. 'The crease that forms between your eyebrows when you are puzzled.'

Evelyn touched her forehead. He raised an eyebrow when she found what she was searching for. She vowed to herself to make a concerted effort not to frown so much.

'What else?'

'The way your lips tighten when you are holding back from speaking your mind.'

'You make me sound horrid.'

'And the way your voice rises when you feel misjudged.'

'You are teasing me now.' She wasn't so sure that he was, his face had suddenly grown serious.

'The way your breath catches when you are about to be kissed …'

He rose up on his side so their faces were close enough to kiss. Her breath caught in her throat. She heard him chuckle as she playfully pushed him away. She lay on her back and stared up to the ceiling, smiling.

'… and the way you groan.'

Her smile broadened. 'You can stop now.'

'And that little gasp when …'

Evelyn reached for her chemise and pulled it over her face to hide her blushes. 'I'm not talking to you.'

'And I love the way you make me feel that *anything* is possible.'

Evelyn refused to come out of her hiding place. He was teasing her, baiting her to ask what he meant. Evelyn's lips tightened.

'And that I can *do* anything.' His voice was sombre, with an edge that unnerved her.

'Like what?' she asked.

'Speak to your father.'

Evelyn dragged the chemise from her face and looked at him. His expression was serious, with no hint of teasing in his eyes.

'What are you going to speak to him about?'

'I've made love to his daughter. I have betrayed him and if I do not ask for your hand, I will be betraying you too.'

Evelyn's throat grew dry as her words tumbled out in a breathless rush. 'He will never grant it.'

'I have to try.'

'He has plans for me. Mawgan—'

'Do you love Mawgan? If you do I will step aside.'

'I would not be here if I loved him, although I do not dislike him.'

'But you do not *love* him and he does not love you.'

'You do not know him to know what he feels.'

'Do you want to marry him?'

'It is what Father wants.'

'And you?'

'No. And Mawgan would not want me either, if he learns about us.'

'Then it is settled. I will speak with him.'

'I don't want Father to know that I came here tonight.'

'I am asking for his permission, not to spread idle gossip.'

'He will refuse to give it.'

Drake did not answer. She knew what he was thinking. What titled man would want their daughter to marry a gardener? Evelyn leaned down to kiss his hand. His skin was warm, with a fine dusting of hair. She felt him gently stroke her hair.

'When Nicholas died everything was thrown into turmoil. My father wants Carrack Estate to remain in the Pendragon family. I am his only surviving child. If I marry you my name will change. Mawgan has the Pendragon name. By marrying Mawgan, Carrack House and all its land will continue to be owned by Pendragons. He will feel that I have let him down again.'

'You have never let him down.'

'I have.' She lifted her eyes to his. 'He tried educating me to take over. I failed him. I was not up to the task.'

Drake wiped her tears away with his thumb. 'Your tutor was a sadistic bastard, Evie. Your father failed *you*. He employed him and he did not give you another chance to prove yourself.'

Why didn't her father give her another chance? Initially, he was adamant that she should be educated to the best standard, but he had easily given up on the idea. She thought at the time they were too frightened of overtaxing her, but perhaps there was another reason. Evelyn frowned. Her father had made it no secret that he believed women had neither the stamina nor the intelligence to own property. So why did he consider training his daughter for such a role in the first place if he did not think she was up to the task? Unless it had all been a ruse to annoy his brother. Had her father always thought Mawgan was the answer to his dilemma? Her father was only too happy to encourage Mawgan's visits after her uncle had died. Evelyn, like a pawn in his game, had fallen into line yet again.

'When will you speak to him?' asked Evelyn.

'This morning.'

'And when he refuses?'

Drake reached for her and held her tight. His voice, hoarse with emotion, chilled her. 'Don't marry Mawgan, Evie.' She felt him swallow and hold her a little tighter. 'You will not be happy with him.'

It was only when she had returned to the silence of her bedroom, before the sun rose and the servants were about their daily tasks, did she realise he had not answered her question.

Chapter Nineteen

Evelyn listened intently at her father's study door, her head bowed in concentration, her hands feeling strangely redundant. The quiet murmur of male voices from within did nothing to calm her nerves. She was unable to decipher their words, whilst their sombre tones gave nothing away. At least there was still hope. Although the tone was not congratulatory, at least it was not filled with anger. She heard Drake speak and there was silence. Evelyn's heart raced as she waited for her father to reply. When his anger finally erupted, any hopes she had held plummeted to the pit of her stomach. Drake had finally broached the subject and asked for her hand and her father was not at all pleased.

Her father's tirade grew in ferocity and drew servants from different parts of the house to the hall. On seeing Evelyn, they quickly slipped away again, one by one, realising it was a family matter and no business of theirs. Tilly was amongst them, but was the only one to remain. Evelyn noticed that she held the banister with a vice-like grip as she looked down upon her from above.

'You arrogant upstart! Do you honestly think I would allow my daughter to marry beneath herself! She is a Pendragon! A Pendragon!'

Tilly's face drained of colour as her father's voice grew louder from behind the oak door. Guilt swept through Evelyn and she looked away. She had shared most things with her maid, but Drake had not been one of them.

Her father's angry voice continued. 'You have no breeding, no assets, no history. Society will laugh at the match. You are an embarrassment, sir. An embarrassment!' Her father drew breath only to begin again. 'Your marriage will bring shame on this family. You are a conceited fool if you think I will allow you to take over Carrack House and lands when I die.'

Drake replied and although Evelyn did not catch what he said, there was a quiet, biting tone to his words. He was in control of his anger, but only barely.

Evelyn glanced up at Tilly, but she had gone.

'Get out! *Get out!*' shouted her father. Something was thrown and hit the panelled door, giving Evelyn a start. Something else was thrown, and Evelyn heard the large mirror fall to the ground and shatter into a hundred shards.

The door opened and Drake stormed out, passing Evelyn without seeing her. She ran after him, but it was not until he had reached the bottom of the granite steps outside did she manage to catch him. She did not need to ask how the meeting went. She had heard it, felt it and now saw it on his face.

She touched his arm. 'Drake, where are you going?'

Drake scanned the horizon. 'I am leaving. Your father has made it abundantly clear about his thoughts on the matter. I expected his anger, but I will not tolerate having objects thrown at me.'

The muscles in his arm felt tense with anger, but his eyes showed his pain. He had been hurt by her father's insults and she couldn't blame him. Despite all his hard work and rise in status, he would never be good enough in her father's eyes.

'Where will you go?' she asked.

'Away.'

'What about us?' For the first time Drake looked at her. His dark brown eyes searched hers, but he did not answer. 'You said you wouldn't leave me,' Evelyn prompted.

'He refused his permission, Evie.'

Evelyn lifted her chin. 'I don't care. We can marry without his consent.'

The outer corner of his eyes creased as her words sunk in.

'You would elope with me?' She nodded. He shook his head. 'Your reputation will be ruined.'

'My reputation is already ruined. We ruined it last night.'

He removed her hand from his arm and held it in his. 'You don't know what you are saying.'

'I do, Drake. I know exactly what it means. My family will disown me and leave me with nothing. But I won't have nothing. I will have you.'

Drake's gaze lifted above her head to the great building behind her. A muscle worked in his jaw and Evelyn wondered if he was looking at all she stood to lose.

'He is watching us,' said Drake. Evelyn stiffened as he let go of her hand, took a step back and bowed his head to her. He was leaving, she thought, horrified. She may not see him again. He straightened and met her gaze. 'Meet me at the end of the drive at midnight. Only bring what you can carry. I will be waiting for you.'

Evelyn lay in bed, watching Tilly undertake the finishing touches before retiring for the day. Picking up a discarded stocking and tidying the dressing table were minor parts of a routine that had shaped her life, but would soon come to an end. Evelyn had tolerated the charade of being prepared for bed knowing that as soon as Tilly left she would be packing a bag. Evelyn felt exhausted by the events of the day, but was still keen for the night to begin.

Following Drake's departure, her father, incandescent with rage, harangued her for an hour on her responsibilities as the heir to the Pendragon fortune, to her cousin Mawgan, and as a woman of her class. Her mother played no part in the lecture. Instead she sent for Doctor Birch and took to her bed complaining of a sudden malady. To his credit, Doctor Birch came straight away to tend to her. After spending an hour providing the attention her mother craved, he was paid handsomely for his service and invited to stay for dinner by her father. Evelyn recognised the invitation for what it was. Her father had no wish to eat alone with his daughter and the doctor would provide a much-needed buffer between them.

The evening meal was a painful affair for father and daughter, who ate very little and did not speak to one another. However, Doctor Birch, whose appetite was as heavy as his consumption of port wine, was in good spirits throughout and did not notice the tension between his companions. Evelyn remained acutely aware that her father's rage still festered and it was not until the men retired to the withdrawing room to smoke their cigars, drink brandy and discuss the deficiencies of the female gender did Evelyn notice that her father's earlier rage was beginning to subside. His spirits even lifted enough to invite Doctor Birch to stay the night. Thankfully Doctor Birch had declined. The less people present on the night of her elopement the better. She would bring shame to the family name. No matter, Evelyn concluded, her future was with Drake, not here.

Evelyn noticed that Tilly had not spoken for most of the bedtime routine. She could not blame her. Tilly had helped her through the Rest Cure and shared so many of her own secrets with Evelyn. If it was not for the gossip she had heard and passed on to Evelyn, she may not have been prepared for her night of lovemaking with Drake. Tilly had taught her things that no lady of her breeding should know until her wedding night and, in sharing those secrets, had unknowingly helped make Evelyn's night with Drake a wonderful experience she hoped to repeat. A surge of guilt prompted an apology from Evelyn for keeping her relationship with Drake a secret from her.

Tilly's reply was curt. 'It's no concern of mine what you get up to.'

'I know you are upset. Yesterday, I didn't know that he would ask for my father's permission.'

'I feel foolish for talking about him to you. For saying the things I did about him.'

'I wanted to tell you, Tilly, but I knew my father would not accept him.'

'So has it ended between you?'

What could she say? Should she tell her? Something inside Evelyn held her back from confessing her plan. 'He has refused to give his consent. What more can be done?'

Tilly left soon after, shutting the door quietly behind her and leaving Evelyn alone with her thoughts. Evelyn waited an hour before she climbed out of bed in search of a suitable bag. The house was silent, whilst the outside world was cast in the inky black and grey colours of the night.

Evelyn had no idea what to take with her. She had never packed a trunk for a journey before, let alone a small bag. Clothes and undergarments were hastily inspected and thrown aside and what was finally chosen had to be quickly reassessed as it would not all fit inside. She abandoned the task to search for something to wear. It must be practical and last. A dress that could be worn at all times of the day. Evelyn found a grey dress, lined with red trim, which would suffice and hastily dressed. Her last task was to pin her hair into a serviceable bun – another task she had never had to do. It stayed in place – just. It would have to do for now. She grabbed a few more pins and a comb and stuffed them into her bag. She would have to look presentable if she was to find work. Shoes, stockings. What else? Of course, undergarments. She would need undergarments. The panic in the pit of her stomach began to rise up inside of her. What if she was not ready in time? What if someone saw her leave? Her throat and lips felt like parchment. She went to the basin in the corner of the room, poured some water and scooped some in her cupped hands. She drank from it, then quickly sluiced her face and neck with what remained. The door opened and Evelyn froze.

Tilly stood on the threshold, with a fresh towel for the morning in her hand. 'I was passing and heard ...' Her eyes widened when she saw Evelyn dressed. Evelyn rushed to the door and quietly shut it. Tilly surveyed the scattered clothes on the floor, then looked up at her mistress. She was horrified. 'You are running away?'

Evelyn touched her lips with her fingers. '*Hush*. Someone will hear you.'

'With him?'

Evelyn nodded. 'Please, Tilly, don't tell anyone. Go to bed and pretend you do not know.'

Tilly absently gave the towel to Evelyn as she tried to take in her reply. 'You will be ruined!'

Evelyn cast the towel aside. 'Don't worry about me.'

'Don't do it, Miss Evelyn. He is not worth it.' Her hands flew up to her face as a thought struck her. 'Your parents! Dear Lord … what will Sir Robert say?'

'Go to bed, Tilly,' ordered Evelyn calmly, trying to walk her to the door.

Her maid resisted. 'He will kill you. He will kill me for knowing.' Tilly broke away and wandered through the warzone of discarded clothes. She picked up a dress and a chemise at her feet, looking at each garment as if she did not know what to do with them. She turned and looked at Evelyn, the garments hanging limply from her hands, her eyes filling with bright tears. 'Please, Miss Evelyn, don't run off with him.' She began to tremble as the full enormity of the situation finally hit home.

Evelyn took the clothes from her hands and hugged her tight. 'It is going to be all right, Tilly. I love Drake and he loves me. We are going to be happy. Just go to bed and pretend you know nothing.' She felt Tilly fall limp against her and begin to sob. Her life was dictated by routine and Evelyn had just turned everything on its head. No wonder she was so distressed. 'Hush, Tilly. Hush,' soothed Evelyn. 'Don't be frightened for me. Now go to bed. In the morning go about your daily routine and raise the alarm when you are due to wake me. You do not have to be afraid. They will never know that you found me packing.'

Tilly fell silent. Eventually she withdrew from Evelyn's embrace. 'When are you going?' she asked sombrely.

'He's meeting me at midnight.'

'You shouldn't be travelling alone in the dark.'

'He is meeting me at the end of the drive. I will be quite safe.'

Tilly wiped her tears on her sleeve. She sniffed loudly and straightened, her expression was unreadable, although the blankness behind her eyes unnerved Evelyn a little. She had hurt Tilly's feelings and was paying the price. It would take time for the warmth in their friendship to return and Evelyn did not have the time to try now.

Evelyn hugged her maid for a final time, painfully aware she did not hug her back. 'One day I will visit you. I promise. Now go to bed before you are missed.'

Tilly left, silently shutting the door behind her and without saying goodbye. Evelyn listened for her footsteps to disappear, before returning to her packing. Her earlier difficulties at choosing what to take seemed unimportant now. She was running out of time and did not have the luxury of being indecisive. She selected a few important items and put them in the bag. Soon, Drake would be waiting for her at the end of the drive. She had no idea where he was planning to take her, but she did not care as long as she was with him.

Tilly fled to the laundry house before she allowed herself to burst into tears again. Miss Evelyn was leaving and she was leaving with Drake. Tilly had tried not to think of Drake Vennor since he'd left. She had even started courting the baker's son with a view to being married. Drake's sudden return had evoked old feelings she thought were a long time buried. Drake's handsome looks now made the baker's son seem a poor substitute. She hated him for coming back and reminding her of what she never had. And now he was going to destroy Miss Evelyn's life too, for that was what would happen if their plan was carried through.

A movement in the corner startled her. It was Abel, lounging on a pile of laundry with a gin bottle in his hand. He stood, swaying a little as he did so, and smiled at her.

'What are you doing here?' she snapped, hastily brushing the tears from her face.

Abel lifted the bottle in his hand. 'Warming my innards. Want some?'

Tilly eyed the bottle suspiciously, before taking it and drinking deeply. She made a face as the foul tasting liquid slid down her throat.

'Finding it difficult to find work and lodgings since Timmins sacked me.' He indicated the laundry pile with a sweep of his hand. 'This place is dry and comes with bedding. Beats sleeping in the woods.'

'Best get back to the woods. This place will be swarming with people by dawn.' Voicing the commotion and panic to come set off a new trail of tears.

Abel noticed. 'Ay, you're cryin', Tilly.' He frowned in concern. She drank some more and would have drained the bottle if Abel hadn't gently prised it from her hands. 'Steady, girl. 'Tis potent stuff. It goes straight to the 'ead. Wham bam.'

'I need it.'

'Why?'

She thought of Drake, handsome and kind, but oblivious to her feelings. She had loved him and he didn't care. He only had eyes for Miss Evelyn and was now prepared to ruin her. And Miss Evelyn didn't seem to care.

'Have you ever loved someone and no one else will ever compare?' she asked him.

Abel's eyes softened. He swallowed; his reply to her question was as gentle as a doting lover. 'Yeah, I've felt that love.'

Finally someone appeared to understand her. Buoyed up by solidarity and gin, she nodded enthusiastically. 'So have I. I think I still love Drake.' And then she told him all that he did not want to hear and more …

A hive of activity by day, at night Carrack House was peacefully silent, however, Evelyn remained wary. Despite no one being around, she knew that Carrack House was like a sleeping, ill-tempered beast. If provoked, it could wake at any moment and turn on whoever had disturbed it. A clock chimed, marking the quarter of the hour. It was Evelyn's cue to leave.

Evelyn stepped out into the corridor and began to make her way down the stairs with her bag clutched tightly in her hand. The full moon, although casting inky black shadows along her route, lit her way, whilst the family portraits that adorned the walls silently witnessed her escape. She had made it down the stairs, across the hall and through the front door before she dared pause again and draw breath.

She had managed to cross the gravel turning circle at the beginning of the drive, before she heard the first shout to raise the alarm. Another quickly followed and servants began to appear from various directions as if they had been waiting for her. Evelyn lifted her hem and bag and began to run. One handle of her bag slipped from her fingers in her panic. It became unwieldly to carry and she almost tripped as she tried to lift her hem and offset the imbalance of her bag. The bag fell from her hands. She halted and turned quickly to retrieve it, her feet sliding treacherously in the gravel as she did so, but when she saw the scattered trail of garments behind her she knew she did not have the time to collect them.

Evelyn turned and ran as fast as she could, aware she was leaving everything behind her. All she had to do was reach the end of the drive where Drake would be waiting for her and then everything would be all right. She was young and healthy and soon the servants' shouts and footfalls gradually grew muffled as she left them behind to be swallowed up in the darkness. She soon found herself passing beneath the trees that lined the drive. It was quieter here and she felt quite alone. In her confidence, she slowed to a gentle jog.

In the far distance she could hear the sound of a horse and gig turning. Drake was waiting for her. Evelyn almost managed a smile before she realised that the gig was fast approaching from the direction of the house and not from the road ahead.

Evelyn attempted to increase her speed, but the mile long race had begun to drain her of her energy. Soon every breath rasped her lungs and throat. She grew clumsy and twice stumbled on the hem of her dress. The sound of the horse and gig grew louder and she called out to Drake to warn him. Finally she passed between the large pillars of the entrance to the estate, watched by the two imposing stone lions, and stepped out onto the road beyond.

Evelyn turned back to look behind her. She could make out the shape of a gig and horse approaching, with the distinct bulky figure of her father sitting beside the driver. She turned to Drake. The road stretched to freedom in both directions, but he was nowhere to be seen.

Chapter Twenty

Evelyn imagined the scene outside her room. Her undergarments abandoned on the gravel drive of Carrack House, their lace trimmed forms appearing like fallen ghosts, twisted and white in the bright light of a winter's full moon. Tilly running down the granite steps, quietly sobbing, before beginning to gather the strewn garments that littered the driveway. She had seen the haphazard scattering and her abandoned bag with its torn handle for herself when they brought her inside. It somehow represented her life – destroyed, torn apart and a stark contrast to the orderly grounds surrounding it.

Evelyn tested the straps that tied her wrists. They continued to hold strong, tight enough to prevent movement, yet just loose enough to allow the blood to flow – not too dissimilar to her parents' care and life at Carrack House. She yelled out in frustration and was startled to hear her maid begin to sob on the other side of the door. She was not alone. Tilly would help her.

'Tilly,' she whispered, 'Tilly, help me.'

Evelyn heard fabric slide down against the door, but Tilly did not answer.

'Please, Tilly. Come in and untie me.'

'I can't, Miss Evelyn. I can't,' whimpered her maid from the other side of the door. Her voice came from near ground level, as if she was sitting on the floor. Poor Tilly, thought Evelyn.

'It's all right, Tilly,' soothed Evelyn. 'Everything is going to be all right. All you have to do is come in and untie me. No one will know it was you.' Evelyn held her breath, hoping she would change her mind.

'I can't,' Tilly replied, sobbing. Her crying grew louder as she gasped for breath between each sob. 'They have sent for Doctor Birch, Miss Evelyn.'

A chill ran through Evelyn's veins. 'Tilly,' she pleaded, twisting her wrists. 'You've got to get me out of here.'

'I'm sorry,' Tilly said. 'I am so sorry.' Evelyn strained to listen. She heard her maid stand up on the other side of the door. Any hope she had dwindled when she heard her maid's footsteps fading away. Doctor Birch. His presence still frightened her as much as it had done when she was a child. She rested her head against the back of the chair. She felt so tired. So very tired.

Evelyn woke and looked at her wrists, which were still tied to the chair. Bathed in sunlight, they felt warm, as wrens warbled and trilled loudly outside. Time had passed, morning had broken and, for a moment, she was confused how she had missed it. She heard someone clear their throat and turned her head to find Doctor Birch standing in the doorway of her bedroom looking at her. He entered and pulled up a chair.

'It is almost six o'clock. You have been asleep. How are you feeling?' he asked.

Evelyn did not reply.

'Are you hungry? Thirsty?' She nodded warily. 'Then let us remedy that straight away.' He gestured for Tilly, who had been waiting outside, to come nearer and asked for a pot of tea, two slices of bread and a dish of jam to be brought. 'What sort of jam would you like? Plum? Strawberry?' he asked, smiling. His gaze dropped to her bound wrists. 'Let us go with plum. I like plum.' Evelyn felt her cheeks burn as Tilly scampered away. She must look a sight, thought Evelyn, for Tilly could not even bear to look at her.

Doctor Birch swiftly untied her. 'You should not be trussed up like an animal, my dear,' he said kindly. 'There is no need to be afraid; I am here to help you. Would you like to use the chamber pot?' He smiled. 'Come, come, Evelyn. I have known you since you were a child. I look upon you as a daughter. There is no need to be embarrassed. Once you have relieved yourself and had something to eat and drink, you can tell me all about it.'

Evelyn did need to relieve herself, but had to use the chamber pot while he remained in the room with his back turned to her. To add to her humiliation, he asked to see its contents before the servant removed it. The inspection felt far longer than it was, and caused Evelyn to seethe inwardly, but she remained silent as she suspected that to make demands now could cost her dear.

Tilly returned with a tray, but disappeared almost immediately, leaving her alone with the man who had been a constant throughout her life. He poured her a cup and handed it to her with a sympathetic smile. The scalding tea was far too sweet, but drinking it gave her something to hide behind and helped to quench her thirst. The food, however, she could not face. She felt Doctor Birch's curious eyes watch her as she drank and suspected that he was locking away every detail in his medically focused mind, so when he began to speak again, Evelyn felt strangely relieved.

'Are you feeling a little better now?'

Evelyn tried her best to not let her trembling hands show as she returned her cup to her saucer and onto the tray. 'Yes, thank you, Doctor Birch.'

His brow creased with concern. 'You must have been greatly distressed to go to such lengths?' He lifted the pot. 'More tea, my dear?' Evelyn shook her head. He replaced the pot on the tray. 'I remember when I was your age and in love for the first time I thought the world would end if I did not make her my wife.' He chortled to himself. 'Of course, it didn't, but when one is young, everything is so much more …' he waved his hand in the air as he searched for the right word '… dramatic.'

Evelyn said nothing.

'Where were you planning to go so late at night?'

'Nowhere.'

'Your father has told me he had refused to grant his permission for you to marry an unsuitable upstart.'

'Drake is not an upstart.'

The doctor smiled. 'Drake,' he mused. 'It is a good name. A strong, no nonsense name. Is that the type of man he is?'

Evelyn nodded cautiously. 'He is a good man.'

'And were you planning to run away with Drake?'

Evelyn did not reply. Drake may have changed his mind about running away with her, but she still felt the need to protect him from her father's wrath.

Doctor Birch patted her hand. 'I am not unsympathetic, Evelyn, dear. Love is a powerful draw. But what of your cousin, Mawgan? Your father says there is an understanding between you. To be betrothed to one man and run off with another is social suicide.'

'I am not betrothed to Mawgan.'

'But there is an understanding.'

'Yes, but—'

'And this man, Drake, your father tells me he is a gardener.'

'He is a landscape gardener. His skills are much sought after.'

'But nevertheless, not of your social standing.'

'I care nothing for social standing.'

Doctor Birch raised an eyebrow. 'Evelyn, my dear, if a woman of your standing was to elope, it would mean her utter ruin. No one of worth would entertain her again. She would be turned away, her calling cards rejected. Husbands would not allow their wives to befriend her in the fear she would influence them to behave equally badly.' He leaned forward, so she could no longer avoid looking at him. 'She would be a pariah. *You* would be a pariah.'

'I would not care, if it meant I could be with the man I love.'

'And you love this man, Drake?'

She might as well confess if he was to take her seriously. 'With all my heart.'

'How well do you know him?'

'Better than I know myself.'

'Have you been meeting him?'

'Yes.'

'It must have been alone as your father does not think him suitable.'

'Yes ... occasionally.'

'More than one or two, I suspect.'

'Perhaps.'

'While you have had an understanding with your cousin?' Evelyn dropped her gaze. She could not deny it. 'You have been seeing two men at once. Have there been others?'

'No! You make it sound sordid. It was never like—'

'But you have to confess, it is unnatural for a woman to behave so wantonly.'

'I don't consider—'

'Have you fornicated?'

The question caught Evelyn off guard and robbed her of a suitable reply. Her blushing hesitation was enough to signal her guilt. Doctor Birch got up from his chair and looked down upon her.

'A woman fornicating outside of wedlock is deviant behaviour. Do you not agree, Evelyn?'

'I loved Drake. I still do.'

'You do not care that this kind of immoral behaviour, this promiscuity, will lead to your ruin?'

'My only shame is not telling Mawgan, but I did not know what was going to happen. The urge to see him—'

'This urge, you speak of, sounds unbridled. Can you control it?'

'I did not want to control it, Doctor Birch, and if I had my time over, I would ...' she searched for the right word and purposely chose Doctor Birch's ' ... *fornicate* with him again.'

'How is she?'

Doctor Birch made himself comfortable in his favourite chair and took the cup of tea offered by Lady Pendragon. He would rather it was a glass of Sir Robert's best brandy, but the day was still young and he had no plans to rush to leave yet.

'I have examined your daughter thoroughly. It is a grave situation indeed and you did the right thing to ask me to see her.' He took his time as he drunk from his cup, aware that Evelyn's parents' eyes were upon him. He placed his cup down and sat back in his chair. 'She is looking a little better now and has eaten and drunk something. You felt it necessary to bind her arms and legs. Why was that?'

Lady Pendragon looked to her husband.

'At the time we had no choice,' replied Sir Robert. 'When I found her at the end of the drive, she appeared in shock and got into the trap quite willingly. I could get no explanation from her and wondered if she was listening to me at all. When we reached the house, her demeanour changed quite suddenly. She became hysterical and refused to enter the house. In the end I ordered the staff to carry her to her room, and because I feared she would run away again, I thought it was best to restrain her.'

'How did you come to find her gone?'

'Her maid informed us of her plans. At first I did not believe her, but she seemed so sincere and fearful for Evelyn's reputation that I grew concerned. I could have locked Evelyn in her room, but in truth I did not want to think she was capable of such behaviour and did not want to give her ideas where none may be forming. The maid was proved right. Our worst fears played out.'

'What is wrong with her, Doctor Birch?' asked Lady Pendragon. 'Evelyn has been so well since her last bout of hysteria. What has made her behave like this?'

'I'm afraid it is more serious than a young fancy of love.'

'Love!' scoffed Sir Robert. 'What does she know about love?'

'Hush, Robert,' soothed Lady Pendragon. 'Let Doctor Birch finish what he was saying.'

Doctor Birch swiped at a fleck on his trousers. 'Evelyn is a slave to unnatural urges. Urges that if left unbridled will lead to prolonged promiscuity. She does not have the insight to see that such immoral behaviour will lead to her ruin and social suicide and, more worryingly, when persuaded that this will be the case, does not care.'

'Promiscuity?'

'She has lost her maidenhood.'

'Dear Lord!' cried Sir Robert. His wife began to sob in the corner, and rightly so. 'Are you sure?'

'She told me so.'

Lady Pendragon, shocked that her daughter would discuss such things, gasped into her handkerchief.

'But she is to be engaged to my nephew,' floundered Sir Robert.

Doctor Birch looked gravely at him over the steeple of his fingertips. 'In my opinion, there are only two cures for her immoral weaknesses. The first, a firm husband who can curb her wanton ways.'

'Mawgan will not want her now.'

Doctor Birch smiled inwardly. If only Sir Robert knew the real truth about his precious nephew. He was, after all, just an illegitimate child with a prostitute's blood running through his veins. Yet, since Nicholas's death, it had given Doctor Birch a queer sense of pleasure to know that the brat had, by sheer luck of a family tragedy, become the only surviving male Pendragon and would inherit the baronetcy title. The pleasure had only intensified when he'd heard that Mawgan was to marry Evelyn and lay claim to Carrack Estate. The brat would become the wealthiest man in Cornwall, and he had engineered it. No one must ever find out, of course. If it was discovered he had swapped a baby at birth his reputation would be destroyed. Even so, to know that one had a hand in such a transformation … like a spiritual healer who had saved a soul.

Doctor Birch shrugged a shoulder. 'The other way, of course, is an admission to hospital.'

Sir Robert looked at him. 'An asylum?'

'Evelyn is afflicted with weak inclinations and a nervous disposition, but I would not wish to see her locked away with lunatics,' said Doctor Birch, looking at Sir Robert over his glasses. He smiled to reassure him. 'Have no fear, Robert. I have Evelyn's best interest at heart. I know of a private clinic run by a colleague of mine. He is an alienist and his clinic is a beautiful manor, situated north of the River Tamar. I will sign the emergency commitment papers today and take her there myself. I have every faith that she can be cured of her ... urges and will make a fine wife and mother one day.'

Lady Pendragon sniffed. 'What if she should marry?'

Her husband shook his head in despair. 'Mawgan will not want her when he hears what she has done.'

'Do you have to tell him?' she asked.

'Yes, I must, as word will get out soon enough. We can only pray that he will forgive her, marry her and save her from herself.'

'And if Mawgan won't marry her, what then?' asked Lady Pendragon. 'Could the man who has taken advantage of her recklessness be held accountable?'

'What? And have a gardener as a son-in-law! I would rather her illness was treated than leave her in the hands of the man responsible for corrupting her.'

Evelyn looked at her fingers. She had paused in her frantic writing to dip the nib of her pen into the inkwell, but as she attempted to remove the excess ink, her hand was trembling before her eyes. She took a deep breath to calm herself, tightened her grip, and began writing again. She was blotting the letter when Tilly finally arrived.

'Where have you been, Tilly?' asked Evelyn. She folded the letter and hastily scribbled an address on the envelope. She made a mistake, scribbled it out and started again. 'I've been ringing for you,' she said, without looking up.

'I'm sorry, Miss Evelyn.'

'No matter. You are here now.' Evelyn got up and left her desk. 'I want you to do something for me, Tilly.'

Tilly took a step back. 'I don't think I can, miss.'

'Of course you can. It is just a letter.' She held out the ill-written envelope. Tilly looked at it as if she had been handed a cowpat. 'It's untidy, but I don't have time to write it again,' said Evelyn, placing the crumpled letter in Tilly's hand and holding it there.

'They are going to send me away to a madhouse, Tilly!' Evelyn was on the verge of laughing at the stupidity of it all. 'I'm not mad. I'm not, really I'm not.' Dear Lord, the more I protest the more I sound like a woman on the edge, thought Evelyn. She realised she was hurting Tilly with the fierceness of her grasp. She let go and stepped back to give her maid some space. She could see from Tilly's face she was scaring her with her desperation. She tried to calm herself. 'I need to get word to Drake. I need to tell him what they plan to do.'

Tilly turned the letter in her hand. 'What good would it do?'

Evelyn felt like shaking her. She was running out of time and no one around her seemed to understand.

'Because he loves me.'

'He was not waiting at the end of the drive for you! Why wasn't he waiting for you?'

Evelyn had asked herself the same question a thousand times. She began to pace the room. 'I don't know, but he is my only hope. Doctor Birch says I show immoral behaviour and wants to send me to a private clinic.' She scoffed. 'He probably has invested money in the clinic and my admission will earn him a pretty penny. I need to escape, Tilly.'

'You can't escape. They will only catch you.'

'Then I am doomed. How do I prove that I am not mad when the world around me is madder?' Evelyn turned to Tilly, tears stabbing her eyes. 'Drake will help me.'

'I heard them talking. They said if you were to marry …'

'Who? Drake?' There was that wild laugh again. 'They would rather I was shut away than marry Drake.'

Tilly shook her head. 'No, your cousin.'

'Mawgan? I can't, not now. It would not be fair to either of us.'

'What choice do you have?'

'I could still leave with Drake.'

'Damn Drake!' shouted Tilly.

Her outburst startled Evelyn. She had never seen Tilly lose her temper before.

Tilly sighed. 'I'm sorry. If I give this letter to Drake and he is unable to help you, will you consider marrying your cousin?'

'Mawgan will not ask me now.'

'But if he did?'

The madhouse or Mawgan? The choices open to her made Evelyn feel sick with anxiety.

'I would have to marry Mawgan,' she said finally. 'But Drake will come for me,' she added hopefully. 'He has to.'

Tilly returned within the hour. Evelyn had hoped for a quick reply, but an hour was far sooner than she had dared hope. She eagerly took Drake's letter from her and opened it. The sight of his familiar hand instantly brought memories of the times she had helped him with his studies. His writing had not changed at all, and it was as if he had stepped into the room and stood by her side. If only the words had given her hope.

Dear Evie,

I am so sorry for the way we parted. I want to explain my behaviour, but there is so little time and so much to say.

Recent events have made it impossible for me to stay. I hope and pray that my departure will, in the end, be a good thing for the both of us. Deep down, I believe we both know that the world is not ready for us to be together. You do not deserve to endure such suffering, so it is a good thing that I leave now. One day you will come to your senses and see me for who I really am.

I will think of you every day I draw breath. I will work hard and strive to be a better man so I can be worthy of knowing you. One day I hope we will meet again and you will look kindly upon me, for I have loved you from the first day I saw you hiding behind the rose bushes, with ribbons in your hair.

My dearest darling, there is so little time left. You have been my greatest friend, my growing passion, my only love. I love you, Evie. Please forgive me.

Drake.

Evelyn blinked away her tears in the hope she would find an offer of help in his letter, but the words on the page remained the same. Drake was unwilling to help her. She was on her own.

Chapter Twenty-One

Evelyn's head broke the surface of the lake, turning its glistening surface into a cascade of ripples radiating towards him. She was smiling, skimming the water with a sweep of her hand in order to spray a circle around her. She looked at him and beckoned for him to join her. He shook his head, smiling and she made a face, before diving below the surface and leaving him with a tantalising glimpse of her bottom as it momentarily broke the surface.

Moments later, she resurfaced again. She was nearer this time. So near he could see the smooth skin of her shoulders dotted with beads of water. She had a happy glow on her cheeks as she looked at him through her lashes. The teasing glint in her eyes held him captive and unable to speak. Silently he watched her slowly rise up from the water and begin to walk towards him. His groin ached for her as the water level fell away to reveal the curves of her body. She wore a chemise, which clung like a second skin to her thighs and breasts, and a corset, which accentuated her seductively swaying hips. She lifted her arms towards him and smiled. Every fibre of his body wanted her and he was powerless to resist.

He entered the lake. Immediately the cold water began to seep through his trousers and chill his skin. Despite his efforts, he could not get nearer. Her smile gradually faded and was replaced by fear as the distance between them appeared to grow. He tried harder and harder, until a white, blinding light stabbed his eyes and forced him to stop. He attempted to lift an arm to shield his face, but the pain he experienced made him cry out and shocked him awake.

Up above, fat, grey clouds hung in the sky. He could not see very much. It was as if he was peeping through a slit in a fence trying to view the world beyond. He tentatively touched his face, knowing something was wrong and found that his eyelids, jaw and lips were badly swollen and tender to touch. There was a metallic taste in his mouth and a piercing pain in his head. How had he come to be in such a state, and why here? He needed to find out where he was and find help, before he grew much weaker.

Like a drunken man, he attempted to lift his head to see his surroundings. His head moved precariously until, exhausted, he let it drop again. He rested, trying to process what he had seen. He was by a river and his legs were partially in the water and numb with cold. The area was secluded and overgrown, with no obvious footpath cutting through it. If he was to survive, it was up to him to find the help he needed as no one would find him here. But in what direction would he have to go?

He rolled over to see behind him. A sharp pain in his chest robbed him of his breath momentarily. Grimacing through his agony, he looked upwards and saw a large sloping embankment. At the top he caught flickering glimpses of a carriage passing along a track behind the trees. Help was at the top and climbing the slope was his only chance of survival. He rolled onto his stomach and attempted to get onto his knees. He failed. His knees were too painful and his hands too swollen to support his weight. A distinct heel shaped bruise on each one told him he had been in no accident. He had been severely beaten and left for dead. But by whom? He remembered waiting for Evie, but little else, except laughter. Someone had been laughing.

He shuffled around to the water's edge, washed the taste of blood from his mouth and drank away his thirst. Finally, he was ready to start the ascent. He crawled on his belly away from the river, supporting his ribs with one arm and levering himself along using the elbow of the other. Inch by inch, he crawled through the broken twigs, leaves and moss that carpeted the muddy ground. As the gradient grew steeper, the terrain grew more littered with broken branches and exposed roots. He made use of a piece of wood to stab into the ground to give him leverage. With each stab he heard his attacker's mocking laughter. With each agonising foot of ground he covered, he thought of Evie, worried and waiting for him, wondering why he had let her down – again. The distress she must have felt helped him ignore his own. He had to let her know he had been there waiting for her, even if it meant he died trying.

'Are you going to tell me why Sir Robert called this morning?'

Mawgan dragged his eyes away from the coach window and settled on his friend's face as he sat opposite him in the cramped carriage. David's smile lifted at one corner, in line with the neat eyebrow on the same side. He appeared nonchalant, but Mawgan had come to know David's mind very well. He often feigned disinterest when in reality he was like a horse straining at the bit.

They had met at university, where similar interests had brought them together. Mawgan had always envied David's easy banter and ability to make friends, skills he sadly lacked. He could not remember a time when he did not feel uncomfortable in company. It was as if the world walked a different plane to him and he was happy to extradite himself away from society rather than experience the pain of emersion into it. A world where everyone seemed to be at odds to how he thought and felt.

His visits to Carrack House were different. Nicholas and Evelyn did not make fun of his social ineptness. Perhaps it was because he was a year older than Nicholas and they gave him the respect children so often give to another older child, after all a single year to a child is worth ten to an adult. He even wondered if they empathised with him as they too felt uncomfortable in their own surroundings. Having a hysterical mother and a father who wanted nothing short of perfection were hard to live with. However, the rest of Mawgan's life had been fairly lonely and out of kilter with the world until David had become his friend. They had parted company when he had set out on his journey around the Empire, but David remained his friend and was the first to welcome him home. He owed the man a great deal and that included being truthful.

'He came to tell me that Evelyn has disgraced herself and he felt it only right to inform me before I request her hand in marriage.'

The curve in David's smile faded. 'I'm sorry, Mawgan. I did not know the reason for his visit was on such serious matters. What did the Angel do?'

Mawgan could not help smiling at David's nickname for Evelyn. David remained irked that after all these years he had still not been introduced to Evelyn and, in his usual spikey wit, had named her after the title of Coventry Patmore's poem of the perfect Victorian woman. Indeed, she was the ideal woman to marry, or at least had been. She was beautiful, healthy, young, of good heritage and rich. Her father had wished it, his father had hoped for it and Mawgan had fallen into line as no alternative presented itself to him on his return from his travels. Now it appears she was not so perfect after all. He should feel shocked, upset, angry. Strangely he felt none of those emotions.

'What did she do that was so disgraceful?'

'She attempted to elope with the gardener.'

David threw back his head and laughed. After a moment he had the good grace to look a little sheepish. 'I am sorry, Mawgan. I hope the gardener is a handsome fellow.'

'He is. I have had the pleasure of meeting him. He has a face that turns heads.'

David sobered. 'You do not seem upset.'

'I'm not sure what I feel.'

'Perhaps you did not love her after all.'

Mawgan considered his friend's words. 'I have known her all my life. Perhaps I am in shock. I think I feel ... sad for her. Are you surprised?'

David's eyes softened. 'Not at all. You would, wouldn't you?'

'I don't know what you mean.'

'I mean—'

Mawgan lifted a hand to parry his words. 'I have never disgraced myself and I plan never to do so.'

'Not even on your travels?' Mawgan did not honour his teasing with an answer. 'Your father did his job well. The Pendragon sense of duty is so overpowering I can actually smell it. I have never met Angel, but at least she attempted to fight against her duty in search for love. I admire her spirit. I am right, am I not? You were going to marry her because of duty, not because you loved her.'

Mawgan gazed out of the window. 'We got on well together.'

'But you did not love her or ever will. You don't have that in you.'

'Do people marry for love these days? Did they ever?'

'They should.' David smacked his friend's thigh. 'At least you are now free of this obligation.'

Mawgan scowled at his friend and moved his leg away. He suddenly felt lost. What would the future hold for him now?

'Let us not talk any more about her,' said Mawgan. He felt David studying him. 'I mean it, David. Let us talk of other matters.'

David conceded with a shrug of his shoulders and leant forward to look out at the passing countryside. 'Where are we going?' he asked as scattered country hovels entered and left his view.

'I have had word that my mother's old maid is dying.'

'How does this concern you? Do you plan to pay her a deathbed visit?'

'I feel I have no choice. She may be dying, but she is not going quietly and is using the time she has left to unburden herself. She has asked to see me.'

'You could have refused.'

'I was about to, but her family was insistent and I felt I had no choice but to hear it for myself.'

'What is she saying?'

Mawgan banged on the roof for the carriage to slow down. 'I will tell you more after my visit.' He softened his reply with a smile. 'I promise.'

David waited in the coach as Mawgan knocked on the door of the small, granite house where his late mother's maid now lived. The door was immediately opened by a woman he presumed to be Mellin's daughter. She had been expecting him and subserviently stepped aside. On entering, he paused for his eyes to grow accustomed to the dimly lit room. A deeply recessed, north-facing window brought little light into the room, whilst a lingering damp smell continued to claw at the air despite evidence of a small fire in the grate. The fire, he suspected, had been built for his benefit alone.

A makeshift bed had been set up near to it and Mawgan could just make out the shape of an old woman beneath its blankets. He heard the death rattle in her chest as a frail arm, sleeved in sagging, fragile flesh, lifted and waved for him to come nearer. He approached and recognised Mellin instantly. Her face may have aged, her body may have shrivelled, but he could never forget her watchful eyes. His childhood and youth had been plagued by them. It was as if she knew something about him and was constantly waiting. Perhaps now he would finally learn what it was.

'Hello, Mellin. I have had word you wished to see me.'

She squinted in the dark. 'Master Mawgan … is that you?'

He nodded and accepted the wooden chair brought to him by the scruffy, flustered woman who had shown him in.

'I do apologise, Master Mawgan,' said Mellin's daughter, positioning the chair behind him. 'It is dreadful what Mam has been saying. I've told her to stop, but she won't.' A sense of unease grew in Mawgan's stomach as he looked at her crimson face and realised she was unable to meet his gaze. 'Pay no heed to her. I don't.'

'Pay no heed to what?' asked Mawgan, but it was too late, Mellin's daughter was already leaving and showed no willingness to remain. He carefully sat down and looked at the old woman. Her watery green eyes stared up at him. He recognised her watchful gaze and felt like a child again. Damn those eyes!

'I remember the night you were born,' said Mellin. Her voice was barely a whisper, but the words were clear. 'It was the month of June but it was blowing a gale. The wind so strong it uprooted the old cedar on the road from Cardin.' Her gaze left his face and she stared into space. 'We were all worried that Doctor Birch would not arrive in time,' she finished lamely.

The old woman lay quietly. Mawgan waited impatiently, forced to listen to each breath as it bubbled and crackled with each rise and fall. He had the urge to cough for her to clear away the infection. The waiting was intolerable and he began to wonder if that was all she had to tell him. He was about to leave, when she drew a deep breath and started to speak again.

'I would never have believed it if I did not see it with my own eyes.'

'See what?'

'That you are not a true Pendragon. Pendragon men are real men. They have an obsession with their bloodline. It is what drives them. You don't have that.'

The woman's mind has turned, thought Mawgan. He had wasted his journey. Even so, the unease in the pit of his stomach would not go away.

'I don't understand.' His voice sounded feeble to his own ears, but that was how he felt, feeble – and vulnerable.

'I have watched you grow. I know what others do not know.' She turned her eyes on him and he felt as if she had stripped him bare. 'I know who you really are. I know, but the question is, do you?'

Mawgan sat back in his chair. Her breath smelt putrid and he did not care for what the old hag was implying.

Mellin reached out and touched his arm. Her feathery light touch felt alien and he had the urge to recoil. He would have done, but she smiled and he was suddenly reminded why his mother had been so loyal to her maid. Mellin had been a constant throughout his life and her devotion to his family was without question. Despite the poison she was spewing, she meant no harm. She was telling him these things to protect him. Not to harm him. Unfortunately, in her poor health and eagerness to speak to him, she had been less discerning in who she had confided in. Whatever she was trying to say could easily sprout wings and be all over the countryside by the end of the month. As if she read his thoughts, she spoke again. For someone who was dying, she had plenty to say.

'I hear you are courting Miss Evelyn Pendragon.' She gave a feeble squeeze of his arm. 'That is a good thing. It will pour water on the fire and keep you safe from harm. Life is cruel. Pendragon marrying Pendragon. No one can question that.'

'Question what?'

'That you should have no place on God's Earth. Marry Sir Robert's heir and you will own everyone. No one will dare speak against you.'

'You think I have enemies?'

'You will have more than most. I was there the night you were put in your mother's arms and I have watched you grow. Marry Miss Evelyn Pendragon and you will be safe from rumour and people who wish you harm.'

Mawgan insisted on leaving the house through the backyard. He needed time, a snatched moment to himself, before the prying eyes of the village could see him. From his countenance and posture, back stiff as a rod with an aristocratic tilt to his chin, Mellin's daughter had no way of knowing the turmoil he felt inside. Relieved that the meeting had gone well and her mother seemed at peace, she scurried back inside and left Mawgan alone.

Mawgan's legs buckled as soon as the door shut behind him. He caught at the yard's wooden gate for support and stood for a moment, trembling and terrified of what was to come. Mellin's protective but watchful eyes, which had haunted his childhood, now held meaning. He had always suspected there was something different about him and today, in a whispered death rattle, she had spoken his fears. It was as if he had written down her deathbed confession for her. He was not like the other men of the Pendragon line. He was not a true Pendragon.

'My God! You look like a ghost!' exclaimed David as Mawgan climbed in the coach to sit opposite him. 'What did the old woman say?'
'Nothing that made sense,' replied Mawgan. He sat back in the seat, a deep frown cutting his brow in two. He should win an accolade for his acting role.

'Were they just ramblings of a dying woman?'

'Yes, something like that,' he said, noncommittally. He didn't want to confide in David. The topic was too raw and the experience, which had left him feeling violated and exposed to society, was too recent. David did not press him further. He had come to know Mawgan well and knew when to retreat. The carriage ride home was a gloomy, silent affair.

Chapter Twenty-Two

A heavy mist hung in the air, dampening the skin and casting a fine veil over the passing landscape. The farmer flicked the reins and encouraged his pony to trot faster. He was in a hurry as he had promised his neighbour he would return both cart and pony by milking time. The mist had hampered his progress, as much of his journey had been through the valley. Now, on higher ground, his vision was a little clearer and he was finally hopeful that he could make up the time before the mist swallowed up the track ahead again.

He frowned. In the distance he could just make out a boulder blocking the track. He would have to move it if he was going to get by. As he approached he slowly eased up the pony until he brought it to a stop. He jumped down from the cart, grumbling at his bad luck.

As he approached, the boulder took on the more familiar shape of a man. He was lying on his stomach, his body wet from the heavy rain overnight, but his lips cracked for lack of something to drink. Whatever time he had fallen, he had not moved since before the rain. He saw some bruising on his face and attempted to rouse him. He received no response and suspected he was already dead. He turned him over and, for the first time, saw the full extent of his injuries. The man's face was swollen to twice the normal size, whilst a gaping wound split one eyebrow in two. The farmer shook his head in disbelief as he allowed his gaze to wander over the man's body. He was someone's son. He could not leave him here to rot.

He knelt down to cradle the man's head in his arms. He felt hot – too hot for a corpse.

'I've got you, boy. I'm going to take you home. Wake up, son. Where shall I take you?'

The man's lips moved, but nothing came out.

'You will have to speak louder, boy,' said the farmer, leaning closer and turning one ear to his lips. 'What are you called?'

'Vennor,' croaked the man. 'Son of … lay preacher's widow … in Perran.'

'That explains how I came to find you,' replied the farmer, as he prepared to lift him into the cart. 'You have God on your side.'

Drake opened his eyes and looked around the familiar bedroom of his childhood. It felt odd to be there as a man. It was as if he had stepped back in time, an interloper that should not be there. His mother came in carrying a tray. She glanced up and almost dropped it when she saw Drake give her a fragile smile.

'Hello.' Drake was surprised how hoarse his voice sounded, but tried not to show it.

'You have been awake several times,' said his mother, putting down the tray, all the while her gaze unable to leave his, 'but I have never seen you smile or—'

'Or what?'

She sat down next to him, in a chair he suspected she had spent a lot of time in lately. 'Or look like you are with us.'

'Us?'

'The man who found you, Albert, has been dropping in regularly to see you, and then there is Doctor Thomas, who has kindly waived his fee and visited you often.'

'Have I been ill?'

'Yes. You were found three weeks ago. We all thought you were going to die.' His mother took his hand. He looked down and was surprised to see a faded yellow bruise covering the back of his hand. 'What happened to you, Drake? Were you hit by a carriage?'

Drake tried to remember. His mind felt foggy and disorganised. He attempted to make sense of the puzzle in his head, but found the process overwhelming. It must have showed on his face because his mother came to his rescue.

'Don't tire yourself, Drake. There is plenty of time for you to remember. Here, have some soup.' She lifted a spoon to his lips.

'I can feed myself.' He reached for the spoon, but discovered he was far weaker than he had anticipated. The spoon tilted in his clumsy grasp, spilling the soup onto his blanket. 'I'm sorry.'

His mother quickly mopped it up. 'Don't worry about that. At least you wanted to try this time. I try to get you to eat and drink each time you wake, but this is the first time you have asked to do it yourself.'

'I don't remember being awake.'

'You were awake enough to take some water and thin broth, nothing more. I am afraid you are nothing but skin and bone now.' She smiled. 'I will need to feed you up and get some meat on those arms again.'

His mother fed him the rest of the soup. It tasted good and Drake was pleased that he had managed to eat it all. He had made his mother happy and from looking at the dark circles beneath her eyes and her unkempt hair, she was in much need of it.

'I need to get better to start earning money again,' said Drake.

'Don't start worrying about that. Sir Robert will have to wait until you are better.'

'I won't be returning to Carrack House again.'

'Why?'

'My designs are no longer needed.' The insurmountable puzzle in his head began to fall into place. One memory at a time, quicker and quicker, with surprising ease. Evie! I was waiting for Evie! What must she think of me?

'I need to go somewhere,' said Drake, pushing away the covers on his bed. The effort exhausted him.

'You need to rest,' said his mother sternly. 'You are not going anywhere. When you are well, then we can talk about earning money again.'

Drake sat back against the pillow. She was right, he felt as weak as a kitten and would be no use to anyone, but he needed to get word to Evie.

'I would like to send a letter to Carrack House.' His mother threw him a questioning look. 'Miss Evelyn may wish to have one of my designs.' It was a lie, but he would have to address the letter to Evie and as he was in no fit state to send it, he would have to rely on his mother.

His mother picked up the tray. 'There is no rush. You can write when they return.'

'Return? What do you mean?'

His mother left his bedside and headed towards the door. 'They are touring Europe for their honeymoon. They left shortly after the wedding breakfast.'

Dare he ask who? His throat was too full of his heart to ask the question.

'Miss Evelyn married her cousin, Mawgan Pendragon yesterday,' his mother answered his unasked question, oblivious to the pain she was causing. 'The weather was sunny, although there was always the threat of dark clouds on the horizon. But it all passed very well, so I hear.'

Drake listened to his mother's footsteps descend the stairs. Her parting news, no more than village gossip, had killed him inside. He pressed his head back into the pillow as he felt an overwhelming, heavy blanket of loss settle over him. Its weight was unbearable, its darkness was draining. He closed his eyes and gritted his teeth, bracing himself against its onslaught, but his defences were weak. A single tear escaped and trickled, unheeded, down his cheek to the corner of his mouth. Its brackish flavour seeped between his lips, as if to mock his pain.

Drake looked at the reflection staring back at him. True, the shape of his face was normal again and his teeth were intact, but the left side of his face had changed – irreversibly. A thick vertical scar divided his left eyebrow. It was as if he had been branded as a troublemaker. Who would employ his services now? he thought. It was not the only sign of his beating. He was blind in his left eye. He should have guessed on the first day he attempted to feed himself. It was not only his weakness that had made him spill the soup. He had misjudged the distance, something he would have to learn to overcome. He looked at his left eye. Its black centre, usually round, now had an odd, keyhole shape. It gave him the appearance of not being from this world. That was how he felt inside, a ghost of his former self.

'I think your war wounds make you look rather dashing,' said his mother from behind him. He had not been aware she was watching.

'You see a dashing man. I see a man who has lost.' He picked up his father's walking stick and turned it carefully within his hand.

'You do not think you were hit by a carriage, do you? Who would beat you so badly?'

Drake looked up at his mother's reflection in the mirror. 'I have asked myself the very same question.' He turned away to avoid looking at her pained expression and limped to the door. His jaw tightened with each painful step.

'Where are you going?' asked his mother.

'Out. To drink away the pain.'

Drake scraped his heel through the sawdust on the floor of the Rose and Crown to reveal the wooden floorboard beneath. He harrumphed at the colour then returned his attention back to his stout. He narrowed his eyes to study his glass. Just as he thought, they shared the same colour, both black as night.

Despite having the money and attire to be accepted into the saloon bar, he had chosen anonymity before comfort and had spent most of the day drinking in the taproom. The crowded patronage and poor light helped him to hide amongst the labourers and unfortunates who loved drink more than life, whilst the drink and hard wooden benches helped him to wallow in his misfortune.

He carefully reached for his glass, fearing he would misjudge the distance. This time he did not and congratulated himself inwardly when he grasped the glass. He had adapted to his blindness two hours before, it was the effects of alcohol that was his new battle now. He triumphantly lifted his glass, before draining it in one and shouting for another. Another stout followed and another. His thoughts turned into thick molasses whilst his head nodded and swayed as he looked about the crowded public house. A sea of faces and bodies surrounded him, their voices a constant tangle of words with the occasional burst of laughter.

One burst of laughter sounded louder than the rest and emanated from deep within the throng of people crowding the bar. The laughter sounded familiar, causing Drake to frown as he searched the depths of his memory. The taste of blood came to mind and the sharp, painful jabs from a boot covered in mud. He heard the laughter again and was reminded of the feel of grit rasping at his cheek and pain throbbing in his head. He recalled the blackness and tumbling, faster and faster, as the sound of laughter grew fainter in the distance. It must be his attacker and he was somewhere in the inn. Drake reached for his stick and struggled to his feet, before lurching forward into the crowd. He attempted to push his way past the wall of bodies. Drinks were spilt and tempers quickly flared, but no one moved aside.

Drake's frustration grew as he realised no one seemed to understand how important it was for him to get through. He forgot the injury to his leg and lifted his stick to beat them back. His leg gave way at the extra strain and he stumbled, falling heavily against a table and knocking over carefully nursed beers. He lay amongst the spillage and broken glasses. Angry faces looked down on him and accused him of being trouble. The victim seeking justice had become the villain. Drake began to laugh at the irony of it all, flaring tempers even more. Rough hands grabbed him and before he knew what was happening, he was tumbling from the public house door and into the road outside.

Drake opened his eyes and saw the hem of a serviceable dress in front of him. He lifted his gaze to see Tilly looking down at him.

'How long have you been sitting here?' she asked.

Drake bowed his head and stared at the grass at his feet. The bright sky and dull ache that filled his head made it hard to look up at her. Moving his head also made him feel sick.

'An hour, maybe more. Since being thrown out of the Crown and Rose.'

'Rose and Crown.'

Drake nodded carefully. 'That's the one.' He wanted to be left alone, but Tilly had other ideas.

'You shouldn't be sitting on a grave. It's disrespectful.'

Drake smiled to himself. 'It is my father's. I'm sure he wouldn't mind.'

Tilly read the gravestone. 'Richard Vennor. Born 1837. Lay preacher of this parish.' She looked at Drake. 'Would he mind if I sat down too?' Drake shrugged and soon Tilly was sitting beside him. He waited for her to scold him on his appearance, but when nothing came he risked looking up at her. She looked worried.

'I must look a mess,' said Drake.

Tilly nodded. 'You look terrible.'

'Mother says my injuries make me look dashing,' he tried to smile, but failed. 'Mothers are often blind to their children's faults,' he finished lamely.

'Your mother speaks the truth, as only mothers can, but you are in need of a wash, shave and a good night's sleep.'

They sat in silence for a moment, Drake staring at the grass, Tilly staring at him.

'Why did she marry him, Tilly? We loved each other.'

'I know.'

He looked at her. 'Did you know we were going to run away together?'

Tilly swallowed and nodded. 'She told me.'

'I was attacked while I waited for her. She must have been so upset to find me not there.'

'She was, but she is now married, Drake. Forget her and move on with your life.'

'Why didn't she find out why I was not waiting for her, Tilly? I thought she loved me, but instead she punishes me by marrying someone else.' Drake cradled his throbbing head in his hands. Finding no relief, he lifted his face again to stare at the trees lining the graveyard. 'I didn't realise her feelings ran so shallow, Tilly, or that she had so little faith in me.' He looked at Tilly and was surprised to see that her eyes were filled with tears. At least she understood his pain. 'We would have been married by now, Tilly. We were going to rent a property until we found one of our own.'

'I cared for her too, Drake, but her family would never have accepted your marriage.'

'She knew that, but she wanted to be with me anyway. That is how much she loved me. At least, that's what I thought.'

'She did love you, Drake.'

'It doesn't feel like it,' he grumbled. 'She didn't try to find out what happened.' He was beginning to sound like a miserable child and he despised himself for it. Yet, losing her to someone else hurt so much.

'She tried.'

Drake shook his head. 'Not hard enough.' He picked up a blade of grass and began to strip it of its seeds. 'They must have been waiting for me. Beaten and left me for dead to teach me a lesson not to rise above my station.' But how did they know? His thoughts and final conclusion sobered him. He lifted his gaze to meet Tilly's.

'I didn't know you would be hurt. I did what I thought was right, Drake.'

'Did you tell her father?' Tilly nodded. Drake couldn't believe it. 'Why?'

'I cared for you both. Running away with you would have destroyed you both!'

'I *am* destroyed!' shouted Drake. 'And so is Evie! Mawgan will never love her like I love her.' Drake leapt to his feet and steadied himself on his father's gravestone. His head began to throb with pulsating pain, but he wanted to know what she knew. 'Tell me everything!' Tilly stood to leave but Drake grabbed her arm. '*Everything!*' demanded Drake.

He listened, with mounting horror, as Tilly told him her part in it. How she had found Evie packing and learnt of their elopement. How, brave on gin, she had found the courage to tell Sir Robert to protect Evie from herself. At first Sir Robert had refused to believe her, she told him, but then he had changed his mind.

Tilly began to sob when she recounted Evie's attempts to leave and how she was caught and carried, kicking and screaming, to her room. 'They tied her to a chair, Drake,' she sobbed. 'I couldn't believe they were treating her that way. Doctor Birch eventually untied her.' Drake waited for her to continue, his throat too full to speak. 'She refused to deny her love for you, Drake,' sniffed Tilly, as she dabbed her nose with a handkerchief. 'It would have been better if she blamed you for her seduction, but she didn't. She was proud of loving you, Drake, but it did her no good in the end.'

'What do you mean?'

'Doctor Birch diagnosed her as morally defective. He wanted her admitted to a private clinic.' Drake clutched the headstone. He needed to feel the pain in his nails to tell him he was not dreaming. 'Her parents were reluctant. Her only other option was to marry her cousin. Miss Evelyn was terrified she was going to be sent away. The Rest Cure still gave her nightmares. She wrote a letter to you, pleading for help.'

'I received no letter.'

'I destroyed it. Marrying Mawgan Pendragon was her only real hope, but she still believed you would come for her. I had to convince her you no longer cared.'

'How did you do that?'

'I gave her the letter you gave me when you were leaving to be a journeyman. I had kept it all these years.'

'Why didn't you give it to her when I asked you to?'

'Because I wanted her to grow to hate you. I wanted to avoid this happening.'

Drake turned away to look at the swaying trees around them. He couldn't bear to look at her any more. 'So she married Mawgan because she thought I did not stay to help her.'

'Yes. The marriage almost did not happen.'

'Did she change her mind?' asked Drake, despising the sound of hope in his voice. What was the point of feeling hopeful when he knew she had married and was out of his reach? He turned round to see Tilly shaking her head.

'No, I'm not sure she ever really made up her mind,' said Tilly, standing up. 'Sir Robert felt it was his duty to inform her cousin that she had attempted to elope. All the staff thought Mawgan would withdraw from their courtship, being a proud gentleman and having a reputation of his own to protect.

'We heard nothing from him so Doctor Birch arranged for the clinic attendants to collect Miss Evelyn a few days later. It was terrible. As they escorted her from the house to the waiting carriage, her mother began to cry and her father locked himself in his study. Neither could watch. Then her cousin arrived and everything changed. Miss Evelyn did not resist and any doubts she had were never spoken of again. They were married as soon as the banns were called. He saved her, Drake. They are a married couple now. I am not proud of my part in it, but it has worked out for the best.'

'Best for who?' challenged Drake as he swung around to face her. He searched Tilly's face for a reply. She was worried too. He could see the self-doubt in her eyes. He would answer the question for her for he wanted her to know the damage she had done. That they had all done. 'It did not work out the best for me, Tilly, and if I know Mawgan, Evie will not be happy either. You have meddled for your own selfish reasons, so don't try to sugar-coat your deception. You have betrayed the very people you cared about. I hope your actions play on your happiness, just as they have destroyed mine.'

Chapter Twenty-Three

Drake set his walking cane against the wall and attempted a step without it. His knee felt weak, but at least it did not buckle as it had done before. He took another step and another, the muscle of his thigh tightened; he took a deep breath and willed it to relax before retracing his steps back to his cane and reaching for it. He grasped it without misjudging the distance. Things were improving. It was time he returned to work.

'Leaving?' asked his mother a week later. 'Where will you go? When?'

'Tomorrow.' Drake showed his mother the letter he had received that morning. 'Mr Morley needs someone to oversee his designs and he has asked if I would like to take it on.'

'Who is Mr Morley?' asked his mother, taking the letter from him to read it.

'A prominent landscape architect. He has designed some improvements to the Earl of Buckinghamshire's parkland and was midway through overseeing its construction, when he was taken with a wasting illness. It is a good opportunity for me and will concentrate my mind.'

'Are you well enough?'

'I have improved, which is all I can expect for now,' said Drake.

His mother chewed her bottom lip as she watched her son limp towards the door. 'Where are you going now?'

'There is someone I wish to say goodbye to before I leave.' Drake turned and looked at his mother's pained expression. 'Don't fret. It is not who you think it is. She is married. There is no place in her life for me now.'

White bulbous clouds cast a chilly shadow over the cemetery, whilst a strong breeze rustled the leaves of the trees that lined its three boundary walls. Drake carefully made his way up the large granite steps, which led up to the graveyard and followed the path around the grey, empty, church to the cemetery beyond. Drake paused and looked across at the grey headstones, which varied in size and grandeur, each one reflecting the depths of the deceased relative's pockets and standing in the world. Today, no one visited them. The cemetery was empty and each grave appeared as abandoned and as lonely as the next. Drake felt the sorrow that emanated from each story of their death. However, he was glad there was no one around. He had no wish to make small talk today. He had come to visit his father's grave and say his goodbyes.

He found Timmins' grave under the trees. It was just a mound of earth as it was too early for a gravestone. He had heard that Sir Robert was going to provide one. He would not object. To do so would cause folk to ask questions and his mother did not deserve to have her secret told now. No one, but Evie, would ever know that Timmins was his father. Some secrets are best kept.

Drake stared at the mound of earth. He thought he would have something to say, to shout, but nothing came to mind. Perhaps some feelings just can't be put into words. Perhaps he was too raw, too mixed-up in his head. He looked up at the swaying branches above his head for inspiration. For help.

What did he feel, *really feel*, deep down inside? Angry? Hurt? Disappointed? Grateful for all that Timmins had taught him? He blinked away the stinging pain in his eyes and shook his head. No, none of those things. He felt cheated. That is how he felt. There would never be an opportunity to get to know him as his father. His future was going to be different to how it could have been. Now it would be littered with missed opportunities and moments they could have shared together if he had lived.

When Richard Vennor had died, he had learned to live with not having him in his life, but at least he had memories of having him as his father. Now he would have to learn to live this way all over again, with a man who had never filled that role in the first place. How do you fill an empty hole inside you when you have no memories of how it could have been?

'The apprentice grieving the loss of his mentor.'

Drake felt the hairs on the back of his neck rise as he recognised the voice. He turned to see Abel Hicks approaching. His dirty clothes hung from his thin frame and he looked in need of a wash, but at least today he appeared sober.

Drake's hand tightened on his cane in readiness. 'I have nothing to say to you, Hicks.'

'Getting too high and mighty for the likes of me?'

'Get a grip man and tidy yourself up. You stink.' Drake passed him and began to walk away.

Abel followed. 'You have always had it so easy, Vennor. Girls … work …'

A muscle tightened in Drake's jaw, but he continued to ignore him.

'Your mother did her best to keep Timmins happy. That must have helped.' Drake stared hard at the ground in front of him as he walked. 'Wish I had a mother who was so willing to offer comfort.'

Drake turned abruptly, his cane slicing through the air and across Abel's stomach. The impact left Abel gasping for breath. Drake grabbed his shirt and pulled him close so he could look into his contorted face.

'Utter another word against my mother,' warned Drake, 'and I will be sorely tempted to give you the beating of your life.'

Drake let the warning hang in the air between them before pushing him away in disgust. He turned to leave, but Abel's angry cry rang out before he had taken a step. Suddenly, his breath was knocked out of him as Abel's body crashed into his. Drake stumbled, but did not fall. Abel quickly lunged again, grabbing at Drake's cane to use as a hold. For a briefest of moments both men held it, knuckle touching knuckle, panting breath mixing between them. It was Drake who broke the standoff, by twisting the cane in Abel's grasp and pulling it painfully upwards. The wrench strained at Abel's taught muscles until he was finally forced to let the cane go. He kicked at Drake's injured leg in retaliation. Drake's leg buckled as a sharp pain shot through his already damaged knee. He grabbed at Abel and both men fell sprawling to the ground.

Neither let go of the other, both twisting and rolling as they tried to aim and parry opportunistic punches. Finally, Drake managed to straddle Abel. A brief respite followed as they stared at one another, until Drake lifted his fist and punched Abel in the face.

Drake pushed himself up using Abel's prostrate body and straightened. He could taste blood. He dabbed his lips with the back of his hand, but found no wound. He explored the inside of his cheek with his tongue and winced when he found where he had bitten himself. He turned away and looked about for his cane. He found it, broken in two and no use to anyone. As he looked about for something else to use, Abel began to stir. He slowly stood up and had fully recovered when Drake finally noticed him. They stared at each other, both bloody and aware there was still unfinished business between them. Silently, they lifted their fists and were ready to spar again.

The first punch came from Abel and landed on Drake's jaw. Drake's head jerked painfully to the side, but he immediately straightened and followed it with a punch of his own. Abel paused, spat out some blood and readied his fists for more.

The two men snorted and sidestepped around each other, on guard for the next opportunity to attack. Abel grunted with the effort of his next punch, but Drake saw it coming and parried with a backward step. Abel's fist fell short. Drake took advantage and aimed a punch of his own. The fight continued for several minutes. Two men, heads bowed and chests heaving, their bodies covered in a slick sheen of sweat, spending their anger at the injustice of life that had brought them to where they were now. The fight was finally brought to an end by a minor mishap of nobody's making. Abel caught his foot on the curb of a grave and fell backwards, hitting his head on the gravestone as he fell. He lay as if dead, his head in the shadow of a gravestone, his body framed by the shape of the grave he had landed on. The bang to his head was no more than a glancing blow, but Drake still waited to see his chest rise and fall. Satisfied he was still alive, he turned to leave.

The breeze that had kept him company all morning, suddenly stilled. The cemetery grew darker and the temperature fell, causing his flesh to prickle as it rebelled against the chill. He looked up at the thunderous sky and saw grey rods of rain hurtling down towards him. The heavy droplets bombarded him, stinging his face and forcing him to look down. He turned up his collar and limped towards the graveyard gate. The torrential downpour roared in his ears. It was unforgiving, soaking everything without respite or a hint of when it may end. Drake hesitated and glanced back at Abel. His arm was moving, but he had yet to get up. Drake swore to himself and retraced his steps.

Abel groaned as Drake prodded his body with the tip of his boot and opened his eyes as Drake pulled him to standing. At first he was confused at what was happening, but the rain soon sobered him and together they made their way to the porch of the church. By the end of their journey, they could not be sure who was supporting who. A wooden bench, no more than the length of a man, lined each wall of the porch. On one of the seats was a blanket and a rolled up bag, on the other an empty wooden crate. Wet, tired and in need of a rest, both men sat on opposite sides, closed their eyes and leant their heads back against the wall to listen to the rain marking a rapid drumbeat on the slate roof above.

'Want a drink?'

Drake opened his eyes to see Abel with a bottle in his hand. He shook his head. His mouth tasted sour with blood, but he had no stomach for alcohol today.

'It is only water from the spring up yonder,' pressed Abel. 'I'm trying to stay off the drink.' He removed the cork and wiped the neck of the bottle with his sleeve and offered it again. Again Drake declined it.

Abel drank a mouthful and rested the bottle on his knee. 'You should have left me lying there,' he said, twisting the cork into the neck of the bottle.

'I had a mind to roll you down an embankment,' replied Drake evenly.

Abel stopped twisting the cork and set the bottle aside. 'How did you know it was me?'

'Your laugh is distinctive.'

'How?'

'It grates on my nerves,' replied Drake evenly.

Their eyes met in challenge, but rather than see an enemy, they saw a wet, dishevelled man looking back at them, just like them.

Abel smiled. 'It grates on mine too.' He rested his head back against the wall again. 'You could have left me. No one would have known it was you who left me to catch pneumonia.'

'You would have used your last breath to tell someone.'

'My word is not worth listening to.'

Drake did not ask why. He had the feeling Abel would tell him anyway. It turned out he was right.

'I lost my job at Carrack. Timmins said I was "unreliable".' Abel kicked at a stone on the floor. 'I worked there since I was twelve and that was how he repaid me.'

'Were you unreliable?'

'Only a couple of times. I had too many drinks and did not wake up in time for work. I don't drink now. The Crown and Rose have banned me.'

'Rose and Crown.'

'I can never remember which way round it is.'

Drake shook his head and tried not to smile. He watched Abel tentatively move his jaw, before leaning forward and appearing to chew on something. He spat an object into his palm and showed Drake.

'That is the third tooth you've knocked out now.'

'Third?'

'You knocked out the other two during our first fight.'

'And you have blinded me in one eye.'

Abel looked away and busied himself by rummaging in his bag, which had been rolled up as if to form a makeshift pillow. He placed his bottle inside it and looked up to find Drake watching him.

'Are you sleeping here?' asked Drake.

'I couldn't pay the rent after losing my job. Been here for several days now … as well as other places. The vicar's not noticed yet. My life has taken a different turn to yours. You have always had it easy. A home, a mother, an apprenticeship, girls …'

'Is that why you attacked me? Jealousy?'

'I was drunk.'

Drake's steady gaze encouraged him to go on.

Abel shrugged. 'I'd just spent the week sleeping in the wood on the outskirts of the estate. Then you turned up in your hired trap and your fancy clothes.' Abel fell silent, preferring to show a keen interest in his own nails.

'Go on,' prompted Drake.

Abel moved in his seat, the discomfort of confessing clearly etched on his face. 'I remember hitting you from behind and then I kicked and beat you. I feared that I had killed you and panicked. I knew I had to get rid of your body so I loaded you on the trap and drove a mile or two. Can't recall how far.' He frowned. 'I can't even remember carrying you to the edge or what I did with the horse and trap. I remember seeing you rolling down the bank.'

'Someone found the horse and trap.'

'That's good. It wasn't me, was it?' asked Abel.

Abel reminded Drake of a confused child. If he hadn't nearly died from his attack, his question would have amused him.

Drake shrugged. 'I don't know,' he said, testing his hand by flexing and stretching his fingers.

'I went too far. I admit it. It's not your fault you had everything I wanted.' Drake remained silent and continued to examine his hand. Abel saw it as a sign to explain further. 'The orphanage took the other bothy lads in as babies. They never knew their mother and father. I knew my mother but she abandoned me when I was four.' Drake looked up in surprise. He wasn't sure if he was ready to hear about Abel's troubled childhood. 'I still remember it. She pretended she found me wandering the streets as she was afraid they would not take me in.'

Now it was Drake's turn to speak. What should he say? He could only imagine how rejected Abel must have felt as a child. He hoped his mother had not given him up lightly.

'She could not look after you?' he asked.

'She could, she just didn't want me any more.'

Outwardly, Drake remained impassive, because he felt that was what Abel needed. He would not welcome platitudes. He just wanted someone to listen, but inwardly, Drake felt Abel's pain and saw it in his eyes.

'I know she didn't want me. She told me often enough. It's a hard thing to hear.' Abel tapped his own temple. 'It never leaves you. I could never understand why you would leave your home to live in the bothy. You had everything I wanted. I hated you.'

Drake felt there must be more to Abel's ongoing hatred of him, but felt it was not the time to press further. Best change the subject to something else.

'You said I had girls. What girls?' he asked

'I saw Miss Evelyn singling you out on more than one occasion.'

Drake waited for him to reveal more. Had he seen them becoming close in the country parkland when they were teenagers? 'And then there was Tilly,' continued Abel, unaware of Drake's watchful gaze. 'I had a soft spot for Tilly, but she only had eyes for you. After you stopped working at Carrack Estate, I thought I would finally have a chance with her. I was wrong. She didn't want to know. On the night I beat you I was sleeping in Carrack's laundry room. Tilly came in. It had been six years since you left and she was still crying over you … I felt so … so … angry. I had been around for years, but you turn up and Tilly realises she is still in love with you. I hated you.' He shook his head as if to clear his thoughts.

So Tilly was the reason his hatred had lasted so long, thought Drake. 'I wish you had told me. I had no interest in Tilly and I would have told you so.'

'I wasn't going to tell you that the girl I was sweet on was sweet on you. How would that make me look?'

'You are telling me now.'

'It makes no difference now. I've recently found out that she's goin' to wed the baker's son. I'd no idea they were courting. Too much drink does that to you. It takes you away from the real world.' Abel jerked his head towards Drake's face. 'Does your eye hurt?'

'It did. Not any more.'

'I'm sorry.'

They sat in silence, both aware of a change between them, yet fearful to speak of it. Instead Abel removed his bottle from his bag and offered it to Drake again. This time Drake took it. The water tasted good and quenched the thirst he did not know he had. He handed the bottle back and watched as Abel drank from it too. He felt the tension in his own body seep away. He was seeing Abel through new eyes, brought about by seeing how the man ticked. Abel was a man in need of some luck.

'I'm leaving for Buckinghamshire today. I'm taking over a commission that has stalled due to the poor health of the designer. I will be taking on men to finish the job. Would you like to come with me?' Abel frowned, but said nothing. 'You will get bed, board, but the hours will be long and hard work.'

'What sort of work?'

'Digging, felling trees, transporting them, building walls. I will be moving on to another commission I have lined up, but will return at intervals to keep an eye on progress. I am offering the job in good faith, but in return I want reliability and hard work. The job will last for two years, but I reward hard workers by using them again.'

'Leave Cornwall,' Abel mused.

'Yes, where no one knows your background or the recent reputation you have acquired. You will have a chance to build a new one.'

'I don't deserve such goodwill from you. I don't know what to say.'

'Yes, will suffice.'

Lost for words, Abel offered his hand. The men shook and the deal was done. Abel leaned back with a smile on his face. For the first time it reached his eyes. They sat listening to the rain and shared more water, chatting about nothing of importance as men do when seeking a respite from their daily trials. However, the sadness Drake felt at losing Evie must have still showed on his face as Abel suddenly returned to the day he had lost his sight.

'Tilly told me you were going to elope with Miss Evelyn. Was that true?'

Drake saw no reason to lie. If they were to forge a new friendship, it should be built on trust and honesty.

'Yes. I loved her.' He ignored Abel's low whistle. 'You see, Abel, we are not so very different. The women we want are not ours to love.'

'I ruined things for you. If it wasn't for me you would be with her now.'

'We will never know,' replied Drake, thoughtfully. 'We loved each other, but she is now married and no one should come between a husband and his wife. Not even me.'

Chapter Twenty-Four

1900, Cornwall, England

Evelyn found Mawgan writing in his study. She entered cautiously, unwilling to disturb his work, yet wishing to speak with him. As she waited for him to glance up, she let her gaze wander around the room. She rarely entered it for the simple fact that she never felt welcome.

Her husband spent much of his time here. It was his sanctuary and she often wondered if he used it to escape from her. From the dark red flocked wallpaper to the strong smell of cigar smoke lingering in the air, the room lacked any feminine touch and she knew that Mawgan liked it this way.

Mawgan glanced up. 'Hello, dear.'

He often called her 'dear'. The endearment tripped awkwardly from his tongue when they were first married. Now it was no more than habit.

'Are we expecting guests?' asked Evelyn. 'Only Lawry is preparing the guest room.'

Mawgan signed his letter and began blotting the paper. 'David is coming to stay.'

'Again? So soon?' He had visited last month and she had not expected him to return until the autumn.

Mawgan folded his letter and sat back to look at her, his right arm dangling from the arm of the chair. 'He has a mind to purchase a house in town. We may be seeing more of him in future. Do you object?'

How could she object? She barely knew him as his visits were to see Mawgan, not her. 'No, although he usually takes lodgings.'

'I know, but his decision to return to Cornwall was hastily made and there were no rooms to be had.'

'As he will be staying with us, perhaps this time I will be able to get to know him.'

'I am sure we will be too busy to trouble you.' There it was. The demarcation line he had drawn between them very early in their marriage. It had plagued them ever since and she felt she knew Mawgan less than she did before they were married. At least when he courted her they had talked. Now they only exchanged pleasantries and discussed subjects of no importance. *Would you like a cup of tea, dear? The roast pork is tender tonight. The storm has caused the daffodils to wilt.* Dear God, she wanted to scream.

Instead, she asked, 'What day is he arriving?'

'Tomorrow. I am picking him up from the station.'

'But we are taking Nicholas to see the sea. You promised you would come with us.'

'You can take him. I am sure you will have more fun without me.'

She probably would, but that was not the point.

'He needs his father, Mawgan. You rarely speak to him.'

Mawgan withdrew another sheet of paper from his drawer, picked up a pen and dipped it in the ink. He studied the nib. 'But I am not his father, am I?' he said, glancing up.

When it became evident she was with child, they had extended their honeymoon. Nine months after they wed, they returned from their travels with a baby. Fortunately, her son had arrived two weeks late so no one outside the marriage suspected that the child was not Mawgan's. Only they knew the truth.

'You knew I was not a virgin before you married me, but you married me anyway. Sometimes I wonder why you did.'

Evelyn turned to leave. Mawgan looked up, frowning. 'Where are you going?'

'To put Nicholas to bed.'

'We have a nanny for that.'

'I am well aware of that, but I wish to do it.'

'It is not your place to do it.'

'I am his mother. My place is to care for my son and how I fulfil that role is up to me.'

Evelyn swept from the room and walked briskly to the nursery. She had spoken harshly to him, but her maternal instinct to protect her son outweighed any desire to curb her anger.

They had married just over three weeks from the night she had made love with Drake, but it was not until the fourth month of their marriage, that Mawgan visited her room to consummate the marriage. Earlier in the day, she had told him that she was four months pregnant with Drake's child. He said very little at the time. They had both been aware of the possibility that she may be carrying a child when they married. However, it must have played on his mind, as later that night he had staggered into her room, with the smell of port wine on his breath. Their union was a clumsy, unfulfilling experience that left them both feeling wretched, but at least the deed was done and their marriage had been consummated. Mawgan had no wish to discuss it or a desire to repeat it. However, despite knowing that Nicholas was not his, he had put his name on the birth certificate to avoid a scandal. She would be forever grateful for that.

Whilst Mawgan appeared content to live his life devoid of physical contact, Evelyn was left wondering how one man had found her so utterly enticing and another found her so utterly repellent. Her husband preferred to spend time at his gentlemen's club rather than time with her. She felt rejected and abandoned, left to wander aimlessly in the barren wasteland of her marriage.

Nicholas, her son, was the only light in her life. She fought to control herself against running the last few steps to his nursery. His face lit up when he saw her, but he too waited until she had dismissed Nanny Bird before launching himself into her arms. They fell laughing onto his bed as Evelyn hugged him tight.

'Quick!' said Evelyn, lifting him off the bed. 'Under the covers.' She playfully slapped his bottom as it disappeared under the blankets. He lay hiding, unaware his dark hair still peeped out from the covers. 'I'm coming to get you!' teased Evelyn, causing Nicholas to squeal in delight. He began to giggle as Evelyn crawled in too. She lay beside him and looked at his handsome little face, both a little breathless and glad of each other's company. How she loved to look at him. His face, with those dark brown eyes and brows, were so similar to Drake's that it made her heart ache.

Nicholas reached out and touched his mother's hair. 'I love you.'

'And I love you too,' whispered Evelyn. They often told each other that when they found themselves alone, yet his words never failed to warm her.

Nicholas lifted one of her curls. It pulled slightly on a comb, but Evelyn didn't mind. 'I love your hair too.' She'd heard those words before, in another time, another life.

'And I love yours. In fact, I love everything about you.'

His eyes grew wide, like a puppy's. 'Everything?' he asked. 'Even my big toe?'

'Especially your big toe.'

'What about my nose?'

'I love your nose too.'

'What about this bit?' Nicholas stuck his finger up a nostril.

Evelyn made a face. 'Perhaps not that bit.' She crawled out from under the blankets and efficiently tucked him in. 'Now go to sleep or you will be too tired for our outing tomorrow.'

Nicholas snuggled down in his bed. 'What are we going to do tomorrow for my birthday?'

'What do you think?'

'Go on a train?' he asked, hopefully.

Evelyn nodded. 'Yes. And can you guess where the train is taking us?'

'To the sea?'

Evelyn nodded again, happy to see Nicholas was as excited about the trip as she was.

'Is Nanny Bird coming?'

'Of course.'

Evelyn was glad to see that Nicholas was pleased. She had gone to great trouble to find a nanny that was both efficient and caring. Nicholas loved Nanny Bird and Evelyn, unlike her own mother, did not feel jealous. She only felt contentment that he was happy.

'Did you visit the seaside when you were a little girl?' asked Nicholas.

Evelyn kissed him on the head. 'No, which is why I am looking forward to it so much. Now go to sleep, or you will be too tired to enjoy it.'

She went to the door, but paused on the threshold to look at him. She could see the shape of his body clearly in his bed for it was still summer and darkness came late in the day. She smiled at his face peeping out from under the covers and he smiled back at her. She loved him so much. If things had been different …

At first she had hated Drake for leaving her, but she no longer felt that way. Her feelings towards him had quickly changed after Tilly's confession and she still wondered if she would have ever learnt the truth if their paths had not accidently crossed.

She had been married for two years when she spotted her former maid in the street. Desperate for companionship, Evelyn had crossed the road to speak to her.

She was glad to see that Tilly looked well. She was married, she said, with a child of her own, but despite their once close relationship, she appeared reluctant to stay. Evelyn, however, would not be discouraged and insisted they took tea and cake at the nearest teashop to discuss old times. Soon they were seated opposite each other, both nursing steaming tea in fine china cups with a plate of delicacies placed between them.

It was meant to be a happy experience, but suddenly tears sprung to Tilly's eyes. Her confession quickly followed, spilling forth in a rush that shocked Evelyn into silence. She finally learnt the awful truth as Tilly told her everything, in detail and in chronological order, as if she had practiced it a thousand times.

Evelyn learnt about her meddling and betrayal. She heard, for the first time, why Drake had not been waiting for her, the beating he had suffered at the hands of a drunken man spurred on by a drunken confession. The injuries he endured had almost killed him. She listened to her former maid's reasons for her actions, how Tilly's concern for Evelyn's future, and her love for Drake, had spurred her on and convinced her that what she was doing was right. Time ticked by. Their tea grew colder and the delicacies remained untouched. When Tilly finally finished, she begged Evelyn to forgive her. Evelyn felt too drained to grant her what she wished for. She could not even look at her, whilst her heart felt too raw to be kind.

Tilly had then let out a sob and stood abruptly causing the table to rock, teacups to rattle and tea to spill into their saucers. She left the teashop, sobbing and Evelyn did not stop her. Instead she watched her leave, frozen with shock and numb to her pain. It was the soft hum of the remaining customers' whispers that finally brought Evelyn back to life. She looked through the window at the street outside and saw Tilly's hat disappearing into the crowd. It was the last time she would ever see her.

Evelyn left Nicholas sleeping and made her way to the morning room. Mawgan rarely visited her here as it was seen as her domain, just as the study was his. She looked round the empty, silent room. The decor remained the same as when her aunt Edith had it decorated and although it was not to Evelyn's taste, she did not dislike it enough to make any great changes. She went to her writing desk, opened the drawer and retrieved the letter she had received that morning. She opened and read it for the tenth time.

Thank you for your article, entitled "The Rest Cure: A patient's perspective". We are writing to confirm that your insightful and harrowing experience of the aforementioned treatment has been accepted for publication and will appear in next month's edition of Health and Home. As per your request, the author of the article will bear the pseudonym, Mrs Turvey. Thank you for your submission. Your account has highlighted that this form of treatment, if used by ill-trained or unscrupulous professionals, is at risk of abuse and, therefore, should be brought to the attention of a wider audience.'

Evelyn neatly folded the letter and slid it back into the envelope. It was a small journal and she had not been brave enough to put her name to it, but for once she felt that she was fighting back and that some good would come from her experience. It was a small step, but great expeditions always started with one step.

Evelyn, Nanny Bird and Nicholas boarded the train and took a seat in one of the first class compartments. Nicholas's excitement for the train journey was infectious, and soon after the train pulled out of the station, his mother and nanny joined him at the window to watch the countryside pass by.

The train stopped at three minor stations bringing with it a cloud of grey smoke and hissing steam, which billowed onto the rudimentary platforms. At one of the stations a small band of buskers boarded a second-class carriage. Evelyn could just hear their joyful music wafting towards them, before it was silenced by the chug, chug of the train's engine as it pulled out of the station. Evelyn would have liked to leave their first class compartment and join the buskers' in theirs, but with no corridor to connect them, they had to remain where they were. Nicholas seemed content to look out of the window and she decided, for safety reasons, it was probably best for them to remain isolated from strangers. After all, they were two women travelling alone with a child and one could not be too careful. Evelyn felt she was being quite daring leaving Cornwall, albeit it was only by the width of the River Tamar.

The distinct noise and iron tubular arches of the Royal Albert Bridge, which spanned the wide river, signalled to the train's occupants that their journey was already coming to an end. Their destination was Plymouth, which was a large sprawling town on the verge of becoming a city and boasted one of the finest natural harbours in England. Their train journey had been short and over far too soon.

They took a short carriage ride from the station to Plymouth Hoe. In recent years, the increased railway network had made it a popular destination for tourists. At the top, overlooking the harbour was Hoe Park. The landscaped gardens were mainly laid to grass and laced with leisure walks made up of sweeping steps and winding paths that led down to the sea.

At the water's edge was the grand promenade and stretching out into the bay of Plymouth Sound was the Grand Pier. Built only a decade before, it's white, Indian inspired, domed canopy provided the final touch of grandeur making Plymouth Hoe an acceptable place for the upper class to visit and mix with the working classes.

A brass band playing in the bandstand, the call of the ice cream vendors from their coloured wagons and the laughter of children playing on the grass overlooking the harbour, provided a relaxing soundtrack to the sunny day. Evelyn finally felt the tension brought about by her unhappy marriage, drain away.

They wasted no time in enjoying the day. They rode on the fair rides at the end of the pier, played hoopla, enjoyed a boat ride around the bay and walked for miles along the promenade. Finally Nanny Bird laid out a blanket on the lush grass of the park and the three of them settled upon it to eat ice cream served in glass cones. From their vantage point they watched women and girls playing in the naturally made water pool, which had been designated for ladies only. Further south, on a small pebbly beach, Evelyn knew that there was a bathing spot for gentlemen and boys. Evelyn hoped Nicholas would not ask to bathe. She had no male companion to accompany him and she would hate to have to refuse him.

Evelyn's gaze wandered over the other visitors, while Nanny Bird and Nicholas counted the ships and rowing boats in the harbour. Evelyn enjoyed people watching and glimpsing into their lives. Perhaps it was because her own childhood had been so isolated, much like her adult life now. Nannies pushed perambulators, met and talked, whilst couples took leisurely strolls as they enjoyed the sea air. Evelyn turned to look behind her where a group of men caught her attention. They were talking and looking around at the gardens, arms occasionally lifted to point at certain landmarks as if discussing future developments. Evelyn's heart began to thud as the men parted and she recognised the man in the middle. It was Drake.

He was speaking, she could tell, although she was too far away to hear. The men around him appeared to be listening intently, before shaking his hand and going their separate ways. Evelyn's heart lurched in her chest. She had to see him, even if it was only to bring closure on their past.

She stood up abruptly, sending a paper napkin fluttering away on the breeze. Why did her legs shake so much? She made a floundering excuse to leave. She would take the glass cones back to the vendor, she told them as she gathered them in her trembling hands. Feeling guilty for leaving her son with his nanny on their day out, albeit it would be for only a few minutes, she asked him if he was content to continue his counting game. Luckily he was and Evelyn, on legs that now felt as weak as water, hastily walked away.

By the time Evelyn reached the spot where she saw Drake, he was gone. She looked for him in the distance and scrutinised passing figures for any signs of familiarity. Disappointingly, none of them was him. The overwhelming feeling of loss she experienced was as potent as a death and confirmed what she already knew – that she loved him as deeply today as she did the day they were going to elope. Nothing had changed, yet everything had. She returned the glass cones and turned to leave, heartbroken.

Drake stood a little way down the path and blocked her way. Tilly had told her he required a walking stick, but she noticed that he appeared to have no need of one now. He looked as sturdy and virile as she remembered, although he did not move, preferring to watch her intently as she slowly approached. Evelyn had often wondered how much truth was in Tilly's confession, but as she drew closer and saw the deep scar, the slash of black in his eye and the sadness in his heart reflected in his eyes, she knew that Tilly had spoken the truth. What should she say to him? She need not have worried; it was Drake who spoke first.

'I waited for you, Evie.'

Her heart heaved inside her chest at the sound of her name on his lips. He had said it so gently, so lovingly. Only Drake could say her name that way.

She knew he was not talking about today. 'I know. Tilly told me everything.'

'She told me you married.'

'I'm sorry. I felt I had no choice.'

'I understand.'

'Do you?'

'You thought I had left you. Your parents wanted to commit you to an asylum. Tilly told me all about it. Of course you had no choice.'

She wanted to cry with relief. She had not realised she needed his forgiveness so much.

'Are you happy?' asked Drake.

What could she say? To say no would help no one.

'Yes ... very happy.' She wondered if he could hear the tremble in her voice. 'Are you?'

'I am very busy with work.'

Evelyn saw his eyes lift to behind her. She turned to see a young woman approaching. She was smiling at Drake. He is married! Can the pain get any worse? Drake lifted his hat in greeting. The greeting was fleeting and soon over as the woman quickly passed by.

'She is the wife of the mayor,' explained Drake. 'I am not married.'

Even now he could read her thoughts. She had better leave before he undid everything that held her emotions in check.

'I had better go, Drake.' She noticed other walkers approaching. 'Good day, Mr Vennor,' she added, politely. She intended to pass him and continue her walk, but as she drew level, she stopped as her body was unwilling to take the final steps forward.

Drake turned his head to look down at her. Their bodies faced in opposite directions, yet they were so close he had only to whisper to be heard.

'I still love you, Evie.'

The words were the undoing of her. The people, the vendors, the sea and the harbour around her no longer existed ... only him. His body, his soul, his power that drove every thought and deed, fed her, energised her and made her brave enough to finally speak the truth. She could hardly breathe from the excitement that flowed through her.

'And I you.' Three simple words and everything changed.

'We need to talk,' pressed Drake.

'When?'

'Now.'

'Where?'

He looked over her shoulder. 'Here.'

She felt his firm grip on her arm and before she knew what was happening he was walking her briskly towards a sun shelter. They stepped inside; its elaborate, decorative ironwork provided both shade and protection from prying eyes. Drake drew her closer and wrapped his arms around her as she rested against his chest. Neither spoke. Neither could.

Eventually Drake said, 'I'm sorry I was not strong enough to allow you to walk away.' Evie felt him brush his lips through her hair. His voice, hoarse and thick with emotion, pulled at her heart and silenced her. 'I know what damage can be done when a man comes between a husband and wife. The consequences ripple outwards and affect others for good and bad. I just needed to hold you again.' He stroked her hair. 'Are you happy, Evie?'

The shake of her head was imperceptible, but Drake felt it. He lifted her chin and looked deep into her eyes. 'You don't love him, do you?'

'Our marriage was not a love match.'

'This is madness,' he said, taking her hand in his and looking down at it. He gently caressed her fingers. 'My belief in the sanctity of marriage has kept me from you, but seeing you again and knowing the pain I will feel when you leave—'

'I will feel it too.'

Drake lifted his gaze to hers. '—has made me realise that my belief in our future together is stronger than any marriage vow promise not based on love.'

His declaration frightened her, but his searing kiss, which ignited dormant sensations she had long thought dead, wiped all worries from her mind. Pure, vibrant passion filled and nourished her and for the first time in years she felt alive again. She craved for more of Drake's kisses, fearful for the moment they would part and she would begin to die again as she inevitably would. She sought Drake's lips when his left hers, she matched the trail of his kisses, with trails of her own. His lips, his cheeks, his neck, his scar tasted exquisite to her. Their insatiable, long denied, hunger for one another were equally matched, finally they paused, breathless and smiling with the joy of it all. Their foreheads touched as their gazes settled on their entwined hands. Drake placed a kiss upon one of hers, before he stole a glance around to see if anyone had seen them. No one had and they shared a fleeting smile, before Drake grew serious again.

'Divorce him. Marry me. Let the newspapers have their day, I do not care. A few days or months living through the scandal will be worth the fifty years we will have as man and wife.'

'I have no grounds, Drake.'

'You said you do not love him.'

'I do not. We exist, we tolerate each other, but there is no love … not like this.' She bowed her head, kissed his hand and held it briefly against her cheek before straightening. 'But I have no grounds to divorce him, Drake. He has not committed adultery. And I would also need to prove desertion—'

'I wish he would leave,' muttered Drake.

'—or cruelty … or another sin against me. He has done none of those things. He is good to me.'

'You could ask him to divorce you on the grounds of adultery.'

'You mean for me to be cited as the adulterer? With you?'

Drake nodded. 'Of course.'

'In the eyes of the law a wife is on the same level as her husband's property. He could sue you for having an affair with me.'

Drake smiled down at her. 'It sounds as if you have looked into this.' His smile left his lips as she looked away. He drew her eyes back to him with a caress of his finger under her chin. 'I do not care,' said Drake earnestly. 'If it means we are together it is worth the risk.'

Suddenly it seemed a possibility. There would be a scandal, but did she care? At least she would be free to marry Drake. She could ask Mawgan. Just as quickly as the feeling of elation had arrived, it died. Nicholas. How could she forget her son?

'What is it? Have I asked too much?' said Drake, searching her face for answers.

'I have a son, Drake. Mawgan is named as his father on the birth certificate. He would never let me take him. What would people think of him if he allowed his unfaithful wife to have influence over his son? He is like my father in that respect. What society thinks of him governs everything he does.'

'What did you say?' Drake held her by the shoulders, forcing Evelyn to look at him. 'Why would you say that his name is on the birth certificate?'

A child's voice called for his mother. It was Nicholas and he was fast approaching. Evelyn pulled away.

'I cannot risk losing my son. I have to go, before his nanny sees us. I need time to think.'

'Is he here?' Drake followed her out of the sun shelter and immediately saw the dark haired boy running towards Evelyn. Drake's face paled.

'Is he mine?' He looked at Evelyn. 'Don't lie to me, Evie. Is he mine?'

'Yes, he is yours.'

Drake turned his attention back to his son. 'He has my hair,' he whispered, hoarsely.

Evelyn looked up at Drake. His eyes glistened with both pride and pain from the revelation.

'I am prepared to shoulder any scandal to be with you, Drake, but if it means I have to give up Nicholas in order to be with you then I can't go through with it.'

Drake swallowed, his gaze never leaving Nicholas. 'And I wouldn't want you to,' he replied. 'Because if you could leave your child, our child, then you would not be the woman I love.'

Chapter Twenty-Five

Drake did not leave immediately, but Evelyn could see that he found the meeting with his son painful. He longed to play with him, touch him and hold him, but etiquette between strangers, particularly adult and child, demanded a distance that he found unbearable. He had just learnt he was a father, but instead of shouting it from the rooftops he was unable to speak of it. It was a secret, something to be ashamed of, yet it felt wrong that it should be so.

As he left, he pressed his card into Evelyn's palm. 'Leave him, Evie. I am willing to wait for you ... for the both of you ... however long it takes. *Whatever* it takes.' He held her hand a little longer than he should, but he did not seem to care. 'Day or night. Send word and I will be there.'

'I can't ask this of you,' replied Evelyn, under her breath.

'You are not asking, I am offering. I have waited all these years for you. There has never been, or ever will be, another woman who has my heart as you do. And today I have discovered we have a son, which makes the notion of never seeing you again unbearable. So I will wait, and hope that one day it will be our time to be happy.'

Before she could reply, he was walking away, his shoulders braced, his stride long and his jaw set tight. Nicholas tugged on her hand, demanding her attention and she gladly gave it. It was a welcome diversion from her anguish at seeing Drake walk away – again.

When they finally reached home, they found Cedar Lodge unusually quiet. The day trip had finished earlier than was planned. Nicholas had grown tired so when fast approaching black clouds, threatening rain, hovered on the horizon, Evelyn decided to return home. Luckily, an earlier train was waiting at the station and soon after boarding it the station bell signalled for it to depart. A short carriage ride later, they were home, but no staff came to greet them. Mawgan must have decided to give the staff time off in their absence. She told Nanny Bird to put Nicholas to bed for a nap, as she removed her hat and gloves. She felt exhausted and meeting Drake again had left her with much to think about.

She stood in the entrance hall and listened to the empty house. The silence was crushing. Suddenly she felt very lonely and desperately sad. She had felt so happy in Drake's arms and those short precious moments shone a harsh light on her unhappy marriage. She could not continue living like this – or without Drake. She must talk to Mawgan – if she could find him.

She placed her hat and her gloves absently on the sideboard and entered the drawing room. Two used glasses were on the table and a faint aroma of cigar smoke still lingered in the air. She left and went into his study. It was empty and had not been aired. The letters he had been writing the day before still lay on his desk, unsent.

Evelyn left, carefully shutting the door behind her. Perhaps her husband had only just gone out. As she climbed the stairs, she decided she would change from her travelling clothes and make the most of being alone by catching up with some correspondence. She walked along the passage to her bedroom and was about to turn the handle when she heard a sound coming from Mawgan's room. He must be changing too, she decided, leaving her own door handle untouched, she reached for his.

Mawgan was lying in the bed, naked, in a tangle of white linen and legs – four legs. Evelyn's mouth opened as she watched the two writhing bodies in her husband's bed. Bodies that were so entwined that at first her brain could not decipher what she was seeing. Mawgan, shining with sweat, rose up on his hands to look down on his lover. His face flushed with the passion she had failed to ignite, his breath rapid and frantic. She must have made a noise, for he looked at her in horror. His lover turned too and she found herself staring into the eyes of David.

'Why did you marry me, Mawgan?' asked Evelyn, when Mawgan finally burst into the drawing room. She had been waiting for him, numb with shock and trying to make sense of all the possibilities that were unfolding before her. He finished buttoning up his shirt and began to tuck it in his trousers.

'I can explain.'

'There is nothing to explain.'

'It is not what you think you saw.'

Evelyn raised an eyebrow. 'I am not a fool, Mawgan. I know what I saw.'

Mawgan took her shoulders and turned her to face him. His face, panic-stricken, still shone with the perspiration of lust. 'I will tell him to leave. I won't have him here again.'

Evelyn shook him off. 'You cannot change who you are,' she said, stepping away. 'You will meet him again, perhaps not here, but somewhere else. It is no way to live.' She turned to him. 'Why did you marry me?'

'You know why.'

'I thought I did. I thought it was because you loved me. After all, despite knowing what I had done and that I loved another man, you were still prepared to take me as your wife.' Evelyn frowned as she remembered the past. 'They told me I was not in my right mind. They told me you were saving me from myself and protecting my reputation. I began to believe them. I was even grateful that I would not be carted away to some godforsaken clinic.' She turned to look at him, her head tilted to one side in pensive thought. 'We both know why I married you, but why did you marry me?'

'I loved you.'

Evelyn shook her head. 'No. You have never loved me. I know what it feels like to be loved and I do not feel it from you.'

'It was our parents' wish.'

It was a feeble excuse. 'Your father was already dead. You no longer needed to please him. Was it for my inheritance?'

'I care nothing for your inheritance. I am happy here, at Cedar Lodge.'

'Then why did you marry me if you do not like women?'

Mawgan looked away, a red blush forming on his cheeks. Evelyn stepped into his line of sight. 'You didn't marry me for any of those reasons,' challenged Evelyn. 'You married me to save yourself.'

Mawgan's shoulders sagged. He pushed past her and collapsed in the nearest chair. He looked exhausted. 'Rumours were circulating,' said Mawgan, resting his head back. 'My mother's former maid became loose with her tongue in the days before her death. I had to stop them.'

'What rumours?'

'That I was not like the other Pendragon men.'

'She knew you preferred men to women?'

He nodded. 'Her exact words were, "You should have no place on God's Earth".'

'That's a terrible thing to say.'

'She told me I should marry to protect myself against society.'

'So you married me.'

'I had to prove the rumours wrong. Society expects it. I knew we got on well. It is what our fathers hoped for. It was the logical thing to do so—'

'But you didn't love me. Do you love David?'

Mawgan snorted. 'Don't pretend you understand. I'm afflicted. I hate myself for what I am.'

Evelyn looked at her husband. He was usually so pristine in his appearance, but today he looked dishevelled and crumpled. Her heart went out to him. She knelt down before him and took his hand.

'Don't hate yourself. I do not.' Mawgan dared to look at her. 'When I was a child I had a governess called Miss Brown. She was kind and loving, but firm and fair. I loved her dearly, but perhaps did not treat her as well as I should.' Evelyn smiled, thoughtfully. 'I was young and spirited back then.'

Mawgan pulled his hand away from hers. 'I don't see what this has to do with anything.'

'She once told me that she was in love. When she was dismissed, for some minor transgression that I do not recall now, she told me she was going to live with someone she once loved and wrote down where I could find her. Her leaving was traumatic for me. I felt that my life was ending. I was able to read the name on the note, before it was snatched from my hand by my father.' Evelyn squeezed Mawgan's hand, demanding that he looked at her. 'I remember the name as clearly as if I was reading it now. Miss Frances, it said.' Evelyn stood and looked down on him. 'I was shocked. Confused. I had assumed the person would be a man, but it did not change how I felt about Miss Brown. She was the same person after I found out as she was before I knew. My love for her did not change and after she left, the pain I felt at losing her was just as unbearable. I do not pretend to understand what it must be like for you, Mawgan, but I do not despise you for it.'

'But the rest of the world does,' retorted Mawgan. He pushed himself to standing. 'I have spent years despising myself. You look shocked. Do you think I want to be different from everyone else?' He went to the sideboard and poured himself a drink. His hands trembled as he did so. 'I will try harder to make our marriage work.'

'You do not have to try at all.'

Mawgan turned to her, his glass forgotten in his hand. 'What do you mean?'

'We both love someone else. Society condemns us for our choices, but the reality is that we have no choice. We cannot control who we fall in love with. We both have the ability, the gift, to love someone deeply. The tragedy is … it is not each other.'

'What are you saying?'

'I want a divorce.'

Mawgan looked horrified. 'Are you mad?'

'Our marriage is not a happy one. If wanting to be free to marry a man I love, then yes, I am mad and proud to be so.'

Mawgan looked at the whiskey in his glass. 'I will not have my private life made into a subject for society's gossip.'

'I have just found you in bed with another man. You have already risked gossip. Are the servants aware?'

'They are not,' he said, swirling the liquid with a tilt of his glass.

'But they may find out eventually.'

Mawgan looked up at her. 'This man you speak of, is it Drake Vennor?'

Evelyn lifted her chin. 'Yes, it is.'

Mawgan no longer looked exhausted. Concern for the future had seen to that. A muscle worked in his jaw. He knew that her love for Drake could not be easily dismissed. Evelyn went to him and placed her hands on his chest to soothe him.

'It will be easier for you to divorce me than I to divorce you. I am willing to be the adulterer, if you give me what I want. I also want your word that you will not sue Drake.'

Mawgan lifted his chin. 'I will not allow it,' he said, refusing to meet her eyes. 'Nicholas will be distraught you have chosen a man over him.'

'I want Nicholas to live with me.'

Mawgan stepped away from her touch. 'Never. He stays with me.'

'You are afraid of what society will think of you allowing him to live with me. However, if we remain friends, society will accept it more readily.'

'I have said my piece. There will be no divorce. I will not have our marriage picked over by reporters.'

Evelyn clasped her hands together, fearful he may see them trembling. She had seen Nicholas with his real father today and could still feel Drake's kisses on her lips. It was a glimpse of what her future could be and she would be damned if she would let this chance go. She had spent her life dictated to by society's rules, etiquette and expectation. For the most part she had found them stifling, at times they had almost destroyed her. She would not let the opinions of others ruin her only chance of happiness. This time she was prepared to do whatever was required to fight back.

'Then I will have to divorce you.'

Mawgan's eyes widened. 'You wouldn't dare.'

'I dare. As a woman I have to have two reasons for divorce, adultery and one other.'

'You intend to recount what you have seen here today?' Mawgan was horrified and rightly so. 'Evelyn, if they believe you, David and I will be sent to prison.'

Evelyn did not let her gaze waiver. He must never know that she would never do that to him. Instead she said crisply, 'And no judge will allow Nicholas to live with you when you are eventually set free. However, grant me a divorce and give me my son and I will never speak of it.'

'The dutiful daughter and wife has turned into a blackmailing viper!'

'If I had the same rights as a man, I would not have needed to!' Evelyn breathed in deeply. Shouting would solve nothing, on either side. She sighed and reached for his hand. 'I just want to be happy. I want you to be happy too and being married to me is not how you can achieve it.'

Mawgan stared at her hands holding one of his, his was taut with tension, hers a warm, soothing balm to calm his fears. Gradually she felt his tension drain away. 'I can never have what you hope to have,' he murmured.

Evelyn gave his hand a gentle squeeze. 'You can. We both can.'

'No. I can't. I've tried.' Mawgan pulled his hand away. With one jerk of his head, he drank the full contents of his glass and returned to the sideboard to pour another. 'I will always have to be on my guard, fearful that a look or an endearment spoken without thought will expose the real me.' Mawgan raked a trembling hand through his hair. 'It is only since our marriage I have admitted that side to my character to myself.' He swung round to face her. 'I have lived my life at odds with the world, not really understanding why I felt so different from everyone else. It was why I jumped at the chance of touring the Empire when my father suggested it. I could escape the world where I did not fit. I see now that I was only escaping from myself. Only I didn't.' He threw her a glance. 'It is easier to succumb to one's leanings in a far-flung colony where no one knows you, Evelyn. Black, white, labourer, employer, trader ... even stranger ... If a man looks hard enough, he will find—'

'I do not want to hear the details.'

'I blamed it on the opium, the heat, the spices, the sound of their drums as they beat late into the night. After each encounter I blamed it on something, someone, other than myself. On my return to England I convinced myself it was out of my system. An illness I'd exorcised and successfully cured. David was waiting for me when I returned. He later told me that he had known the first time we met at university. He was just waiting for the day I accepted it. I think he was hoping the tour would bring me to my senses. I, on the other hand, took longer ... right up until the day we were wed. After that I could no longer deny the truth, but by then it was too late.'

'It doesn't matter now. I just want to be free.' Evelyn took the glass from his hand. 'Please, Mawgan, I beg you. We have both tried to live up to the expectations of our parents. Isn't it about time we lived for ourselves? You could live here with David, with minimal staff. No one need know. I will not tell anyone.'

'It is illegal.'

'It should be a crime to be in a loveless marriage and waste years in a relationship neither of us want. An uncontested divorce has a better chance of not attracting scandal. We can remain friends. We are cousins and will always be so.'

Mawgan touched her cheek and smiled sadly as she looked up at him. 'You have it all planned.'

'For once in my life, I do. I just need your help.'

'We are a fine pair,' mused Mawgan.

Evelyn's heart lifted. Was Mawgan considering her request? Dare she hope such a thing?

Mawgan smiled. 'You are being very brave.'

'Brave is not the word I would use.'

'Yes it is. A woman's reputation is delicate and therefore the easier to damage. Divorce is a heavier burden for a woman than a man.'

'I can bear it.'

'If you can, then so can I. You have your wish, Evelyn. I will divorce you and give you custody of Nicholas in exchange for your silence ... and continued friendship. But I have one condition.'

Evelyn's heart skipped a beat. 'What is it?'
'That you break the news to your parents.'

Chapter Twenty-Six

Evelyn was informed by the butler that her parents were taking tea in the Rose Garden. She chose to delay the inevitable by meandering through the other gardens for one last time as she had no doubt that what she was about to tell them would mean they would not wish her to visit again.

It had been several years since she had entered the gardens. Her visits to Carrack House in recent years had been conducted either on the great lawn or in the house itself. The last time she had seen the orangery was shortly before her failed attempt to elope. The tall elegant building was missing Timmins' proficient management. It was empty of orange trees, as an unchecked disease had ravaged the collection several years before. Even the woodwork required a fresh coat of paint.

The Italian and French Gardens had fared better. Drake had worked in them all, his tender care and management bringing life and freshness to the designs. She dipped her fingers in the fountain as she passed, fondly remembering the times she had watched him work. However, it was the maze that brought Drake's presence vividly to life. She could see him now, as a young lad, waiting for her to step inside the tall green hedges and into his arms. Evelyn smiled and walked on.

The Fern Garden was next. Amongst the graves was Duchess's. She hadn't told Drake that Duchess had died or what had become of her kittens while he was away as a journeyman. They had so much to tell each other, but at least now they had the rest of their lives to share it.

Evelyn was pleased to discover that Lady May's Garden remained unchanged. It had always been her favourite. She felt tempted to climb the lion for one last time and look out towards the country parkland to see its ancient trees where, in the shadow of an ancient ash, Drake had told her he loved her. She did not have time to visit the White Tower where they had secretly met. She wondered if other lovers would meet there in the future.

Her parents' voices interrupted her memories and reminded her why she had come. She left Lady May's Garden and approached the Rose Garden. This is where I first saw Drake, she thought, this is where it all began.

Rose fragrance filled the air. Her parents sat at a table covered in white linen and laid with tea and cake. She was not surprised to see they had company. Doctor Birch was with them – as he always seemed to be.

Her mother was the first to greet her. 'Evelyn,' she cried. 'What a surprise.' Her smile faded as her gaze lifted to her daughter's hair. 'Where is your hat and parasol, Evelyn? The sun is strong today.'

'I am not stopping long, Mother.'

'Even so,' insisted her mother, 'one cannot be too—'

'I do not want to wear a hat or carry a parasol,' interrupted Evelyn. Her curt response caused her mother to set down her cup and her father to look at her. There was no point in wasting time. 'I have come here to tell you that Mawgan and I are getting a divorce.'

At first no one spoke or moved. They all looked at her dumbly as if she had spoken in a foreign tongue. It was Doctor Birch who spoke first.

'On what grounds?'

'Adultery.'

Her father finally found his voice. 'That is no reason. So Mawgan has been indiscreet. He is young and inquisitive. He is not the first husband to seek comfort elsewhere and will not be the last.' He selected a scone and proceeded to spread strawberry jam on it. 'Turn a blind eye, girl. I will have a word with him to be more careful in the future.' He lifted the scone to take a bite.

'Mawgan did not have an affair,' said Evelyn. 'It was me.'

The scone hovered at the entrance of her father's open mouth, before he dropped it onto his plate. 'What are you saying?'

'His friend is to be our witness.'

'What friend?'

'David Marsden. He is an old university friend of Mawgan's.'

'And who is the man you have supposedly had an affair with?'

'It is not supposedly, Father. I did.'

'I don't believe it.' He frowned. 'Who is this man? Name the blackguard.'

Evelyn tilted her chin. 'Drake Vennor.'

Her father abruptly stood, tipping the table in anger as he did so. Tea, plates, cups and saucers, tumbled to the ground. Her mother remained seated, staring up at her.

'What is the meaning of this?' roared her father. 'Have you gone mad?'

'No. I am not mad.' Evelyn turned her gaze on Doctor Birch. 'I have never been mad.'

'You will stop this ridiculous plan right now. I will speak to Mawgan and soothe the waters. Persuade him to change his mind. Vennor has taken advantage of you. Seduced you. Yes, that is what he has done. Mawgan will have to forgive you.'

'I do not want him to. I asked him to divorce me. It will be easier—'

'Easier?' Her father kicked his chair out of the way. 'Have you any idea what a divorce will do to our family name?'

'It will help sell a few papers then all will be forgotten.'

'Our name will be splashed on every paper in town. The scandal will never be forgotten.'

'I do not care if it means I can spend the rest of my life with Drake.'

'That upstart! If he thinks he can worm his way into my family—'

'He wants to marry me *despite* my family!' shouted Evelyn.

For a moment her father was lost for words. The silence did not last long.

'And what is that supposed to mean?' he blasted.

Dare she tell him what she really thought and felt? Yes, she would dare!

'You have spent your life protecting the family's inheritance and name, Father, but it has come at the cost of the very people that you profess to love.'

'Mind your tongue, girl,' warned her father. Evelyn would not.

'You had very little to do with me before Nicholas's death. When I became the sole heir, you were quick to conclude that I was not up to the task.' Evelyn tilted her head as she studied her father. 'But I should not be surprised. You have always felt that a woman is not capable of owning property.'

'And your behaviour today does not convince me otherwise.' He turned to Doctor Birch. 'I am sorry you have had to witness this today. I trust it will go no further.'

Doctor Birch nodded in agreement, infuriating Evelyn. She would not allow her feelings and needs to be brushed under the carpet.

'You had no desire to hear my side of the story when I was a child. Rather than listen to my cries for help, you were quick to condemn me. How could you stand by and watch your daughter undergo the Rest Cure? I did not have hysteria. I was pleading for help. While I was being robbed of my childhood, your main concern was who would take over Carrack House and lands. It did not matter who I wanted to marry. You had made up your mind it would be Mawgan.'

'And now you are married and it cannot be undone. You made your choice.'

'What choice did I have?'

Her father thumped the leg of the upturned table. 'You had every choice!'

'I had no choice at all!' Evelyn shouted back. She pointed at Doctor Birch. 'You preferred to be taken in by that charlatan.'

Doctor Birch stood, tugging his waistcoat down in his anger. 'I will not stay here to be insulted.'

'Stay or go, it will not stop me saying what I have longed to say,' retorted Evelyn.

'Which is what, exactly?' the doctor challenged.

'What are your tonics made from, Doctor Birch?'

'I'm not listening to this,' said the doctor as he attempted to leave. He found his escape blocked. Sir Robert and Lady Pendragon, too shocked by their daughter's recent accusation, felt unable to move. In front of him lay a carpet of broken crockery.

'In my opinion, the cure rates of your tonics are very poor,' pressed Evelyn.

Doctor Birch attempted to pick his way through the broken cups and saucers on the grass. 'I am leaving,' he muttered.

'Then I will follow you, Doctor Birch. I *will* be heard! Your administration of the Rest Cure on me was barbaric and far too long for a child. You look surprised that I should know this,' observed Evelyn. 'I often wondered where my life went wrong. When a husband prefers to spend his time in other people's company rather than his wife's, there is much time spare for reading and research on the subject.' Doctor Birch gave her a nervous glance. 'The Rest Cure is not for children, Doctor Birch, and it should not last the length of time you ordered me to endure it.' Evelyn stood in his way, forcing him to halt. 'You must have earned a pretty sum from your visits. You are a charlatan.'

Doctor Birch stared at her. 'I am not.'

'You are not an alienist yet you tried to have me committed to a clinic in which you have shares!'

'Is this true?' asked her mother.

Doctor Birch turned to her, smiling. 'I am a partner, but it has no bearing on my professional opinion. Your daughter is overwrought.'

'If a charlatan claims to have skills he does not possess and profits from the misfortune of others, then yes, I believe you to be a charlatan.'

Her mother whimpered. Everyone ignored her.

'How many women have you committed, Doctor Birch?' questioned Evelyn. 'Innocent women who have done nothing more than acknowledge the same desires that men can freely indulge in … inside and outside of marriage!'

Doctor Birch began to pick his way through the debris at his feet. 'You were not of sound mind.'

'Because I wanted to be with the man I love?'

'Because you would not acknowledge that such an act would ruin you!'

'But marrying my cousin would cure me! What a miraculous cure,' Evelyn scoffed. 'If you could bottle it and label it, no doubt you would sell it as a tonic. You sell everything else as a tonic. You are a disgrace, Doctor Birch. I believe there is little you would not do to further your own name. It may interest you to learn that I am going to have my account of the experience published so all of England will learn of the dreadful practice and the misery patients have to endure.' Doctor Birch brushed passed her and began walking away. 'I believe you would stop at nothing!' she shouted after him. 'Nothing! And I intend to expose your malpractice, if it means writing to every journal and newspaper in England! No one will want you as their doctor. Your career will be at an end.'

'Enough!' ordered her father. 'You are making a spectacle of yourself.'

Evelyn turned to her parents. Her mother had not moved since her arrival. She still held a teacup in her lap, despite the absence of any furniture to put it on.

'I love Drake, Father, and I will marry him. I have loved him since we were children.'

'You are married.'

'And I will love him until the day I die and beyond.'

'I will not allow you to divorce.'

'It is not up to you. It is up to Mawgan and I.'

Her father frowned and looked at her, as if she was a curiosity of the most grotesque kind.

'Why would you want to ruin our good name? No person of worth will want to socialise with you.'

'If they make that decision, then I do not consider them worthy of my friendship.'

'Vennor will not get his hands on my property.'

'He does not wish to. He wants to marry me because he loves me.' She might as well tell him everything and start how she meant to go on. 'Nicholas is his son.'

Her father, stricken, looked about him in bewilderment. His orderly life was dismantling around him and Evelyn was aware that she was to blame. However, her bid for freedom was long overdue and she would not be made to feel guilty. She knew what was concerning him now, it would not be her future happiness, but who would inherit his precious legacy. However, despite her resolve, her strong formidable father now looked like a lost child who was unsure of the strange new world he found himself in. A pang of sympathy tugged at her heart.

'Nicholas is from my body, Father,' she reassured him. 'He has the Pendragon name. He has Pendragon blood. He may be Drake's son, but he is also *your* grandchild.'

'He is too young.'

'For now, but he will soon grow. He will be strong, determined, but also well loved. He will know both his real father and Mawgan.' Her father looked at her, with that same curious look as before. 'Yes, Mawgan and I plan to remain friends. There will be no animosity between us. I don't want there to be any between us either.'

'You ask too much.' Her father braced his shoulders and looked past her as if he could no longer bear to look at her. 'I think you better leave.'

The dismissal was expected, but it still felt brutal. She could not blame him. She had just destroyed all he had hoped for. She looked to her mother. A pained expression had come to settle on her face and she could not meet her gaze. There was no more to be said. Evelyn turned and walked away.

Evelyn had already reached the gravel path when she first heard her mother call her name. At first she ignored her, unwilling to listen to her mother's scolding. However, the pleading in her voice when she called her name again, made her stop and turn to face her.

'I will not change my mind, Mother,' she said as her mother approached. 'I love Drake and I want to spend the rest of my life with him. You cannot persuade me otherwise.' Evelyn braced herself. She saw that her mother was slightly breathless and her hat a little askew, but she would not soften towards her.

'I know,' said her mother, coming to a halt.

Evelyn felt a sense of unease sweep over her as her mother straightened her hat and looked at her. Her mother looked odd. There was a flush to her cheeks and a light in her eye that she had not seen before. This woman was not like her mother at all.

'What is it you want to say, Mother? That you are disappointed in me?'

'No.' Her mother heaved a sigh. 'That I envy you.'

Was this a trick to persuade her to change her mind? 'I don't understand,' said Evelyn warily.

'You are far braver than I. I have spent my life being afraid,' said Lady Pendragon. 'Do you know why I married your father?' Her mother did not wait for a reply. 'I was afraid I would remain a spinster. Many of my friends were already married and I was led to believe that marriage or caring for my aging parents were my only options. Your father had not long been widowed and was keen to take a wife. He was wealthy, titled and my father approved of him, so when he asked, I accepted. It was not a love match, but it was acceptable to me as I was afraid I would not receive another proposal.' She stepped into the shadow of a tree to seek shelter from the warmth of the sun. Evelyn followed her.

'It was my duty to be a good wife and mother. I did my best to fulfil the role and prepare my children for adulthood. I have not been perfect, but I did what I thought was best.' She reached out to touch Evelyn's cheek. 'I tried to mould you into a young lady,' her mother's eyes strayed to her hair, 'but you were always losing your ribbons and not sitting still.' She let her hand fall and smiled. 'And being quiet in chapel seemed beyond you. The number of times I had to scold you not to turn and look at the staff. You were so inquisitive ... so full of energy. The more I tried, the more you rebelled. I couldn't understand where we were going wrong.'

'I disappointed you.'

'No! I was never disappointed in you. I was afraid for you. There is that word again … afraid. I feel I have spent my whole life being afraid.' Uncharacteristically, her mother ignored the lichen that might spoil her dress and leaned against the trunk of the tree. 'When I discovered Nicholas was so fragile, I had to be strong to protect him. Your father was no good. It was me who had all the responsibility of when to call the doctor and to ensure he had his medicine. I felt on constant guard for any deterioration. I was always in fear that he could die at any moment and it would be my fault. It was a heavy burden, but not as heavy as the burden a mother carries when she loses a child. My children were all I have, but I am losing them one by one.'

'You do not have to lose me. And you still have Father.' Her mother did not reply. 'You do not have to be afraid for me, Mother.'

'Is he kind to you?'

'Drake?' Evelyn nodded. 'Yes, the kindest.'

'Do you love him?'

'With every fibre of my body.'

'And Mawgan has agreed to this?'

'At first he was fearful of what others might say. But now he is as eager as I am. I think we will become closer. We will no longer have to live the lie we have had to endure these past few years.'

'And Nicholas?'

'He is well. Drake will be a wonderful father to him. He does not wish to force his new role upon Nicholas and will take all the time Nicholas needs to build their new relationship. He understands that Nicholas will experience a lot of changes in his life and he wants to help him through it, not make the adjustment worse.'

'He sounds an understanding man.'

'He is.'

'And can he support you financially?'

Evelyn smiled. Her mother was meaning well by asking such a question. 'Yes he can.'

'Then I can only wish you both well. You are far stronger than we believed you to be. And far braver.'

Her mother moved towards her and for a moment Evelyn thought she was going to hug her, but she should have known better. It was not her mother's way. Instead her mother placed a rather chaste, awkward kiss on her cheek.

'I hope you will still visit and bring Nicholas with you, but perhaps we should leave it until after you are remarried. Your father will have had some time to calm down and you will be Mrs Vennor by then, rather than a divorcee.'

Evelyn did not argue. Her mother was offering an olive branch in the best way she knew how.

Her mother looked towards Carrack House. 'You accused Doctor Birch of malpractice. Is it true?'

'Yes.'

'Then I am glad you are going to bring attention to it, although I think it would be better for the family if you used a pseudonym.'

Evelyn smiled. 'I have used a pseudonym, Mother, but I cannot promise that it will always be so.' Evelyn felt this might just be the beginning of a long campaign to highlight the medicalisation and mistreatment of women who rebelled against society's rules. However, she did not feel it was the right time to share her plans with her mother. Bridges were being made, but they were too fragile to support such news for the moment. Her mother, however, had other ideas.

'For my part, I will not use him again and I intend to advise my acquaintances and friends to do the same. It won't be long before he is treated as a pariah by the society he so craves. Let him be forced to take his methods elsewhere, although I believe you are right when you say that no one will receive him once word spreads.' She offered Evie a shaky smile. 'You see, I am trying to make amends.'

'And what about Drake? Will he be welcome in Carrack House one day?'

'I will work on your father and send word. Your father blames him for the breakup of your marriage, but I will do my best to persuade him otherwise. When he sees that Mawgan is content with the outcome and Nicholas is happy, he may relax his stance on the matter.'

Her mother tucked a stray curl behind Evelyn's ear. It was a gentle gesture, given by a mother to her child. Evelyn suppressed a smile when her mother, realising what she had done, turned stiffly away to look at the view.

'I think his opinion may relax a little sooner when he remembers that his future son-in-law has an expertise in horticulture. You know what your father is like about his gardens. They are a powerful bargaining tool. I have used them many times in the past.'

Evelyn raised her eyebrows at her mother. 'You surprise me.'

'Do I? Good. It has been a long time since I surprised anyone by my behaviour. Perhaps I should follow your lead and find the courage to do it a little more often.'

Evelyn looked up at the canopy of leaves above her head. The heavily laden branches swayed gently above her, dipping and rustling, as if they were waving her goodbye.

Her mother had turned back some moments before, leaving Evelyn to walk the remainder of the drive alone. Evelyn breathed in deeply and let it escape in a joyful sigh. She felt happy. Her mother's candid confession bode well for a better relationship with her in the future and they had parted on good terms. The heavy burden of telling her parents of her plans was now lifted from her shoulders and lightened her steps. She felt like dancing, but instead reached up to her hair and began to remove the pins and combs that held it. She raked her fingers through her locks until they lay untidily about her shoulders and enjoyed the feeling of freedom it gave her. Soon the end of the drive was in sight where she could see Drake and Nicholas waiting patiently in a trap, their heads bowed as if in deep conversation. Nicholas was the first to see her. She waved back at him. They were her future and what a glorious future she was going to have.

'Is that Mother?' asked Nicholas.

Drake followed his son's gaze. 'Yes,' he replied fondly when he saw Evelyn coming towards them.

'What has she done to her hair?'

Evelyn had taken it down so her fair hair lay loosely about her shoulders. Her hair shone like liquid gold in the sunshine and lifted gently in the breeze behind her.

Drake smiled. 'She has unpinned it.'

A slight crease formed on Nicholas's brow. 'What is she doing?'

Drake's smile broadened. 'She appears to be dancing.'

'Why?'

Drake thought for a moment. She was a woman whose spirit had been caged, but now she felt free. Her heart had the power to love deeply, yet it was a love she had had to deny. She had endured so much. Drake understood. He had watched her grow behind her gilded cage. He had loved her for so long that he also felt the joy of being free to declare it.

But how could one explain all this to a child who has yet to experience such a deep emotion? He watched Evelyn dancing along the drive and heard the joy in her laughter. Suddenly he knew how to answer him.

'She is dancing, Nicholas, because she can.'

Drake stepped down from the trap and went to meet her. Her meandering, dancing steps were forgotten as she walked into his embrace. Her soft yielding body pressed against his as he kissed the top of her head and deeply inhaled the fragrance of rose water which drifted up to meet him.

He tilted her chin to see her face. There was a youthful sparkle in her eyes that confirmed that she had told her parents. It hinted at hope and excitement for the future and showed him the happiness filling her heart. He did not need to press her to know how her parents had reacted. It did not matter. She was going to live her life how she wanted to live it and her family's opinion, or the strict rules that were placed on women by society, would not prevent her. He wondered if she saw the same sparkle in his eyes for he felt the same emotions as she – hope and excitement for their future and the feeling of pure joy from loving and being loved.

Thank You

Dear Reader,

Thank you for taking the time to read *Daughter of the House*. I hope you enjoyed Evie and Drake's story about an enduring love across the class divide.

Daughter of the House was initially inspired by an archived newspaper article about a young Victorian woman who had been diagnosed as insane. Her illness? She simply wanted to live with her lover rather than marry him. Her family and doctor concluded that, as she was unwilling to accept that her 'immoral behaviour' would lead to her social suicide, she must be insane.

Thankfully her friends' successfully obtained her early release, but the article set me on a path to research the expectations placed on an upper-class woman in the 19th century. My research eventually led me to the tortuous Rest Cure.

Thankfully the rights of women have improved greatly over the years, although I acknowledge there are still improvements to be made. I hope this work of fiction, which was inspired by real events, would somehow shine a light on the women from our past that endured, and eventually challenged, the limitations placed upon them by society. They started us on a journey to gender equality and I would like to thank you for taking the time to read Evie's journey.

If you enjoyed reading Drake and Evie's love story, and the hurdles Evie faced to be with the man she loved, I would be grateful if you would leave a review on the online retail site where you purchased it. It doesn't have to be long as a single sentence would do. A collection of positive reviews are very important for the life of a book. They help influence purchasing choices, online distributors and high street selection. Ultimately they will help *Daughter of the House* to reach a wider audience so more people can learn about how far women have come to have equal rights and how much further we have to go. The story may be fictitious, but it is inspired by truth and sometimes historical facts are more palatable when wrapped in a blanket of love and romance.

Love,

Victoria

PS. If you want to find out what is in store for Evie and Drake's son, Nicholas, you can read his Cornish tale in *A Daughter's Christmas Wish*. In *Daughter of the House* Drake recalls his father, the lay preacher, talking about his cousin who gave birth to an illegitimate child. His father lamented that if only she asked for God's help she may have survived. To find out what happened to his cousin's illegitimate child, Beth, follow her tale in *The Daughter of River Valley*.

About the Author

Victoria Cornwall grew up on a dairy farm in Cornwall. She can trace her Cornish roots as far back as the 18th century and it is this background and heritage which is the inspiration for her Cornish based novels.

Victoria is married and has two grown up children. She likes to read and write historical fiction with a strong background story, but at its heart is the unmistakable emotion, even pain, of loving someone.

Following a fulfilling twenty-five year career as a nurse, a change in profession finally allowed her the time to write. She is a member of the Romantic Novelists' Association.

For more information on Victoria:
www.twitter.com/VickieCornwall
www.facebook.com/victoria.cornwall.75
www.victoriacornwall.com

More Choc Lit from Victoria Cornwall

The Thief's Daughter

Hide from the thief-taker, for if he finds you, he will take you away …

Eighteenth-century Cornwall is crippled by debt and poverty, while the gibbet casts a shadow of fear over the land. Yet, when night falls, free traders swarm onto the beaches and smuggling prospers.

Terrified by a thief-taker's warning as a child, Jenna has resolved to be good. When her brother, Silas, asks for her help to pay his creditors, Jenna feels unable to refuse and finds herself entering the dangerous world of the smuggling trade.

Jack Penhale hunts down the smuggling gangs in revenge for his father's death. Drawn to Jenna at a hiring fayre, they discover their lives are entangled. But as Jenna struggles to decide where her allegiances lie, the worlds of justice and crime collide, leading to danger and heartache for all concerned …

Visit: www.choc-lit.com for more details.

The Captain's Daughter

Sometimes you need to discover your own strength in order to survive …

After a family tragedy, Janey Carhart was forced from her comfortable life as a captain's daughter into domestic service. Determined to make something of herself, Janey eventually finds work as a lady's maid at the imposing Bosvenna Manor on the edge of Bodmin Moor, but is soon caught between the two worlds of upstairs and downstairs, and accepted by neither, as she cares for her mistress.

Desperately lonely, Janey catches the attention of two men – James Brockenshaw and Daniel Kellow. James is heir to the Bosvenna estate, a man whose eloquent letters to his mother warm Janey's heart. Daniel Kellow is a neighbouring farmer with a dark past and a brooding nature, yet with a magnetism that disturbs Janey. Two men. Who should she choose? Or will fate decide.

Visit: www.choc-lit.com for more details.

The Daughter of River Valley

Can you trust a man with no name?
Cornwall, 1861
Beth Jago appears to have the idyllic life, she has a trade to earn a living and a cottage of her own in Cornwall's beautiful River Valley. Yet appearances can be deceptive …

Beth has a secret. Since inheriting her isolated cottage she's been receiving threats, so when she finds a man in her home she acts on her instincts. One frying pan to the head and she has robbed the handsome stranger of his memory and almost killed him.

Fearful he may die, she reluctantly nurses the intruder back to health. Yet can she trust the man with no name who has entered her life, or is he as dangerous as his nightmares suggest? As they learn to trust one another, the outside threats worsen. Are they linked to the man with no past? Or is the real danger still outside waiting … and watching them both?

Visit: www.choc-lit.com for more details.

A Daughter's Christmas Wish

A Cornish Christmas wish sent across the ocean ...
Christmas, Cornwall 1919
A promise to a fellow soldier leads Nicholas to Cornwall for Christmas, and to the teashop managed by Rose; the youngest daughter of a family whose festive spirit has been blighted by their wartime experiences. But as Nicholas strives to give Rose the best Christmas she could wish for, he begins to question whether his efforts are to honour his friend, or whether there is another reason ...

Visit www.choc-lit.com for more details.

Daniel's Daughter

Sometimes the truth is not easy to say and even harder to hear ...
Cornwall, 1895
Grace Kellow is a young woman with a strong sense of who she is and where she comes from. As the daughter of a well-respected Cornish dairy owner Daniel Kellow, her existence in the village of Trehale is comfortable and peaceful.

But then handsome Talek Danning comes striding over Hel Tor, and soon after his arrival Grace is hit with a revelation that leaves her questioning her identity and her place in the Trehale community.

In her hour of need, Talek and his sister Amelia offer Grace sanctuary – but wherever Grace runs, her secret will follow ...

Visit www.choc-lit.com for more details.

Introducing Choc Lit

We're an independent publisher creating
a delicious selection of fiction.
Where heroes are like chocolate – irresistible!
Quality stories with a romance at the heart.

See our selection here:
www.choc-lit.com

We'd love to hear how you enjoyed *Daughter of the House*. Please visit **www.choc-lit.com** and give your feedback or leave a review where you purchased this novel.

Choc Lit novels are selected by genuine readers like yourself. We only publish stories our Tasting Panel want to see in print. Our reviews and awards speak for themselves.

Could you be a Star Selector and join our Tasting Panel?
Would you like to play a role in choosing which novels we decide to publish? Do you enjoy reading women's fiction? Then you could be perfect for our Tasting Panel.

Visit here for more details…
www.choc-lit.com/join-the-choc-lit-tasting-panel

Keep in touch:
Sign up for our newsletter for all the latest news and offers:
www.spread.choc-lit.com.

Follow us on Twitter: @ChocLituk Facebook: Choc Lit
and Instagram: ChocLituk

Where heroes are like chocolate – irrestible!

Printed in Great Britain
by Amazon